LIVES OF THE ARTISTS

ROBERT CLARK

Lives of the Artists

A Novel

HARPER PERENNIAL

Lives of the Artists

Published by Harper *Perennial*, an imprint of HarperCollins Publishers Ltd

First published in original trade paperback by
HarperCollins Publishers Ltd: 2005
This trade paperback edition: 2006

HarperCollins books may be purchased for educational, business, or sales promotional use through our Special Markets Department.

HarperCollins Publishers Ltd
2 Bloor Street East, 20th Floor
Toronto, Ontario, Canada
M4W 1A8

www.harpercollins.ca

Library and Archives Canada Cataloguing in Publication

Clark, Robert, 1952–

Lives of the artists / Robert Clark. — 2nd trade pbk. ed.

ISBN-13: 978-0-00-639409-9
ISBN-10: 0-00-639409-4

I. Title.

PS3553.L2878L48 2006 813'.54 C2005-905502-2

RRD 9 8 7 6 5 4 3 2 1

Printed and bound in the United States
Set in Garamond

FOR CARRIE, AS EVER, AGAIN

1.

Porta Romana

In the city of Florence, on the far bank of the dusky Arno, a short distance from the Porta Romana at the bottom of the Bellosguardo hill, there is a house of uncertain age and provenance, lately restructured to form *appartimenti.* In one of these, an American couple had taken up residence a little over five months before. They were named Mary Bruckner and Alex Hansen.

Were you to enter and find them at home, you might see Mary reading, her feet up on a dark blue couch of Swedish manufacture, and Alex, perched in a wicker chair opposite, drawing her as she read. Or, were you to enter when they were out—Mary at the *mercato* (buying blood oranges for juice, asking when the first artichokes would arrive) and Alex supervising the restoration of the villa they had acquired up on the hill—you might survey the rooms and the objects within at your leisure.

There would be flowers on the dining table (Mary insisted on flowers) in a clear glass cylinder purchased from the same concern as the couch. The table itself, you would quickly apprehend, was of more local provenance, rectangular and thick and grave in the Italian manner. Atop it, a little forlorn, rested that morning's coffee cups, Mary's not quite empty, and adjacent to these, that day's *International Herald Tribune*, a pen, and a piece of notepaper upon which were the words "tile delivery," "water heater (how to say in Ital.?)," and "gardener—ask rental agent."

Just beyond this, closer to the windows that overlooked the

street, opposite a fireplace, sat the aforementioned blue couch, at one end of which was a low round table. This held Mary's books and papers, and were you to search through them—and, since the house is empty, the stairway silent, why not?—you would find a copy of John Ruskin's *Sesame and Lilies,* a highly regarded contemporary American novel about a boy with a stutter, and a fat paperback of Thomas Mann's *Doctor Faustus* that you might imagine has gone unread (you would be wrong). Together with these, you would find two notebooks, the paper within ruled into squares, *quaderni,* in the European manner. And in these volumes—one devoted to ideas, sketches, quotations, lists of books read or desired; the other to longer stretches of writing, observation, and experiment—you would encounter yards and yards of Mary's precise, italic handwriting, and you might wonder what possible harm could come of settling on the blue couch for a few minutes and seeing what account she gives of herself in these. Lunch is still some way off, and, although you might not be aware of this, it is Mary and Alex's custom to eat lunch out nearly every day; at, in fact, the same trattoria off the Piazza Santo Spirito where, just over an hour from now, they will rendezvous over a *mezzo*-litre of wine and Mary will eat roast chicken with braised black cabbage while Alex eats fava beans in concert with pecorino cheese. But you have scruples. Or at least the patience to see how the story unfolds in its own good time. Good then. Let's go on. You mustn't expect much, of course: this apartment is meant to be only a temporary home while the villa is made ready (although the lease has been extended twice due to delays).

In the rudimentary galley kitchen, there are few signs of habitation beyond the disconsolate coffee pot standing sentry on the stove, the crumbs milling on the breadboard, and a knife swathed in apricot preserve. To one side of the kitchen lies the single bedroom, which bears looking into long enough to see that there's a Victorian "three-decker" edition of a novel on the nightstand on one side of the bed (Mary's, in fact) and a small spiral-bound artist's pad with two pencils on the other. There's a wardrobe full of clothes (mostly jeans, shirts, various pieces of synthetic fleece, and a few tops and skirts of white linen or black wool) and little else; and your eye might well return to the bed and your mind reflect on what—one is curious about these things, go on, admit it—transpires there, but the bed itself, made up in a blank white coverlet, yields no testimony.

So you continue to the bathroom, which may be more forthcoming. There is a shower, a toilet, a bidet (looking either very clean indeed or simply unused), and a sink set into a marble counter upon which sit toiletries and personal sundries: a comb, a hairbrush, the rolled butt-end of an American tube of toothpaste, a few cosmetics, and—yes, here we are—vials of medication. You will recognize the anti-depressant tablets (you've taken them yourself). There's also a British-made compound of paracetamol and codeine (bought at one of the London airports perhaps). So who is the melancholic? Who gets headaches (or is it cramps)? And no sign of contraceptive pills or devices—oh, you looked in the drawer of the nightstand with the three-decker? Sly fox.

You might well ponder these mysteries at greater length (did it occur to you to look for condoms in the drawer on *his* side?), but there's a faint thunk from somewhere downstairs, akin to the slam of a door. You bolt from the bedroom, retrace your steps across the terrazzo of the *salone,* and go to the window. The postman's just exiting below you. You exhale, relieved, but your hands and arms are still taut, and the backside of your wrist brushes against something on the windowsill. Careful—you've nearly knocked it over. It's one of several glass jars of coloured powder, blue as lapis. Oh, you realize, it *is* lapis. It's pigment. You move it back in line with its mates in what you hope was its original position.

You will be thinking you'd best go. You're not supposed to be here. You let yourself out, descend the stairs. You glance at Mary and Alex's mailbox on the way out, but don't look inside. So you miss, among the flyers and bills, the letter postmarked Seattle. No matter. You'll find out everything eventually.

Mary came home a little after two o'clock, carrying the morning's grocery shopping. She retrieved the mail from the box, and once she had closed the door and caught her breath and set down her bags, she rifled through it. There were the usual statements and confirmations and proxies and quarterly reports forwarded from the brokerage firm—they came at least once or twice a week, but she was determined not to let her wealth intrude upon her unless it was with the aim of doing something finely appreciable—and these she consigned straight to the trash. There were advertising flyers from various outlets and hypermarkets on the edges of the city proffering beds, garden furniture, long underwear, and video cassettes. And there was, unmistakable in the cramped, upright handwriting—devised, surely, to promote an impression of singularity but conveying nothing so much as diffidence, of things not merely unfinished but never begun—a letter from Tom Hirsch, from whom they had not heard in some weeks.

Mary put the teakettle on the stove, settled herself on the sofa, and began to read. It was a long letter (the kettle boiled before she was half done) and she laughed aloud in places. She might have cried in others, save for the fact that in some sense there was no one present to cry for; that while there were events and, indeed, injuries reported, they seemed to have happened at a great remove, even from Tom himself. There was a voice, to be sure, but no body.

By the time she was done, Mary's tea was well steeped. She poured a cup and went to the window. She could see the rise of Bellosguardo, the "olive-muffled hills" as Henry James had put it, where, she supposed, Alex was now back at the villa, sorting through the endless business of the plumbing but especially of the tiles—tiles for the roof, for the floors, for the ceilings, for the bathrooms, the kitchen, and the cantina.

This was now to be her life, out there, above and before her; and behind her, manifest in the teapot, the flowers, the books, and the journals. She might just then have been seeing it whole. It was, thanks to the money, of her own making. It consisted of more than merely getting by, avoiding suffering or averting boredom; she had scarcely retired; rather, she was doing precisely what she wanted and needed to do. For quite a while after Noumena, and then again after the Critic.com buyout, she had felt awkward, even ashamed, that by a small measure of work and a great deal of happenstance, other people had to labour while she, now, did not.

But it was surely not her *fault* that Noumena, a fledgling when she hired on and qualified for stock options, had since become perhaps the largest software and electronic media company in the world, nor was it her fault that Critic.com, a start-up she had joined precisely to escape Noumena, was subsequently bought for an immense price. Unlike many of her cohorts, Mary scarcely ever flattered herself by maintaining that her quotidian tasks there had played much of a role in making Noumena what it was today. Neither did she insist that her fortune constituted the just desserts of hours that were sometimes long and occasionally tedious. That was the past, and she kept herself well insulated from the money (and the money's attendant accountants, brokers, prospectuses, schedules, advices, and statements) the past had produced. Her true purposes lay entirely before her, in the future.

She could hear the traffic beginning to stir after the early-afternoon hiatus. Her eye fell to the windowsill, to the jars of pigment, so saturated, so fully realized in themselves. And that was how she had come to feel about the money: that it had given her the gift not of leisure but of herself.

Mary returned to the couch. She would finish her tea and read some more Ruskin, of the transcendent and necessary work of the sculptor, the painter, and of course the writer. She was content, but she was not idle or smug. In fact, since coming to Italy she was improved in every way. She even felt prettier, and perhaps she was, if Alex's ardour was any proof. Her own desire for him, too, was more urgent, in some way more essential and necessary. So the money—though she could never say this aloud—had made her more beautiful; and perhaps, she could not but think, it would make her better, even good.

She was still holding Tom's letter, extracting a fragment of tea leaf from her mouth with a corner of a page, and it occurred to her that the effect of money was not the same on everyone. Tom, for example, could acquire a great windfall, and while it might change his material circumstances it would not alter his life one iota. He would still be a loose end, his purpose to find a purpose. Money, infinite freedom and choice, would only confuse him more.

Mary would read Tom's letter to Alex tonight. He liked Mary to read to him, even from Ruskin (whom, he opined, was "full of shit"). Alex cared about Tom. He called him "our mascot." Tom had called Alex the "ur-slacker," but perhaps failed to understand how Alex's insouciant manner freed him to achieve whatever struck him as interesting or needful almost without apparent effort, whereas Tom's constant preoccupation with the need to find a suitable persona for himself had pretty well paralyzed him.

So Alex wished Tom well, would raise no objection to his visiting them for as long as he liked, but would scarcely give him the push he needed to launch him into life. But Mary, in her good fortune, might be just the one to do it. Opening *Sesame and Lilies,* she thought again of Tom Hirsch; of how she might save him, or at least put him to some good use.

That evening, Alex and Mary sat before a little fire of chestnut and oak boughs. Their lunch had been substantial, so they supped on olives, bread, and morsels of pecorino, drinking red wine. Alex was midway through his fourth glass and lay sprawled in his paint-spattered jeans and chambray on the couch, blue on blue. Mary sat on a cushion with her back to the fire. She began to read.

Dear Mary and Alex,
It's been quite a day. I got fired. I got a little drunk. On the way home I got mugged. Hope you guys are well.

You remember Michael Sullivan? He did the deed, denying he was doing it, even while the dronebots from Human Resources were cleaning out my desk and wiping my passwords. Our friend Michael.

"I don't remember him, this friend of ours," Alex inserted.

"You wouldn't. He's a content developer. I knew him at Noumena a little."

"So really, Tom's being . . ."

"Rhetorical," Mary said, and continued reading.

He'd called me over to talk about the encyclopedia, "Founders of the Modern" (a.k.a. My Favourite German Guys). He says he wants to go through my Wagner entry. Just a couple of comments. We go back and forth a little and then he says, You're just supposed to be reporting about Wagner, not making him look good. And with that and the links—besides Schopenhauer you've got Nietzsche and Hegel and Heidegger and Rilke—it's like you have this whole parade of anti-Semites and proto-Nazis.

So it's like I've single-handedly made this thing into "Founders of Third Reich"? I say. That's really unfair. And bogus—

"Nietzsche—he's hip these days, right?"

"Right."

"But not Wagner?"

"No."

"So Tom's way behind the curve with some of this stuff."

Mary shrugged. "Or way ahead." Her eyes returned to the text.

Michael interrupts, saying, In which you mention Heidegger, like you do practically everywhere. So the whole thing starts to reek of Heidegger. Who was a fucking stone Nazi.

A lot of things constellate around him, I say. And the Nazi thing's really overstated.

But that's the perception, says Michael. And the perception ends up compromising the objectivity of the whole project.

I make a lame reply. I say, The project's about doing good work, I hope.

But good work in the context of team work. I don't think you get that.

So I'm not good at my job? I say. He says, Not in the team context, no, you're not. Not any more.

Are you trying to tell me something? I say. He doesn't reply right away. We're just standing there in the cubicle desert, in the glare of the noonday sun, so to speak.

Look, he says. Yes. This isn't working.

I'm thinking he's talking to me like we're lovers and we're going to break up. I say, What isn't working? For who?

You aren't, he says. So you're being outplaced.

I'm being fired, I say.

No, you were never hired, Michael says. You were a contractor. That was no secret to anyone.

Whose decision was this? I ask.

Alex rose and went to the table to refill his glass.

It's just being done, he says. He's looking away.

I say, So this is like a sentence without a subject? No one's doing the firing. It just kind of happens?

This isn't about personalities, says Michael. You can talk to Human Resources. But they can't tell you anything.

This is just fucking Orwellian, I say. Kafkaesque. No wait, it's Carollian, it's like Alice in Wonderland. It's fascist and *absurd.*

"Ha," said Alex, still standing by the table.

"It gets better."

Tom, none of this is helping anybody, Michael says. Just accept it isn't working. Do yourself a favour and—

I interrupt, What is this "it" that isn't working? That's a straightforward question. Come on, Michael, unmask the signifier here.

He says, "It" is you. Okay?

Sure, I reply. That helps a lot.

So do yourself a favour, says Michael. He's getting out a piece of paper and shows it to me. He says, Sign this and there's a severance package. It just extends the non-disclosure thing you already signed and adds a non-disparagement clause. Or you can bitch and moan and get nothing. I think it would be a smart thing to do. I know maybe it doesn't feel that way right now, but I'm still your friend.

Oh, you care, I say. How nice. For you.

"Bad move, Tom," said Alex, returning to the couch with his glass.

He says, Now you're just being an asshole.

I'm *being an asshole? I say.*

"Well, as a matter of fact—"

"Shh," said Mary.

Sign it, Tom, he says.

I ask, How much is it worth?

10K, says Michael. I have the cheque right here.

I ask him, So I should take the money?

Yeah, take the money, he says. Move to Portland, where it's still cheap. Maybe do the same gig there if you want. You get a nice letter of reference with the cheque.

I don't say anything. I take the paper from his hand. He gives me a pen. I sign.

Now I start talking a little nicer because I'm ashamed. I say, You know, I always thought we were going to do some great things. Some cool things.

"Is that regret or self-pity?" said Alex. "I can't tell."

"Both. Now shut up."

This isn't nothing, Michael says. You think most companies let you work on Wagner or Gertrude Stein?

I say, It's a product. That's what it's called here. That's what you *call it.*

It's still creative work, he says.

What, so it's art? I ask.

I don't know. Maybe everyone's an artist now, he says.

I say, So we're all artists now. That's nice. I like that. And we're all millionaires now too.

He says, Some of your *friends are artists and, yeah, they're millionaires.*

"I changed my mind. This Michael guy is the asshole," Alex interrupted.

How about you? I say. You going to be a retiree soon?

"Okay, Tommy lands one."

None of your business, says Michael.

"Got him on the run."

"Alex, please." Mary waited an instant and began again.

I say, But it's not exactly irrelevant to your point of view on all this.

Oh, fuck you, Tom, he says. Just go. Go have a life. Send me a postcard from Portland or wherever. Call me in a year.

I say, Okay. I guess I need to go back to my desk and get my stuff.

But Michael says, I think it'll already be at reception. And then he hands me an envelope. The one with the money. I gave him my ID. We shook hands in a limp sort of way.

I drove back across the lake and dumped my stuff at home. I looked around my apartment and realized I wasn't going to be able to afford Belltown any more. The 10K might get me through four months. I could move. I could sell my car, which arguably wasn't worth anything. I went to the Emerald Grill to think.

You remember Kevin the bartender?

"Good guy. A sweetheart."

"Alex, will you just stop? With these—I don't know—inane, drunken interruptions."

"I'm not drunk. I'm working on it. But I'm not drunk."

Mary exhaled.

He was cool about the whole thing. He told me to forget about the bar tab. And I'd had four drinks plus the goat-cheese appetizer thingy. I decided to go home and listen to Parsifal.

Which turned out to be a really stupid idea. I was walking on Blanchard. There were three guys, big but kind of short, like refrigerators or sumo wrestlers. Indeterminate race, like the people on airplane safety instructions.

They had me down on the sidewalk that quickly, kicking me. I tried to offer them my wallet and one of them just kicked it out of my hand and said—I swear this—"Don't want your fucking money, yuppie." They kicked me some more and I tried to yell at them, but I couldn't speak. I could have killed them. They'd called me "yuppie." That really galled.

I went home and looked at myself and called a taxi to take me to the emergency room. I'm bruised all over and ache like hell, but there's nothing broken. So here I am at home, writing you guys.

Alex sat up, put his hands in his lap, the fingers entangled, and stared downward.

You might imagine I'm not feeling awfully well disposed to Seattle right now. You might say Seattle doesn't love me either. Anyway, I don't want whatever it is people think they're going to get here: leather club chairs, stock options, the Ford Behemoth SUV, more bandwidth, a pug, love with the right dronebot. I'm ready to settle. You can have love and money and all the rest.

And here Mary laughed in what Alex heard as a sad way, and then continued to read, more slowly.

So listen. What if I take my blood money from Noumena and come see you guys? You said you had room before, but people always say that. But now I'm really asking if it truly would be okay. For maybe a month. Really think about it and don't be afraid to say no. That's why I wrote instead of calling—so you guys could really think it over.

I imagine it's really exciting and busy now you've found a house (I can't get myself to write "villa" without wanting to put quotation marks around it). But I hope everything's really great: that you love it as much as you thought you would and of course that you're managing to get some good work done, that Alex is painting great things (If I came, I could model. [ha.]), that Mary has started her novel (The novel could be about me. [meta-ha.]).

But really, I want to try to finally do some serious work. (Maybe

I could write that essay about Morrissey and the Smiths in their early period. In relation to Baudelaire. I really was serious about that. Or about Rilke. I've got some ideas. Or at least some thoughts about some ideas.) I suppose this is an opportunity, bruised ribs and all. Anyway, you guys are an inspiration.

Love,
Tom

Mary put the letter down on top of her books and journals. She said nothing, aware that Tom's proposition to them required Alex's assent.

Alex looked up at last. "Poor fucker," he said.

"Poverino," said Mary.

"He does kind of go on," said Alex. "Sheesh, what, eight pages?"

"He's a writer. Or at least a writer *manqué*."

"I don't know. Maybe just a wannabe rock critic, one of these people that's so blown away by some music they heard when they were a teenager that they have to spend their twenties and thirties *explaining* it to everyone. As if the music needed that. As if it were about the music and not just *them*."

"That's not really fair," said Mary. She paused. "Maybe it's slightly accurate. But anyway, I feel some responsibility. I got him that job."

"You got him every real job he's ever had."

"He got the barista jobs on his own."

"I said *real* jobs. And if he screws it up, it's not really up to you to fix things. I mean, frankly, you could see how somebody would almost *want* to fire him."

"And beat him up?"

"*Especially* beat him up."

"So that justifies—"

"No. Of course not. His personality just kind of gets up some people's noses."

"That doesn't make it any easier for him."

"But he's kind of his own worst enemy. Always taking these stands about stuff that's beside the point."

"He's intense," said Mary. "That's sort of *different* these days. It balances out the obnoxiousness and makes him kind of lovable."

"He fucks up at love too. Remember that nice guy—the guy who was going to be a composer. He broke up with him because he didn't want be a 'down,' or whatever they call it."

"A bottom, I think you mean. Tom wasn't comfortable with it. He wasn't even sure if he was really gay."

"How can you not know who you want to fuck?" said Alex.

"I remember a time when you wanted to fuck pretty much everyone."

"I had convictions," Alex said. "Tom's just . . . nowhere at all. Anyway, so let him come over. Should we call him? It's . . ."

"Ten in the morning. Too early."

"So later? Maybe after . . ."

"We find some way to pass the time?"

"So come here, you."

"*You* come here. Closer to the fire." Mary patted the other cushion next to her. Alex drained his glass and went over to her. They undressed and made languorous, oblivious love as the heat and light of the fire radiated across them, beating against the ancient walls, floating up towards the *cotto* ceiling and its heavy beams. Of that, and all else, they were scarcely aware.

Mary had, unusually, an orgasm. She did not give this much thought, but kept herself swaddled inside the feeling of it for a long time afterward, even after Alex had lifted himself up and fetched and refilled his glass. The feeling expanded and diffused into one of general well-being, of happy potential; no longer so much constituted by the ascent to and arrival at the instant of her climax, but by the sense of continuing progress, of a vista before her. She felt herself launched into a great project, of having purchased a villa—as, she reminded herself, she had indeed done—and of now having the pleasure of ordering and furnishing each of its rooms exactly as she saw fit, like chapters in a well-wrought tale, and then of peopling them as well.

2.

Agli amici, all'arte, alla vita

Maddalena was twelve years old and lived, insofar as she lived anywhere, in the central train station of Florence, the Stazione Santa Maria Novella, named for the great Dominican church across the street. Maddalena had begged for change with her mother in front of the church, she had been inside, and she had done things she supposed you shouldn't do in the cloister, in places you were not supposed to go.

But lately—since her mother had gone off again, had left her under the vague supervision of some acquaintances her mother used with—Maddalena lived more or less in the station with Laura, Pietro, and various other kids whose domestic arrangements were similar to her own; who slept in empty coaches, who cadged spare change at the entrances, who grabbed unattended bags, who scoured recently arrived trains for forgotten belongings and food; who, for five or ten thousand lire from a man in a hurry, a lonely man, would touch him or let him touch them in one or another of the station's hidden crannies.

Maddalena went to her mother's friends' apartment every other day or so to check in, to wash clothes, to watch television, to see what food was available and what money might be lifted from sleeping or stoned adults. But as often as not, no one answered the door, or some friend of her mother's friends would bother her, or it was just boring, whereas at the station, although it was noisy and dirty and sometimes cold, there was always somebody around, there was always something happening.

Just then, at around eleven in the morning on the first Thursday of March, they were waiting for the Eurostar from Milan, a train that was especially well provisioned with businessmen and bleary tourists fresh from all-night flights. As the train drew in, Maddalena, Laura, Pietro, and a kid Pietro knew named Jacopo were down at the far end of the platform, where the first-class coaches would stop.

When the doors opened, you had to stand back at first or the businessmen lunging forward would practically knock you down. Nor were they susceptible to the girls' entreaties for donations, even from Laura, who, although older than Maddalena, made a very persuasive waif, of whom people might say *"molto carina"* even as they passed her by. Even then, Laura did rather well, better than Maddalena, who was no more mature, but had what she called "*un* look" constituted of bright tops and hip-hugger jeans. They were still girls' clothes, but reflected Maddalena's aspirations to be a pop star or a supermodel. She was pretty enough. Even the kids who teased her admitted that. None of them would say—and perhaps they didn't see, for the same was true of them—that her clothes were frayed and smudged in places.

Now they waited for the tourists, especially the Americans, to appear. They came a long while after the businessmen and the Italians, descending unsteadily to the platform, towing wheeled luggage that scarcely fit through the doors, that must contain everything one could want or need, although the Americans did not look rich. They almost always dressed in lumpy, drab clothes and fat, thick-soled shoes. Even when they didn't, you could spot them: dress them head to toe in Italian attire, and they would still waddle, or stride as though someone were chasing them, or let their heads loll; or simply wear a perpetual expression of needing to please and to be pleased, of wanting the world to be as happy as they; of wanting to consume it entirely.

The children on the platform knew this, depended on the inevitability of certain habits and tics. For example, as soon as they descended, rather than move down the platform to the concourse, the Americans would stop, often for some time, as if accustoming themselves to the light. And then they would begin to reorganize themselves, opening bags, packs, and suitcases, taking things out, consulting maps and books and hand-held computers. Sometimes they looked pleased to have arrived, but more often they seemed to be in the grip of various agonies: fatigue, disorientation, vertigo, swoon and collapse under the bulk of their baggage, and you might see the couples among them hiss or glare at one another.

This was a boon for the children, for however badly off the Americans were, the children were seemingly worse so and Italian in the bargain. And as often as not, wallets and bags and those strange pouches Americans cinched just below their bellies were already open, their contents—tickets, travel documents, credit cards, and banknotes—to hand. When the children greeted and encircled an arriving party, things tended to get overlooked or dropped or lost. If one American was gruff, another would be generous (perhaps, ignorant of the value of the local currency, unintentionally so) or give them something simply to go away, out of irritation or fear.

That morning, the children netted six thousand lire plus an American dollar bill each. Then, once they were certain the conductors had left, they boarded the coaches and scoured them for bags, change lost in the seat cushions, food and sundries—bottles of water, sandwiches, pastries, cigarettes, gum and candy, sunglasses, return tickets, gloves, scarves, coats, and magazines (Maddalena liked these)—abandoned or overlooked. After checking three or four coaches, the children sat down and assayed their salvage, trading it or simply bestowing it on one another, for the children were generous with one another, as generous as Americans.

Around that time, as always happened, the cleaners came aboard the train and with shouts and imprecations attempted to drive the children off. The children simply ignored them or moved down a coach. The cleaners weren't even Italian—they were Arab or African—and, unless they threatened violence or attempted to seize some of the booty, were of no concern. For their part, the cleaners knew that no one, not even their own supervisors, would do anything to help them.

When the children were all ready, Pietro proposed they go back to the concourse to see what was happening or at least to change the American dollar bills. At the *cambio* booth, they saw that a teller who was ill-disposed towards them—who would either refuse to deal with them or who would take half of what was due to them as a *tangente*—was on duty, and so they returned to the platforms.

They turned up platform one, running along the far north wall of the station, and saw at a little distance an unmistakably American figure using the normally broken and somewhat isolated telephone kiosk there. As they continued towards him, he hung up the handset and began to root around in a large nylon pack, the possession of which revealed him as a student or someone posing as a student, friendly perhaps but unlikely to render them any charity.

"Non darsi la pena—" Laura began to say, but Pietro's friend Jacopo cut her off. "No, no—*andiamoci*." He strode towards the American, calling back to the other children, *"Dai, dai."* They followed after him.

As they approached, the American stood up from his pack and faced them. He was, Maddalena saw, about her mother's age. She had never seen her father, but imagined him, too, to be roughly similar to this man: perhaps thirty-five years old, dark and slight, and somewhat preoccupied or distracted; or at least too distracted for him to take part in her life.

Jacopo sidled up to the American, his thumbs locked into the pockets of his jeans. Jacopo was at most fourteen, an unknown quantity to Laura and Maddalena, but Maddalena could see that the American was afraid of him, even before he spoke, asking him what was in the pack, first in dialect and then in Italian.

The American stood there, his mouth slightly open. He looked over to the other children, and then down the platform to the concourse. Then he said, *"Non capisco,"* and smiled. He looked down the platform again.

"Oh, *inglese*. Okay. Okay." Jacopo looked back at Pietro and cocked his jaw to indicate Pietro ought to join him. Pietro shook his head. *"Non preoccuparti,"* he called out.

"Un attimo," said Jacopo, and turned back to the American. "You want to suck me cock? Ten thousand lire. Okay?"

The American moved a step down the platform towards the distant concourse, his hand clutching the open flap of the pack, which made a scratching sound as it dragged along with him.

"It you good?" Jacopo continued.

The American halted, and moved back a further step. He scowled and said, "Oh, fuck you," and then louder, "Just fuck off."

Maddalena recognized the word "fuck," although she was unsure of the rest. He was speaking too fast for her, as foreigners tended to do. Pietro now came forward to Jacopo's side, whether in defence of his friend or for some other purpose, and together they pressed towards him. Red-faced and trembling, the American simultaneously took several more steps back and shouted, "Just fuck off, you fucking maggots," and broke into a run, towing his pack behind him.

They stood and watched him, Maddalena and Laura, Jacopo and Pietro still standing together by the telephone, as he disappeared into the concourse. Maddalena had not understood much more of what the American had said, and this was a disappointment to her, for although she had pretty much given up on school, she wanted to learn English, needed to learn it, she averred, to become what she wanted to be.

She had caught the last word, and much later, Alessandro would explain to her what it meant, laughing, because it was a sort of silly word, something disgusting, a worm that you'd want to throw away, like a bad painting, *un aborto di quadro,* he'd said. One of the last times Maddalena had seen her mother they'd had a terrible fight, she had called her mother a whore and a junkie, and her mother told her she had nearly had an abortion when she got pregnant with her, that Maddalena ought to be grateful to her for saving her, for not aborting her—like, Maddalena supposed, a maggot. And that was more or less when Maddalena decided the station was her home.

Tom Hirsch arrived in Florence just before noon on the second day of March, having transited—as best he could remember—three different airports in three (or was it four? *could* it have been four?) aircraft, plus the second-class train car he had just stepped down from. He had arranged with Mary that he would telephone her when he got in and she would come to the station and fetch him.

"I can handle this," he said, steadying himself and his pack as he descended what seemed to him vertiginously steep steps to the platform. He looked up one end and down the other, increasingly aware that bodies—Italian bodies, moving at high speed, as often as not brandishing ignited cigarettes—coursed around him, and, for safety's sake and for want of any other idea, he let himself be borne down the platform along with them. At the delta of this river, where the flood of persons dispersed and disappeared into a score of smaller streams, he saw a newsstand. It was here, he thought, that he might buy a phone card.

Tom advanced and then stopped perhaps four feet in front of it. There was no identifiable line in which he might wait his turn, but there were, it seemed, an infinitude of customers, who did not so much stop and purchase a newspaper as intercept one in mid-flight, money and goods changing hands wordlessly, telepathically, at a frequency that Tom could not hear.

At last there was a break. Tom stepped forward, holding a five thousand lire note. The vendor would say *"Mi dica"* and Tom would reply *"Vorrei comprare una carta telefonica"* and that would be that. The man's back was to him, but then he swung around alarmingly fast and from between the bales of periodicals made eye contact with Tom. Or simply glared at him.

"Yes?" he said.

This threw Tom off his plan. He blurted out, "Buon giorgio," followed by "Card telefono."

"No," the man said.

"No?" Tom said.

"No."

Tom attempted to shrug, to walk away, lest he begin crying. But then the man continued. "Not here. There," he said, flinging his arm out to Tom's left. "Tobacco."

"Tobacco," Tom said, feeling he ought to give his assent, even if he did not understand in the slightest what the man meant. *"Va bene,"* Tom added after some time, but the man had turned his back again.

He moved in the direction the news vendor had indicated to see what he might have been referring to. There was a cafeteria to his right and the baggage-check room to his left. Then it occurred to him that the man must have thought he wanted to buy cigarettes. Which was stupid, because no one (like him. From Seattle.) smoked. Maybe Tom had garbled the words and said something that meant "cigarettes" in Italian. The play, the possible interpretations, of a text were limitless. Imagine how much more so in a foreign language.

But just then, to the right of the door of the cafeteria, Tom saw another stand, this one selling candy, gum, and, yes, cigarettes. He moved closer. There was a sign illustrating things that looked like tickets or coupons. Tom threw himself forward—the vendor was unoccupied—and pleaded, "Card telefoni?"

"Quanto?"

"Cardi telefonese," Tom explained again. He held out the banknote.

"Sì." Now he had been understood. His heart stopped pounding. *"Cinque mille?"* the vendor was saying.

"Whatever," Tom offered. The vendor took the bill and handed him an orange and white card. *"Va bene grazie,"* he said, backing away from the stand. "*Ciao mille.*" He made a little bow and turned to find a telephone.

These, he assumed, would be close by. But there was none in sight. He stood still. The metal names and numbers on the announcement board fluttered and clattered. Gusts of Italian issued from loudspeakers. People poured by. Tom felt immobilized, but he was determined not to have a panic attack. He had already done that, back at the newsstand. He made himself move forward, dragging his pack along behind him, down towards the left flank of the station, which gave the appearance of being a place where Italians might put telephones.

He worked his way past the baggage-check room and the long queue of people with packs waiting in it, people who looked reassuringly like him, or at least as he was ten or twelve years ago. He felt safe in their proximity and so continued down the platform.

There was an empty train parked alongside it and it seemed to grow emptier and more ramshackle and abandoned with each car he passed. When he was nearly even with the stained and rusted locomotive and just preparing to turn back, to haul the burden of his pack and his body back to the concourse, he saw a telephone.

Tom set his pack down next to it and dug out Alex and Mary's number. He inserted the card into the telephone. It hummed for a moment and spit the card back out. He put it in again with the same result and then once more. He tried to remember to breathe, to breathe and remember—recollect in tranquility—what Mary had instructed him. Slowly, calmly. Yes, tear off the corner. He hadn't done that. Now he did. He put the card into the phone. As though in greeting, in order to reassure him, the little screen lit up and displayed the figure "L5000."

Now he dialed all the numbers on the paper except for the first five. There was a sound, not a ring, but a long bleat, followed by a silence, and another bleat and then a voice. *"Pronto,"* it said. Tom feared he had reached an Italian by mistake, that he had the wrong number—that all was lost—but then it spoke again, unmistakably Mary. "Hello?"

Tom's heart (or rather his serotonin levels, he supposed) leapt. "It's me," he said breathlessly. "I'm here. At the station."

"Great. I'm on my way. It'll take me maybe twenty minutes."

"Sure. No problem."

"Wait at the bus stops. They're on the side of the station, out on the left as you face towards the front, as your back's to the platforms."

"I think I'm pretty near that."

"Good. Just hang out there. I'll find you."

"Okay. Hey, thanks."

"Oh, it's nothing. This is going to be great."

"Okay," Tom said, and hung up. The telephone spat out his card and he bent down to his pack to place it and Mary's information back inside. Then, as he rose, he saw a group of children, surely no more than pre-teens, coming towards him.

"Not five minutes in Florence and you're set upon by urchins," Mary remarked.

"I was really a little afraid. I mean, they were definitely kind of menacing."

"Well, it seems that way, the way they kind of pack in around you. Usually they have a sign they push at you and while you're distracted one of them picks your pocket."

"They didn't have a sign. And the girls kind of hung back. But still, kids . . ."

"They're not even really Italian," Mary said. "They're gypsies. Or that's what the Italians call them. There are gypsies, and then there are the black guys who sell the handbags. The Italians can be pretty racist about them."

"These didn't look like gypsies. Just white kids. Not that I know how gypsies are supposed to look."

"This isn't a violent country. You're safe here. Maybe not your stuff, but *you* are. So don't let the one experience put you off."

"I'll just think of it as local colour," Tom said. Mary had led him to a bus stop, and they stood there a few minutes. Tom had not bargained on Florence being cold, not in March—he had pictured the weather being rather like Los Angeles's—and he was relieved when, shortly, the bus pulled up. As he hefted his pack aboard, he said as much to Mary.

"It's not an unknown fact," she replied. "Cold in winter, hot in summer. Henry James was always mentioning it. That's why they took villas up on the hills. It's cooler in the summer, less damp in the winter."

"I guess I was relying on *Lonely Planet*, not James."

"Don't worry. We'll keep you warm." The bus shuddered and began to lurch across the Piazza Santa Maria Novella. Mary added, "I suppose you don't have a ticket?"

"For the bus?"

"No reason you should. I've got a pass. For you, we'll just have to pray that the inspectors don't come."

"There's a big fine?"

"A medium fine. But lots of scowling and gesticulating. Lots of shaming and loss of face."

"I don't need any more of that. Noumena was enough. And getting mugged. That and the kids just now."

Mary patted his hand, the one clutching the rail by the ticket-cancelling machine. "I know. But now that's all far, far away and over. Now you're going to have fun. You're going to be happy."

"I suppose if I can't be happy here, I can't be happy anywhere."

Mary didn't reply but began to point out the window. "See that church? Santa Maria Novella. The hotel to the side of it is where James lived for a while, where he wrote *Roderick Hudson*. William Dean Howells lived there too."

"Wow," said Tom. He hadn't read *Roderick Hudson* (except for *The Portrait of a Lady* in college, he hadn't really read Henry James at all: one didn't need to read him to know he sucked) but he knew James was one of Mary's passions. As for William Dean Howells, he, presumably, was a friend of James.

"And I found the place near our house where Rilke lived."

"Really?" Tom exclaimed. Rilke, together with the lyric oeuvre of Morrissey, was more or less the culmination of all art in the mind of Tom Hirsch. "Can you go in? Is there a museum?"

"It's a hotel, on the river. I suppose you could rent his room if you wanted. Sleep there, if the notion took you."

"Shit," said Tom. He was a little muted by his journey—Seattle to Salt Lake City to Atlanta to Milan to the Stazione Santa Maria Novella—and looking to acquire a second wind. He wanted to have coffee or a nap or some other restorative and then have Mary tell him all this again.

Mary was continuing. "It gets worse. You know the house we're buying? Villa Donatello? It's almost next door to Villa Castellani, where James set *The Portrait of a Lady*."

"Jeez, really?" said Tom. He felt that was quite enthusiastic, under the circumstances.

"Wait," said Mary, scarcely suppressing a giggle. "Our next-door neighbour—well, practically next door—is Wright Turner."

"The—?" Tom began, but just then the capacity to speak, together almost with the capacity to breathe and metabolize, seemed to have escaped him; thanks, he supposed, to the travel, the lack of sleep, the sheer surfeit of novelty Mary was throwing at him.

"The one you're thinking of. The art historian, and of course the guy who wrote the diaries. The principal one, I suppose, among the Wright Turners of this world."

"Cool," said Tom. He had heard of Turner. He was an eminent gay, an expatriate art connoisseur, writer, and all-purpose savant who had known and often slept with most of the major post-war artists and writers. When he published his journals in the 1970s and '80s they'd caused quite a stir. There'd been no further volumes as far as Tom knew.

They crossed the Ponte alla Carraia over the river, travelled some further blocks, and then Mary indicated they should get off. "I need to pick up some things on the way home. Some food."

Mary led him down a narrow pavement and into the entrance of a delicatessen, or some kind of store at which cheese, cold cuts, and miscellaneous groceries were being sold. It was a little before one o'clock in the afternoon, and there was a line, or rather a mob, a crush of persons pressing up against the counter. The place echoed with amiable shouts and cries and canoodling chatter, the bustle and froth of the great henhouse that is Italy.

Prompted by a cue unrecognizable to Tom, after some minutes Mary suddenly put herself front and centre and became the object of the counterman's attention.

Good day, madam. Tell me, what would you like?

The prosciutto. Some of prosciutto, please.

Which would madam like, the Parma or the San Daniele?

A littleness of the San Daniele, I prefer.

And how much?

Give me of it two hundreds gram.

Very well, madam.

The counterman set to work and Tom said to Mary, "You've gotten really fluent. You just get in there and do it like a native."

"Really, to them, I sound like I'm talking baby-talk."

Tom reflected that there was very little in life with which Mary did not "just get in there." But he added, "I don't think so. I mean he's taking you completely seriously."

"For a presentable female or an infant, Italian men will do *anything*," Mary said as the counterman returned to her with a paper bearing the prosciutto, now sliced into translucent leaves. Tom saw that she had her hand propped on her hip as she spoke with him, that she had at some point pushed her sunglasses up and back into hair.

And what else, madam?

Some of bread. Not too cooked.

With salt?

No, without. Tuscan bread, please.

Excellent, madam. Madam has a taste for the authentic. And how much?

That one here. Give me of it one half.

Very well, madam.

The counterman sawed through the loaf and wrapped it. Tom whispered in Mary's ear, "I'd say he kind of likes you."

"It's just flirting," Mary said. "No, not even flirting. It's just . . . aimless aestheticism. Which happened to land on me."

And what else, madam?

That's of it all. I am enough.

Very well. Thirteen thousand lire then, if you please.

Here there is of it. Thank you very much.

Thank you, madam. You speak Italian perfectly.

You are a great gentlewoman. Good day, sir.

Until we see you again, madam.

They went out and began to walk. "It's just a couple of blocks to our place," said Mary. Tom looked around him: at the tan and sorrel walls of the buildings, the throb and spew of traffic rent by blitzkriegs of motor scooters, at the paper-wrapped food parcels Mary held against her breast. He was here, and it was almost more than he could bear. But Mary was here too, and had already acclimated. So perhaps he could too.

Of course, Mary had her overarching confidence to see her through. Not to mention her money. But it was her beauty, her *bellezza*—one of the few words in Italian Tom felt sure about using—that must have seen her through in the store. If she spoke well, it would be exquisite, and if (as she had protested) she spoke badly, it would be charming. She could scarcely fail here; and she might well bring him along with her.

The first thing Tom noticed in Mary and Alex's apartment were the shadows; or rather the manner in which the light, strained through the tall windows and their veils of curtain and shutter, fell upon the floor. There was more floor than anything else, as there was little furniture: a few pieces from the landlord, Mary explained, and some inexpensive things they'd bought locally. Most of their own belongings were still sealed inside a shipping container, awaiting their move to the Villa Donatello.

"Which is where Alex is," Mary said. "He's supposed to come back around now. For lunch. He really wants to see you."

"Has he been working up there?"

"Well, not on *his* work. But on stuff that needs doing. Some plumbing problems. Tiles. Staying on top of the contractors."

"So are they bilking you American homeowners in their colourful and charming way?" said Tom. "I mean, I read that book."

"Everybody has. But no. Actually, they show up and work. I suppose we're being overcharged, but if that's the worst of it, who cares?"

"So when do you move in?"

"Two or three weeks, if we're lucky. We're not doing much to it, really. Adding a second bathroom. Fixing the roof. We agreed we want it to feel intact, old, even if that means it seems a little funky, a little dilapidated."

Just then, Alex entered, himself looking a little rumpled and spattered, as was usual. He gave the impression of being a painter even when he had been nowhere near canvas in weeks. He was tall and broad-shouldered with a great thicket of wavy blond-brown hair on his head. He had large and supple hands, from one of which just then hung a bottle.

"Hey, hi Tom. Here you are," Alex cried. "Here we *all* are." He raised the bottle. "I got some prosecco. Actually, it's Bollinger. It's an occasion, to say the least. So why fuck around?" He moved closer to Tom and bent down a little to look at him closely. "So how was it? The eastward journey and all?"

"I'm a little wasted. Somewhere around Bologna on the train I think I lapsed into a fugue state. It's like I'm outside of myself. And I'm watching this person who seems to be me walking around and trying to do stuff. I hope I've got the right guy. That it's not somebody else. That I didn't lose myself somewhere along with my luggage."

"Then some gypsy kids hustled him at the station," Mary added.

"Nothing a beverage won't cure." For Alex, life was but a succession of occasions that called for a drink, for some fortifying or celebratory device to cement the fabric of the day.

"I'm not sure I should. Might knock me out—"

"Well, of course, you shouldn't," said Alex. "But of course you must."

"I suppose," said Tom.

"Good," said Alex. "Just let me get the Ikea champagne flutes out of the Ikea cupboard and we can settle down on the Ikea sofa. It'll be just like home for you, just like Seattle."

"I guess I can handle that," said Tom.

"This is all temporary," Mary said to Tom. "Actually, we've bought some nice things that are stashed up at the villa."

Alex wrenched the cork from the bottle. "Hey, Ikea's good basic stuff. Good design."

"So there's an Ikea in Florence?" Tom asked.

"You're surprised?" Alex said.

"I suppose not. It's just a little . . . incongruous. Somehow."

"Here in the cradle of the Renaissance, you mean?" added Mary.

"It's not exactly what you come here for, that's all."

"Oh," said Alex, "it's not what we came here for either. But it's handy." He handed Tom a glass and one to Mary. "We came here for the art and the food."

"And of course the real estate," Mary said. "Or so people might believe."

"Those would be the stupid people," said Tom.

"We should toast your arrival," said Alex.

"We should toast your villa," said Tom.

"That can come later," said Alex, raising his glass. "May you get what you came for. May you get what you deserve."

"Be careful of toasts like that," said Mary. "Let's just say, to friends, to art, to life. To our work."

And they tapped their glasses together and drank.

3.

Things in Themselves

Tom had begun to find his bearings a little. For the first few days things had felt artificial and brittle; the world seemed a great dry mouth, a bag of fidgets and itches. Mary had taken him to see Michelangelo's tomb in Santa Croce and Alex showed him the Masaccios in the Brancacci Chapel near their apartment. While they were standing there, Alex said, "I want to paint like this."

"I thought you wanted to paint like Rothko or one of those fifties guys."

"Not now, I don't. To tell you the truth, I think I'm a little tired of that stuff."

"You mean the Moderns? In general?"

"I don't know. It all seems a bit . . . sterile. Too intellectual. Like a lot of blueprints or manifestos." Alex stopped. "God, don't tell anybody I said that."

"I won't."

"Maybe the paintings are fine," Alex continued. "Maybe it's me. Maybe *I'm* fading."

"Or maybe," Tom offered, "it's not the paintings or you, but that historical moment that's slipping away from us. It's not our fault. It's just that our capacity to see it is sort of disappearing into the distance. Or only exists in dreams."

"I don't know. Maybe so. But it wouldn't make me any happier. I mean, I don't think I even like Picasso any more."

"Wow. Does Mary know?"

"Oh, she'd be thrilled. She thinks Picasso was a prick. A self-promoter, she says. Warhol with genius."

"That's a little out there. I didn't know she felt that way."

"Well, you can't just say these things. At least you couldn't in Seattle. I mean, what she said about the Beats—she lost friends over that."

Tom felt entirely too frangible to pursue the matter further, but it registered as a rather remarkable transformation, and not a little strange.

He had also visited the villa twice; once, as promised, on the afternoon of his arrival, and then two days later. On the first occasion, moved by the champagne they'd been drinking, he remarked, "So this is Gilbert Osmond's next-door neighbour's house." After unpacking, Tom had made a quick scan of Mary's copy of *The Portrait of a Lady* in order to reacquaint himself with the plot and characters.

"Or at least," said Alex, "Wright Turner's neighbour's house."

"Well," said Mary, "Turner is supposed to have known Bernard Berenson, who knew Henry James, so there's actually kind of a connection."

"Not," inserted Tom, who didn't want to insult his friends by association, "that there's anything spooky or . . . devious about this place. Really, it's heaven. It's perfect."

That seemed true enough; and it is not difficult to impress a bookish and sensitive young man if you show him a small walled garden studded with olive trees and vines; a terrace roofed with wisteria; and a view of the city and the river. The house itself, smaller than the word "villa" had suggested to Tom, had four bedrooms (one, he imagined, for Mary and Alex, one for him, a writing studio for Mary, and maybe one for *his* studio), a spartan but generously sized kitchen, and two sitting rooms (the latter of which would serve as Alex's studio). It was, as he had observed of the apartment, a little dark inside, but he could not truly imagine

Gilbert Osmond—rearranging his artworks and *objets,* setting his net for the good, lovely, and rich Isabel Archer—anywhere nearby.

Still, Tom put it more than once to Mary that she must be writing a sequel to *The Portrait of a Lady*, not always to good effect, for Tom tended to alternate too often between obsequity (which he mistook for kindness) and presumption (which he mistook for concern), and for Mary the contrast was often less bracing than disconcerting. The last time he pressed her, as they stood in the villa's upstairs hall, she merely shrugged and admitted little more.

"But you are working on something, aren't you?" Tom continued.

"I think I'm just on the verge."

"So what's it about?"

"I can't say. It would jinx it. It would spoil it."

Tom nodded, and chanced another subject he was curious about. Pointing down to the large bedroom at the end of the hall, he said, "So I guess that's the master, for you and Alex. What are you going to do with the others?"

"Well," Mary said, "that one"—indicating the room adjacent to her and Alex's—"I figured I'd use for my study, my writing room, or whatever you want to call it."

"That sounds cool. And—"

"And that one"—here Mary did an about-face and pointed down to the opposite end of the hallway—"will be the guest room. Which means your room, if that's okay."

"Okay? I hadn't even thought—"

"Well, of course you're staying. And for as long as you want."

"Shit, Mary, that's really—well, I don't know what . . ."

"Oh, it's nothing. I mean, what would we do with all this space, a bunch of empty rooms?"

"Well, it's still really amazing, really kind."

"I imagined you'd just take it for granted. It just goes without saying, okay?"

"Well, sure." Tom was relieved but also a little taken aback by Mary's nonchalance about his appropriating the villa's space, and could not help but put a further question to her. "So what about *that* one?" he asked, nodding towards the door of the room between what was to be his and what was to be Mary's studio.

"Oh," she offered agreeably, "I suppose that's the other guest room. Or maybe the nursery. Who's to say?"

"Oh. Okay."

Tom had never pictured Mary and Alex as parents; could no more imagine them in that role than he could himself, which was to say never under any circumstances whatsoever. But he let the thought go, and returned to basking in Mary's announcement that he was already fully installed as a member of the household. That was more than enough for Tom. He had simply wanted assurance that they were all going to be artists together (although he had never really thought through how he would be able to remain in Italy). He pictured each one of them working happily in their respective rooms, and then of an evening—surely every evening in summer and not a few in April, May, and October—sitting outside together, eating and drinking and talking. Even now, while it was still a little chilly outside, he could imagine it. But it would have to wait a while for the workers and painters and plumbers (who were installing central heating in addition to the second bathroom), at least, by the latest estimate, until April.

The construction delays at the villa had, in fact, been few, something Mary attributed to Alex's rapport with the workers and contractors.

"I thought he couldn't speak Italian," Tom had said. "So I don't understand how he . . ."

"Communicates?" said Mary. "Me neither. But he does. It's like he's gone straight past Italian and into dialect. Anyway, if it wasn't for him they would have mounted the bidet on the bathroom wall or something. Maybe it's the visual art thing—he's into all the building materials and stuff."

That seemed likely enough to Tom that very evening when, at dinner in a trattoria near the Porta Romana, Alex launched into an explication of the different varieties of tiles in use at the villa.

"It's really a whole different building medium here," he said. "I mean, at home it's essentially framing lumber and sheetrock and siding. Here, it's stone and mortar and tile and brick. There's wood beams, but everything else is stone and terra cotta." Alex stopped and drank. "There's *mattone* and *mattonelle,* different sizes and shapes—"

"Kind of like pasta," Mary offered.

"Yeah," Alex continued. "Those are your bricks. Then there's tile. There's *coppi* for the roof and *mezzane* for the ceiling and *cotto* for the floor."

"So there's kind of a grammar of tile," Tom said.

"Maybe. I don't know," said Alex. "But anyway, we haven't even gotten to the decorated tiles, the field tiles—"

"Do we really need to get to them?" Mary asked. "Right now? Tonight?"

"Sorry," Alex said. "I didn't mean to be boring." Alex strove to never be boring to anyone, anytime, a vocation he felt nearly as strongly as his desire to shield Mary from boring phenomena in general and bad news in particular. But now she had forced his hand. "The thing is," he continued, "is that there's a little mix-up with the tile."

"At the villa?" Mary said. "Oh, shit."

"Yeah," said Alex.

"Grandissimo or *piccolino?"* she pressed.

"Maybe kind of *moderato,*" said Alex, and leaned back in his chair, his glass cradled in his palm. He turned to Tom, as though by explaining it to him the problem would be somehow less noisome to Mary. "See, we wanted to use old tile, to keep the character of the house. And we needed *mezzane* for the ceilings and *cotto* for the new floor in the second bathroom and for the kitchen."

"Yes?" Tom heard himself say, as if he understood, as if this had anything to do with him.

"Well, the guys did the floors with the *mezzane*."

"Oh, shit," Mary said.

"Is that bad?" inquired Tom.

"Yeah. *Mezzane* is softer, rougher, thinner. Doesn't wear as well."

"Alex, why did they do that?" Mary said.

"Why? I don't know why. It's not like they had . . . a motivation."

"Okay," said Mary. "*How* did it happen?"

"Well, I suppose I fucked up." Alex said this in an unremarkable tone. "I should have checked when they started."

"You couldn't see the difference?" Mary said, more evenly than harshly. Still, Tom thought, he was glad it was Alex rather than him.

"I should have," Alex continued. "They laid them paint-side down, so I didn't see that they were *mezzane*."

"You didn't see," Tom said in affirmation of his friend Alex, and offered, "and they're painted."

"On one side. Because they used to be somebody's ceiling."

"Oh," said Tom, mystified.

Mary's jaw had been thrust out for some moments. She retracted it and said, "So how long? How much?"

"Maybe a week, maybe two. Because now we're short tiles for the ceilings too."

"And how much?" Mary repeated.

"Don't worry about it."

"Okay. I won't."

That was the end of the matter. It seemed to Tom that it had been no big deal and, on the other hand, that there had been palpable tension; that great things were at stake. He thought it might help if he made a show of solidarity, of being a genuine housemate.

"You know, about my room—you guys are so great—my room in the villa? We never talked about rent—"

"Rent?" Alex said. "There's no rent. Come on."

"Well, wow. I don't know what to say. But still, I want to put in something. For the groceries, the electric bill. Although, really, I couldn't pay much. I've got maybe five thousand dollars to my name."

"We don't want you to pay anything," said Mary. "I mean, what are we going to do with more money? And you're our friend."

"I'd want to contribute something." Tom said.

"You can pick olives. You can cook. You can do the shopping. Whatever," said Mary.

"Wow," Tom said. "I guess that's a deal." He added, "I guess I better learn how to pick olives." But, in fact, this opportunity would never arise.

After a few more glasses of wine, they managed to get the waiter to bring the *conto* ("You have to fight them for it, go mano-a-mano," Alex explained. "They don't want you to leave—*ever*"). Tom made a limp effort to put in his share, but was waved off by Mary, who produced one of her several platinum credit cards and laid it over the check. "You're incorrigible," she said. And then they went home to bed.

There was indeed no false urgency about Mary's wish to make the villa habitable as soon as possible. Tom was a considerate, even fastidious, guest, and during the daytime you would scarcely guess that the blue couch was his bed and the kitchen his lavatory (the toilet, of course, was only accessible through Mary and Alex's bedroom; and you would be impressed were you to consider the amount of urologic rigour he brought to bear on this problem after they had retired for the evening).

That night, Tom lay on the couch, the glow of Mary and Alex's offer still warming him. They had given him not just financial largesse, but succour, support, and counsel without the smallest hesitation, without any suggestion that, like so much else, these were not qualities they had in excess. He could not but think that coming here, to these now dark and silent rooms just within the gates of this city of pocked and riven stone, was one of the few smart things he had done in his adult life.

At some point when he was beginning to fall asleep he thought he heard something. In the week he had been here, he had never heard any sound traceable to their room, but he surmised that Mary and Alex were fucking. He supposed they did this every night. He thought some more and found himself imagining that Alex had a big cock; that Mary's lovemaking was assertive and lubricious; that their bodies together made a sort of seething noise as they rubbed against the linen. Tom realized he had an erection.

He touched himself shyly, as though it might be someone else's penis, and then with more confidence. He found himself imagining more things about Mary and Alex separately and in tandem, and he could not say which of these aroused him most or to whom he was more attracted. Could Alex's cock trump Mary's beautiful ass, or could the two of them locked together, pressing and thrusting, be said to demonstrate that the whole exceeds the sum of its parts?

Then he thought of all of them being in bed together—of all three of them, and especially of himself—and in the space of a moment ejaculated with tremendous force and volume. He lay quietly for a moment. Whatever sounds he had heard before were stilled, and now he pondered the matter of how to clean himself up.

Clutching his genitals, Tom got up and made his way to the kitchen, hoping the trail of drips he was doubtless leaving on the terrazzo would go undetected. He could see almost nothing. He felt along the counters, and when his wrist struck the breadboard it seemed to him to make a tremendous clatter against the tiles, sufficient to wake the whole household. He stood stock still and waited, but there was no sign anyone had been awakened. Then he rifled the drawers, and found a paper napkin.

Having cleaned himself and disposed of the napkin in the trash, he moved back to the door of the *salone*. Tom could just make out where the window must be, betrayed by a sliver of light between the massive drapes. He shuffled towards it, his hand stretched out in front of him, parted the curtains and slipped past them. He pressed up against the windowsill, against Alex's little shrine of ground pigments.

Tom could see out onto the street and, if he craned his neck hard enough, up the way to the house where Mary had said the Brownings and Hawthorne had lived. Adjacent to it were the rooms where a brokenhearted and bankrupt Dostoevsky had written *The Idiot*, a book people had said he ought to read but which he had not taken up, feeling there was something a little pointed, a little cruel, in the suggestion. Below him were rank upon rank of motor scooters and a few bicycles, chained to a lamppost or a rail or ring of thickset wrought iron. There was a scant moon, and he saw two cats crossing the street, and from the other direction, the distant buzz, click, and slam of some person being admitted to a locked and shuttered palazzo. He had in that moment of near-perfect silence and stasis, of a thousand or two years of human life pausing between breaths, a great instant of recognition; of where, at last, he was, if not who; and of the necessity to seize it and make something of it, and not least something of his own self. He heard another sputter of motor-scooter noise, not so very different from distant gunfire, and then he parted the drapes and returned to his bed.

Tom slept deeply, so deeply that Mary and Alex were already in the kitchen making toast and coffee when he awoke. Alex came out carrying cups. He saw that Tom's eyes were open and said, "Hey, hi. Sleep well?"

"Oh, yeah. Sure," Tom said as his hand slithered out from

beneath his blanket to retrieve his boxer shorts from the floor. He glanced at the terrazzo between him and where Alex was standing and saw a trace, broken and faintly sheened, that looked like a slug trail. He wriggled into his shorts, stood up and pulled on his jeans, and stepped towards the breakfast table, buffing strategic spots of the floor with his stocking feet as he went.

Alex had returned to the kitchen and now re-emerged with the coffee, Mary behind him bearing the toast. "And you guys?" Tom asked. "Well rested?"

"Pretty well," said Mary. "I had one of my headaches." She twisted off the lid of a jar of apricot marmellata. "Gone now, thankfully."

"Good," Tom offered.

Alex was applying butter to his toast, saying nothing, as Tom joined him and Mary at the table. He grabbed a piece of toast from the platter. "So what's on for today?" he asked brightly.

"I'll be up at the villa," Alex said. He turned towards Mary and added, "Until dinner, probably."

"Suit yourself," responded Mary. She turned away from him to Tom. "I'm going to read. Maybe write a little."

Tom could not help but detect a chill in the air, or at least the absence of any residual goodwill from what he had assumed was the previous night's lovemaking.

"And what about you, Tom?" Mary was asking.

Tom felt caught out, unawares. "About what, about me?"

"I mean, what are you going to do today?"

"Oh," Tom said with some relief. "I don't know. Take a walk. Whatever. Maybe I could have a look at that Ruskin when you're done."

Alex lifted his head. "You'd be better off looking at some real art. Maybe tomorrow—"

"I'm sure Tom can decide what he wants to do," Mary inserted briskly.

Alex seemed to pull back a little. "Sure he can. I just think maybe the work ought to come before the criticism, the secondary stuff."

"Ruskin's a classic. He's a primary work of art in himself."

"Well, okay. But it's still . . . contingent on somebody else's painting or architecture or whatever."

"It's parasitic, I suppose?" Mary had, Tom saw, put down her coffee cup and was looking straight at Alex.

"I'm not going to go that far."

"Good. You don't need to be threatened by people writing about art, you know."

"I should go," said Alex. He went to the door, and then turned back and said to Mary, "You know, I could probably make it down for lunch. If you wanted."

Mary was silent for a moment. "No, it's okay," she said finally.

Alex merely nodded and went out. After he was gone, and Mary dressed and went out herself to get a newspaper, Tom wondered if what had just transpired was a fight or merely some variety of bad weather, a squall or shower, that had drifted across the breakfast table. In Tom's recollection Alex and Mary did not fight: not about money—they hardly had reason—or sex (but how would he know?), but only about art, and then scarcely at all. Of course, Tom barely knew even to whom he was attracted, never mind anything about the secrets of couples. But it seemed to him that when it came to art, it was very important to like the same things. Kant had said this, he thought.

Alex boarded the bus to Bellosguardo in Piazza Romana. They were going to buy a car—a little one—but there was no place to park it anywhere near the apartment, so that would have to wait, like so many things, until they were in the villa. Sometimes he almost hated the villa, its refusal to gel. You'd stuff one problem—say, a vent for the new bathroom—back inside the box and another—say, the heretofore undiscovered rotten beam between the bathroom ceiling and the roof tiles—would pop out somewhere else. There was never a crisis as such, only an endless concatenation of niggles and distractions.

The villa, in short, was *hassling* him. And its hassles metastasized and cross-fertilized and made little baby hassles that got *into* everything, that smeared grape jam on the freshly primed walls. Last night, he and Mary had had sex and afterward they were lying there. Mary said something like, "I could have had a really nice orgasm if Tom wasn't ten feet away in the next room."

Alex said, "He can't hear anything. You'd have to scream—"

"Maybe I'd like that. To scream."

"You don't scream. Not ever with me anyway," Alex had said, and then thought, Dumb move, Alex.

Mary did not address this point which, Alex knew, did not mean she hadn't taken it in, wasn't processing it, didn't intend to address it in a footnote somewhere; she was simply laying it down in the cantina for bottle-aging before uncorking it on some later occasion. Now, she said, "It's just the feeling of being hemmed in, of not having the space. Just to be able to have the apartment to myself, to be able to read and write . . ."

It seemed to Alex that he might reasonably point out that Mary had been mightily enthusiastic about Tom coming over; that, for that matter, Tom had initially been *her* friend, and was now—what? Her project.

But Alex saw that would be the wrong thing to say; that, kind of like the plumbing at the villa, Mary's response would not necessarily follow the line of argument Alex had intended to lay down; that it might burst forth under the kitchen sink rather than the main drain or the cold supply. She might say, "So really, you weren't levelling with me about it being okay for him to come," or, "So he's not your friend too?" Then she might, for good measure—because psychoanalysis had become unfashionable to such an extent that she was keen to take it up—call him "passive-aggressive."

So Alex congratulated himself for having the brains to say,

"Well, it's a temporary situation," in a tone that was meant to be both neutral and reassuring. Now if Mary had said, "I guess you're right," or "I suppose," or even "Whatever," that would have been fine. But she merely rolled over and, saying nothing, went to sleep.

Mary's silences were not like other people's: words were her medium, so their absence was no less meaningful than was a white space on one of Alex's canvases. In fact, her silence could be her most profound comment, her ultimate rhetorical weapon, and, as Tom liked to say, interpretations were limitless. Although Alex thought Tom was full of shit about this, he rolled over and began to make some interpretations of his own. These boiled down to the belief that Mary thought it was all his fault for not getting the villa (*her* villa? He wasn't going to touch that.) finished; that, and the insuppressible notion—stupid and insistent, like an erection—that if his sex skills were better, his cock mightier, she wouldn't have not had an orgasm in the first place. Alex thought of mellowing himself a bit by going out to the kitchen and pouring himself a little glass of wine, but, yes, there Tom was.

He had gotten up that morning feeling testy, and maybe Mary had too. He had ragged her about Ruskin and all the air had gone out of the room, replaced by the stuff they put in refrigerator coils and air conditioners. He had tried to make it better as he was leaving, but she wasn't buying any.

So when he descended from the bus, he was adding that—fixing things with Mary—to his punch list, the tally of repairs necessary that day to undo the previous day's outbreaks of chaos and fuck-up; to get back to where they were the day before that. This, together with a couple of glasses of wine, would be by Alex's lights, a fair definition of success.

Alex was actually good at fixing things, or at least persuading others that they weren't as broken as they appeared. It was his own version of *sprezzatura*, the knack of making difficult things look easy, and on account of it Italy suited him. The workers at the villa seemed to genuinely like him, perhaps because he gave no sign that it was especially important to him that they work. So things got done.

To reach the villa, Alex had to walk down a lane for a half mile, and he always liked this part of his daily journey. It reminded him of where he grew up on the eastern side of the Cascades. Like Tuscany, his had been a dry climate and the light seemed to fall in much the same violet-blue zone of the spectrum. Where these hills had olive trees, they had had apple trees, not so different in shape and stature, and sometimes the leaves had a similar tint.

Alex was walking between two opposing sets of walls, broken now and then by a gate, and the olive leaves hung over them. He saw what bullshit it was to say the leaves were "silver" or "dusky" or "pewter" or "burnished green." They were, in fact, the colour of olive leaves, precisely, exactly, no more or less, the colour itself of the thing itself. That wasn't, as Mary might have said, tautologous, but merely essential. It was the facts of the matter. It was what the world was. He was walking through it: olive leaf, stone wall, early morning light tending to violet, heat forming on the asphalt, pebbles in the asphalt, bump in the road, crack in the wall, lizard—hello, lizard!—emerging from the crack out into the purpling light, junction in the road, another road—but not just another but entirely distinct, *like* other roads but really itself—with parked cars, like stumps and boulders but still absolutely cars, that villa, this villa, and now the gate, the guys—thank god—inside working.

Alex said hello to the two guys outside mixing plaster, and called up to the two inside, and he heard voices boom back from within, saying who knows what (Mary had studied Italian for two years at the Seattle Language Academy, unlike Alex, but he got along. She might be able to speak Italian, but he could, he felt, *talk* it a little). He looked around the garden. They needed a gardener, and Mary was supposed to be asking around, but it would be easier if he just handled it himself; if he just asked one of the guys who they knew.

Meanwhile, he saw there were flowers coming up—camellias, he thought, but what did names matter?—and that if he cut some of these, dressed them out with a little wisteria, and brought them down to Mary, that would, with luck, go most of the way towards repairing the breach of this morning. And it struck him that, as at his dad's shop, there was always *something* lying around that would do the job, patch things up, more or less, if you only looked around carefully.

Most of what he knew, he had learned from his father (or, later, from Jens Hammershøi, his painting mentor) or taught himself from dealing with his mother. His father had an auto repair and body shop which, as far as Alex could see, distressed cars entered, but never emerged recognizably repaired and completed. Rather, a car might limp in with a crushed front left fender and a ball-joint knocked all-to-hell akimbo, and roll out a week later with the fender hammered out and filled with body putty, the wheels apparently tracking straight, but now with inexplicable pulmonary difficulties in the region of the manifold.

Alex's father, seated among bales of manuals and parts catalogues and oily rags in his office or out on the curb next to the pop machine, explained more than once that this was the law of thermodynamics in action; or, on other occasions, that of diminishing returns or of Hobson or Heisenberg. In any case, it meant that while one thing might be made better, another would get worse; and the point therefore was to maintain an overall steady state, to keep one's head above water and a smile on one's face. It was Ockham's Razor and Gödel's Ontological Proof. It was, as iron laws went, Dad explained, The Champagne of Bottled Beers.

This philosophy did not make the Hansens wealthy—it

wasn't until he came to Seattle after high school that Alex realized they had been, by some people's definition, poor—but it served, as Dad promised, to keep their heads above water; and in this they were much aided by Dad's capacity for friendship, by his legion of buddies, who hunkered around the shop and when needed would rise off their haunches and stick their heads under the hood in question. They might not effect a solution, but they were generally ready with a hypothesis or a line of inquiry, from which profitable speculation might result. One or another was always ready to go the parts store, or swap or borrow or conjure up by alchemical means the necessary thing, or the baling wire, tin foil, and electrical tape to approximate it.

Alex's mother—grey eyes and grey hair—lived with, perhaps even assented to, this dispensation through the first ten years of his childhood. Dad was a good man, idle and tending to overdrink, but authentically good. And Mom had set her store in Alex's older brother, Peter, who was set to amount to something, when, at age seventeen, he was killed in one or another automobile at the Blewett Pass cut-off of U.S. 2. Dad started drinking more, spending the night at the shop while Mom stood for hours in the kitchen, ironing and re-ironing Peter's clothes.

Peter had been a heroic figure to Alex, less a brother than a visiting dignitary whose autograph he had been lucky enough to obtain. Alex might have been asked, this being 1970, how he felt about it all, about the tragedy. But no one did, not in Wenatchee, and he was too busy to ask himself. A vacuum had formed in the Hansen family, and he was sucked into it, was the fodder that filled it insofar as a boy could; ran interference and shuttle diplomacy between Dad and Mom. Over the next seven years, he learned to apply Dad's lessons to a variety of problems and situations with considerably more imagination and energy than Dad himself had ever brought to bear upon the world. In dealing with Mom—how to keep her upright and on course, to fend her off when the sheer deadweight of her, the lead ballast of her grief, threatened to take them all down—he learned how to make women happy.

These skills—he scarcely gave their origins a thought, just as he forgot Dad and then Mom, once they were buried—had stood him in good stead; had, if not made him happy, given him the assurance that happiness was possible; even afforded him (once he got his brain chemistry adjusted and tuned) contentment. He had learned, perhaps most all, to love—to take satisfaction in—a good day's work; less in any particular task or achievement than in merely keeping the decks clear so that there was space and time to let the world show itself. That was how it was for Alex as he walked back to the bus stop, taking in the same things—the walls and lizards and olive leaves—he had seen that morning, all the same yet entirely new because the light had heated up, because the cicadas pulsed and the lizards skittered noiselessly in counterpoint, because it was now and not then, because he was walking back from and not to the villa and was in a better mood.

He sat on the bus, holding Mary's flowers, looking forward to a few glasses of wine, to dinner, and to, yes, he was sure now, seeing Mary; and not least to telling her he thought they'd gained back some time today at the villa. As the bus swung around the Piazza Romana, he saw a new piece of graffiti sprayed on the massive city wall that towered over the street running northward. It said *Amore perchè anticipare la nostra fine,* and he thought, as Dad would have said, "Ain't it the truth."

Alex was right. Mary took the bait, accepted the tribute paid. She knew what it was, what it symbolized, but she received it gladly. Because they *were* lovely flowers, flowers from her garden, and they were easily commensurate to the task of forgiving him. She drove a hard bargain, but he knew the value of things.

Alex and Tom and Mary sat happily for an hour, drinking wine and eating nuts and olives. Tom had gone for a long walk and had managed, rather to his own surprise, to find his way to the other side of the Arno and back again without getting lost, except in pleasant and serendipitous ways. He had stumbled upon the Uffizi during a lull in the press of the crowd and had to wait scarcely ten minutes to be admitted. Once inside, he bounced along in the wake of a group of Japanese who were following the beacon of a rolled umbrella held aloft. That group's forward march was bisected by a similar group following a similar umbrella. Tom heard the words *"Schönheit"* and *"malerisch"* and naturally followed them into an adjacent gallery. The convoy of Germans disappeared, and Tom saw he was alone with a legendary Botticelli. He had just an instant to consider whether this might qualify as an epiphany when another group poured through the cataract of the gallery and swept him up.

"So was it?" Mary asked.

"It might have been. But before I could decide, the painting turned into this thing I'd seen a million pictures of—this . . . celebrity—and then I wondered if I even cared."

"Well, that's a lousy environment to see art in," Alex said. "I mean, you can't *look* at things in a place like that."

"Because of the crowds—"

"Because the work's been penned up in an institution. Like a fucking zoo. Almost none of it was made to be seen in that context. It's all a byproduct of Berenson and people like that wheeling and dealing."

"The Uffizi predates Berenson," Mary put in.

"Maybe, but it's still a black hole for art. I mean, look around it, the kind of thing it attracts. Bad, really bad consumer junk—the guys selling Prada-bag knock-offs and those posters of the Raphael angels and Bart Simpson and the cat doing chin-ups and the close-ups of the David's cock. It's not coincidental."

Tom said, "But it's democratic. People can see this stuff that used to be hidden away—"

"Which now they pay to see. When it was all in churches, you could see it for free. You could see it where it was meant to be, see what it was *for*."

"Alex, you almost sound like Ruskin," said Mary.

"I don't know about that. But listen. I've got an idea. Let's all take some time tomorrow and I'll show you something really great. It's a museum, but it's not a museum."

"Sure," Tom agreed.

Mary nodded, but then added in as neutral a tone as she could muster, "They don't need you at the villa?"

"Not really," Alex said. "Actually, I've got some good news. The *mezzane*. It turns out they didn't lay them upside down after all. They just misplaced them."

"They lost them?" Mary said.

"Yeah, but now they're found."

"Was blind and now I—"

"No, Tom. Please," said Mary, a little sharply. "And so?"

"I'd say we gained back a week."

"Which means?"

"Well, if you don't mind some rough patches here and there—there'd be running water, toilets, and a working kitchen, so to speak—we could probably move in a week from now."

Mary pressed her palms together and then slapped them down on her thighs. She said, "Oh, Alex, you really are so absolutely good," and then she beamed at him.

"Well, I guess we ought to celebrate," said Alex modestly, and so they did. They went to a happy, noisy trattoria on the south-west corner of the Piazza Santo Spirito. They had to wait until nine-thirty to get a table, but they bought a bottle of wine and took it out to a bench on the edge of the piazza and drank under the moon in the budding night. The piazza was almost silent, almost free of other people, like an empty theatre, save for a brace of lovers and an old woman dishing out food to a pride of feral cats. They felt themselves for the first time to be a kind of family planted here in the great empty heart of Tuscany.

The next afternoon, around five o'clock, Alex took them to the Convento San Marco, which was a museum but also not a museum in the sense that it was a decommissioned Dominican priory. They had pressed forward, upward through the city's touristic core—the Palazzo Pitti, the Ponte Vecchio, the Duomo and Baptistery, and the Accademia—beating against the crowds, and when they arrived at the Convento they were surprised at the stillness of it, at how much it remained a place of silence. It struck Tom to such an extent that he repressed his urge to observe aloud that they were paying to enter it.

The three of them wandered for a little under a half-hour on the ground floor, in and around the cloister. Mary circled the cloister several times, noting that merely to sit here, undisturbed save for the striking of the bell on the quarter-hour, book in hand, every day, just her and the lawn and the geraniums, for the rest of one's life, would be heaven, more or less. The villa, of course, would be a little like that.

Tom's reaction was initially more guarded. In the refectory, he imagined how it would be to sit here, three times a day, with the same people, year after year, eating dorm food (they did call the place they slept a "dormitory"). But he liked the library and the cloister, and the information brochure had given him to understand that it was in the cloister that the monks did their writing, which consisted mostly of what the brochure called "marginalia" and "commentary."

Tom could live with that; that and the free room and board and, when he thought about it, the reassurance of never having to go out and find a job, of becoming something and being and doing it successfully. Of only having to study and pray. He was not sure about the latter. He had tried meditation several times and hadn't gotten anywhere with it. But anyone, he had always heard, could pray.

Alex, too, imagined a vocation of sorts here; of the task of filling all these walls with images. That had been Fra Angelico's job, and he had all the assistants and materials he needed, supplied by this, his community. He was artist-in-residence, here and up the hill in Fiesole at the home monastery. It would be pretty close to the ultimate gig, except for the lack of women and decent beverages. The notion of someday painting, perhaps even frescoing, all the walls in the villa, was just forming in his mind's eye when Tom and Mary came up to him.

"So is that it? Should we go?" Tom was asking.

"Oh shit, no. The best part of all is upstairs," and with that Alex led to them up the stairway. They rounded the landing and as they ascended an image hove into view at of the top of the stairs. It was a fresco of a slight woman, seated on a stool in an arcade of Tuscan columns, her arms crossed in self-defence or deference, her head somewhat bowed, her expression a little fearful and dumbfounded, as well she might be, for an angel was standing opposite her.

Alex motioned Mary and Tom forward, and the colours, muted from a distance, swelled up, surfaced out of their depths, into brilliance.

"It's beautiful, stunning," Mary said.

"Shit," Tom said. "Holy shit."

"It's all you need," Alex said. "Just this one."

Tom, on what impulse he could not say, found himself reciting, "'And there—that one's holding nothing but itself.'" He stopped and then he said, "That's Rilke. 'The Bowl of Roses.' I've been waiting for the right time to say it."

"It fits," Mary said. And then they stood silently a little longer. Tom noticed this, and he thought that it was perhaps the hardest thing in the world—at least in this present world—to remain silent and let something simply act upon oneself; not to deflect it or push it away, to fear what it might say or do to you if you let it. And yet, here they were, in a building that was consecrated to exactly that purpose, to putting yourself before, in the path of, certain things, almost at their mercy, some of them things you couldn't even see. Maybe that was what the prayer part was: a means to see the invisible.

When Alex finally spoke, it was a kind of release, as though he had been holding his breath all that time. "There's more," he said.

He led them down the corridor past door after door, each one the little cell of a monk, each one frescoed with a scene from the life of Jesus, all in the same style; all, Alex told them, by Fra Angelico or one of his assistants.

The frescoes were mostly crucifixions—grisly and absurd, blood spurting in jets and streams from the impassive body—or annunciations in the mode of the one at the top of the stair, or madonnas with their infants.

Of one of the latter, Alex remarked, "What I like about them is they're *soft*. But not in a fluffy way." He paused. "You could almost see them as a series of abstractions, just changing the colour field a little, changing the tint of the sky."

"But really," Tom offered, "the whole subject, the whole composition is prescribed. By tradition. It's nothing new. It's a formula."

Alex took what was, for him, umbrage at this. "It's *all* new, every time," he said. "In one, she's looking a little more to one side or up or down. Or the baby's doing one thing or another. Or the weather's changed." Alex was in the home stretch, bounding towards what Mary knew to be his aperçu, his truism. "They're all completely the same and completely different."

Alex stood and let this remark steep a while, and then Mary said, "She's never looking *at* you, is she? The baby does, sometimes, but he's . . . a baby."

"You know what she doesn't do," Tom said, "is look right at the baby. Like you'd expect her to, like a mom's supposed to."

"She can't bear to. It's too painful. She knows this child was born to die," said Mary.

Alex moved still closer to the painting, to Mary and Tom, and said, "That's why she so . . . composed. She's not happy like a mother should be, but she's totally self-possessed, complete in herself. She's . . . intact."

"Of course she's intact, Alex. She's a virgin," Tom offered.

Alex wasn't done. "No, I mean she's in this picture and she's oblivious to it. She couldn't care less."

"Well, come on," Tom said. "She's there to be looked at. She's being objectified, silenced."

"She can't *talk*," Alex said. "She's in a fucking painting."

"Alex, please," said Mary.

Alex went on. "No, listen. Trust me. I'm a painter. In this painting, the madonna's like . . . a force. She doesn't know she's being looked at. She doesn't care. Maybe everything about her is tragic, but she's a thing, a force unto herself."

Mary had said very little all this while. She was slightly annoyed by Alex's pronouncements, which she sometimes felt did not really add up but were merely designed—if they had any design—to produce a mood of off-hand profundity. He had the right of course, as a painter, to hold forth on painting, and sometimes he was very smart about how a painting might have come about or how the artist might have felt or thought as he worked.

But on the subject of madonnas, of motherhood, he knew nothing. How could he, given his own mother? Mary had met her but once, and that had been more than enough. She was a monster—not actively evil or even openly unpleasant—but a monster of despair, of despair suppurating into rage and self-pity. When she entered a room, she drank down all the oxygen in it. She left you gasping.

For that, Mary cut Alex some slack. But she had some ideas of her own about motherhood, its imperatives, the way it came upon you like that angel did to the girl, and made you assent to it, made you think it was the most important thing in the world and that it had always been your idea in the first place.

Mary thought that thought and more, but she had the wit to keep them to herself.

Meanwhile, Alex was having what seemed to be an epiphany. He was holding forth, ostensibly to Tom and Mary, in a manner that was both abstracted and manic, as though seized by an invisible force. He might as easily have been talking *to* the wall as talking about it.

"You want to paint like Fra Angelico?" Tom was inserting.

"No, not just like him," Alex began to explain. "But figurative and nude and kind of lapidary, like these. Like the world's shimmering, like it's breaking apart into . . . photons."

"And nude?" said Tom. Mary still wasn't saying anything. "I don't quite see—"

"I'll tell you why," Alex continued. "Because if Fra Angelico—or, really, any of these Renaissance guys—were alive today, that's what they'd be doing. Not madonnas and that kind of thing, because that's an image we don't know how to see any more. It's all emptied out, used up. But they'd still want to paint women. They'd want to paint beauty, naked beauty." Alex rubbed his hands together, exhaled, and smiled. "So that's what I'm going to do."

"Sounds great," Tom said.

They returned to the annunciation at the top of the stairs. Tom noticed an inscription along the bottom. Turning to Mary, he inquired, "Any idea what it says?"

Mary had, among the various arcana in her possession, a little Latin, which was in any case not all that different from Italian. She said, "Let me see," and then, after a moment, "I think it's basically saying that every time you pass this image you should remember to say an 'Ave,' a 'Hail Mary.'"

"You could almost talk me into it," said Alex.

"We'd love to see you convert, Alex," Tom laughed. They all had felt the pervasiveness of religion here. Just leaving the Convento, merely passing across the piazza to the bus stop, it assaulted you from every direction: churches (three or four within a block of here) and their bells, squadrons of nuns, old ladies with their rosaries (dressed, more often than not, in nun-like black), beggars wailing, *"Prego, per caritá,"* the saints' names of almost everything, the music store just behind the bus stop selling, of course, Palestrina and Monteverdi vespers.

Their bus drew up, sucked them in, surrounded them with convivial Italian chatter, itself the result of an inbred assurance of the availability of infinite forgiveness and grace. As the bus lurched towards Saint Mary's train station and its children, Tom might have reflected that this irrational and unexamined belief was so integrated into Italian life that you couldn't separate it out or pry it loose. It was why the Italians didn't worry about being killed by the insane, lunging drivers of their buses, scooters, and cars—they were all going to heaven, which they must assume was full of good restaurants (smoking permitted) and designer outlets. If you wanted to simply enjoy the food, the art, the buildings, and the general lifestyle apart from all that, as Alex and Mary and most other Americans did, you had to fabricate a kind of willful oblivion.

The bus crossed the river and followed the city wall towards the Porta Romana. Alex signalled Mary and Tom to get off just short of the piazza, just to be on the safe side—you never knew where a bus might land you if you simply accepted the route on faith. There in front of them was the graffiti he had seen the day before. It was large and clearly applied and it was not an anarchist symbol or the initials of a soccer team, so they noticed it.

Tom pointed it out to Mary. "So what's it mean? Something about love, I guess."

Mary worked her mouth as if chewing as she repeated the

phrase, trying to get a fix on it. She said, "Okay, 'Love because . . .' No, 'Love in order to anticipate our end.' Maybe 'end' as in 'our purpose.' How funny."

"How Italian," said Alex.

Mary continued. "Maybe it's really closer to something like, 'Love, because it reveals our purpose.' Our final, ultimate purpose."

Alex thought to himself that this was not quite right, but what did he know about literary Italian? He said nothing. Mary was entitled to her interpretation of things, and things, after all, were going pretty well.

At home, Tom had a shower and Mary went through the mail, pitching flyers and bits of paper from her broker and accountant into the trash. Then she stood, went to the window, and drew the drapes. Alex meanwhile laid a fire, had a glass of wine, and then another glass of wine.

The Convento San Marco came into his mind. He wouldn't say an "Ave," but somebody somewhere ought to be thanked. Debts were owed, even if to the unlikeliest people like Jens, who had taken him in hand when he'd come to Seattle and shown him how things worked in the world and on canvas. Then there was Mary. She was too good for him, of course; too pretty, smart and, lately, rich. He'd always be in arrears with her, perpetually in the red, no matter how hard he worked. But he would work anyway. It was his métier, trying to catch up, to make amends. Sometimes, awake in his cold pre-dawn sobriety, he had the unmistakable sense that he must have once done something so terrible and grave—so awful a betrayal, somewhere in or between Wenatchee and Seattle, by way of Blewett Pass, at sometime he had since forgotten—that he would spend the rest of his life atoning for it. So even now, when he felt content, the thought came easily upon him that he could do worse things in this life than do some good.

4.

The Agony

They were settled, the three of them, into the Villa Donatello by the third week of April. Tom established himself in the promised bedroom at the far end of the hall, Mary and Alex at the other, with Mary's studio and another empty room between them which Tom still hoped might become his studio. But in truth, the two windows, the oak table and chair, the old-but-not-threadbare red easy chair, and even the Ikea bed suited him very nicely. It was, as he cheerfully noted aloud many times, "a room with a view," but then all the upstairs rooms of the Villa Donatello might have been so described.

Alex's studio, the smaller of two salons, was downstairs, reached by a dark corridor. The studio itself, a corner room, was filled with light from the north and west, and was perched high above the far verge of the garden where the hill fell steeply away. It was, Tom felt, the most complete room in the house. Alex's easel, his stacked blank canvases leaning against the wall, his as yet unused tubes of paint and brushes, and especially Alex himself, in jeans and a blue workshirt, looked as though they belonged precisely there.

The total effect of the other rooms was in many places rather less congruous. The furniture that had been most at home in Mary and Alex's house in Seattle—various Stickley and other Arts and Crafts pieces—looked a bit forlorn in the Villa Donatello; what in a bungalow suggested integrity and painstaking simplicity here seemed provincial and crude. Mary and Alex's local purchases fit in better, but even these appeared rather small and spare, a little retiring for rooms like the *salone* that, while neither vast nor precisely formal, had terrazzo floors and patches of fresco on their walls. By day, the rooms seemed empty even when occupied by all the members of the household; at night, where Mary had pictured the rooms exuding an amber sheen, they seemed merely dank.

"So much for bungalow-style," said Alex. "Everything should be more baroque. More junky. But with refined junk. Seedy, but pretty too."

"You mean slutty," said Mary.

"Yeah, slutty. That's exactly it."

"You could put brocade and velvet over the furniture," Mary said. "I don't mean like slipcovers or tablecloths, but just sort of dump it right over things, like sheets. Like the house has been vacated for the summer."

"That's good, Mary," said Alex. "That's really good. Plus we hang some big paintings. Some big, *bad* paintings. Virgins having religious ecstasies and stuff."

"Why don't you do some?" Tom interjected.

"Oh, I will. But it'll take time. I'm going to do those nudes, you know."

This remark was still in the forward portion of Tom's mind a few days later when, walking into the centre of Florence, he and Alex stopped at the church of Santa Felicità. "Wait until you see what I found in here," Alex said.

Just inside the door, to their right, was a chapel dominated by a vast and looming *Descent from the Cross*, a crowd of bright pastel figures in stunned postures of grief.

"Pretty cool, huh?"

"Wow," said Tom. "The colours are like Valentine candy hearts. But then everybody in it is totally losing it. It's a little disconcerting."

"It's agony. Gorgeous, total agony."

Tom stepped over the threshold, into the chapel itself, but just then the lights went out. He startled.

"Relax," said Alex. "Nothing five hundred lire won't fix." He put a coin into a box on the wall, and the lights came on again. "You buy your time with art here. It's like a taxi. Or a hooker. Anyway, the painter's name was Pontormo."

Tom had gone back to looking, and then he looked at Alex and said, "I think all the faces are the same. That's kind of weird."

"The same model. I figure two models. A man and a woman. The men all have the same nose and mouth. And the women all have these hooded eyes."

"They're kind of erotic," said Tom. "The men too. Maybe even more so."

Alex didn't seem to hear him. "Not that it matters," Alex was adding. "You don't need a lot of models. Anyway, this is it. This is what I'm aiming for."

"I thought you were aiming for Fra Angelico."

"Whoever. Better not to get too grandiose. Just paint a nice painting." Alex put his hands in his pockets. "Want to get lunch?"

"Sure." They left the chapel and the church; left their last two hundred lire's worth of light for the good fortune of whomever might come in next, if they were quick about it.

Alex and Tom walked east along the Arno, crossed the Ponte alle Grazie, veered towards and then past Santa Croce, into an unprepossessing neighbourhood Alex said was called San Ambrogio. They entered a restaurant opposite a large outdoor market. They were seated at a large wooden table in a plainly furnished but handsome room. Before they could resume talking, they were approached by a man, also handsome in face and dress, and about Tom's age, who proceeded to sit down at their table and speak to them. It dawned on Tom that this, although he gave no indication of it, was their waiter.

He spoke to them in English, with the terrifying perfection of well-educated Germans, and he told them what was on offer that day; or, really, what he was going to let them have. Alex, who had been here before, responded with nods and shrugs, his only declarative sentence being a call for a particular bottle of wine. This they drank happily enough, and then another.

The food—very good, actually, though not what Tom was used to in either Italy or America—came and went, and they talked with what seemed to Tom heretofore unknown frankness and even abandon. Alex avoided pat summarizations and glib pronouncements, and Tom neither whined nor flattered. This state—drunkenness, Tom realized, but so much more—was perhaps what people like Jens Hammershøi saw in alcoholism. He didn't even mind when Alex pressed him (perhaps even needled him), because he realized it rather entitled him to press back.

"So what are you going to do with yourself?" Alex was saying. "Now that we're all settled in."

"I'm going to do something about Rilke. About the time he spent here."

"What kind of thing? Poems?"

"Creative non-fiction. I guess. A sort of meditation in prose. With maybe some memoir with it."

"So, really, you don't know. Right?"

"It's not totally clear to me yet, no. But it's not a lot of bullshit either."

"I didn't think you were bullshitting."

"Sometimes *I* think I am," Tom said. "So I figure it must be pretty plain to everybody else. Especially you and Mary."

"We don't think that. I don't think that. And I don't think Mary thinks that."

"You're great. So's Mary." Tom realized that somehow a third bottle of wine had appeared on the table, and that they were rounding the home stretch of it. Alex was talking, apparently to no one in particular, but then turned to Tom.

"Yeah, she's great. She can be a bitch, of course. But I love her. I love that I get to . . . *tame* her every day."

"Shit, Alex. Where'd you learn to talk like that?"

"From Zoloft. I suppose it emboldens me," Alex said. "But I mean it in the nicest possible way."

"That Zoloft emboldens you?"

"That Mary can be a bitch."

"Oh. But why do you take Zoloft? If anybody doesn't need Zoloft, it's you." Tom was surprised, not least because he had already surreptitiously inspected the contents of Mary and Alex's bathroom and seen the pills, but assumed they were Mary's.

"I wouldn't be 'me' without it. I'd be living alone in a cave. In some Nordic slough of despond, drinking myself to death."

"You'd be Jens, in other words."

"Jens wasn't a bad painter. He might have even been a good one."

"You talk like he's dead."

"He could be. I haven't heard from him in a year. We don't hear a lot from anyone from home. Or Seattle, or whatever you want to call it."

"Not even from Mary's friends? From the *CityReader*?"

"No. Not that Mary really has many friends. Most people can't handle the money thing. And, like I said, she can be a bitch."

"You don't mean that."

"I do, but like I said: in the nicest possible way," Alex said. "Which is why we're suited to each other. It's a perfect relationship. We love each other and we're totally selfish. Too selfish to let anyone else in."

"That's not true. You let me in. I'm living off you guys."

"You're family," Alex said, and poured the last of the wine into his glass. "You're one of our needs. We're having you instead of a baby."

"Mary doesn't want one?"

"She talks about it sometimes. And then at the last minute she backs away. She sees we couldn't be Scott and Zelda any more, the arty expatriates."

"That's not really her model, is it?" asked Tom. "Or yours?"

"I don't know. Maybe." Alex drank, and the waiter brought the check. "Did you know that they moved to Rome because Zelda read a Henry James novel that was set there? And that's where Fitzgerald really started hitting bottom, getting into brawls with the police during his benders." Alex extracted a credit card from his pocket. "And here *we* are. Because Mary read *The Portrait of a Lady*."

"Oh, come on. It's not like you don't want to be here, that it's not inspiring you."

"I suppose," he said, and put the credit card on top of the check.

"Shouldn't I be contributing something? I could give you some cash."

"Don't worry. It's taken care of."

Then Tom found himself saying, "By whom?"

"By me. Really. It's okay." Alex looked up at Tom. "Oh, I see. You want to know if it's really me. Or if it's Mary."

"Shit. I didn't mean it that way."

"Sure you did. People are curious. I'd be."

"I guess."

Alex leaned back and locked his hands behind his neck. "Well, it really is me. I've got my own money. I'm independent. I'm even a little bit rich."

"How?"

"Same way as Mary. She's been sharing with me right along. Her options. Because there were more than she knew what to do with. Because it would have felt weird not to. Awkward. And Mary's nice."

"Even though she's a bitch. She's generous."

"Oh, it's not like she knew we'd end up like this. Really rich. It kind of snuck up on us. Like giving Christmas presents over a period of a couple a years. And then you realize it's turned into a lot of money."

"So you have like . . . half?"

"No, not that much. But plenty. Enough for me."

"It's invested?"

"Yeah, in nice conservative things. Bonds and stuff."

"And Mary's . . . ?" Tom was conscious of leaving off the word "money."

"It's still in Noumena and Critic.com stock. She doesn't want to think about it. She wants it to just go away, like it doesn't exist." Alex began to get up from the table. "Anyway, it's all worked out well for me. I mean, coming here. Because making this big a move *and* being the kept man—I don't know if I could have gone for that. It gives me freedom, even to screw up. Like with the tiles. I could have just bought new ones."

"Interesting," Tom said, and left it at that. He was a little stunned by the knowledge he had just attained. He would have sooner asked Alex if he and Mary had anal sex, or voted Republican.

After the *conto* was settled, Alex and Tom walked in silence, the streets themselves silent in the ebb of the lunch hour, until they reached Santa Croce, where the tourists milled about waiting for things to open, frustrated by the afternoon intermezzo. Tom could no longer decide whether he and Alex were drunk, or had passed beyond that into some happy dream state. They crossed the bridge and as they approached Santa Felicità, Alex said, "How about another look?"

"It's open?"

"Sure. Even though hardly anyone goes in. If it were popular, the Italians would have it closed most of the day, maybe all the time. But it's not popular. That's the logic, I figure."

They went inside the church and Alex put a coin in the meter. The lights surged on, and they both looked a long while. "You see, this is what Mary *really* wants: gorgeous, remarkable suffering. Agony in pink."

"I don't see it," said Tom bravely. "I don't see the religious obsession or any of it. She's not a masochist."

"Oh, I don't mean she wants to suffer. I mean she wants to make an impression. She wants to leave a trace in the world, an image of herself. And it's kind of a dark image, I think. Of being a woman and suffering."

"I don't know. She's a strong woman."

"Trust me," Alex said and pointed upward. "See, there she is. Just to the left of the Virgin. With the pink scarf and her mouth kind of frozen. Not looking at Jesus, but at how the Virgin is reacting, like the true horror of his death is just dawning on her. And this other woman, this other Mary—my Mary—is realizing that this is bigger than grief, that it changes everything, makes everything sad forever. Mary would buy right into that."

"She might like the image, but that's not the same thing."

"She'd love it. And it's really dangerous to fall in love with images. Trust me. I'm a painter. I can tell the difference between what's real and what's a painting, an image. Some people can't."

Tom did not know what to say to this. He changed the subject, or at least pursued a different avenue of it. "So, these nudes you're going to paint. Who's going to be in them? Who's going to pose for them?"

"You, if you want. And Mary, of course."

"I don't know. I mean, maybe. But, really, I'm not very . . . imposing naked."

"Oh, I'll make you look like a god. Like Apollo. Or Big John Holmes."

"And Mary? She said she'd do it?"

"I'm not sure. I don't think I've asked her yet."

And what of Mary? As Alex and Tom talked about her, she was at work in her studio at her desk, her Craftsman writing table, which she had bought with her first options money. She was writing in a chestnut brown notebook, the one she had reserved for the project she was about to begin: her book. It would be set among Florentine Americans, it would be a novel, and Mary would be the novelist.

The last thing went without saying. The notion that she was incapable of it, could be hindered by either herself or anyone else in bringing it forth, was inconceivable to her. True, sitting at this very desk just a moment before—and not for the first time—she looked out into the garden and then imagined looking back upon herself: a woman, framed in a window, pen in hand, pen to paper, writing; framed, inevitably, not just by the window but by a conception, the phrase "a room of one's own."

But Mary scarcely needed an icon of a woman writer in order to *be* a woman writer, particularly one so peevish and spoiled as Virginia Woolf. If Mary took anyone as a model, it might be Dorothy Parker or, better still, Mary McCarthy; women who drank, fucked, and played the game on the same terms as men. She didn't need a room of her own. She already had one. She'd bought it herself.

Mary planned to bring her whole life and being to this novel; to bear down on it with immense force and impress within it pretty much everything she thought and felt. That she was born in the San Fernando Valley, in Woodland Hills, California, in 1963 would not be very pertinent to this, except insofar as it was the *nihilo* out of which she had created herself.

As a child, a conventional child living happily in the avocado-green arcadia of American suburbia, Mary was told she was pretty and told she was smart, and doubtless both these things were true; and she came to them almost by right, as they seemed to come to most every other child she knew. Her father taught chemistry at UCLA and was funny and kind. Her mother, who was busy and read a lot, stayed home with Mary and her two elder sisters and younger brother. Mary's mother was an aggressive competitor at tennis, had marched against the war at Century City, and maintained connections with really interesting people from the movement, from campus, and from Venice plus Laurel and Topanga Canyons, which constituted the main avant-garde within reach of the Ventura Freeway. They came to the Bruckner living and dining rooms, drank her sangria and ate her ratatouille, and told her she was smart, committed, and with-it. But for all that, she was unhappy.

Seeing this was Mary's first great act of intuition, which was to say compassion; and, even more so, you might say, of imagination—of picturing the interior landscape of another person. She was unhappy: Mary was sure that this was what her mother must be trying to say the Sunday morning she told them she was leaving. Lots of parents, mothers and fathers, were leaving just then, in 1972, at least two or three just on Mary's street, maybe five or six in her fifth-grade class.

Sometimes, of course, parents left because they hated the other parent in their house, or preferred a parent from another house. But most of the time they just needed to leave. It didn't mean they didn't love the kids or even the other parent they were leaving behind. But you couldn't love anyone else until you learned to love yourself. Mary's mother said this to them; said she was leaving to learn how to do this thing.

But Mary pointed out an inconsistency to her: that surely she had been loving them for all the time up until now, so she must have known how to love other people. So either she already did love herself or maybe the whole business ran just the opposite way: that you came to love yourself by loving other people.

This did not sway Mary's mother. She said of course she had loved them, but now she had to find her authentic self and learn how to love it, and then maybe she could come back and live with them again in a self-actualized way. Anyway, she had to get all the bad conditioning out of her. It wasn't anybody's fault; or maybe a little bit Dad's fault, but not in a way he could completely help.

Things did not change that much after Mary's mother went away to northern California. Dad had always poured the cereal and reminded them to get dressed and helped them with their homework. Now Mary and her sisters took over cooking dinner and supervised their little brother—walked him to school and walked him back and generally kept after him. They did more for him perhaps than really needed doing, for as a teenager and then a young man he showed himself to be diffident and aimless, possessed of a viscous potential that refused to harden into any particular interest, talent, or ability. But then, Mary would later reflect, this was pretty much the way something like two-thirds of the men she knew were.

On Mary herself, the changes in their home had nearly the opposite effect. Her duties and responsibilities transformed her from a dreamy and complacent little girl into a serious young person. When her mother returned after ten months, the household was indeed more complete, more vibrant, and even happier. The cat the children had adopted some weeks before had kittens, and this set a kind of seal on their rejuvenation as a family. Mary's mother could not help feeling it was her doing, that by imposing a new dispensation based on female self-reliance and male altruism, they were now all actualizing, individually and collectively.

Mary was not sure this was precisely right, but she was not going to argue about it. As her responsibilities—on her mother's return not so much diluted as having been rendered routine by Mary's growing competence and the passage of time—preoccupied her less, she lost herself in novel reading, nineteenth-century novels in particular. It was an unique moment in the history of the San Fernando Valley, but one that was mostly lost on her. When other girls were dreaming tube tops and crocheted vests (later establishing the Sherman Oaks Galleria as a phenomenon not unlike Seattle in the 1990s, Paris in the 1920s, or Florence in the 1500s) Mary dreamt muslin, linen, the starch and rustle of the world of venerable books.

At some point, after making the acquaintance of a stream of Jane Austen and George Eliot heroines, it struck her that she was in truth a nineteenth-century woman marooned in the opening chapters of Ronald Reagan's America. She felt estranged, not least from her mother. It seemed to Mary that her mother had simply missed the point of becoming a woman, of the need to seize the immense essential, the great thing, and thereby *arrive* at oneself. As a result, Mary had a sensibility, whereas her mother had only a psychology.

After Mary removed to college in Seattle (which, if it was a backwater, was a real backwater, as opposed to a phony backwater like the Valley), she returned home (how flat the roof of their house, she thought; how strangely nacreous the light, like fog illuminated from within) mainly to see her father and brother. She talked with her mother without any great awkwardness, but when matter of Mary's achievements at college or her future came up, Mary could not but feel that her mother wished to lay claim to these for herself, or at least take credit for their being possible. Yet surely, Mary thought, these—no less than infinitude of sandwiches made for her brother, the GoBots and Ninja Turtles animated for him in play, the clothes washed—belonged entirely to her alone.

She did not dwell on this. She simply stayed away and took in the diversions of college. She discovered sex. This was problematic, because she found she liked sex; liked it, in fact, as much as she did books and art, but she feared the entanglements it engendered would take her away from herself, would prove her mother right. Sex with the boys she met at the University of Washington was thrilling, but also rather too frivolous. She wanted to aim for passion, not merely fun; she wanted to fuck, but she wanted to fuck as the Brownings had fucked, as Mary

McCarthy and Edmund Wilson fucked after they had finished beating the shit out of one another in a literary argument. She felt that she and Alex had come awfully close, at least in their early years.

Alex, of course, had come along some time later, at a time in fact when Mary was tired of sex and certainly of men. By the time she had graduated, she believed she had done nearly everything there was to do and had done it with a strikingly diverse selection of partners. She worked for two years waitressing and, later, as a freelance copy editor at the Seattle *CityReader*. She returned to the university, spent six months in the creative writing program, and took one of her professors as a lover. He was old enough to have spots and grey hairs on his body, he was married, and, for her pains, showed not the slightest enthusiasm for her work, inside or outside of class, even when it was (as frequently happened) attacked by the other students. Later, when she'd left to take a staff editor job back at the *CityReader* and was happily celibate, she reflected that he had been no better a lover than he was a writer.

Alex wandered in one day to bring some freelance artwork he'd been assigned by Amy, the managing editor. She, it happened, was out, and the receptionist sent him to Mary's desk.

"Hi, I'm Alex Hansen," he said to her. He held up a sheet of illustration board with paper taped over the front. "This is for the 'Should Gay People Act Gay?' piece." He began to pull the paper off. "It's a frieze—"

"Really, I don't have anything to do with that." She noticed he was nice looking. He had acute eyes, fine lips, sandy hair, and a strong nose and chin. "You can just leave it—"

"A frieze, you see," he continued, holding the board up. "It's kind of parody of the Village People."

"Who were a parody themselves."

"Sure. Of course. Anyway, on one side they're these gay stereotypes, but on the other, it's the same figures looking like conventional straight people."

"It's good," Mary allowed. In fact, it actually was. "I'm sure Amy will be really happy with it."

"Good, good." He hesitated and then he picked up a Pantone book—hundreds of oblong colour chips fastened together with a brad at the top—from Mary's desk. "You know, they introduce about a hundred new colours every year?"

"No, I didn't. It's not mine, really." Mary had taken it from the desk of a recently fired employee, of whom there was a steady crop at the *CityReader*.

"Oh, yeah. It's like this year's colours—which ones are in and which are out."

"Well, I suppose they'll run out eventually. But really, I'm kind of on deadline—"

"They can't run out. It's mathematical, an infinite series of numbers. Subtract a little blue, add a little red, crank up the white. Endless combinations—"

"That's very interesting. But—"

"Well, it *is* interesting," Alex Hansen said, and then with a conjurer's flutter of the hand, he fanned out the book to reveal a cascade of blues. Against it, his hand was ruddy, his hair golden, his eyes a creamy azure.

"Some of these," Mary heard him say, "absorb light. And some of them reflect it. The colours are really abstractions. Only the light's real."

"That's what you believe." It seemed to Mary that her own voice was far away, or was issuing from some other person.

"It's what's true." He was challenging her. He was also, she now realized, hitting on her; and if she had had the wit of one of her Victorian heroines, she would have declared herself affronted. But it was too late. "Well," he said, the spread feathers of the colour book still hanging from his hand like a brace of pheasants he'd shot, "I suppose I should go."

"I suppose you should," Mary managed to say. Then she added, "I'm on deadline." Mary normally loved to say this. It marked her as a professional, as someone of consequence. It was even true today. She *was* on deadline. But just now it felt like an admission of failure.

"Well, I'll see you around." He smiled and revealed his comely teeth to her.

She did, in fact, see him around. In successive weeks ("Smack-Down: Grunge's Dirty Heroin Secret," "Breakout Chefs of '94," "Can Blacks Be Racists?" "A Valentine's Guide to Condoms") he spoke to her, and then, at an office party ("Best of Seattle") she found herself, somehow, pressed into a corner with him as he drank and held forth on art.

After what must have been a half-hour, he said, "You ought to come over and see my paintings."

"I can't believe you're saying that. It's so—"

"A pick-up line?"

"And a lame, clichéd—"

"But it's true. I really do have paintings. I can't help it. I'm a painter."

"Not etchings?"

"Oh, I fooled around with some drypoint once."

They talked and drank for another half-hour and then, at about eight o'clock, they left and went to Alex's tiny and not inconsiderably shabby Belltown apartment. He showed her fifteen canvases and a portfolio of drawings and then they made love.

"I can't believe I did this," she said afterward.

"But you did," Alex said, and then they drank another glass of wine and did it again.

Things proceeded apace, as they do in a new romance. They exchanged sexual histories (Alex's was prodigious). They met each other's friends: Mary's regiment of lady journalists, authoresses, and displaced humanities graduates; Alex's frequently seedy and tobacco-stained acquaintances from the world of art and alcoholism. But then Alex seemed to know everyone. Once, when they were walking on Second Avenue, Alex was greeted quite warmly by someone just exiting the storefront of the city needle-exchange program. It was just someone he'd met, that he'd seen around the neighbourhood, Alex explained. Mary told him he had very catholic tastes in his acquaintances. No, we were all Lutherans, Alex said, and they laughed and continued on their way.

Then there was Jens Hammershøi, whose impenetrable silences gave Mary the creeps, who smelled like he must have been preserved in formaldehyde, though it was only vodka. But for Alex, Jens was non-negotiable. He was part of the package. Mary told Alex she might like Jens better if Alex sent him out to be dry-cleaned. But she learned to accept him. He was part of their mutual furnishings, their souvenirs and photo albums, he and Tom Hirsch.

All or some of this—not the whole history, but surely some of the moments—might go into the book, which just now was open before her, blank and transparent like the window through which she could see her garden—her rosemary and lavender oiling the air, her wisteria entangling the light (coiffed by the gardener Alex had found)—from her own room of her own house. So Mary began to plan, to sketch. She wrote in her notebook:

> PLOT
> X and Y (lovers) entice Z (single male at loose end) to father child with X, Y being sterile. ???
>
> ~~X and Y (lovers) entice Z (single male at loose end) to raise their love-child, Z being rich and X and Y poor.~~
>
> X and Y (lovers) entice Z (single male at loose end) to become their lackey, for their amusement. YES?

CHARACTERS
X—Brilliant, icy, beautiful, mysterious (like Zenobia in *The Blithedale Romance*?) Name her Honoria, Arabella, Clotilde?

Y—Her "consort." Amiable, alcoholic, but with terrific sexual magnetism. Name—Phillip, Morton?

Z—New to Europe, easily taken-in—not because of innocence but self-absorption. Gay? Has trust fund? Or is a sponger? Name—Nicholas, Jason, Piers—

Just then, Mary heard Alex and Tom come in downstairs, with the boisterous force of a mob, of a blast of wind. She imagined they must be drunk.

Alex and Tom had taken the bus up to Bellosguardo from the Porta Romana, and walked from the closest stop to the Villa Donatello. This distance, uphill, was sufficient to give them the illusion that their brains had cleared somewhat, while in fact rendering them breathless and addled. And it was in this state that they met, walking in the opposite direction, Wright Turner.

It was Turner who spoke to them, addressing them in English. "Say, aren't you from the Donatello? The new owners?"

Alex and Tom looked at him a little longer than was strictly polite. He wore a loose-fitting linen yellow shirt and carried a walking stick. He was tall and silvery, handsomely conserved in the manner of persons whom age has not corrupted but merely burnished.

It was Tom who recovered himself, and said hastily, "Yes. I mean, he is. Not me."

Alex smiled in his easy way and introduced himself, speaking as though he were meeting a potential friend or perhaps some later version of himself. "I'm Alex Hansen. We—my partner Mary and I—moved in a few weeks ago. You must be a neighbour."

"Very much so. Two doors down. In the Villa Castellani."

"Oh," said Tom, still winded and now becoming breathless again. "You must be Wright Turner."

"I think I must be," said Turner. He said this in a tone not only devoid of condescension, but one that suggested that the joke was somehow on him.

"We've wanted to meet you," continued Alex. "Mary especially. She's a writer. As is my friend Tom here."

"Well, not really," said Tom, and Turner's charm was so uncanny that, by not responding, but merely shifting his body towards Tom and then back to Alex, he suggested that "not really" being a writer must be a very grand thing indeed. Then he said to Alex, "And you? What *are* you?" He said this in an equally friendly manner, but overlain by a glint of appraisal, of testing.

"I'm a painter," said Alex, and he said this in a way that was either blind to the air of challenge in Turner's query or felt itself equal to it. Tom caught Alex's tone and thought it was a little presumptuous, or at least at a great remove from his own deference. Although Alex *was* a painter, or, at any rate, much more one than Tom was a writer.

"Well, I should come see your paintings," said Turner slowly and with precision. He turned to Tom, looked at him deeply (or that was at least how it seemed to Tom), smiled, and said, "And you. You must come see me. We'll talk."

As Tom reported this to Mary, who had come down to the *salone* when he and Alex had come in, she interrupted him to say, "I think he wants to fuck you."

"You should be flattered," added Alex. "I don't suppose Wright Turner fucks just anybody."

"Actually, if you read the diaries, he apparently does," Mary said.

"Well, still . . ." said Alex.

Tom objected. "I can tell about these things. He was just being friendly. And generous."

"You, more than anyone, can't tell for shit about these things," said Mary.

"And I suppose you wouldn't care one way or the other if he invited *you* over?" Tom asked.

"Sure I would. He's a kind of monument, isn't he?" Mary said. "And I'm sure he'll get around to it sooner or later."

"You're pretty confident." Tom was still feeling bold from the afterglow of his and Alex's lunch. "And that'll be because he wants to fuck you?"

"He's welcome to fantasize. Makes no difference to me."

"Mary suffers from high self-esteem," Alex said to Tom. "Not that I don't think she's entitled to."

"You always say the right thing," Mary noted. "Even when you're shit-faced."

"I am?" said Alex. "You can tell?"

"I know you better than you know yourself. Not that that's difficult, sweet child that you are."

Tom thought that Alex ought to take umbrage at this: that it may have been a tender remark but also a condescending one. He felt he ought to be making common cause with Alex, on account of brotherhood or the three bottles of wine and the intimacies they'd exchanged over them. But Mary had turned back to him and the matter of Wright Turner.

"So when are you going over there?"

Tom thought, and said, "In a while. Maybe a week. I want to get started with my project. I want to have something to talk about. Or some inspiration."

"You want to make a good impression," said Mary.

"He wants to play hard to get," Alex added, at which Tom thought, Fuck brotherhood. Out loud he said to Mary, "Come on, I'm serious. Give me some credit. This isn't like you."

"How would you know what I'm like?" Mary asked.

This seemed, however true, a hurtful thing to say, but Tom only responded, "We're friends."

"Okay." Mary smiled at him. "So what is it you're going to do about this project? To get started?"

"I want to go stay for a couple of nights in that hotel Rilke lived in. In the same room, if I can."

"Sounds like a really good idea," Mary said. "We'll check you in. If you want."

"Sure I do."

The following afternoon, Tom stood with Mary at the desk of the Hotel San Remo. Alex had stayed home. He was not, after yesterday's lunch, feeling well. Tom himself was a little befogged.

"Why don't you let me handle this?" Mary proposed, and Tom was happy to assent. He had been studying Italian in an informal fashion, but had no enthusiasm for trying it out today. So Mary turned back to the man at the desk and began.

We would like a room.

Of course, madam. With a matrimonial bed and bath?

He is not my spouse.

Of course. That is no concern to us.

But truly the room is entirely for my friend. For his needs. He is an author.

Of course. His needs are his own affair. So you would prefer the single with bath?

That is not of the question. He lacks the room of Rilke. Where he is staying here many years.

There is no Rilke registered here.

No, no. Rilke is dead. He was here in the past.

I can assure madam that no one has died here since I have been manager. The building has been fireproofed.

No, no. You don't grasp me. Rilke was a most great poet. He died in—

"Nineteen twenty-six," Tom supplied.

—nineteen hundred and twenty-six. He remained here since several months. In—

Mary looked at Tom. "When did he stay here?"

"Eighteen ninety-eight."

Mary halted, stared at the man, and gathered herself together.

No. Approximately nineteen hundred.

That is rather before my time. I'm afraid I don't quite understand.

Tom saw he must somehow insert himself in the conversation. He searched his memory for the appropriate phrase to at least introduce himself, and flung himself in.

"Ich küsse die Hand," he said.

The hotel manager looked at Tom. *"Ach. Wir sprechen Deutsch. In Ordnung? Dieser Rilke ist ein Deutscher? Schweizer? Oder ein Österreicher?"*

"Er ist ein Prager." Tom felt dizzy, felt the floor seeming to open up underneath him. "*Er* war," he added, before vanishing beneath the terrazzo, "*er* war *ein Prager.*"

"Prag ist sehr schön," the manager said to Tom. *"Aber ziemlich melancholisch, nicht wahr?"*

Tom was simply staring at the floor. Mary touched him on the arm and said, "I think you better let me handle this." She turned back to the desk.

In fact, my friend solely seeks to—

"Perhaps we should speak English," the manager said.

"Don't you patronize me," said Mary sharply.

"All our clients are also patrons. Surely this is so."

"Please," Mary said. "All right. Look, there's a room he wants to stay in. Where Rilke stayed."

"Oh, so this Herr Rilke has checked out?"

"He's dead. He's fucking dead."

"That is no problem."

"Please. The room he stayed in."

"We have no record of that. Of this Rilke."

Mary touched Tom again. "You know which one it is, right?"

Tom slowly looked up. Then he said, "Sure. I guess. It's in the diary." He opened his little backpack and rummaged in it, took out a book, paged through it, and read aloud.

"At the Lungarno Serristori, not far from the Ponte alle Grazie, stands the house whose flat roof—both its closed-in part and its part wide open to the sky—is mine. The room itself is actually no more than the vestibule (it also includes the stairwell leading up from the third floor), and the living quarter proper consists of the high, wide stone terrace—"

"That is surely number 42. Our best."

"It's expensive?" Tom asked. Mary spoke to the manager.

It's dear?

A little dear. On account of the terrace.

How much costs it?

Two hundred eighty thousand lire.

Mary turned to Tom. "Two hundred and eighty thousand lire."

"I don't think I can manage that."

"I'll manage it for you. It's no problem."

"But this is my project. I don't want to base it on freeloading off other people."

"It's not freeloading. It's a privilege. For me. To help get you started. To save you . . ."

"Save me?" said Tom. "That's kind of a weird expression."

"Well, not 'save' you like rescue you. Just help you a little," Mary said, and then paused. "For something important. Like this." She took out her credit card.

"I could repay you. When I get some money or another job."

"You're repaying me right now. Right here. Doing what you're doing," Mary said. "You'll see." And with that, Mary passed the manager her credit card.

Upstairs, Mary surveyed the room. "It's nice. Especially the terrace."

Tom did not think it was that nice. "I suppose it's been remodelled since Rilke was here."

"I suppose. But still. His spirit . . ." Mary said. "I guess I should go." She walked to the door and turned back to Tom. "You going to be okay?"

"Sure." And added, "Hey, thanks."

"No problem."

Mary shut the door behind her and Tom sat down on the bed alone, all alone. He was going to spend three days here. He did not think he was ready for it. He opened Rilke's Florence diary and read a favourite passage, which must have been written in this very room. Now it seemed cruel and dreadful:

"But art is also justice. And you must, if you wish to be artists, grant all forces the right to lift you and press you down, to shackle you and set you free. It's only a game, don't be afraid."

He got up and went out on the terrace, wondering if it were too late to see Mary walking home. But she was nowhere in sight.

Tom put his clothes in a drawer, and his toothbrush, toothpaste, razor, and comb on the shelf over the bathroom sink. He took out his new blank journal and his black fountain pen, both just purchased yesterday, and set them on the desk. Then he backed slowly away from the desk until he reached the foot of the bed and sat down. Everything was ready.

He sat a while longer, and then he decided it was time. He went to the desk, sat down in the wobbly, spindle-legged chair, and wrote:

April 25, 2000

So here I am, in the Hotel San Remo, in Rilke's room. He checked in here one hundred two years and ten days ago.

The room is nothing special, a good room I guess, but the terrace is the main thing. Here's what Rilke said about it:

My room's outer wall is blooming everywhere with yellow roses, their fragrance at full strength, and with little yellow flowers that are not unlike wild hedge roses, except that they climb the high trellises more quietly and obediently, two by two, rather like the angels of Fra Fiesole bringing recompense and songs of praise for the Last Judgment.

The yellow flowers are still here, or at least I think that's what the ones I see are. I should be excited about that—about this whole experience, really. Occupying the same space, practically sleeping in the same bed as Rilke. (I suppose it's not really the same bed, not literally.)

But, really, what's on my mind is feeling kind of sad and lonely. I looked out from the terrace and the view is beautiful, but I was hoping to see Mary—one last time. But she was gone. I felt a little bit like she'd just dropped me off at my first day of kindergarten. I still do, to tell the truth.

That seemed like enough for the moment. He thought about what he would have for dinner, and then he picked up the remote control and switched on the TV, just to see what might be on, here in Italy, in Florence, in Rilke's room.

The next afternoon Mary was sitting, or half-leaning, on a sofa in Alex's studio, naked. She had been in this position for some twenty minutes, not unhappily, for the window was open and she could see the wisteria and hear the pulse of the crickets rising in the sun. From time to time she was aware of a half-warm breeze moving across her body and it felt pleasant, pleasant and deeply sexual.

"What do you think about when you paint? Now, here, in this house?" she finally said to Alex.

"The same as before. It's not about thinking. It's about looking."

"I know that. But something's going on in your mind. You're not a paramecium."

Alex lowered his hand, which held the piece of charcoal he had been using to incise a rough sketch of Mary on the canvas before him. He picked up a can of fixative and sprayed the area he had been working on. Then he said, "Okay, I'm looking. But I guess I'm also *solving*. I'm figuring out how to get what I see *down*. On paper. Or whatever." He raised the charcoal stick. "How's that?"

"That's very nice. Nicely put."

"This is better: it's about thinking in images, not thinking in words. It's thinking with *light*."

"And when you draw me?"

"I have a great big boner."

"Really?" said Mary. "Show me."

"That would be kind of distracting."

"It's not already distracting?"

"No, it's kind of nice. Makes you feel on your toes. Sharp. Cocked and ready to fire."

"Ha," laughed Mary, and threw her head back.

"Don't move, okay?"

"Sure." Mary was quiet for a moment. "So, when you look at me, right now, what are you seeing? Or solving?"

"I see beauty."

"Tell me more."

"If I did, I might have to come over there and do something about this boner. It would break my concentration."

"That's a good answer. Stay there, but tell me more."

"I warned you," said Alex. He sprayed another puff of fixative at the canvas. "But here goes. I see your face. It's like the face of a madonna. It's beautiful and serene, but pondering. Thinking about deep things. Like we were talking about at San Marco."

"Okay. So far so good," Mary said. "What about . . . the rest?"

"Your mind? Oh, I kind of covered that, I guess. So you must mean"—and here Alex released a little gust of breath—"your body."

"Yes."

"Okay. Just making sure," Alex said. "Well, I love your body."

"Can you be more specific?"

"About the whole or the parts?"

"Whichever."

"I'll stick with the whole. If I start talking about the parts I'll get too hot."

"That's such a guy thing," said Mary. "Why is that? It's like men want women dismembered—the breasts over here, the face over there, the ass somewhere else. To contemplate and jerk off to."

"The whole is too much to handle. Too hard to grasp all at once."

"Then men have a terrible lack of imagination."

"Maybe too much imagination," Alex said. "I mean, the female body is our great mystery. The deeper you go, the more lost you get. It's our spirituality, our religion."

"That's a little bizarre," said Mary. "Bizarre but interesting. So go on."

"I guess you could say I *worship* your body. It's my sacrament. I could eat it and drink it."

"Oh my," Mary said.

"It's perfect. Like a madonna. Untouched by corruption. By . . . the ravages of childbirth."

She thought to object that a madonna's body was of necessity touched by childbirth. But only said, "Oh my." She laughed, or, she felt, at least someone did.

Alex had moved around and was in front of the easel. "I can't get enough of it. It's like I'm starving *and* I'm going to burst."

"What's going to burst?"

"My brain. My heart. My dick."

"That's kind of apparent," said Mary. "You better come over here."

He was before her in a moment, his jeans around his ankles, his hand between her legs, touching her.

"God you're wet."

"God you're hard."

He began to bend down. "Let me . . ."

"No. Just fuck me."

"That's okay? Even if you don't . . ."

"No, no. It's fine. Just fuck me."

He pressed into her and came quickly; with a shudder, calling her name, saying he loved her. And as he did, Mary almost laughed.

Alex lay panting, half-propped against her. "Jesus," he said, after a time.

"You burst."

"I burst."

"But you're still starving?"

"Not exactly. But I will be. Always. Forever."

"Even when I'm old?"

"Sure."

"Or after . . . the 'ravages of childbirth,' or whatever?"

"Well, that's not very likely."

"But not impossible," said Mary.

Alex was silent for a moment, and then he laughed. "Oh, like a madonna. An immaculate conception. A virgin birth."

"Maybe. Or maybe not. It's not like I couldn't get impregnated," Mary said. "Would you mind?"

"It depends. Could I watch?"

"Be serious, Alex."

"But *you're* not serious."

"Well, maybe I am. Or at least I'm thinking out loud. I mean, in theory, wouldn't you want a baby from my body? Seeing how it's your . . . religion?"

Alex felt his penis, now slack, slipping out of Mary's body, though their skins still seemed combined, adhering to one another, on account of the secretions, his and hers, that still clung to them. He answered. "It's my religion, but it's not our arrangement. Our understanding. Us." He paused, feeling the need to keep talking. "I mean, my . . . the snip, it was both our ideas. I remember what you said. You said 'We're perfect together.

We love each other and we're totally selfish. Too selfish for a baby.' That's what you said, Mary."

"Yeah, I did."

"So now you're kidding, right?"

"Yeah. I guess so. Don't worry. It was just a little thought, a little thought experiment."

"Well, that's good. I mean, if you were serious—"

"Don't worry. I was just talking. You're not going to lose me."

"Not you, Mary. Lose *us*."

"I know. Don't worry." Mary looked at Alex. Alex rose and dug a handkerchief from the pocket of the jeans pooled at his feet and gave it to her, and she wiped herself off. She smiled lightly, a wry and wistful smile, the smile she knew would pacify him. "So let's get back to work," she said. Alex nodded and smiled too.

"Then," Mary added, "we'll shop for dinner. And have a bottle of wine and a bowl of olives. We can sit and listen to music. Really old songs. Then we can do this again, if you want."

"I want."

"All over the house. What with Tom being gone. The whole big empty house, all to ourselves."

"We can box the compass. I can worship every little part of you."

"We can consecrate every room. Even Tom's. You can fuck me on his bed, if you want."

"Sure."

Tom was just then setting to work on his journal, bringing it current with the events since his last entry:

> <u>April 26, 2000</u>
> So here I am. Still.
>
> I went out last night just long enough to buy a bottle of wine, some olives, and a piece of cheese. Mary and Alex's

favourite wine bar is maybe a hundred yards from here, but I thought, What if I ran into them?

So I come back here and read the D. H. Lawrence Mary gave me. But I can't concentrate. I feel like I'm <u>wading</u> through the prose, that it's thick, gelatinous. So I drink most of the wine and nibble at the olives and cheese. I try to read some more, but I still can't get focused. So I masturbate. Then I turn on the TV and watch CNN.

This is how <u>low</u> I am.

<u>Afternoon</u>

I go out and get a ham sandwich. I'm not eating much these days, and that's okay. Last night, looking in the mirror, I was thinking how being skinnier really makes my dick look bigger. Like those big dangling hands on Michelangelo's David.

I come back here and now I'm writing this.

<u>Later</u>

I miss Seattle. Or least I feel sad in a "missing" kind of way. And I wouldn't mind doing my laundry at the laundromat near my old apartment. I wouldn't mind having Kevin serve me a drink at the Emerald. I wouldn't mind a plate of pad thai or hash browns. I wouldn't mind going to Restoration Hardware with Alex and Mary, mocking the whole thing but maybe buying something anyway.

But we're all here now. Nobody, really, is <u>there</u> any more.

It gets up my nose that when Rilke was here, he wasn't sad. He wasn't even pensive. He was thinking, but he was manic. He was on track.

The following morning Tom repacked his bag with his clothing and toiletries. When he was done, he sat down to write one final entry in this room. He wanted it to be a good one, so he got up and opened the doors that gave onto the terrace, to let the breeze and yellow flowers wash over him. Then he sat down and began to sum it all up:

> April 27, 2000
> My last day here. I'm not sure I know what I'm up to with this writing. It's either
> a) notes
> b) a diary
> c) a draft of my "project"
> d) a sort of "counter-diary" to Rilke's. Which is maybe what my "project" really is.
> e) the notes for the counter-diary?
> Anyway, there's a lot of problems so far. A lot of bad writing. To wit:
> 1) "telling" instead of "showing"
> 2) telling the reader what to think and feel
> 3) undisguised gimmicks or stylistic ticks like underlining
> 4) self-consciousness. Or the wrong kind of self-consciousness. Boring, ranting, overly-serious self-consciousness. Instead of interesting, charming, amusing self-consciousness.
> Maybe I have an unpleasant authorial persona. Which is to say, maybe I'm an asshole—at least on the page. Nobody would aspire to my life or think it was entertaining, never mind moving or funny.
> Maybe I haven't really found my material as an artist. Or my artistic vocation. Or the love to make it happen. It's like that graffiti we saw the other day: Love shapes our purpose, or whatever.

And with that, he was done. It was still two hours until check-out time, but he felt he had exhausted the possibilities of the room. There was nothing on television and his penis had begun to feel a little frayed.

Tom returned to the Villa Donatello just after lunchtime. Alex and Mary wanted to know how it had gone—whether he been moved or inspired—but he begged off, saying he really needed a nap. He went upstairs to his room and looked around. He decided to add another entry, by way of conclusion, to his journal.

April 28, 2000

I'm back at Mary and Alex's now, at the desk in my room. They asked me a lot of questions, but I didn't feel like saying much. The San Remo thing is another failure I'd just as soon not dwell on.

I think they were fucking in my bed. There are stains. Or at least it's rumpled.

5.

It's Only a Game—Don't Be Afraid

The following day, Mary could not but think Tom was being strangely unforthcoming about his three days at the Hotel San Remo.

"So, how'd it go?" Mary asked.

"Okay."

"So what did you do?"

"I wrote some. I sat on the terrace and read."

"Do you feel like you got anything figured out?"

"Maybe."

"Maybe?"

"You know what you say about not talking about your work? About keeping it in a separate space inside yourself?" said Tom. "It's like that. I just want to keep it inside, intact—not let it get diffused. Not until I get a real grip on it. Does that make sense?"

"Sure," said Mary.

"It's nothing personal."

"Of course."

In fact, Mary did rather think it was something personal; that having negotiated his registration, paid his bill, and virtually tucked him into his bed, she was entitled to hear a little more. Of course, she understood the notion of letting work gestate in peace and privacy. She was herself right on the verge of getting past notes and sketches to drafting some actual pages, any day now. But she also felt her relation to any work Tom might produce was deeper than that of her work to him; that she was in a very real sense its handmaid and patron.

They had a pleasant dinner that evening. Mary and Alex talked about their painting sessions ("I never knew how dull modelling was") and they all went to the studio to look at the canvas, at this point not much more than a six-foot-tall rectangle of gessoed canvas marked with broad shadings of charcoal and a few dabs of bright pastel colour. You could not say it was Mary, but it was, it seemed to them all, definitely something.

The next day Tom announced he was going to take up Wright Turner's invitation to call on him at his apartment in the Villa Castellani. The villa lay perhaps one hundred yards from Mary and Alex's. There was a little courtyard inside the door, white and austere as though it were a cloister. Tom found Turner's apartment up the stairs that wound around the outside of the courtyard. Next to his door there was a little brass nameplate reading "Sig Dott W Turner" and beneath it a doorbell. Tom pressed it.

Turner opened the door, wearing what Tom guessed would be called a dressing gown, and that in itself rather threw him, it being early afternoon. But Turner smiled and said, "Oh, the young man from the Villa Donatello. I'd *hoped* you'd come."

"Well," Tom managed, "you said if—"

"Of course, of course," Turner continued, gesturing for Tom to enter.

The apartment was composed of broad rooms with high ceilings and big windows, but despite all the windows there were vast areas of darkness. On either side of the windows hung heavy drapes and between the window and door casings were rows of bookcases. In the centre of the room they had just entered, the *salone,* were several Breuer and Eames chairs and a huge sofa and coffee table. On the walls hung modernist prints and drawings together with a number of older Italian paintings with heavy gilt frames.

"Well," said Turner. "You're just in time for a glass of wine."

"Sure," said Tom, not a little nervously.

"I'll be just a moment then."

Tom sat down on one of the chairs. He felt his feet didn't quite reach the floor and, although he knew this to be an illusion, he almost bent over to see if it were the case. Then he scanned the coffee table to see if there might be something to read, but there were only great hulking volumes of art history, in Italian at that. An instant later Turner came back with a tray holding a bottle, two glasses, and a bowl of mixed nuts. (They were very big on mixed nuts in Italy, Tom had noticed.) He put this down, filled the glasses, and handed Tom one of them across the expanse of the glass-and-steel coffee table. Turner then sat and adjusted himself into a near-reclining position on the couch opposite Tom. He looks, Tom thought, like he's floating down a river on Cleopatra's barge.

"So," Turner said, "tell me all about yourself. What brought you to Tuscany? I hope it wasn't that fucking book."

Tom was surprised to hear him say "fucking," but he said it, Tom reflected, in such an elegant way that it came out as though he'd merely said "dreadful."

"No," Tom began, "I'm here because Mary and Alex invited me. I was at . . . a loose end. I thought I could do some writing, some critical writing or creative non-fiction." Tom paused to drink. "Or at least figure out what it is I want to do with my life."

"Oh, don't do *that,*" Turner said with a little laugh. "Stay . . . flexible. Life's full of lovely surprises for young men like you."

"I hope so."

Then Turner smiled as though to offer Tom every assurance that the world was all before him, and continued, "Now tell me about your friends."

So Tom told him. About how they'd met in Seattle, about Noumena and Critic.com, and how about how, yes, Mary was indeed retired before the age of forty, a not uncommon thing in Seattle.

"I think I've seen that—Critic.com—on the internet," Turner inserted.

"You have the web here?"

"Oh yes. Italy's very high tech, except for the post office. American don't like to think that, of course. Spoils the fantasy promoted by that fucking book. I suppose the internet saves me a fortune in magazine subscriptions. Which never used to arrive anyway, because of the post office."

Tom felt a little taken aback, not by Turner's possession of a computer and a modem, but by the sense that, having disposed of Alex and Mary, the discussion was about to return once again to Tom and his own life, or lack thereof.

Just then Turner asked, "And you—will you be going back soon? To find another—what did you call it?—"

"Dronebot job?"

"Yes, dronebot. Lovely. Lovely and droll."

Tom began slowly. "I hope not. But I can't live off Mary and Alex forever."

"It sounds like it wouldn't be a problem for them."

"But it's awkward. I mean, they're almost *too* generous."

Turner sat upright and raised the wine bottle, motioning for Tom's glass. "One should learn to accept generosity *generously,*" he said, pouring with abandon.

Tom, spurred by some urge he could not account for, told him about the Hotel San Remo. About how Mary paid and how he didn't accomplish anything.

Turner smiled at Tom and said, "How can anyone know whether he's accomplished anything? So much is accidental."

"With me, everything's accidental."

"No, no. None of that now." Turner continued. "Look at me. I just *washed* up in Europe after I got out of the army in 1945. It was *inertia,* indolence. Then I got interested in things. I met people, interesting people. And from that came the diaries, living here, my whole life, everything I am. You only see the connections retrospectively—how everything fits together so delightfully."

"For example?"

"For example, I met this attractive, intelligent young man on the road the other day, purely by chance. Now I find he's just stayed at the San Remo, where I stayed in 1947, when I first came to Florence. Well, I didn't stay there. But I was there a lot. I was having a fling with an army officer. Who was from Iowa. Where I'm from. Not thirty miles from the town where *he* was from."

"That's an interesting coincidence."

"Not coincidence," Turner said. "*Connection*. Because it goes on. Because this young man—you—were at the San Remo because of Rilke. Whose stepfather I knew."

"Balthus?" Tom said.

"Exactly."

"Tell me about him," and Tom found himself leaning forward.

"About Rilke? Because Balthus didn't say much about Rilke. Of course, I have *opinions* about Rilke. I have opinions about most everything. But you want stories, no?"

"Whatever you want to do."

"Well, they were both almighty pieces of work. Rilke especially, and like stepfather, like son. I never understood why neither of them were gay—why they insisted on being hetero. Just so they could be that much more *difficult*, one suspects."

Tom sat back. "You think it's simpler, easier to be gay?"

"Well, I think so. For an artist anyway. It's a solitary business. It doesn't really lend itself to attachments, children and so forth. Of course, Rilke was about the most selfish artist who ever lived. Abandoned his children, his wife, his lovers willy-nilly. And half of what he wrote is about how being an artist justified it all."

"That kind of comes across in the diary I've been reading. It's addressed to Lou Andreas-Salomé."

"Never met her. She died before I got here. I think she ran with the Freud crowd, the psychoanalysis crowd. That was a big distraction for a lot of people. It doesn't seem to have amounted to much now, does it?"

Tom said, "I don't know. Not among people I know. Or maybe only as it relates to theory."

"Theory?"

"Literary theory, queer theory, that kind of thing."

"You'll have to tell me about queer theory sometime. I've got a few theories about queers myself," Turner said and emitted an almost inelegant little snort. "But shall I go on, about Rilke? Or at least Balthus."

"Please."

"I met him in Paris, late in the '40s. The Countess of Noailles had taken him up, and there were a lot of us—gifted expatriate fairies—in her crowd. Of course, he fancied himself a count, too. It was bullshit, but he bought a château and rather lived the life. How, I don't know. Then he took over the French Academy in Rome, the Villa Medici. I'd moved down here maybe ten years before, so we saw each other again. It was a quite a scene. This was the early and mid-sixties, of course."

Tom had drained his glass and he found himself thrusting it towards Turner. "And were there lots of little girls around?" he asked, as Turner topped him up.

"Oh, I don't know about *little* girls, but girls, yes. Nubile, I suppose. Children of the domestic staff at the villa. He was painting the cook's daughters, I think. But there were so many beautiful kids around. I can't say it concerned me a lot."

"But he was painting these girls nude."

"I suppose he was. He did that a lot. It was a big part of his oeuvre."

Turner stopped, leaned towards Tom, and grinned. "I suppose you want to know if he was fucking them? And the answer is, I don't know. I don't think it's terribly important, one way or the other." He settled back on his couch.

Tom looked into his glass for a moment and then said, "A lot of people would say it *is* important, if he was abusing them or even just eroticizing children."

"Eroticizing?" Turner shook his head slowly, as though airing himself. "They're already eroticized. I eroticized myself by the time I was five or six. Playing doctor, playing house, playing *with* myself. Didn't you?"

"Sure. But that's their own sexuality. It's not the same thing as an adult appropriating it, exploiting it."

"Oh, my dear Thomas," Turner said. "You can't seriously believe it's exploitation. It's art. Art of a very high order. Very brave art, considering what everyone else was painting at the time. And he always had permission from the families. It was always above-board."

Tom felt himself bristle. He did not like to be condescended to. "Of course it's art. But if he was sleeping with them, it's also sexual abuse." He halted and looked at Turner. "So was he?"

"I really don't know. But this business about 'abuse' is so off the mark. One of these self-regarding tempests in the American teapot. One of these witch hunts where the purpose isn't so much to find witches as to give everyone the chance to attest to their own purity."

Turner tuned his voice upward into a whine. "Oh *no,* they all say, *I* would never do such a thing. I'm not a child molester. I'm not a Red. I'm not a sissy. I'm upright. I'm *good.*" He resumed his conversational baritone. "The whole thing is infantile. It's an evasion of life as it actually is. Hypocrisy in the classic American mode."

Tom was surprised at Turner's vehemence. He wondered what else Turner hated. With a little hesitation, he began, "Maybe that's true, but real lives have been destroyed. By sexual abuse. I've known people—"

"I'm sure you have. I gather everyone in the United States has been abused. Life is always affronting Americans, don't you think? Not giving them what they're entitled to."

Tom thought he must be feeling the wine. The bottle was empty. "I don't think anyone deserves to be abused," he said rather weakly.

Turner leaned back, and it seemed to Tom that he sighed as he did so. "You misunderstand me, Thomas. Let me tell you about what you call abuse. Or what people might call abuse. In my case. I was fourteen. My uncle must have been forty or forty-five. It was summer. At night. I don't know where everyone else was, but we were alone. He touched me. And touched me again. Finally I touched him back and one thing led to another. It went on all summer, and by the end of it I knew who I was and what I wanted."

Turner stopped, and then said, "So I owe him a great debt, really. He saved my life in a way. After that summer, I knew where I was going. At least as much as you can at that age. I found my own lovers. Of course, he and I couldn't continue on. That's in the nature of these things, I guess. He wanted to. So I suppose his was the first heart I ever broke."

Tom looked at Turner and then at the floor. He felt moved, but also, he realized, a little aroused.

Turner surveyed the coffee table. "Oh, we need something more to drink, don't we?"

"I guess we do."

Turner stood—Tom saw he needed to brace himself to get up, to splay his long white fingers against the glass tabletop and give himself a push—and he came back a moment later with another bottle of the same wine they'd been drinking. He sat down and began to insert the worm of the corkscrew into the bottle. Tom said, very evenly, he thought, "Your story—I understand. But it's not like that for everyone."

Turner looked up and said, "No. Of course not. But it was for you, wasn't it?"

Tom looked down and then over to one of the windows, towards the bloom of light, surprised to find it was afternoon rather than evening. He was offended at Turner's presumption, his inadvertent and unerring ambush, but he wanted it to be true, the thing that Turner had said. Because it was, or might as well have been.

Turner poured the wine and Tom took a mouthful and finally said, "Well, there was a friend of my older brother. I was thirteen or fourteen. He must have been eighteen. I had a sort of crush on him."

"So you see," Turner said. "It was scarcely abuse. Perhaps it was you who seduced him."

"I'm not sure. I don't remember," Tom said, and he realized that he didn't care, because he wanted it to be the same way for him as it was for Turner. "It probably was."

Turner said, "And then?"

"Not much of anything until I got to college." Tom added, "Then there were some girls, too."

"Of course. Girls are nice," Turner said quickly. "You'd be a fool to forgo them. I've had a few myself."

"I just feel like I should make up my mind about who I really like."

"Nonsense. Do what moves you. Follow the connections. Only connect, Morgan Forster said—E. M. to you—a great and wise fag. Don't think. Act."

"I guess I should do that," Tom said. "That's my problem in all sorts of areas."

Turner patted the couch. "So," he said, "come over here. Sit with me."

Tom felt himself get up, knowing what he wanted to happen, assenting to it. His cock was hardening.

He sat down and Turner leaned over and kissed him. The kiss was not what Tom had thought it would be, but better. He'd imagined that Turner would smell, that beneath the tidy clothing and the charming talk, he'd be decrepit and his breath would stink. But he smelled like nothing at all. Or maybe like paper with a little cologne sprinkled on it.

After a long while Turner said, "Come to bed." Tom followed him to his room, to the big four-poster bed, and the dark heavy furniture, and the brocade on the walls, hanging like moss. There were statues—busts and torsos. Turner settled himself on the bed and jerked his head upward to indicate Tom should undress. "Let me get a good look at you," he said. Tom pulled his shirt up over his head. His trousers and briefs fell, were pushed away.

"Oh, lovely," Turner said. "Now come here."

Tom went over to the bed and sat next to Turner. Turner pressed him down, laid him down by the shoulders. Then he started to suck Tom's penis.

Tom was already ahead of where he wanted to be. He tried to squelch himself, but it was too late, he was beyond stopping. Between his teeth he said, "I think I'm going to . . . right now, so maybe . . ."

Turner stopped just long enough to say, "So much the better." And Tom was rocketing out of himself in big waves and pulses. Then he lay there. He thought he must be shaking.

After a moment he reached over to Turner, inside his robe. He found Turner's silk undershorts and started to pull them off. "Oh," Turner began, "there's no real need."

"But I want to," Tom said. He touched Turner's penis. "Tell me what to do."

"Whatever is your heart's desire."

Tom pulled the robe away and looked at Turner's cock. He thought it would be shrivelled up, but it was actually pretty substantial. Not hard. Very pale, almost transparent. His whole body was like that. Like a bird with the feathers off. His dick and foreskin like the neck and the head. Tom put it in his mouth. It was as soft as an old lady's cheek.

"Don't expect too much," Turner said, seeming very far away. "I'm not much for fireworks in my dotage. But I'll enjoy myself."

So Tom sucked him. He felt Turner's cock stirring, but it never firmed to the point of absolute hardness. He tasted something. He wasn't sure if it was come.

After a while Turner said, "That was very nice," which Tom surmised meant he was done. Turner sat up. "Now you can let me watch you dress," he said.

Tom dressed, looking at Turner, wondering if he—whom Tom now saw was an old man—was trying to hustle him out the door. But Turner merely looked at him intently, with a smile.

"What a handsome cock," he finally said. "Cut. A long time since I've seen one."

"Well, yes. But in America, most guys are . . ."

"Of course. I forget, having been on a diet of Italian *ragazzi* all these many years."

Tom found himself saying, "So you've had a lot of lovers?"

Turner didn't answer. He stood up and said, "Perhaps you'd like a little more wine? Or something to eat?"

"No," Tom heard himself say, "I think I'd better get going."

"But you'll come back soon, of course. We'll have dinner. And talk. I'll know to take one of my pills. You'll see there's more to me than meets the eye."

"That'd be great," Tom said, and then felt immensely stupid. They walked towards the door together, Turner's hand just brushing Tom's hip. Tom wanted to say something smart or definitive. But before he could imagine what that might be, Turner said, "Soon" and Tom was outside the door, overlooking the courtyard with the whole day now leaching into dusk.

All the way home Tom felt very strange, like something was

draped over him and he couldn't quite breathe, like dread or shame but without the fear. He went inside and Mary was there. She put her hand on her hip and said, "So?"

"It was interesting," Tom said. He did not want to talk.

"How interesting?" Mary said, and then detecting Tom's reticence, shrugged and said, "Maybe later on, okay?"

"Sure," Tom allowed, and then added, inanely, as it struck him an instant afterward, "I really need to get up to my desk—there are some ideas I want to write down."

Tom showered, tried to read, changed his clothes, wrote nothing, and went downstairs again at six-thirty. The three of them drank wine and picked at cocktail nuts, and about every ten minutes either Mary or Alex brought the conversation back to Turner and Tom said something banal and neutral. He volunteered that it was "no big deal"; that Turner merely told stories and reminisced and made skeptical remarks about the contemporary art and literature scene. He was surprised they didn't take the hint.

The next day Tom thought of little else than contriving a way to see Wright Turner. He thought of writing him—but how? ("Dear Dottore Turner" wouldn't really do)—and by afternoon he resolved to simply call him. He waited until Mary and Alex were off working in Alex's studio, as they were every afternoon these days, and dialed the number from the phone in the kitchen. When Turner answered, Tom stammered out his name, and Turner cut him off in the nicest possible way—"Oh, *dear* Thomas. How lovely of you to call"—and simply invited him to come over the next evening for dinner.

Upon hanging up, Tom decided that, against all expectations and appearances, Wright was in fact a good person. He was kind and he was even nice, although he doubted this was a word Wright would ever wish anyone to apply to him.

So Tom passed the afternoon calmly and happily. He was even able to make some progress with the D. H. Lawrence book

Mary had thrust upon him, with the Etruscans and their tombs and their phallic mojos. But at dinner Mary and Alex relaunched their inquisition and pressed Tom to invite Turner over to the villa. Tom could not but think that they must have been speculating about him and Wright all the while they were in the studio.

Finally, to placate them, Tom said, "I'll ask him when would be a good time for him to come over. I'm seeing him tomorrow."

"Really?" Mary said. "So soon?" She hung fire another moment and added, "For . . . ?"

"He invited me to dinner. He called today."

"Really? I never heard the phone ring," said Mary. "And there's one in the studio."

"Well, it did," Tom said, with surprising firmness.

Alex put in, "Could be, Mary. You know these Italian phones."

Alex, too, is good, thought Tom.

Mary shrugged. "Well, be sure to mention it to him."

"I'd really like to have him see my paintings," said Alex. "He wrote some amazing art criticism back in the '50s."

"I know," Tom said.

This seemed to satisfy Alex and Mary, and their conversation moved onto other topics. The three, as in old times, drank themselves into a calm and genial harbour and then said goodnight. Later, in his bed, Tom wondered if he really wanted Wright to see Alex's paintings; if he really was all that thrilled to have Wright feted at the villa, oiled and rubbed with Alex and Mary's money, charm, and sophistication. Mary and Alex, he thought, don't have to have *everything.*

It occurred to Tom at lunchtime that he ought to get Wright some flowers, this being not only an Italian custom but one thing among many that he quite simply found himself wanting to do for and because of Wright. But he quickly learned that today was a national holiday—holidays rather than work days seemed to be the norm in Italy—and the bus down the hill scarcely ran, and everything, Alex and Mary assured him, would be closed. Tom thought about asking Mary if he might take some blooms from the garden, but decided he didn't want her involved; didn't want to let her inside the circle he had begun to draw which enclosed just him and Wright. So he waited until she and Alex were settled in the studio and then stole out into the garden and cut some gladioli, stashing them just outside the gate to pick up on his way out that evening.

Tom arrived at the Villa Castellani at seven on the dot. Turner opened the door dressed in white linen pants and a white linen shirt. Tom gaped, realizing that Turner looked terribly handsome. He didn't know if he'd noticed that before. Wright took the flowers and held them against his chest. They seemed to illuminate him.

They sat together in the *salone,* the young man and the old, and had a drink. Turner got up a couple of times to put things on the stove, but it seemed to Tom to happen without interruption or impediment. Their talk was easy, as though it were a fragrance hanging in the air. You merely had to breathe it in. They ate nuts and olives, and by the time Turner announced that dinner was ready, they'd a finished a bottle of wine.

Turner had made some pasta and a chicken with rosemary and roast potatoes. It was a simple dinner. Tom could not have said later what they had talked about or how the food had tasted; except that it was all easy, and there had been, after all, very little in life that Tom found easy.

Afterward, they went to Turner's bedroom without speaking. Turner had set out candles, and lighted them while Tom undressed. Tom was lying on the bed with an erection when Turner came over to him. He touched Tom, ran a long stroke down his chest to his belly, and then grasped his cock.

Tom said, "Now you." Turner nodded and began to undress. He folded his clothes and put them at the foot of the bed, taking his time. It's like a ceremony, Tom thought.

Turner lay down next to Tom. His cock was flaccid, and then, as if by fiat, it was not. Tom lowered his head to it, and realized it was rather impressive, particularly in relation to the rest of Turner's body which, Tom now saw, was rather slight. It was his head that made him look big. That, and now his dick.

After a few minutes, they changed positions. Turner took Tom in his mouth, but after half a minute, Tom touched the side of his head, pulling him away. "I don't want to come too soon. I want it to last. I want to do more, do everything," Tom said, each word an exhalation of breath. He knew the words sounded lame and clichéd, but he wasn't in charge of them any more.

Turner said, "Do you want me to fuck you?"

This should've thrown Tom. The last guy he'd had sex with said Tom had "issues" about being penetrated. But now Tom said, "Yes. Please. Yes." He would, just then, have begged him to.

Tom rolled over as Turner busied himself with something from a drawer in the oak nightstand next to the bed. A fleeting shape loomed over him, pressed down on him, and he felt the heat, the breathing, the little sharp burst of light as though something was breaking free. It hurt and it felt beautiful, Wright going in. He went on for quite a while. Tom wondered if he was going to come—if he *could* come. But he went way deep and then he shuddered.

Turner withdrew himself, still a little bit hard. He pulled Tom around, put some lubricant on his hand, and rubbed it onto Tom. "Please," he said and turned away. He looked back over his shoulder at Tom and smiled. "You have to be a bit gentle. I have the ravaged innards of an old man."

All this while, Tom had been sleepwalking, letting himself fall towards this gravity or that. He entered Turner slowly, but then something told him it wanted him to get deep, fast and deep. He didn't want to hurt Turner, only to come inside him. So Tom went on, and then he saw himself watching himself fucking Wright. Just then, he thought he might be losing his erection.

Tom said, "Am I hurting you?"

"Oh no," Turner said. "You can't *really* hurt me."

Tom felt himself get very, very hard again. He thrust and thrust, then came, powerfully.

Tom rolled over onto his side. Turner was right next to him, breathing shallowly, saying nothing. Tom felt very quiet too, and they lay that way a long time together.

After a while, Tom felt like he was floating over the bed, looking down at the two of them—as though he was the soul that had left his body: that his body, far below, might be dead. He thought about Wright fucking him, and about whether he really liked it, and, if he did, what that meant. It made no sense, but Tom felt himself wanting to cry.

He hadn't sobbed or really shed a tear, but just then Turner rolled over and put his arm, his long white hairless arm, over Tom's shoulder. He said, "You're fine. Just lovely, in fact." He added, "You *were* fine. And you don't do this very often, do you? What I did to you."

"Well, no," Tom said. "Not really. Not ever, actually. Or just experimentally, with that friend of my brother's. I didn't really like it then."

"And now?"

"Oh, I don't know. It was fine, I guess. I feel a little confused, that's all."

"Well," Turner said, "you gave as good as you got."

"Thank you."

Turner slapped Tom on the bottom. "Why don't we go have a little post-prandial, a little grappa or some such?"

"That sounds great," Tom said. But he still felt sad, and now he felt dismissed, as if the weight of what had just passed between them hadn't amounted to much.

Tom sat down on Turner's great couch. He imagined his expression was simply impassive, but then he felt it tugging itself into a pout. He didn't care.

Wright was busy organizing a bottle and a couple of glasses, then filling them. He put on a CD. "Some après-fuck music," he said.

"It sounds like Wagner," said Tom. "Like *Parsifal,* maybe." He waited for Turner to respond, waited to be found correct, to have made an impression.

Turner sat down and appeared merely to be listening. "Pfitzner," he finally said. "Hans Pfitzner. His big opera, called *Palestrina.*"

"I don't know him," Tom said.

"It's about a tortured artist. Just your thing."

"Did you know him?" Tom felt that evened things up.

"Of course not," Turner laughed. "I'm not *that* old. I don't really like Germans, except for their music."

"I do," Tom offered.

"So who are your favourite Germans? Aside from Marlene Dietrich?" Tom tried to laugh, but the laugh got lost inside his glass, which he was just then trying to drain. "Schopenhauer. Nietzsche. Wagner. Heidegger and Rilke, I suppose."

"Oh my," Turner said. "We *are* very serious, aren't we? And Wagner. You can like Wagner the way all fags like Wagner, for the showmanship and excess. But with you I suspect it's in earnest."

"Why bother otherwise?" Tom came back. "Life's too short. I want mine to amount to something, something with consequences."

"Oh no, life's too *long.* I know. And art can't save you. Neither can geniuses. Trust me. I've known a few. The Germans believed in art and genius and big ideas. They gave the world Marx and Hitler. Hitler was the biggest artist of them all."

"That's kind of out there."

"You think so?" said Turner. "Hitler thought he was a genius, a superman. He thought he was an artist."

"I think that's really a stretch, Wright."

Turner grinned. "It's you who thinks ideas and art are so powerful. So why can't they be *that* powerful?"

Tom said nothing. The fight, or the ardour for it, had left him. Turner took another sip of his drink and said, "I don't mean to be contentious."

"It's okay." Then Tom added, "I suppose I should be getting home."

"You're not going to spend the night?"

Tom hesitated. "I think I better not," he said at last.

"I haven't scared you off?" Turner's eyebrows rose as he spoke.

Tom thought that, in truth, Turner had done exactly that—or maybe he'd scared himself off; he didn't know quite how to feel about staying. Or about having Mary and Alex knowing he stayed.

"No, I'd just like the comfort of my own bed. Personal fussiness, I guess."

"I suspect we could make my bed very comfortable for you, if we set our minds to it."

"I'm sure we could," Tom said, and thought to add, "I'm sure we will."

"Fine," Turner said brightly. "But do come back tomorrow. For lunch, or an afternoon drink, all right?"

"Sure."

"Good," said Turner. At the door, he kissed Tom. "You know, adults can have disagreements among themselves and it means nothing."

"Of course," Tom answered, and as he trudged down the stairs and into the dark, he wondered if that remark, too, was a little condescending. But the truth was, Tom did not like disagreements. They made him feel like a child. Wright, he supposed, made him feel like a child. Except in bed. There, he made him feel like a stud. At the gate of the villa, he stood a moment, unsure of which made him more uncomfortable.

In the morning, when he went downstairs, Tom was surprised to find that Mary made no effort to debrief him on the previous evening. She merely sat with her newspaper and her coffee cup. Alex, of course, was already in his studio, or down the hill running errands. But as Mary continued to sit—she looked up occasionally and smiled, as if in greeting or general commiseration—Tom began to feel irritated. He was sure that she knew—or, worse, thought she knew—exactly what had happened at Wright's last night; or imagined she could extract it from Tom whenever she felt like it. So Tom made a cup of coffee and went back upstairs to pretend to work on Rilke.

He came down again at lunchtime, and Mary still offered no more than small talk or simple requests in the kitchen; and then just before two, Tom said, "I'm going out," and Mary said, "By the way, did you invite Wright Turner to dinner?"

"No. But I will. I'm on my way there now."

"Oh," said Mary evenly.

At the Villa Castellani, Tom and Wright Turner worked their way slowly through a bottle of wine and a tray of nuts. They were polite but tentative with each other.

Towards the bottom of the bottle, Turner said, "You know you're a wonderful lover?"

Tom squirmed and, he feared, blushed. "No. I guess I didn't."

"Oh, yes. Your whole body is, how shall I say, *sincere.* Unjaded."

"Well, I guess I'm a little inexperienced."

"I imagined that. But in your case it's rather a gift. To me, at least."

"Even after all the people you've known, the things you've written about?" Tom spoke a little rapidly.

"Especially after all that," Turner said. "But you, you haven't had many lovers?"

"Maybe . . . a dozen or so."

"Boys or girls?"

"Half and half, I guess," Tom supplied. "Maybe two-thirds boys, one-third girls."

"How even-handed of you," said Turner. "How modern. But then you're one of these baby boomers, I suppose."

"I'm not a baby boomer," Tom said. "Technically speaking."

"Oh, you're the generation after. I ought to know these distinctions better." Turner picked up a nut. "The baby boomers are the hypocrites. Whereas you are the cynics. Or the ironists. Have I got that right?"

Tom tried to stay calm. "We're not cynical," he said as steadily as he could. "Or ironic. We're just not sure of everything. We have low expectations. We're not very confident. About what to think or what to be. Or at least that's what I think."

"That pretty cock of yours is full of confidence."

Tom looked at his feet. This was not what he wanted to hear just now. At any other time, yes. But not just now.

Then, miraculously (so it later seemed), Turner added, "And you have a quick mind. And it seems to me you offer your opinions—your ideas—with great conviction. So I don't quite understand the lack of confidence."

Tom raised his head and looked straight at Turner. "But I don't feel I have the *right* to say anything—that I don't really know anything. That I don't amount to anything." He did not know how or why all this was coming out.

"But you say things anyway."

"I can't help myself."

"Well, there you are," Turner said, and Tom would not have been surprised if he had slapped his knee for emphasis. "You already have convictions. You shouldn't be so shy about it. You should be braver with yourself. For yourself. Like your Rilke says, 'You must change your life.'"

"And if I change my mind about what I think?"

"That merely follows from it, from thinking. From living a considered life."

Tom thought about—considered, he supposed—that last phrase, "A considered life." He wasn't sure what it was, but he wanted it. "And how do I know," he asked, "when I'm doing that?"

"You don't, not exactly. That's why it's difficult. It's a habit of mind. You exercise it by exercising it. Which you are already doing." Wright leaned forward. "You think you don't know anything, because you're still looking, because you still have an open mind. When in fact that's precisely what knowing consists of."

"I've always felt like an artist," Tom allowed. "Except without a medium."

"That's not really important. And it will come." He held out his hands. "Look at me. I think I've created *something*, however slight."

"It's hardly slight. It's a whole history, really, of modern culture, of an important movement."

"Well, that's how it may seem to have turned out to you. But it began with my simply being in the right place and being attractive and clubbable. And then putting pen to paper."

"Actually," Tom said, "I'm putting pen to paper. I'm keeping a journal right now."

"Oh," said Turner. "Are *we* in it?"

"Not exactly. It starts when I was reading Rilke in the hotel. But it's not current. Not yet."

"But it will be soon."

"Sure, I guess. Soon, yes."

"Will you be mentioning . . . the pills?"

"I don't have to, not if—"

"Oh, I don't suppose it matters. My reputation is intact. If not entirely firm." Turner laughed a dry laugh, rather too dry, Tom felt, as it seemed to have caught in his throat. He cleared it. "And turnabout is always fair play." He smiled and added, "I just happened to take one before you arrived. Why don't you come fuck me and then you can write it all down afterward, all the savoury details?" After he'd come, Tom remembered to invite Turner for dinner. When he returned from the bathroom to get some tissue, Tom mentioned it to him. "I'd be delighted," he replied, and lay down on the bed to stroke Tom's chest. He would come over the day after tomorrow.

As he walked home Tom surprised himself. He took a sort of personal inventory and, tallying it, realized he was pretty much complete. He had a relationship, he was bright, he was a stud, he had a creative vocation, and now even a medium. As he entered the kitchen, he might have been bearing gifts, or at least several bags of groceries. Above all, he had Wright Turner, and even before Mary could open her mouth to ask him, he announced that he would be bestowing a piece of him on the Villa Donatello in a couple of nights.

6.

In Which Wright Turner Comes to Dinner

He came, the great man, a little after seven-thirty, carrying flowers, and Mary thought, they do cast him in a different light; they turn him from bronze into silver, if not quite gold.

The entire household had gone down to the Porta Romana that morning to do the shopping. As they made the circuit of the stalls and shops, it seemed to Mary that Tom hung back for long stretches of time and then inserted himself into the business at hand with questions that were both pointed and pointless.

"Do you think that's enough pasta?"

Mary said, "Well, it's half again as much as what's always enough for the three of us."

"But, I mean, it's ravioli. It's *filled* pasta."

"Then it'll go that much further, won't it?"

Tom paused, looking away. "I suppose it will."

Mary adored marketing and she wasn't going to let Tom's fussing ruin it. She moved deliberately among the stalls, taking in the heaps and landslides and banks of vegetables and fruits; four sorts of artichokes at one stall, violet, blue-green, olive, and nearly umber, tumbling, trailing leaves and stems. Eight varieties of tomatoes at another, crying out to be subsumed with the neighbouring eggplant, oregano, and flattened spheres of onion. It wasn't a matter of abundance—any American supermarket had abundance—but of density, of all this pressed together, purple and crimson, sweet, sour, and bitter, phallic and ovoid—

Mary heard Tom saying something. "Maybe, for dessert, these—" and then an interruption by another voice, accented and brisk.

"No touch, okay?"

Mary saw that Tom had his hands in a pile of fruit, and that its proprietor was shaking his head at Tom, who turned to her and said, "Christ, I'm just *looking*."

"No, you were touching," Mary explained. "You don't do that here. Either he picks some for you or you wait until he invites you to choose your own."

"Okay. I didn't know." Tom said this with a note of surliness, but Mary, not a little flustered, needed to apply herself to assuaging the stallholder.

Excuse me so much. My friend fondles your melons. He is an idiot. I pity you.

It's nothing, madam.

We shall with a free will colonize the ones he touched.

Please.

Mary took the two Tom had been holding, plus two more, and handed them to the proprietor.

And what else?

These beautiful crucifixions—

The artichokes?

Oh, yes, the artichokes. I was confounded.

A simple mistake. You speak Italian beautifully.

You are too pliant. The artichokes, the roots of them, I see, are thick and husky. It is all potable?

Just peel them until there's no green showing. Some people think it's the best part.

Very well. Of them give me also four.

The stallholder chose Mary's artichokes, took her money, and bagged them with the melons. Mary said goodbye, and she Tom continued on their way. "You have to understand this isn't just shopping, it's ritual."

"Okay, I'll watch," Tom said, and so he did, without enthusiasm, as Mary bought big salad tomatoes and little ones for sauce, two kinds of lettuce, and a great fistful of basil. "We just need cheese now," she concluded.

Alex had meanwhile gone ahead to the wine shop where they habitually purchased their oil, wine, and nuts. The owner had already poured him a wine to assay by the time Mary and Tom entered, having bought a leaf-wrapped pecorino and a big ball of mozzarella. Alex was gazing happily into his second glass while his benefactor held forth enthusiastically in Italian about the merits of the wine, which had slept a long while in an oak bathtub (or this is at least what Mary understood him to mean). On seeing her, he beamed and spoke.

Oh, the lady of the house. What a pleasure. Let me offer you and your friend a little taste of this. They vinified it with a full malolactic fermentation.

The morning is early. But a littleness doesn't afflict me, so I submit.

It'll do you good.

Would that it be a consolation to myself.

"It's good shit, Mary," Alex added. Then, just as the proprietor was in the midst of pouring two more glasses, Tom broke in.

"Are we going to have enough white?"

"We already do," said Mary. "In the cantina. There's most of a case."

"He likes white."

"Fine. We all do."

"But I mean he *really* does."

This assertion struck Mary as deeply vacuous, and it was all she could do not to respond, "Well, bully for him." But she simply said, "I think we're really all set in that department." And then it struck her that Tom must be in love with Wright Turner and it had turned his brain to mush.

In the afternoon, Tom hovered in the kitchen, where Mary was making preparations for dinner. At four, he left, apparently to go pester Alex in his studio. At five, he reappeared in the kitchen, wearing a fresh linen shirt Mary had never seen before. He poured himself a tumbler of wine and sat up on the counter. He drank perhaps half the wine and spoke without any preface. "So how much of Wright's stuff have you read?"

Mary gave the pot of tomatoes a stir. "I've looked at some of his art writing. And I think I read half of the first journal—the one that covers the early '50s."

"*Ignorant Armies*?"

"Yeah, that was the one."

"Only half?"

"I wanted to read the parts about Mary McCarthy. The rest I didn't care about."

"Didn't care?"

"About the Italian film directors and the fashion photographers and the Paris crowd. It's not my area. You know that."

"But what about the book on its own terms? It's a sort of classic now."

"I don't know," Mary said. "I suppose it is. But to me, it's just diaries with famous people in them. I don't really want to read anyone's diary."

Tom said nothing. He looked at his empty glass and slid down off the counter to recharge it from the bottle on the table in the middle of the room. He came back and stood next to the counter, farther away than before. He looked at Mary hard, seeming to screw up one eye so as to see her more sharply. "But the diary—the journal. It's a valid form, a genre in its own right. He made it one."

"I think maybe Samuel Pepys did that a little before him."

Tom looked down and then he drank. He looked at Mary again, not hard but mistily. He said, "If you think so little of him, why did you want to invite him to dinner? Maybe you should call him up and cancel."

"That's not fair, Tom. Actually, it's really stupid too."

"Well, I just have to wonder now what your . . . *motivation* is. If you think that's stupid, I don't know what the fuck to say. It's not stupid to me."

Mary thought of several devastating things she might say in reply, but wisely only offered, "He's a neighbour. He's your friend. And, yes, he's an eminent, interesting person. That's why I—no, that's why we *all* invited him."

"Okay. I'll accept that."

"You'll *accept* that? You know what, Tom? You're being an asshole. And it's unbecoming. So stop, okay?"

Tom drained his glass and looked at Mary softly, imploringly, she might have thought. "All right. I'm sorry. I'm a little wound up, I guess."

Mary nodded. She wanted to say, by way of being kind, "I know," but realized just in time that this would raise the question of what exactly she knew and how she had come to know it. In any case, Tom seemed to have been mollified. He said, "Well, okay. I suppose I'll just go upstairs and change my shirt or something."

As Mary handed him a glass of wine, Wright Turner surveyed the *salone* of the Villa Donatello with a gaze that seemed to her at once intense and offhand. He turned to Mary and Alex and smiled. "I haven't been in here for, oh, twenty years, but I'd say you've done *wonders* with it. Because although I don't recollect exactly, I'm sure it had that dark stuffy aspect these old Italian rooms always have. That . . . packratty baroqueness the World War I generation cultivated—the Gabriele D'Annunzio look, I suppose you could say."

"Miss Havisham's dining room with *putti*. And goblets of absinthe," Mary offered.

Turner laughed. "Exactly."

"Or," Tom (who had thus far been silent) added, "Walter Benjamin's Paris as a consumerist attic. Baudelaire as *flâneur* in the department store."

"You'll have to explain that one to me, Thomas," Turner said after a hesitation.

"You didn't *know* Baudelaire, did you?" Alex asked slyly.

"Only in his dotage."

Mary and Alex laughed, but Tom had been occupied assembling the explication of his previous text. He began, perhaps too quietly, he realized, "It's the idea of nineteenth-century Paris being a locus of display, of people putting their stuff out to show, and the *flâneur*—the artist—puts himself on display, and commodifies himself . . ." and there Tom trailed off.

Turner was saying, "And the furniture. Very inspired. I wouldn't have thought," and there he indicated the Stickley rocker and sofa, "to put that in here."

"Neither would we," Alex shrugged, and they all laughed, Tom without much conviction, and Turner looked over at him and said, "Now Thomas, I'm sorry, I fear I stepped on your lines. You were saying?"

"Benjamin . . ."

"Ah, I knew Ben Britten. And all his crowd. Auden, of course. I must tell you about Auden sometime. You would have found him very intriguing." And then he turned back to Mary and Alex.

"Now you," he said to Alex, "are reputed to be a painter. But I don't see anything hanging."

"We thought we'd go to the studio after dinner," Mary said.

"Fabulous," said Turner. "I can't wait. Well, actually I can wait, because I feel rather desperately hungry, and Tom tells me you're a fine cook."

"That's very nice of him," said Mary. "I just hope you won't be too disappointed."

Tom, for lack of anything to do or say, fished a handful of peanuts from the bowl on the coffee table. He reflected that these people were hypocritical and cruel. All except for Wright, whom he believed must adore him.

* * *

Dinner did not go as Tom had imagined, although he could not have said exactly in what particular. He supposed he had thought he would be introducing Mary and Alex to Wright, exhibiting them and their various qualities to him. Or at least in some sense preside at the table, mediate their relations, taking a certain pleasure and pride in showing his fine friends to his distinguished lover, his smart and charming lover to his attractive and sophisticated friends.

But he found that, even once he had decided he had made too much of the interchanges in the *salone,* he had no great urge to take charge of this encounter. There was, in any case, no need. All that was essential for Tom was not to visibly sulk, and after the second time Wright gave his thigh a furtive squeeze under the table, he was, in fact, almost content. They were outside, under the pergola, at the edge of the garden, and the sun had mostly gone down, although it was still warm. There were five bottles of wine on the table, and only the last of these still held any wine. They had just finished their *secondo,* and Alex brought out some cheese and a further bottle of wine to drink with it. They might have been in paradise.

Turner was saying to Mary, "Thomas tells me you are a great Jamesian, that you've come here to walk in the master's footsteps. That you followed him to Bellosguardo."

"Oh, you might say that. In a manner of speaking." Mary's own manner of speaking just then was a little hurried. She was happy enough to talk about James, but she had no desire to be seen as a fan, as a wealthy lady hobbyist "of a certain age," rather than an artist in her own right. She added, rather cleverly, "Of course, you get to walk in his footsteps every day, don't you."

"Oh, in the villa? I suppose I do. Not that one tends to think of it. You can't, not really. Or you'd go a little mad. So much past. So many ghosts."

"James always strikes me as a little bit of a ghost himself,"

Mary said. "Lurking in the shadows of ancient rooms, overhearing the conversations of the living."

"And you admire that?"

"I don't know. I admire the writing that comes out of it."

"I hear from Thomas that that's a minority view among your contemporaries."

"I guess it is. I can't really be bothered about it. About the opinions of people who generally haven't even read him."

Tom broke in. "They don't have to read him. The facts speak for themselves. He was a priss. He was effete and sexless. He wrote about pointless, elite people. His books are dull. Ergo, he sucks." Catching himself, Tom added, "Or that's the consensus."

"A little strong surely," Turner interjected.

"It's all right. It's something Tom likes to say to amuse us all," Mary said, and indeed felt the remark must represent a thawing in their relation since the exchange in the kitchen that afternoon. She added, "Tom's the voice of his generation."

"Somebody has to do it," Alex said.

"But sometimes I think *everybody* wants to be the voice of our generation. It's kind of a preoccupation," Tom said. "Of our generation."

Alex faced Turner. "So what I want to know is, Did you *know* Henry James?"

"Alex, that's ceasing to be funny," said Mary.

"No it's not," said Alex.

"I knew his sister Alice," Turner said. "No, I'm kidding." They all laughed heartily and then Turner continued. "But I met Bernard Berenson, who knew him. Of course Berenson knew everyone."

Alex said, "It seems like everyone you knew knew everyone."

"Which is how *I* know everyone," Turner said. "It gets to be a habit, knowing everyone." Alex emptied the remainder of the bottle he'd brought out with the cheese into their glasses and said, "Berenson was the guy who invented the Renaissance. Or at least the idea of it."

"You're thinking of Burckhardt. Or Pater," Turner said. "Really, he was the first great expert, making attributions and such. And dealer. He got the collectors and museums in play, made it *de rigueur* to own a Florentine or Venetian masterpiece."

"And he would have known Ruskin, right?" Tom asked.

"I don't know. They would have hated each other."

"Mary's been reading Ruskin," Tom offered.

"My, all this very earnest interest in fusty dead writers and critics," said Turner. "Quite remarkable. Quite unexpected. Henry James. Ruskin, for Christ's sake."

"Why 'for Christ's sake'?" Mary said.

"Well, he's rather the epitome of all the things Thomas was objecting to in James. Plus the carrying on about the morality of art. With the usual Victorian hypocrisy, of course."

Mary said, "Where's the hypocrisy?"

"He was one of these Victorian fetishists of little girls. A pedophile. I understand from Thomas that in America you all get quite exercised about that these days."

"Really?" said Mary.

"Oh, yes. There are things he wrote that are quite salacious. I'll show you some examples, if you're interested. When you come by. As, of course, I hope you will."

"I'd love it," Mary said.

There was a pause, and then Turner looked at Mary and said, "Now I know your husband is here painting. And Thomas is here . . . *discovering* himself and his métier. And you, I understand, are writing a novel. Perhaps it's a sequel to *The Portrait of a Lady,* which would be another reason to come by."

"It would."

"So that's what you're working on? Or something in that mode?"

"I don't like to say. And I'm not sure. Sometimes I think I'd like to write something more Italian, a saint's life or something." Mary laughed. "With all that devotional fervour, the raptures, that erotic love of God."

"I've got just the one for you," Turner said. "Maria Maddalena de' Pazzi. Girl from Florence. Eminent cinquecento family. Went completely overboard, of course. I'll show you her memoir."

"Sounds interesting."

"She has a church. There are paintings of her, too."

Mary said, "I'd like to see them. Sometimes I forget we're here—that these things are out there, just down the hill. Which is why we came. Or why we thought we did."

"Not to get away?" asked Turner. "That was very important in my day. To get away from America, from the conformity and stultification."

"I guess it's something like that."

"But really, Mary," Alex said, rising to refill their glasses, "there's not much you can't do in America these days."

"Everything is permitted, I should think," said Turner. "And Seattle is supposed to be lovely and prosperous. I daresay most Italians would think you were mad to leave and come here."

"There are drawbacks," Mary said. "Seattle's still provincial. All this gloss and money and pseudo-sophistication have been laid over the provincialism, but it's still there. Too much money with no object, no purpose. Among the people we know, there's all this ambition, but it's aimless."

"I got mugged just before I left," said Tom. "Because some gangsta kids thought I was a yuppie, a dot-com-er."

"You *were* a dot-com-er," Mary inserted.

"As of noon that day I wasn't."

"Well anyway, it rains all the time. It really does," Alex added. "Especially when you don't want it to."

"The climate's incorrigible," said Tom.

"It's melancholic. People are nice in the sense of being polite," Mary added. "But they're a little ghostly. They don't have edges. They've been washed away."

"And we're the heroin capital of the West Coast," said Alex. "It's our little secret."

"Seattle," Tom said, "where rain is ubiquitous as junk." He felt, even as he formed the words, that this was a lame and stupid comment and resolved to say no more.

"Well," Turner was saying, "we have all that here. Perhaps less rain. But heroin, yes. I think Florence is supposed to be the heroin capital of Italy. A few years ago the Piazza Santo Spirito was scarcely passable for the addicts and dope peddlers. There were needles in the street."

"But they've cleaned it up, apparently," Mary said.

"Oh, I think it's only moved a little farther out of tourist range. But it's all around the *stazione*. You know about the children? *I ragazzi della Santa Maria Novella?*"

"No," said Mary, and Alex and Tom shook their heads.

"Oh, I suppose you don't read the Italian papers," Turner said. "Just the *Herald Tribune.*"

"That and the English Sundays," said Alex.

"Well, it's rather a scandal. There are children in and around station, quite a few. Children of addicts, or already addicts themselves. As young as eleven years old, it's said. Committing petty crime or selling drugs or selling themselves."

"Those might have been the kids that hassled me," said Tom.

"Tom had a run-in with some gypsies at Santa Maria Novella," Mary explained.

"Well, in any case," Turner said, "it's not exactly *la bella Toscana,* is it?"

"Somehow," said Alex, "it seems more shocking here than it would in America."

"But this place has always had all the evils, all the misery. That's what Dante was recording in the *Inferno*. The life of this city as he knew it. It's not hell, it's just Florence. Then as now. That's why one lives in Bellosguardo, I suppose—we expatriates."

Alex stood and picked up his glass and the bottle. "Maybe we ought to go to the studio now. If you're up for it."

"Of course we are," said Turner. "I'm sorry if I cast a pall over the evening. But art's the great remedy. So, yes, let's go."

"I'll bring another bottle," Alex said. "Just in case."

They went inside and down the long corridor to Alex's studio. It occurred to Tom that he had not been here in some time. There was still a little light, moonlight perhaps, pressing in through the windows. In the middle of the room there was a couch and at the other end an easel and a small table cluttered with tubes of paint.

Alex switched on the candelabra overhead. "Here we are," he said, leading them around and behind the easel. "And there it is."

"Just the one?" Turner asked.

"Well, the only one I've done here."

Turner considered the canvas before them for a moment. "Not that it's not . . . formidable in and of itself."

Alex had set his glass down on the table and was refilling from the bottle he'd carried. Mary stood off from the rest of them at a little distance. Tom was studying the painting. "Jeez, Alex," he finally said.

The canvas was six feet tall and perhaps three feet wide, with a background of soft cerulean-blue glaze. The rest of it was filled with Mary, Mary quite naked and almost life-sized; Mary's dark hair and green eyes, her strong face; but Mary's body quite ruddy, in places pink as a Valentine candy heart. She seemed to be resting on something yet to be floating in the blue space; or perhaps to be suspended while bearing a great weight.

Turner backed away from the painting, and Tom followed him. The painting insisted on being seen from a distance to be comprehended even as it pulled you towards it (or so it seemed to Tom), asserting the need almost to be touched.

Alex charged Turner's glass and then Tom's. Mary, who had left her glass at the table, had moved still farther to the edge of the room, almost to the darkening window.

"So, what do you think?" Alex asked Turner.

"It's very arresting. I'll say that for it. The colour's rather baroque. And of course the figure itself is . . . luscious."

Alex looked over at Mary. "Painted strictly from life. I didn't gild the lily." Mary returned his gaze and smiled, and then looked at Turner, who had his back to her, still regarding the painting. She had been prepared to feel scrutinized—to have the strong sensation that Turner and Tom were seeing her stark naked (which indeed they more or less were)—but she was surprised to find there was virtually no discomfort in it. In fact, as she pondered it, she took a certain pleasure in having Turner—gay or bisexual that he was—know her body so intimately, know what it had to offer. It occurred to her that Alex had indeed made her into an object of adoration, as he had intended.

Turner faced Alex and said, "Where do you get these colours?"

"From a tube. It's acrylic. Not very Florentine, I guess."

"But the painting *is* Florentine, rather. Perhaps in spite of itself. A sort of cotton-candy Florentine."

"Is that a compliment?" Alex asked.

"I'm not sure yet." He gazed at a painting for another quarter-minute, and took a long sip of wine. "Cotton-candy Venetian, perhaps. What with all that blue." He turned and faced Alex. "So what were you aiming for?"

"I don't know. Maybe Klimt," Alex said.

"Oh," said Turner. "I think I see the Klimt. There's the etherealness, but with that odour of raunch. And that's Bellini's blue, perhaps."

Alex still had said nothing. Tom could not help thinking that Alex was looking terribly proud of himself. That he was inviting Wright to become a little sharp, to take a swat at him.

Finally Alex said, "You're warm. But not quite there." He

swallowed some wine. "Really, it's Pontormo, from the chapel in Santa Felicitá."

"Really," Turner said.

"Alex and I spent a long time there after lunch a few weeks ago," offered Tom. "Actually, it was the day we met you on the road."

"Really," Turner said. Then he added, "I suppose I can see it. The colour in particular." He stopped. "And it's rather beautiful. Doubtless because Mary's a beautiful woman. But it's not glorious, like Pontormo."

"Not glorious," Alex repeated, not sounding in the least bit stung, Tom thought.

"It's not stunning or audacious or bizarre the way Pontormo is."

"That's not really what I was aiming for."

"No, doubtless not. But the painting was. Art always is, I think."

Alex drank again. He scratched his chin, as though this all were merely a small problem he and Turner were puzzling out together. "So what would it take to get it to 'glorious' and 'bizarre'?" he said at last.

"Well, Pontormo has all those bodies tangled up together. That's rather key, I think. So you might add a body or two. Not to this canvas. It's too small. And it's nice in its own way."

"So?"

"A new painting. With a couple of bodies. To start, a couple of boys or girls or a girl and a boy if you like. The point is: stick your neck out a little."

"Nude?"

"Of course," said Turner. "And Mary's a lovely model." He stopped and drank, and began to speak almost before he'd swallowed. "And here's the thing—yes—paint her with Thomas. He's just right for it. It'll be lovely."

Tom looked at Mary, who still stood expressionless and

distant at the window, looking as if she were having a cigarette, but for the fact that she didn't smoke.

Alex was smiling, smiling very broadly indeed. He said, "So, are you two up for that?"

Tom began haltingly. "Well, I suppose. . . . But I'm kind of modest about my body, about being—"

"Well, you shouldn't be," Turner interjected.

"But, well, I guess it's okay. If it's okay with Mary. If she *wants* to." Even as he said this, he saw that for him it had everything to do with what Wright wanted, that he would do it for Wright.

Mary had left the shelter of the window and now came towards the easel, towards Alex and Tom and Wright Turner. She said to Alex, "Sure. Why not. It might be fun." She looked at Turner. "It might even be glorious or brilliant or whatever. But you have to give me the grand tour of the Villa Castellani. And show me this Ruskin stuff and this Santa Maria Maddalena whomever."

"De' Pazzi," said Turner.

"*Pazzi*—that means 'crazy,' right?" Mary said.

"Yes indeed," Turner replied.

"She's perfect for me then. So it's a deal."

"Of course," said Turner. "As you wish. Tomorrow if you like."

"Fine. We'll all come. After lunch."

"Or perhaps on your own? Alex and Thomas are certainly welcome, but I doubt they'd find my showing you dusty old books very diverting." He looked to Tom and Alex.

Mary said, "He has a point."

"If you two don't mind," Turner added.

Alex said, "No problem. I'll take Tom out for lunch or something. Or I'll round up some stretcher bars and stuff." Tom nodded.

"Good then," said Turner. "It's done."

7.

The Turin Girl

Tom and Alex watched Mary go out the gate of the Villa Donatello.

"She's bringing him flowers," Alex said.

"I always do that," said Tom. "He likes it."

"What else does he like, *Thomas*?"

Tom held back a moment. "Alex, with all respect," he said, "fuck off."

"Just asking."

A few minutes later, Alex and Tom themselves departed the villa, on their way down the hill to purchase Alex canvas and stretcher bars, and then settle into a three-bottle lunch.

They stopped first at a framer's workshop in the Oltrarno behind the Piazza Santo Spirito, a whole neighbourhood apparently consecrated to framers and furniture repair, none of them marked with signs or any indication of the craft practised within.

"How do you know about this place?" Tom asked.

"Oh, I found it when we were renting the apartment down here. Bought the stretchers for Mary's nude here. The owner and I are kind of friends."

They went in and the proprietor greeted Alex in a sputter of Tuscan.

So, painter, how goes it with you?

Could be worse. And you?

I'm well-nigh befucked with work. Look at this place.

The proprietor indicated a huge work table awash in half-gilded frames.

I'd say it always looks like this.

Very funny. And I suppose you want something done too, right now.

As a matter of fact, yes. Stretcher bars. I can come back after lunch.

You can come back next year.

Please. They're standard sizes. One metre by two.

So, the golden rectangle. By Saint Pancras's balls, you take yourself for a master now.

No way. Really. But I can bring you down something to frame. Something you'll like. A pretty lady without any clothes.

Well, I might have something lying around. Come back later. We'll see.

That'll work. I'm grateful.

You can kiss my grandmother's twat. So go.

Thanks a million. See you later.

Alex and Tom returned to the street, and Alex said, "How did you do that? I mean, talk to him. I couldn't understand a thing he said."

"Oh, it's just joshing around. Universal language. Same thing in my dad's body shop when I was a kid."

"But you haven't really studied much, taken classes. You're not fluent like Mary is. I'm impressed."

"I get by."

They crossed the river and stopped at an art supply store where Alex asked for linen and managed to have it cut and rolled while they waited. He also bought various tubes of Liquitex, plus a tub of gesso and one of gloss medium and some brushes. By one-thirty they were ready to eat.

Tom and Alex sat down in the same restaurant as before, and the same waiter came over, speaking his preternatural English, proffering the same jellied tomato concoction and little livery toasts to get them started. Alex ordered a magnum of something red and profound, and they began their long row into the backwater of the afternoon.

At some point into the second magnum of the same wine ("I don't want to jinx things," Alex explained) Alex brought Tom up a little short.

"So what's the deal with you and Wright Turner?"

This inquiry made Tom uncomfortable even though he had expected it; had, in fact, already composed a reply.

"I don't know. What does Mary say?"

"Mary doesn't say anything. Why should she?"

"She might have ideas," Tom said. "She's a . . . young person of many theories."

"Of what?"

"Never mind. It's a . . . joke."

"Ha," said Alex. "A joke." He drank. "So talk."

"I'd prefer not to," Tom said very deliberately.

"Is that a joke too?"

"Actually, yes. I guess it is."

"So come on. Last time we were here, I told you about the money. I opened the fucking *vault*."

Tom considered, or rather feigned considering, as he had already assumed the matter would come out today. He merely wanted to extract what he felt was the proper due for intelligence of this interest and currency. Finally, he said, "Well, we're lovers."

"Congratulations. I mean, that's good. Or I hope it is."

"It is. I guess."

"You guess?"

Tom had not planned to say what he had just said; had not, in fact, known he was in any way disposed to think it, never mind give it voice. He attempted to follow the thought down the hole from which it had emerged, to its burrow.

"I guess I mean that it's . . . not really clear what the relationship is. At this point."

"You mean you don't know whether it's just fuck pals or fuck chums—well, whatever it is they say—or something more."

"I suppose," Tom responded. "He says really great things to me. About me. But I don't know how to take them. I mean he's so fucking . . . knowing."

"He's jaded?"

"Or world-weary. But then he'll say something really—I don't know—encouraging. And nice. Really nice."

"Nice," Alex repeated. "I wouldn't have figured him for 'nice.'"

Tom found himself taking umbrage at this. "Oh, he's supposed to be a bitchy old queen, I suppose?"

"No, I don't mean it to sound that way. It's just that, well, his reputation is kind of for kiss-and-tell."

"There's a lot of smart critical thinking between the lines."

"Between the sheets too." Alex held up his palm. "Sorry. That's *my* joke."

"It's really lame."

"I know." Alex laid his palms down on the table. "So what's the problem? If there is one."

Tom thought. He did not know. He said, "I suppose maybe there isn't." He stopped again. "Well, maybe last night, he was a little . . . condescending or something. I mean he was all over you guys, being charming and so forth."

"He wasn't exactly charming to me. He was critical. In a useful way. Maybe to Mary he was charming."

"I guess," Tom conceded. "Anyway, I kind of felt like the third wheel."

"Instead of like a couple."

"I suppose."

"But you didn't want us to think of you and him as a couple. You came home from there and you weren't telling us anything."

"I'm talking about how he related to me, not how you and Mary related to us."

Alex drained his glass and then he said, "Still, maybe that's it. You aren't owning up to the relationship, acknowledging it. So why should he?"

"I don't have any basis to do that. He hasn't told me—"

"Why should he? Why don't you tell *him*? Somebody has to, right?"

Tom thought about this, about how wise and brotherly it sounded. He sometimes forgot that he loved not only Mary, but also (nearly as much) Alex, who just now seemed fully to understand that Tom indeed loved Wright Turner.

Tom said, "I guess you're right—"

"No, *he's* Wright. Ha ha. Sorry. I've had a lot of wine."

"Okay. But, anyway, really, it's just not my style to do that."

"Maybe it's not his either. I mean, he just doesn't strike me as someone who's going to fucking gush over anybody. So tell him, okay? You tell him."

"Well, I suppose."

"You won't regret it. At least you'll know the score."

"Okay," said Tom. "But promise me one thing: that you won't tell Mary."

"Well, I mean, she can guess—"

"I just don't want her misinterpreting things."

"She's not going to misinterpret anything. She'd be happy for you, if it's a good thing."

"I just want to tell her myself. So she'll understand that it *is* a good thing."

"Sure. If that's what you want." Alex regarded the half-spent magnum before him. "Shit, we're not going to finish this, are we? Oh well. A pity."

Afterward, when they had recrossed the Arno and Tom waited outside the framemaker's workshop while Alex went in for his stretcher bars, Tom reflected that, in truth, he had no intention of telling Mary just now; that telling Wright what he needed to tell him precluded telling Mary anything.

Alex came out carrying his timber, laughing. "Boy, these guys. You think they're, you know, old world craftsmen, dignified, venerable, salt-of-the-earth. But no: they're good old boys. They don't give a shit. They're fucking *dudes*."

He laughed again and they walked to the bus stop and continued on their way up to Bellosguardo, where Mary was presumably waiting for them after her visit to Wright Turner.

Mary was indeed already home, having returned only a few minutes before. She was upstairs changing her clothes after showering when she heard Alex and Tom coming into the garden and through the kitchen door. When she was done dressing, she went downstairs and found them in Alex's studio.

Alex was laying stretcher bars out on the floor in a rectangle. He looked up at Mary. "Hey, how'd it go?" he asked.

"With Wright? Oh, fine. He lent me a couple of books. The things he talked about last night."

"And?" Alex continued.

"Nothing much. We had a couple of glasses of wine. Some olives. Maybe another glass of wine."

"You look kind of . . . flushed."

"I just got out of the shower. It seems . . . *close* today."

"I suppose. Seems cool up here," said Alex. "In town, it might be in the high seventies. I don't know." He stopped and picked up one of the wooden triangles near his feet. "We're kind of tight, you know?"

"I gathered," Mary said, and looked over at Tom for an instant, though their eyes did not meet. "But you got your canvas and stuff."

"Yeah, we did."

"So when do you start? Or, I guess, when do *we* start?" She looked at Tom more deliberately now, but his eyes were locked upon the floor.

"Well," and here Alex stopped and walked over to the chest where he kept his materials. "Where's my fucking staple gun?" he said. "Okay. Well, if I got this all put together now, then I could gesso it tonight. So we could start tomorrow. After lunch."

Tom looked up and said, "I can't wait."

Mary went out of the studio and, for fifteen minutes or so, Tom watched Alex assemble the bars and begin to stretch his canvas. Then he went up to his room. He tried to add something to his journal, but the journal refused to be written in. He was still, he realized, a little drunk, not high but certainly addled. He put on his headphones and listened to Morrissey singing "How Soon Is Now?" and then he listened to it again. After a while he went downstairs and stood in the kitchen, picking through a bowl of olives. From the direction of the studio, his ears registered the sound of voices raised, emphatic if not angry. He was tempted to slip down the hall and get within earshot, to find out what the discussion was about. But instead, assured that Alex and Mary were occupied and that he would have privacy, he dialed Wright Turner's number.

The phone rang a long time before Tom gave up and put down the receiver. He could not imagine Wright being out, so he imagined him sitting on his big sofa, sitting in the half-light, holding a wine glass or perhaps a long-stemmed rose, deliberately letting the phone ring and ring, knowing it could only be Tom.

He heard a door and footsteps, the brisk tap of Mary rather than the shuffle of Alex. He caught a glimpse of Mary's face, stern but etched by two or three strands of tears, as she turned up into the stairwell. So, he thought, even couples like Mary and Alex fight, make one another weep. And it's normal, it's okay, it's part of the deal. That was all he wanted with Wright.

The lunch consumed at the Villa Donatello the next day was lengthier and more formal then what Mary, Alex, and Tom were accustomed to. Indeed, they were not generally in the habit of sitting down collectively for lunch at all. And they drank two bottles of wine together, whereas none of them normally drank at home until evening.

Mary asked herself, "Is Alex drinking more?" but she could not decide, Alex's drinking being a tide that might rise or ebb several feet over a cycle of days. She certainly wasn't going to bring it up, not when they were negotiating something so important. Last night, after a round of lovemaking and sheepish discussion, they had just managed to retrieve a middle ground in which Alex again agreed to keep an open mind, to consider the matter. But yes, she was sure Tom was drinking more, and then she thought, And me. I'm drinking more. But this is Italy. This is Bellosguardo. Everything is different here.

At that instant, Alex stood and said, "So, let's do it." They went down the hall to the studio, and Alex went over the big canvas, now clenched upright in the jaws of his easel. He touched the surface. "Seems okay," he said. He nodded to Mary and then to Tom.

The store of ease Tom had built up over lunch had almost entirely drained off once they entered the studio. He knew it was lame and infantile and silly, but he could not adjust himself to the idea of taking his clothes off in front of Mary and Alex; he had no precedent for it in his life to that point save in locker rooms, sexual encounters, or medical examinations, none of which seemed apropos to his present dilemma. He said, with what was meant to be insouciance but became strangled in a gulp, "So, do we . . . strip now?"

Alex—good and kind Alex—said, "You don't have to. Not just yet. Maybe just try to get into the idea of what we're doing here together."

Tom took consolation in this reprieve, but Mary had already taken off her shoes, her russet sneakers of a chic Italian manufacture. And now she was pressing her shoulder blades against the wall as she set to work extricating herself from her jeans. As Tom watched this, a whole further vista of discomfort began to open out before him: he was going to see Mary naked.

Mary had one leg free by the time Tom thought to reiterate Alex's suggestion. "Yeah," he said. "Let's just sort of plan things out for a minute."

"Sure," said Mary, now extracting her other leg. She walked over bare-legged and stood next to Tom, facing Alex. Her panties, Tom could not but notice, were light blue.

Alex began, "So I'm thinking you guys could be on the couch, but we won't see the couch in the painting. It'll be more like you're . . . hovering somewhere. Or crouching."

Mary turned around and sat down on the sofa behind them. Tom joined her. He faced Alex, hunched forward, his hands on his knees.

"That's not quite it," said Alex. "Mary, why don't you kind of lean into him a little—just enough to be touching, just so Tom's bearing a little of your weight. Then maybe, Tom, you turn towards her a little bit so she's pressing on your left shoulder."

Mary sidled up against Tom, rather like a cat pressing against a leg.

"That's good," Alex said. "But look away from him. Turn your neck. Like you're . . . entangled with him, but you're not really quite all there." Mary moved a little and Alex said, "Good." Tom guessed she was looking serious, which she was indeed quite good at.

"Now you, Tom," said Alex. "Turn a little bit to your right—from the waist up. And look, I don't know, just a little short of dejected." He stopped, and then said, "Yeah, that has possibilities. Let me get this down."

Alex took a digital camera from a chest, lined himself up in parallel with the canvas and the easel, and pressed the shutter. He studied the screen. "Okay. That's close. Now we can try some other things. But really, I'm going to have to get you guys naked to decide on anything."

"Ah, what," asked Tom, "are you aiming for, exactly?"

"I'll know it when I see it. Maybe something a little like the one I did of Mary. Only these two figures are stuck together, even though they're not exactly interacting. They have a sort of common fate. Or something. They're naked and they're beautiful, of course, but kind of devastated. Okay?"

"Sure," said Tom. "So do you want us to . . ."

"I think Tom's feeling shy," Mary interjected.

"Oh, not shy. No, not shy," Tom said hurriedly. "It's just that I've never done this before. I don't know the . . . protocol."

"There's no protocol," Alex said. "You just get naked."

"Oh," said Tom. "Okay. That's simple." He leaned down and began to untie his right shoe.

"You guys might want your robes or something to put on when we're taking breaks."

Tom looked up, and said, "Good idea. I'll go get mine right now."

"Mine too, if you don't mind?" Mary said. "On the back of the bedroom door—no, wait. On the chair in my studio."

"Sure," said Tom. "Be right back." Tom nearly bounded for the door. Exiting the studio, he felt safe; so safe, it did not occur to him until he reached the stair that he was wearing one shoe.

He grabbed his flannel robe from his room and went into Mary's studio, seeing her robe—long and flowered in a cotton print—draped over the chair at her desk. As he picked it up, he saw there was a printout of a manuscript next to her laptop. The top page said:

The Villa Donatello
A ~~Novel~~
Romance
by
Mary Bruckner

He carefully lifted a sheath of pages and read a few sentences and then a few more. His hand shook as he returned the pages to the stack.

As Tom came down the hall, carrying the robes, feeling as though he were hopping on his unshod foot, he heard Mary and Alex talking. He heard Mary say something to which Alex replied, "It comes down to the same thing. We should have thought of that before . . ." but he stopped as Tom entered the studio.

Tom saw that Mary was naked and he tried not to look. He quickly busied himself with removing his own clothes, and when he looked back Mary had sat down on the couch with her body turned slightly away from him. He sat down next to her and tried to arrange himself in the position they'd been in before. Alex came over and rearranged them, pressed them closer together with Mary's head against Tom's upper arm.

"There. Good," Alex said. "Now close your eyes. Not Tom, just you, Mary. Good. But Tom, you look away. Not that much. Maybe more looking down. Yes. Look dejected maybe. Spaced out."

"Abstracted?" Tom asked.

"Sure—be abstracted." Alex stood back. "One more thing. Tom, you need to put your hand on Mary's side, along her chest." Tom placed the palm of his right hand just where her ribs began. "No, further up the torso, and more onto her chest."

"On my boob?" Mary said.

"Well, not over it—not, like, cupping it. But on the side of it, yeah."

"I'm not sure I'm comfortable with that," inserted Tom.

"Well, here," Alex said and moved back over to them. He took Tom's hand and positioned it so the fingers rested just on the flank of Mary's right breast. "Is that okay?"

"I guess," Tom said. He held his fingertips against Mary's breast as lightly as he could. The flesh felt cool. Cool and very white.

After a while, Tom was scarcely aware of being naked or of Mary leaning against him, of her dark hair and slightly damp skin touching his skin; of its tang of good soap and citrus fruit, of its being no more than a rose containing precisely itself.

Later, when he tried to recollect what Mary's body actually looked like, he could not say; or rather, it was the same body as in Alex's painting of her, which now lay facing Tom against the studio wall by the window.

When Alex said it was time to stop, Tom stood and put on his robe. He turned slightly and saw Mary pulling her own robe over her back, wrapping its cord around her waist. She looked at him and smiled. "So that wasn't so bad, was it?" she asked him. "It's mainly just boring, really."

"I guess so," Tom said.

"Sometimes Mary reads," said Alex. "Aloud. It kills the time and doesn't really interfere much with the modelling. Or we can have music."

"Whatever," Tom said. He indicated the canvas. "So can we . . . see?"

"Oh, I guess. Sure. It's just a lot of chicken scratches right now."

Tom came around to the other side of the easel. The canvas was still almost entirely blank, except for an arrangement of ovals that, he realized, represented loose balloon-man renditions of his and Mary's bodies. They might have been a pile of potato sacks or a bunch of grapes.

"It's just to try to locate where the figures are going," Alex was saying. "Just to see where they're comfortable. Then maybe I'll paint a glaze over the whole thing—maybe kind of gold and teal green. Then we'll get serious."

"How long does that take? To get serious?"

"I don't know. It takes as long as it takes, to coin a phrase."

"To coin a tautology," Mary said.

"Anyway, I promise," said Alex, "that you won't have to pose more than a hour or so a day. Okay?"

"Sure."

"And like I said, Mary can read or whatever."

Tom looked at Mary, who was standing next to the couch, the robe fallen over her body. She looked very beautiful, almost as beautiful as in the painting leaning against the wall.

"Maybe you could read some of your work-in-progress," Tom said.

"Maybe. Maybe I could," Mary replied. "Or you could read some of yours. About Baudelaire and Morrissey, or whatever Wright's put you up to." She raised her eyebrows and then tilted her head in a gesture of query.

"I suppose," said Tom. "But I think maybe it's pretty dull stuff at this point."

"Oh," Mary said, "I doubt that."

Tom was singularly relieved that the modelling session was over. He had not (as he had feared he might) gotten an erection. It had been, as Mary promised, basically dull, but dull in the manner of a three-hour final exam back in college: tedium gilded with panic.

The residue of that morning's anxiety left Tom edgy for the rest of the afternoon, and his own racing thoughts—about the modelling, about Mary (her novel, her general closed-mouthedness and opacity of late), and about Wright—compounded and replenished it. Finally, around five-thirty, he could stand no more. He strode out of the house, checked the beds closest to the gate for flowers, and, finding none in good condition, thought, I'll bring him herbs, things that smell nice. He made a bouquet of lavender and rosemary and hurried to Wright Turner's apartment in the Villa Castellani.

"Oh. Thomas," said Turner when he opened the door. "Come in. Come in." He took Tom's bouquet and regarded it.

"This is nice. Rather original. I suppose I'll roast a chicken for the one, and put the other in a little vase for the bathroom." He was still standing in the doorway and Tom was still standing in the corridor. Turner said, "Oh. Yes," and backed away from the door. "Do come in," he repeated, without (so Tom thought) much conviction or urgency.

Tom went to the couch and settled himself upon it. Turner still stood near the door, and began to move towards the couch, but stopped and said, "I'll just get us some wine, all right?" Tom nodded and Turner nodded in response.

When Turner came back with their glasses, he sat down on the couch and said, quite affably, "So *how* are you? Have you started posing yet?"

"We started today," Tom said, and drank a sip of wine.

"And how did you find it?"

"A little awkward. Then kind of boring."

"I suppose that's quite normal," Turner said. "After all, you have someone scrutinizing you very . . . fiercely. And you're in close proximity to another naked person."

"I think it's more the proximity thing that made me nervous."

Turner said, "So you and Mary had never seen each other naked before?"

"No."

"Oh, I'd rather imagined you might have been lovers at some point."

"No. Never."

"She's an attractive woman, and very smart as well."

"I guess she is."

Turner drank and then put his glass down on the coffee table. "So you might well be attracted to her," he said. "Anyone might."

"No. Not at all." Tom paused, took a breath, and—so it felt to him—leapt. "Besides, doesn't it occur to you that my being here with you—having done the things we've done—means that's not what I'm interested in?"

Turner said nothing and then smiled. "You needn't become so . . . vehement." He picked up his glass and drank. "And of course," he continued, "that *occurs* to me. It was purely a matter of curiosity. You three constitute this rather unusual ménage, after all. And precisely because of our connection, it seemed like something that I might want to know about—about you. But it's not, I suppose, really my concern."

Tom felt both ashamed and boxed in. His words came out in a low bleat. "That's not what I meant. I mean, you can ask me anything you want." He paused. "Anything. I just feel sometimes like Mary sort of takes over things. Everything."

"She's impressive. But rather forbidding. One doesn't exactly . . . warm to her, does one?"

"Oh, she can be very thoughtful. Very kind. When you least expect it, though," Tom said. "I owe her and Alex pretty much everything."

Turner sat up. "Now why would you say that? Beyond the financial aspect, which of course, given their wealth, really costs them nothing?"

"Because they've been my friends when nobody particularly wanted to be," said Tom. "Because they don't care that I haven't amounted to much."

"I shouldn't think true friends would care one way or another if one hasn't amounted to much. That's not the principle in friendship."

"Well, sure. I mean we all support each other with our work, no matter how it's going. In my case, though, it's just not very advanced."

Turner was cradling his glass in his palms. He said, "Well, Thomas, it's not as though they're advanced, either. Alex, apparently, has one painting to his name."

"That's not true. He left a lot of things behind. In Seattle."

"Which may say something about how consequential they were," said Turner. "And Mary. Where is this novel of hers?

Where can one read all this literary output of hers? I don't quite see what she's really accomplished, I'm afraid."

"Oh, she's done tons of things," Tom said. "Really. It's just not what she's interested in right now. I mean, at the *CityReader* she published something every week. Reviews mostly."

"Of books?"

"And art. Restaurants too. Her restaurant reviews were really sharp. Funny too. They were like this whole commentary on the social scene in Seattle—the new money and so on. She called them the 'nouveaux faux bohos.' It was really trenchant."

"Doubtless, she has a gift for that," Turner said. "But it's essentially journalism: here today, gone tomorrow."

"But that's just one thing. She had this whole other career in software, in dot-coms. She was in on some groundbreaking things," Tom said rather firmly.

"I thought it was along the lines of very well-paid technical writing. She said as much."

"That was at first, at Noumena. At Critic.com, she created some really cool stuff. The 'Edge-A-Sketch.' It was this graph that averaged out all the hip critical opinions in the country for books and films and music, so you could see where the buzz was, even in advance."

"Very clever."

"And she got very rich, too."

"Surely that was rather accidental. The stock had a run-up or whatever."

"Maybe, but she had the foresight to be there," Tom tried to conclude.

"She might have been anywhere. She might have worked just as hard and just as cleverly and ended up with nothing."

"But she didn't," Tom said. "So you could say she kind of earned it, couldn't you?"

"You could. As you might say someone earns the winning lottery ticket. Or being struck by lightning."

"You know, I thought you liked her. But I'm not so sure."

"I like her perfectly well. She's rather compelling in a way," Turner said. "Even though you know she's really withholding herself, you feel you're getting something. Or that if you wait a while, you're *going* to get something."

"So you had a good time? When she came over yesterday."

"Oh, yes. Perfectly fine."

"I tried to call you last night. To see how it went. You weren't home."

"No, I wasn't."

"Oh," said Tom.

Turner lifted his glass and drank slowly. Then he said, "If it matters, I was at I Tatti, Berenson's villa that he left to Harvard. I'm a sort of unofficial trustee."

Tom looked away and said, "I wasn't snooping. I just wanted to talk, to see how you were."

"It's very sweet that you do," Turner said, and patted Tom's thigh. He left his hand there.

"So how *did* it go? With Mary?"

"You don't let up, do you? Well, she talked. She's quite funny. She wants one to know she's not easily impressed. But then she's quite apologetic about some aspects of herself and that's rather charming. She dwells on having come from the San Fernando Valley. As though it's her tragic flaw. I tried to console her."

"How?" Tom asked.

"I told her I was from Iowa. Where everyone in the San Fernando Valley was originally from, before they improved themselves by moving to California."

Tom laughed, and so did Turner. It was, Tom thought, the first time they had laughed that day, or even since before Wright had come to dinner at the Villa Donatello. "And what else?" he asked.

"I gave her the books and papers I'd mentioned to her. She was quite excited to have them."

"The Ruskin?"

"Yes, I have the complete works. Twenty-some volumes, which are of absolutely no use or interest to me."

"So why do you have them?"

"They were Jeremy's," Turner said. "He was my companion for many years."

"You never mentioned him. And I don't remember him from the journals."

"I don't put everything in. I keep some things for myself. We were together six years. He was an art historian, an independent scholar, I suppose you'd say, with an inheritance. English, one of these classic Anglo-Catholic fags who like religious ritual and art, who are comforted by the notion that their aestheticism is spiritual and profound. Even though they must know that, if there is a God, just being who they are defiles him. It strikes me as a rather death wish."

"Did you tell him that?"

"Oh, yes. Especially when he threatened to convert to Catholicism. But he always finessed it. He said that if there was no God, there wasn't any harm in it. And if there was, and it turns out he hates queers, he was going to get you anyway. He called it Auden's Wager."

They laughed again, and Tom asked, "So did you break up over that?"

"No," Turner said, and took a sip of wine. "We didn't break up. He died." He drank again. "Right here in this apartment."

"How?" asked Tom, and added, "I'm sorry."

"It was twelve years ago. The plague, as it were."

"AIDS?"

"There's always one plague or another in this place, isn't there?" Turner said, gazing away, his voice trailing off. "'*Non averei creduto/che morte tanta n'avesse disfatta,*' Dante put it. But, yes, AIDS."

"But you were okay?" Tom asked, and then stopped himself.

"Oh, I mean *were* you okay *then*, not whether you're okay now. I didn't mean that—what I might have seemed to mean."

"It's a perfectly reasonable thing to want to know, Thomas," said Turner. "And I was okay. And I *am* okay." Then he squeezed Tom's thigh.

Tom said nothing because there was, he felt, nothing he could say that was not stupid or lame. He took a drink from his glass and waited, hoping Wright would say something, and after a breath or two, he did.

"It wasn't as awful as you might have heard, not in his case. He worked until the end. He was translating the memoir of this Florentine mystic drama-queen, Maria Maddalena de' Pazzi. He said it was a consolation. It's one of the susceptibilities of sickness and old age, I suppose—the inability to sustain disbelief. May God protect me from it." Turner gave a strangled laugh.

"So what happened to it? To the translation?"

"I gave the manuscript to Mary. I thought it might as well be of some use somewhere, to someone."

Tom said, "That's a good thing to do. She's excited about it."

"I'm glad to hear it," said Turner. "And I would have gotten around to telling you about Jeremy, Thomas. I'm not keeping anything from you. It was a long time ago. It's worth forgetting, if it's worth anything."

"I'm sure it was worth a lot," Tom said. "It's worth something for me to know that about you."

"That's very sweet." Turner squeezed Tom's thigh again. "I wish I'd taken one of my pills."

"That's okay. But maybe next time you go to I Tatti, you can take me."

"I doubt you'd like it. It's a lot of art-history graduate students and old farts."

"I think I *would* like it."

"We'll have to see," Turner said. "But to be frank, I don't want to be seen playing the doddering old queen leaning on the arm of his young Adonis. Which is how it would be taken."

"And why would you care?" Tom said as evenly as he could.

"For the same reason you might have cared what your friends made of you and me the other night. Don't make me tell you it was on your mind."

"Okay, fair enough," said Tom. "But that was then. I feel things are beyond that."

"That was two days ago."

"Well, I guess it was just in that time that I figured out what I felt. What I wanted."

"Which is?"

Tom thought carefully of what he had meant to say, of what Alex had said he should say. "I want," he said, on a long exhalation of breath, "us to be a couple."

Turner settled back against the cushions of the couch. "Oh, Thomas," he said, "that's very sweet. Not merely sweet. It's moving. It truly is." Turner put his hands behind his neck and leaned back a little more. "But, really, it's very inadvisable."

"What's advisable isn't really the point," Tom said quietly.

"I know. And I won't tell you you're wrong. How could I? It's flattering; rather miraculous, I suppose. But you have to consider your own future. You have to do that precisely because *I* care about your future. You need to indulge me in that regard."

"And how do I do that?"

"You should take a look at what it all adds up to," Turner said. "I'm old, Thomas. I'm going to get older. I'm going to be wizened and stale and smell like pee. And you would become my nurse. Because there isn't any money for a real nurse. There's this apartment, which I don't own, and a few nice paintings I've picked up over the years. Those and the odd government cheque—plus some spare change in royalties and such—are what my finances amount to."

"And what difference does that make?"

"Because you mustn't condemn yourself to what it all entails. I forbid it."

"You can forbid it," Tom said. "But suppose I decide to just . . . disobey you?"

"Then you'd stay until you saw how it really was, until you understood that you had to go. And that would be very sad. For everyone."

"You're not so old. And I'm not so young," said Tom. "I'm not twenty or something. So if you just think that I'm going to get bored or restless, if you're saying—"

"I am not condescending to you in the least," Turner said, and sat up. "Really. Think of this as my expressing *my* preferences in the matter."

"So what your preference is," said Tom, "is that I should go away."

"Oh, don't be childish, Thomas. My preference is that we go on as we are."

"And if I want something more?"

"What would 'more' be? Really. Because every day there's a little *less* of me. And in a couple of years, there'll be nothing at all. I'd say you're getting a good measure of what I have left to offer."

Tom saw that this line of argument could scarcely be gainsaid, at least not by him. Tom took a drink of wine, and it came to him to say, "I'd just like to offer you what I can during that time. Which is longer than you're allowing."

"That's kind," said Turner after a moment. "And well put, even true. I'm not sure I *want* it to be longer. It's 2000, for god's sake. Everything that matters to me happened in the last century. This century belongs to you and your friends. I don't belong in it. I'm an alien now."

Tom wanted to look in Wright's grey eyes, to take Wright's slight chin in his fingers and hold it while he explained. "No," he said. "You don't understand. I'm—we're—aliens here too. I don't belong either."

In the days that followed, Tom modelled for Alex with Mary. He went again to the Villa Castellani, and this time he and Wright made love. He thought, too, of returning to Mary's studio to have a longer look at her novel. But she scarcely left the house, and when she did (to visit, in fact, Wright Turner), shame prevented him from doing so.

So they posed together, and he became accustomed to the feel of her hair and skin against him until it was not so very different from a familiar chair or his own bed. He became inured—if not indifferent—to her beauty. He admired rather than desired her. She was too close, it seemed, for him to feel intimate towards her.

Alex, through these days, was mightily content. He spoke hardly at all, but his little smile never left his face. Music played and sometimes Mary read aloud, though it could not be said if Alex heard either the one or the other.

Tom, however, listened deeply; felt the words and the Górecki and Pärt they all favoured as palpably as the faint adhesion between his and Mary's flesh when the session was done and they pulled apart.

During their fourth session, towards three o'clock, when the heat was beginning to build even inside the house, Mary read, in lieu of one of the Dorothea passages from *Middlemarch* she was presently absorbed with, a piece of Ruskin's Italian journal that Wright Turner had given her.

Tom listened intently, clutched at the text to see what it might reveal about Mary and Wright, because he was too principled and too cowardly to read Mary's novel or to ask Wright what was transpiring between them. What Tom heard was this.

> *A girl of ten or twelve, lying with her arms thrown back over her head, all languid and lax, on an earth-heap by the river side (the*

> *softness of dust being the only softness she had ever known), in the southern suburb of Turin, one golden afternoon, years ago. She had been at her play, after her fashion, with other patient children, and had thrown herself down, full in the sun, like a lizard.*

Mary stopped a moment to get her breath.

> *The sand was mixed with the draggled locks of her black hair, and some of it sprinkled over her face and body, in an "ashes to ashes" sort of way; a few black rags about her loins, but her limbs nearly bare, and her little breasts, scarce dimpled yet,—white,—marble-like—but, as wasted marble, thin with scorching and the reins of time. So she lay, motionless: black and white by the shore in the sun; the yellow light flickering back on her from the passing eddies of the river, and burning down on her from the west.*

Mary waited a moment and then said, "It's kind of beautiful, isn't it?"

Alex raised his head to her and said, "It's like a painting. It would make a painting, actually."

"So you should paint it," Mary said.

"But it's kind of sick," Alex considered. "Fantasizing about little girls."

"He's not fantasizing. He's just looking. Like all these Victorians did. Like Lewis Carroll," said Mary. "They didn't touch. Just looked."

"If you say so," Alex shrugged.

It seemed to Tom that he also ought to be venturing some remark, for the journal passage had struck him too. But just then what was striking him still more was the realization that his penis had expanded considerably in the course of Mary's recitation, perhaps not to the point of full tumescence, but substantially. Just now it rested languidly on his thigh, but was poised to begin levitating upward. And should it bank to the left in so doing—the most likely trajectory, given the slant of the pose he and Mary were in—it would come to a halt sidled up against Mary's waist.

At the moment, Tom's penis was out of Mary's line of vision, hovering just below the horizon, but Tom feared the worst. The Ruskin text—the diffuse and inexplicable text—had conflated itself with images of Rilkean and Renaissance angels, that Tom had not consorted with since the Hotel San Remo; erotic visions that on every previous occasion had insisted on being spent in orgasm and ejaculation.

It was Alex who saved him, whose face appeared from behind the canvas, gazed straight on at Tom, and unmistakably registered the fact of Tom's engorged phallus. He looked and then he shrugged, and Mary said, "So you ought to consider painting it," and Alex said, "I suppose I should."

Tom realized only after an instant that neither the remark nor, perhaps, the shrug concerned his near-erection. But it in any case provided a sufficient jolt to cause his penis to withdraw into the burrow of its flaccid state. And there, thankfully, for the rest of the session, and the two after, it remained.

Mary was rethinking her novel, thinking of abandoning it for a whole new conception. It would have something to do with Maria Maddalena de' Pazzi, with art and faith and eros and Italy. This, admittedly, was Wright's contribution (she had begun to address him by his first name; it had come very naturally after their most recent encounter). But it struck her as a way forward into the work, as a means to put herself before the world a little, and that—that was the great thing.

Moreover, Mary had to admit to herself that Wright had turned out to be more substantial than she had expected. She had imagined him a kind of irrelevance, an artifact from the long steel-grey Gallery of the Modern that ran between her beloved late Victorians to the postmodernism of her contemporaries. But he lacked, for all his "grand manner," the pretensions of either his generation or hers, and this was a happy and intriguing discovery. After a bottle of Pinot Grigio he happily admitted to her that the reputation of *Ignorant Armies* and his subsequent books owed not a little to luck.

"I was fortunate in who I knew," he said. They were sitting together on his big couch, the afternoon light blooming through the window like a cloud of gauze. Turner's hand rested just shy of her neck on the back of the couch. She could sense it behind her, white, languid, avian. He seemed to sigh, continuing, "Fortunate too, I suppose, in being rather fetching. Or so it was bruited at the time."

"I'm sure it was more than true," Mary allowed. "Even now, you're very—"

"You're going to say 'distinguished,' aren't you?" Turner interrupted.

"I was. But I could try to do better, if you want." She smiled and opened her green eyes wide.

"No need."

"All right," said Mary. "So tell me about Mary McCarthy. You knew her, right?"

"Indeed. Rather well, in some respects. She was here for a while in, oh, 1957. Or '58. She'd had her heart broken by some English cad. I comforted her."

"You sly old thing," Mary laughed.

"I wasn't old. I was about *your* age. And a good dozen years younger than her." Turner paused and looked at Mary. "You know, you rather resemble her. The eyes and mouth. Pretty and steely at the same time."

"Thank you. I think," said Mary. "So what was she *like*?"

"Oh, very sharp. Acute all around. Very self-involved, of course. But charming. *And* guarded. Simultaneously."

"Really. Even," Mary said, her voice lowering, "in—"

"Oh, you are a very curious girl," Turner broke in. "A very

curious girl. Well, let me think. Yes, I believe she was. Voracious. Voracious and hard, somehow."

"Maybe she simply knew what she wanted."

"Maybe. There were people who thought she might have had lesbian inclinations."

"That's so predictable," Mary said. "That people would think that. Anytime a woman's genuinely sexual . . ."

"I never thought so. She wasn't a dyke. She was a fag, really. A fag trapped in a woman's body. I mean, she lusted after men the way a gay man would. Like I did. Or, rather, do."

"That's an unusual idea. Did you lust after her?"

"I think I did. And maybe that was why," said Turner. "I've had a number of women lovers, and it was all very fine and pleasant. But my passions have always been homosexual. And Mary wasn't like other women. Or like anybody else, of course."

"She's kind of a role model for me, actually."

"Well, don't go the whole hog. Please. But by all means write well. She wrote like an angel. With mastery. Not like me," said Turner, and laughed.

"That's a little unfair. You're a real writer. Your journals are classics."

"Well, I did get to fuck some very interesting people. But my art criticism never got as much play. And there you are. My literary career, such as it is. Or was."

Mary did not know how she might disabuse him of this last notion, or if attempting to do so was any of her business. Finally she said, "It's going to endure. You'll see—"

"I rather expect, being nearly eighty, that's something I *won't* get to see."

"Well, perhaps," Mary said, more weakly than she would have liked. "But the point is, you added something to your experience. You didn't just present it as raw material, as gossip. You transformed it into art."

"One makes one's art with whatever's at hand, whatever's

lying around." He paused and smiled at Mary. "I was rather good at lying around myself."

"You were also good at writing. Which is where the art comes into it all."

"Oh, perhaps the art was in the fucking, not the writing."

"I kind of doubt that."

Turner leaned slightly in Mary's direction. His hand, which had never left its perch, slid closer to her neck and her dark hair. "Oh," he said. "You have *no* idea how good I could be."

Mary was gazing into the far corner of the room. She was wondering what the hand signified, or what she was meant to do about it. "I bet Tom does," she said and turned towards Wright. She smiled and gave him the force of her eyes.

"Now who's a sly old thing?" Turner said.

"Not me. Tom thinks I'm a madonna or an angel."

"He told you this?"

"Not exactly. But it's something I know."

"So he imagines you're sweet or holy," said Turner. "Or perhaps you're a dark angel. That's what I'd say."

"Is that good or bad?"

"It's good, as far as I'm concerned."

"Well, it's all part of his Rilke thing," Mary said.

"Poor dear boy. Another of his delusions. I really ought to take him in hand a little more. Not, I gather, that you haven't."

"We try."

"He talks as if he landed on your doorstep in a foundling basket."

"And we took him in."

"Exactly. But really, it's ridiculous. I knew people who knew Rilke—"

"Why am I not surprised?"

"Ha!—and they all agreed he was an ass, that he had no . . . human capability. Maybe 'negative capability,' but he hadn't a clue about people. Roses and angels, yes, but persons were absolutely lost on him."

"Well, there's Tom for you," Mary said. "In a way."

"In a way, yes. But Tom is sweet. Even good. And I'd hate to see him become that sort of heartless aesthete, believing that his big vague feelings and ideas—his rhetoric, really—amount to the real world."

"So he lives too much in his mind."

"And his mind's in the clouds."

"And his body?"

"You *are* persistent," said Turner. "Or at least very curious."

"I've seen him naked. There's not much for me to wonder about, if that's what you mean."

"Oh, yes, the modelling. Alex is nearly done, isn't he?"

"Yes, thank god," Mary said. "Then, the other day Tom got a hard-on."

"You saw it?"

"Not exactly. But a woman senses these things."

"And this was in tribute to you, I would imagine."

"I couldn't say," Mary responded slowly. "Perhaps his thoughts were farther afield."

"But you said he thinks you're a madonna."

"A madonna isn't someone you want to fuck."

"Oh, I suspect with Tom it would be," Turner said. "Everything's all mixed up and topsy-turvy with him. 'Conflated,' as he likes to say."

"That's more of his postmodern cant."

"'Cant'—there's a word you don't hear much any more," said Turner. "Now, how goes the writing?"

"It's coming along. There were a couple of false starts, but I think I found the way into it."

"So when do I get to read it?"

"When there's more. When I'm a little surer about it. When I know it's serious work."

"Serious? I hope you're not aiming for something ponderous and 'important.'"

"Oh, no. Although I suppose I am in deadly earnest about some things."

"Which are?"

"Writing a novel. This novel. Living a certain kind of . . . considered life."

"That's all?" Turner asked. "Not that it's not enough."

"I'd like to have a baby."

Turner pulled back a little from Mary. "Now that *is* a surprise. Not that it's not understandable, I suppose. Not that I know anything about children, or traditional straight family life."

"I didn't say anything about traditional straight family life. I hope you're not being condescending."

"No, of course not. I'm just taken aback a little."

"It's really what most of the women I know want," Mary said. "Their work and a child. The book *and* the baby."

"Well, I live and learn," said Turner. "One has these images of motherhood, of the maternal woman—"

"You don't have to be maternal to be a mother."

"God knows mine wasn't."

"Well," said Mary. "There you are."

For his part, Alex merely wished to do some good in the world, to paint a good painting and perhaps ease a portion of the affliction that beset the city that he just then had come to feel was his home. It was, for all its beauty, a raw, wounded place of inhospitably narrow pavements and high, thick walls. It was practiced in the arts of betrayal and revenge. It needed soothing, assuaging, sacrifices.

Alex was sitting in the car outside the villa, thinking, with the engine running. He knew he was close to finished with the double nude of Tom and Mary, or at least with working from them as models. He drummed his fingers on the steering wheel and thought some more, and at some point in his thinking he drove off. At the Porta Romana he decided to go see the frescoes in the Strozzi Chapel in Santa Maria Novella; di Cione's renderings of Dante's universe, of the anguish and pity that this world carries into the next.

He parked the car some distance away and went into the great church. And while in the chapel, standing before the fresco of hell on the right-hand wall—stratum descending upon stratum of suffering beyond hope of expiation—Alex had an epiphany; a sort of annunciation, it seemed to him. In the grip of it, he went straight across the street to the *stazione* to find a girl, a heroin child, an angel and virgin, thin with scorching and the reins of time.

8.

An Epiphany

At the end of May, on the cusp of June, when the heat was beginning to build and Mary was visiting Wright Turner and Alex had gone down the hill on an errand of some kind, Tom went again to Mary's studio. He approached her desk and looked for the manuscript he had discovered ten days before, titled *The Villa Donatello*. But that manuscript was gone, and in its place was a sheath of perhaps four pages, headed *The Florentine Hours of Maria Maddalena de' Pazzi*. It began—Tom could read the crossed-out parts (sometimes struck out twice) without too much difficulty:

> Maria Maddalena de' Pazzi entered the convent of Santa Maria dei Angeli on the ~~far bank of the dusky~~ Arno in ~~the city of~~ Florence in the ~~beastly~~ seething heat of August, 1582. She was sixteen years old, and had an ~~active rich~~ fevered imagination ~~but~~ She possessed a finer mind than most of ~~the persons among whom her lot was cast,~~ the merchant classes and aristocratic factions of Florence. She took her vows the next year, and then the visions began, visions of ~~Christ~~ the Incarnate Word as her ~~husband and~~ lover, mystical reveries tinged with the unfamiliar, ~~palpable, fulminating with eros erotic.~~

Then, on the next page, Tom found a stretch of text that Mary was apparently satisfied with, or that at least passed muster for a first draft:

> I came here in August, August of 1582, I think. It was hot—I remember that much—and when they cut my hair and gave me a novice's gown to put on, I was grateful to shed the heavy clothes that a decorative girl from a society family like mine is made to wear. It wasn't that they couldn't have married me off—I wanted to come here.
>
> I wanted to marry God. I wanted Him for my lover.
>
> He came to me the first time just after I took my vows, just after our wedding. He is Love, the Incarnate Word, His body is Love's Body. So I called him my Lover, my Amorous Word.
>
> He ravished me again and again. I wanted Him and I couldn't bear Him. It's said that Love is unbearable. But I wanted to go on with Him forever. I wanted to die with Him, for Him. I wanted Him to drive the nails of His crucifixion into me. No, I wanted to be the nails driven through Him.

Tom read this and then he read it once more. He wondered where the *Villa Donatello* manuscript had gone, and if Mary had abandoned it in favour of this strange new project. Mary had only shelves for storage in her studio, and he didn't see anything there resembling the bundles of pages he'd found before. He wondered if she might have burned them. No, that was too dramatic for Mary. But then, for the Mary who had written this, it would be right up her street.

Tom heard noise below, emanating from the kitchen. He tidied the pages of Mary's new project and replaced them on her desk. There was more noise from downstairs, and then the unmistakable sound of the door, Mary returning from another visit to Wright; Wright, who had put this idea into her head, who, Tom imagined, had enchanted her even as she imagined it was she who was enchanting him.

With the onset of summer, there were more sleeping cars coming into the Stazione Santa Maria Novella, idling along unused platforms and through the night, for days on end, in the yards. The German, Swiss, and Austrian sleepers were the nicest, the French a little less so. In the former, you could lock the door in the first-class cars, round up some linen, and fashion yourself a very comfortable little suite. On the windowsill of the one Maddalena had claimed for her own, she had placed a blue flower, a bottle of nail polish, her grandmother's rosary, her brush, and two elastics to bind her hair. There were magazines—mostly in German, but she had some English ones too. It was very important to learn English, so as to get on in life, especially as a *supermodella*.

So Maddalena might sit in her compartment for an hour or two at a time, happily reading *Brigitte* or painting her nails or merely dreaming. She might look up and expect to see countryside racing by outside her window—perhaps the Alps or one or another riviera—only to be confronted by a wall of disconsolate, motionless empty railway cars. But had you asked her whether she travelled frequently, she might scarcely be able to help saying "Yes, of course, always by train," having spent so many hours here in this compartment and others like it. She would have been to Milan, of course, but also to Paris, Berlin, and London. Or she certainly would be going there shortly.

Still, Maddalena had been going back to her mother's friends' place every three or four days, and had spent the night a few times. One morning, when the grown-ups were in the depths of their sleep, she'd found a fifty-thousand lira note in one of their bags. She bought herself a new top—a T-shirt, really—and treated her friends to pizza and Coca-Cola in the station restaurant.

When she returned to the apartment two days later, no one said anything about the money. They'd forgotten or didn't care or simply knew she'd say she didn't know anything about it and let the matter drop. None of them, her mother's friends, was much good at persistence, at plans and intentions, at getting from A to B or remembering why they'd wanted to go in the first place. They weren't really all there. They weren't quite dead, but they were definitely a little disembodied and ghostly.

When they weren't high, they left her alone, were oblivious to her, although mostly they were either asleep or out scoring. She'd lock the bathroom door and take long baths. When they were high, they were nice to her. They thought it was sad that she was on her own. They offered to share their stash. Most of them had been on their own a long time, too. They were all from someplace else. None of them was from Florence. Neither, Maddalena felt, was she. She was from the *stazione*; at least she would be until she went to Milan and starting modelling.

Really, her mother's friends were no worse than Pietro's friend Jacopo, who was a creep and conceited. He'd come into Maddalena's compartment in the very nice Deutsche Bahn InterCity car and tried to get her to smoke with him. She declined, but he went ahead and smoked anyway, stinking up her beautiful room. Then he took his thing out. It was a noodle with four or five long hairs sprouting from the base. Maddalena laughed at it, and he buttoned his pants and left. Since then, he'd been more respectful.

This morning, they'd all been sitting outside by the bus terminal. Pietro was sharing out the chocolate from a Kinder egg three Carmelite nuns had given him for helping them with their luggage. Jacopo was holding forth.

"In Milan, all the designers and models use."

"You don't know anything about Milan," Laura said.

"My father's from Milan. That makes me a Milanese."

"You said your father was from Rome."

"That's his other father," Pietro put in. They all laughed.

"Still," Jacopo continued, "Maddalena should get used to the idea—should stop being such a priss."

"You don't know anything about it," Maddalena said. "Using wrecks your skin. It makes you a hag."

"The designers make you suck their cocks too, Maddalena. You'll really love that."

"Fuck you, Jacopo."

"They're all *froci,*" said Laura. "So why would they want a girl to do it? They'd want a boy. They'd want you, Jacopo." She and Maddalena laughed.

"Anyone want the puzzle from the egg?" Pietro asked, but just then a man approached them. He had dark blond hair and walked like an American. Jacopo stood, hurriedly put his hands in his pockets, and cocked his hip. He began in English, *Okay, dude. You got*—but the man cut him off, and started talking in Italian.

"Nice English. But never mind that. I wonder if you guys would do me a favour?"

"Depends," Pietro said.

"I just want to take a few pictures."

"Oh, I heard about that," said Jacopo. "I'd do it. But it'll cost you big time."

"That's not what I'm after. Really, I'd just like to take a few right here, just the way you are. Just sitting around."

"For free?" Pietro asked.

"Oh, no. How about, say, five thousand for each of you."

"Sure. What do we do?"

"Just keep sitting there, just like you were. Don't look at the camera or anything. And you," the man said, indicating Jacopo, "just stay where you are."

The man snapped several photos. Pietro pretended to be contemplating the Kinder egg puzzle. Laura folded her hands in her lap. Maddalena leaned back on one hand and looked up towards the sky. Jacopo scowled.

"That's great. Really great," the man said. "You guys are very professional."

Indicating her friend, Laura said, "Maddalena wants to be a model."

"Really? Is that right?"

"Well, yeah," Maddalena said, looking down at her feet. "That's my goal," and then she looked straight up at the man.

"So would you mind if I took some shots of you by yourself? Just you, right here?"

"I guess not."

"I could give you, say, ten thousand extra. Would that be okay?"

"Sure," said Maddalena.

"Okay. Just stay there. But maybe lean back a bit more, look off to the side."

Maddalena let her weight go, let herself slump. Her new top rode up just past her navel.

"That's perfect. But maybe not quite so much of a smile. It's a lovely smile, but it's not what I'm after."

"I'm sorry. I'll try to be sad."

"You don't need to be sad. Maybe just look like you're thinking."

So Maddalena did that. Her thoughts, in fact, were racing. She was wondering if it all—her life—was beginning right now.

Downstairs, Tom found Mary in the kitchen. She looked at Tom and smiled. She struck him as very pretty at that moment.

"Alex was telling me this morning that he's almost done with us—with the double nude," she said.

"Hey, great," said Tom. He ought to have been excited or at least relieved, but his thoughts were elsewhere. What he really wanted to do was ask Mary how she was, how she was doing; how she was *really* doing.

But just then Alex came in, beaming. "Hey, hi," he said.

"I was just telling Tom you're nearly finished. With the painting."

"Oh, yeah. I want to have a party for it," Alex said. "An unveiling party or a hanging party or whatever. Anyway, a bash. Just for us. And for Wright. I mean, the painting was his idea. Maybe tomorrow. This week, anyway."

"I don't think Wright can make it," Mary said.

"Why not?" said Tom.

"Well, I got the impression he had obligations this week, that's all."

"He didn't say anything to me," Tom said.

"He can't tell you everything, Tom," said Mary.

"Well," Alex said, "I really want him to come. I'll have to go over there and insist—"

"We can just call him," said Mary. "I'll do it. Maybe he can rearrange."

"I was going to see him tonight," Tom added. "I could mention it."

"It's all right, Tom. It really is. I'm the mistress of the house, so to speak. I'll organize everything. Really."

"Well, okay," Tom agreed.

"And how was the great man today?" asked Alex.

"Oh, fine."

"Did he give you something to eat? Sometimes I get the impression from you guys that he's this old squirrel living on nuts and olives."

"That's what we had," Mary acknowledged. "That and some wine."

"I worry a little that he drinks too much," said Tom.

"But you had some good talk, yes?" Alex said.

"Oh, sure. He does kind of go on about his own work and the old days. But he told me about Mary McCarthy."

"Anything juicy?" asked Alex.

"Not really."

"He told me they were lovers," Tom said.

Mary looked at him. "Well, there you are, Tom. You've got special access."

"But you're going back soon?" asked Tom.

"I told him I'd show him some of my new work."

"You could just show it to him when he comes over," Tom continued.

Mary shrugged and said, "I think that'd be boring for everyone else. It's supposed to be a party."

"I don't want anything boring at this party," Alex said. "I want riotous fun and frolic. For my painting—your painting, really, you two."

"Our painting," Mary suggested.

"And Wright's, too," added Tom.

"Yes, Wright's too, Tom," Mary said.

Wright Turner, Tom, Mary, and Alex were sitting in the *salone* at the Villa Donatello drinking wine and eating olives and nuts. This was preparatory, Alex had explained, to going into his studio for the real party, for the unveiling. Here they were merely priming the pump with two or three bottles of Vernaccia while Turner amused them with a story about Picasso.

When Alex determined that the wheels of the evening were greased to his satisfaction, he led them back to the studio. All the lights were on, candlesticks had been placed here and there, and in the centre of the room stood the painting itself on the easel, covered by a purple sheet. On an adjacent table was a big spread of food—prosciutto, several cheeses, cold dishes of peppers, artichokes, and eggplant, and *fettunte* with tomatoes, chicken liver, olive paste, and mushrooms, plus two magnums of champagne. Alex opened a bottle and they raised their glasses and Alex gave a toast, the same toast Mary had given when Tom had first arrived.

"How charming," Turner said after they'd drunk.

"It's corny," said Mary. "But it's our little team cheer."

Then Alex, smiling, his face roseate, moved to the easel and pulled the sheet off the painting. For a long while they stood silently before it, as though it were a fire before which they were warming themselves. They waited for Turner to speak.

"It's really rather fine," he said at last. "Full of good, surprising things."

"You think so?" said Alex. He began topping up their glasses.

"Oh yes," Turner said.

Alex pressed him. "What sort of good things?"

"Well, to begin with, the colours, the whole palette. They're lovely, like in the earlier one of Mary. But these have a luminous quality, as if there's gilding underneath."

"There's not," said Alex. "Just a lot of glazes. But yeah, I was even thinking of calling it *Flaming June,* just because of the colours, because of the way Tom and Mary look sort of burned up. Anyway, I like the phrase."

"It's the name of a painting by Lord Leighton," Turner said. "One of those late-Victorian symbolist atrocities that are over-refined and vulgar at the same time. Not what you want, I'd think."

"Well, it's just a working title. So what do you think about the composition? And the bodies?"

"Oh, it's all very good. You could just fall into it. And I like the little morsel of Thomas's cock. Just enough so it's not academic." Turner looked at the painting again and continued.

"Now that's just technical, of course. Because, really, Alex, it has something to say. It's a fine nude. But it's not just bodies prettily arranged. In fact, it's not pretty at all. Not that you two"—here he glanced over to Tom and then to Mary—"aren't beautiful. But it has a tragic feeling to it."

"How so?" Alex asked eagerly, his colouring now almost magenta. He recharged Wright's glass and then his own.

"What I mean," said Turner, "is that there's the pleasure and the beauty of the bodies, but the composition and the postures are telling the viewer something else: that the whole scene is overshadowed by despair, by some sort of grief. Or even agony."

"Eros and agony," said Mary.

"Yes. Exactly," Turner said, and drank.

"Well, that's incredibly generous," said Alex. "But, really, I got the composition off Pontormo's *Deposition* in the Santa Felicità." He drank deeply, and thrust the thumb of his free hand into the front pocket of his jeans.

Turner was silent for an instant, and then said rapidly, "Of course, Pontormo. Old queen who lived with his apprentice and lover—Bronzino, another great Mannerist—in the via Laura, near the Santissima Annunziata."

"I didn't know that," Alex offered.

"Neither here nor there," said Turner. "In any case, you're scarcely saying this is just some sort of knock-off."

"No. I just want to give credit where credit's due."

"Be that as it may," Turner continued, "I don't really see the resemblance. So perhaps you were merely inspired. As you were by his colours in your last painting."

"Well, if you want."

"If I want?" Turner said abruptly, and then laughed.

"I mean, I'm pretty clear that I looked at that painting a lot. I looked at it with Tom and I looked at it by myself. And I thought, this is how to do it."

"But really, you *didn't,*" Turner said, measuring out his words. "Because, to begin with, Pontormo was a Mannerist. And there's nothing mannered in this painting. That's one of the reasons I was inclined to like it. So you may imagine—"

Alex laughed. "I'd say I imagined the whole thing. I painted it." Then Alex tilted his head back, and threw down the last of his champagne.

A pool of silence gathered itself and began to fill, but Mary had the wit to speak. "You two are talking about two different things," she said. "Alex, you're talking about executing the picture, but Wright's talking about interpreting it."

"Thank you, Mary," Turner said. "That's a good distinction to observe." He drained his glass, and turned back towards Alex, his arm stretched out in the direction of the painting. "So, Alex," he began, "you may *feel* you were influenced by the Pontormo, but in critical terms it's perfectly reasonable to say that that's interesting but beside the point. It's a simple idea."

Tom took a step forward, forming the apex of a triangle with Turner and Alex at the other points. "Really, you can say there is no painting as such," he said. "There are only interpretations of it."

Alex's forehead wrinkled and his mouth contorted for a moment. Then he shook his head back and forth. "So you guys are saying that the painting doesn't matter? It's just something to, like, riff on?"

"No, of course not," Turner said quickly.

Alex took a step forward, his empty glass dangling from one hand, the magnum from the other. He said, "So, maybe you can elaborate for me."

"Well, in fact," Turner began hesitantly, "it's just the opposite."

"The opposite of what? Please. Explain it to me. I know it's a simple point, but I'm a simple guy."

"I mean," Turner said and took a long breath, "that the painting is the essential thing, the only thing. It deserves to be addressed on its own terms as a work of art."

Alex gave no response, nor did Turner elaborate further. Tom stepped forward so he was now between them. "But really," he began in a helpful tone, "you could argue that it doesn't have any terms of its own. That it's just what the viewer brings to it. It doesn't bring anything to the viewer. Except the social constructions it encodes—"

"Thomas, please," Turner said briskly. Alex backed away from Turner, and then stared at him. He shook his head again and said, "So in all this, what's the artist? A hand puppet? The fucking dancing horse?"

"I don't think there's really anything to fight about here," Mary said quickly. "We're all friends. We're just discussing different ways of talking about art." She looked at Turner and then at Alex. "And most painters," she added, "would think they were pretty lucky to get their work critiqued by Wright Turner."

Alex held fire for a moment. "Okay," he said. "But let's be clear that somebody painted the painting." He went to the table and got the second magnum and began to open it, ratcheting the cork furiously.

"Fine. But to be fair," Mary continued, "you ought to acknowledge Wright." There was a faint, desolate pop from Alex's direction. "He gave you the concept the first time he came over."

Mary looked back at Turner and Alex looked at them looking at each other. Alex refilled everyone's glass, and then he sighed, as if tired. "Okay," he said. "But really, you want to know the truth?" He looked straight at Mary. "I painted this for you."

Mary nodded. "Okay," she said.

Then Turner spoke. "And it does her great justice, great—"

"Let me talk. Let me say this," Alex interrupted.

He continued, speaking to Mary. "It's for you. It's all about you. Especially because of the Pontormo. Tom and I went into that church one day, and we were looking at it. And I found you in it. Tom remembers."

"Sure," Tom offered.

Mary looked intently at Alex, almost squinting. "So," she said, "that's where you got the pose I'm in?"

"Not exactly. I got the feeling from one figure, up high, but the pose is from farther down. It's Christ and Mary Magdalene, I guess."

"Mary Magdalene," she said. "Well, I guess that suits me."

"Actually, no. Tom's in that position. You're the Christ figure."

"Oh. So much the better, I suppose."

"Except for the inconvenience of being dead," Turner said with a laugh.

Mary continued, "So you painted Tom as Mary Magdalene and me as Christ. Nude. Is that blasphemy or something?"

"It's transgressive," said Tom.

"Oh, Tom, please," Mary said. "Enough of your fucking cant."

"Cant? What's cant?" Tom asked, but no one replied.

"Well, you're in those poses," Alex said carefully. "Not necessarily in those roles. You're not dead, you're exhausted. From love. Or life in general."

"Oh," said Mary. "So that's how you see me?"

Alex shrugged. "It's a painting. It's not like my secret journal or something."

"But you said it's about me."

"It's only about you in the way it's about light or shapes or life in general." Alex looked away, and then said softly, "Hey, isn't anyone going to eat?"

Now Mary raised her hands to her chest and shrugged. "That doesn't seem like what you said before." She let her hands drop. "And you want to be, like, feted as the author of the painting. So tell us what you meant."

They stood in a rough circle now, Mary and Turner and Tom, with Alex a little out to one side of the circumference, near the table, upon which the food lay untouched.

"What I said before was all to do with the Pontormo business," Alex finally said.

"That's kind of a cop-out," said Mary.

"It's not a cop-out. It's an influence."

"Well," Mary said. "I've read about Pontormo."

"Oh, in Vasari—" Alex began.

"He was kind of a crank, agoraphobic and rigid. It says in *The Lives of the Artists* he had an *"orrore dello spazio."* He was afraid of space, in life and in his painting. That's where the Mannerism came in. Everything's flattened down. It's floating, but there's no air, no space around it."

"Yes," said Alex. "So?"

"So maybe that's what you like about him. The disconnection from life, the not really being grounded."

Alex looked at Mary, and then cast his eyes downward. "Well," he said, "I'm going to eat something. Even if no one else is."

Tom spoke. "Mary, I don't think it's really fair to, like, go after Alex for having some influences. I mean, you have all these absolute heroes who've all been dead for a hundred years."

"That's not what I'm talking about, Tom," said Mary. She looked at him and then shifted her gaze to Alex, who was thrusting a little piece of toast heaped with tomato into his mouth. "I'm talking about not having your own ideas, or at least not knowing what they are. Or being afraid to articulate them."

Alex licked his lips, swallowed, and looked off to one side of the room, towards the shuttered window. "I do my articulating in paint, not words," he said.

"Fine," Mary said. "But then don't use words to discredit Wright."

Turner put his hand on Mary's arm and shook his head. "Please. I'm perfectly capable of defending myself. I don't want to be a source of contention."

Tom broke in. "Really, everything an artist does comes from someplace else. There's no 'originality' any more. Everything's borrowed. That's the whole postmodern condition."

Turner, bearing a melancholic expression or perhaps one of pity, looked at Tom and said, "That's the despair—the anomie—*you* feel, Thomas. It's not necessarily a universal reality."

"I don't know. I mean, I think it *is* real. Now. And even more so in the future."

Mary said, "Not in my future, if you don't mind. But you go right ahead and live there. And Alex, too, if he wants."

Tom continued. "Oh, come on, Mary. Look at your own work. You don't just borrow the style. You borrow the plot—from history, from a dead nun."

Mary stared at Tom. "And how do you know about that?"

"Oh, Wright must have told me."

Mary looked at Turner. "Oh?"

Turner lifted his hands. "I don't recall," he said. "I may have. Or not. Of course, I'm generally inclined to keep confidences to myself."

Then Alex said, "I told him."

Tom looked intently at Alex for an instant, licked his lips, and said, "Oh, yeah. That's right. Now I remember." Then he glanced away and shifted his weight from one foot to the other.

There was a long silence. They stood in the debris: the half-empty magnums, the glasses, the uneaten food, the sheet crumpled on the floor by the easel.

Turner suddenly pressed his palms together and smiled. "I'm sorry if we misunderstood each other, Alex," he said brightly. "I think very highly of this painting and of you as an artist."

"Well, I appreciate it," Alex said evenly. Then he added, "And Mary's right. It's an honour to have you critique me."

"And so," Turner asked, "what's next in your oeuvre?"

"I'd like to know, too," Mary said. She smiled at Alex.

Alex smiled back. He went over to the smaller table where he kept his supplies and picked up some sheets of paper which revealed themselves to be photos.

"This," he said. He handed around the pictures.

"A ragamuffin," Wright said.

"One of those gypsy kids," supplied Mary. "The ones that come at you with the cardboard sign and try to pick your pocket."

Tom looked at the prints. They were all of the same girl, mostly alone or, a couple of times, sitting with other children. "Hey," he said, "these almost look like the ones that hassled me the day I got here. At the station."

"Well, that's where I found them," Alex said. "I guess it's another concept from Wright. You remember? The *ragazzi della stazione*?"

"Yes," said Turner. "Yes, I do. The heroin children."

"Well, it's that," Alex continued, once more animated. "That and something I got from Mary's reading. From Ruskin. The description of this half-naked girl in Turin."

"Oh," said Turner. He turned to Mary. "That I gave to you," he added.

"Yeah. She read it to us," said Alex. "Anyway, I thought: paint it."

"So you're going to work from these?" asked Mary.

"Oh, no. I'll have to get her to come up and do some sessions. This one—," he said, pointing to the girl posed by herself.

Mary looked again at the print and said, "So you're going to go find her and bring her up here? What about her parents?"

"I doubt that's an issue. Not with these kids," Turner offered.

"If it is," added Alex, "I'll just work it out. I mean, it's art. People here support that."

"I don't quite get this, Alex," Mary continued. "You just went down among the junkies and pickpockets and found a girl, what is she, maybe twelve? And she agreed to this?"

"I'm going to pay her," said Alex. "These people are really poor."

"And so she's going to be in our house—"

"In my studio."

"—maybe with her friends and relations, wandering around and ransacking the place."

"Oh, come on, Mary," Alex said sharply. "That is so middle-class paranoid, so . . . Woodland Hills."

"No, Alex. Excuse me. It's being realistic. These people are fucking petty criminals. You don't invite them into your house."

"This is a girl, a child. Who I'm going to pay for honest work. To make a painting."

Mary paused and put her hands on her hips. "And when," she said, "did you get interested in children, Alex? I was under the impression you didn't have much use for them. Or is it just pubescent girls that interest you?"

Turner suddenly spoke, clearing his throat. "Well, I'm sorry, but it's awfully late for an old man like me. So I must thank you for your hospitality and go home and take to my bed."

Alex and Mary detached their stares from one another. Mary said, "Oh, of course."

Alex looked at his watch. "Wow. It *is* late." By a tangible but unspoken consensus, the party left the studio and conveyed Turner to the door. Mary kissed his cheek. Alex shook his hand. Tom hugged him limply, and Wright disappeared into the garden and the night.

Then Mary looked at Tom and said, "I think we're going to bed." And Alex nodded. They ascended the stairs.

Tom stayed downstairs for a few minutes. He went into the kitchen, regarded the unwashed pots and open food packages, and switched out the light. He went down the hall to put out the light in the studio, and it seemed to him the candelabrum over the table was swinging ever so slightly on its chain. But of course, he realized, they had all gotten pretty tight.

Tom turned off the last of the lights and went up to his own bed, confused and discomfited by the strangeness of Mary and Alex's relationship, of their weird love—to say nothing of his and Wright's.

One might walk from the Villa Donatello to the Villa Castellani in scarcely two minutes, but Mary took five. She paused just outside her gate to admire the wisteria, to let the violet cool of it pour down on her as she stood in the shadow of the wall, to catch her breath. She and Alex had just had words and she had walked out. Through her gate. And this was her wall, of course, and a good one, she could not but note. She had never imagined she would own a venerable stone wall, still less, one on an olive-studded lane overlooking Florence.

She began to walk towards the Villa Castellani, moving into the stronger light, and as she did a lizard raced across her path and halted a few feet from her, holding itself so still that after an instant it seemed to disappear. He was dusky green, she supposed, the general green of the place; or he became it so as to blend in.

Mary continued along the verge of the lane, and as she did, she realized she was more content than she ought to be, considering the frost that lay over her and Alex as a couple. They had fought last night and again this morning (the subject of that second altercation being, of course, the usual one). On every such occasion for the last six years, mending the breach would have been for both of them the day's most urgent and essential priority, on the order of a burst pipe or a wound that needed stitches. But today, Mary realized, while she still cared, she did not care so much. Neither, she could not but conclude, did Alex.

After Wright had welcomed her and they sat down and had coffee, she continued to think about this. In fact, her conversation with Turner was more or less an unfolding of these thoughts in an unedited and inchoate stream. She was rambling. It was as if someone else was speaking while she herself took in the apartment and made a separate set of observations: that she would have given the world, ten years ago, to sit in this room, in this building, in this place, with the likes of a Wright Turner as her interlocutor.

It was altogether more than she could have then ever imagined: the golden darkness of the apartment, tinted with ivory and olive, and at the windows the light raining down outside. She was definitively here, arrived; she had obtained her heart's desire and perhaps more. The fact of her happiness now had little or nothing to do with Alex. She was—in fact, just now, in this light, from this day forward—another person entirely.

"So if," Turner was saying as he refilled Mary's coffee cup, "you've made this decision that you and Alex have to redefine your life together, what does that amount to? For you, not to say him?"

"I don't know what it means for him. Do you?"

Wright considered the matter. "I don't pretend to know what people are meant for. I only know what I can do with them."

"Well, I can't do anything with Alex," Mary said. "Not that he would care. He's gone completely overboard with his work. He's monomaniacal. He doesn't have any use for other people except as models to paint from."

"Perhaps you should be more like him."

"More selfish?"

"More careful with yourself," Turner said. "Italy's lovely. There are . . . impressions one can only get here. But it's also spoiled a great many people, made them idle and dilettantish and second rate."

"And you think that's a risk for me?"

"If you don't take hold of yourself, yes. I assume you have the means. You don't *have* to do—"

"The financial means, yes. Complete freedom, in a way. But it's still easy to feel fragmented, pulled in all directions," said Mary. "By the house. By Alex. Tom. Wanting a baby. And my writing got lost among all that. But now"—Mary set down her cup and leaned forward—"now I see a way forward, a way out."

"Which is?" Turner asked.

"I simply see that my life—what I want from it—is one thing. That there shouldn't be a boundary between what I write and how I live."

"So you're going to write your autobiography?"

"Of course not. I'm a novelist."

"I was attempting a joke," said Turner. "And what's to become of Alex and Tom?"

"I don't know. You see how Alex is. He's a child. He goes his merry way and then he's horribly shocked when anyone objects. We've had a lot of fun together, but ultimately I've come to think he's just not a serious person."

"Could he manage without you? I suspect he's become accustomed to a certain style of life."

Mary raised her arm and batted the air with her hand, as though shooing something away. "Oh, he's got his own money. I gave it to him."

"That was rather kind of you."

"It was our arrangement. To allow us to come here. So that if it didn't work out, Alex wouldn't lose everything by having given up his work in Seattle. He'd be independent."

"And having a baby was his half of the bargain?" Turner said.

"Maybe it wasn't set down in so many words." Mary had laid her hand across her heart. "Obviously, he doesn't think so."

"So he simply doesn't like children?"

"It's more that he thinks our life is perfect as it is," Mary said. "That anything more would be superfluous."

"So he refuses to consider it? I suppose you could simply stop taking the pill or whatever—"

"I don't use birth control."

"Then how is it that you haven't gotten pregnant?"

"Well, Alex and I haven't slept together for three weeks. I declared a moratorium."

Turner smiled. "So your plan is to starve him out."

"Not really. I mean, anyway, he can't."

"Can't what? He's impotent?"

"Can't impregnate me," Mary said. "He's had a vasectomy."

"Oh, this is getting rather complicated. So, really, he's of no use to you in that area anyway."

"No, but that's not the issue. I don't mind that he can't. It's that he *won't*."

"In the sense that he wouldn't if he could, if he were capable."

"Exactly," said Mary.

"I suppose he doesn't see the logic of your position."

"He thinks I'm basically insane in that regard."

"But he wouldn't stand in your way," Turner said, "if you sought other means to achieve the same goal."

"No, probably not. But there'd be no point to it. I'm not going to bring up a baby with him being indifferent to it. I'd rather raise it on my own."

"So that's your plan?"

"I suppose it is," said Mary. "I mean, the issue is the lack of support. No, not even support. The indifference. He won't even argue *against* the idea. It's that infuriating passivity of his. You saw."

"He seems to be mostly interested in painting his paintings."

"It's all he's interested in. That, and amusing himself."

"And what about Thomas? He's rather a fledgling," Turner said.

"Oh, he can stay. He's been my surrogate baby all these years, my son."

"And when you get your real baby?"

"He can be the nanny."

Turner took a sip of his coffee and set the cup back down. "I have to say I'm not terribly surprised that it's come to this. As a couple, I found you and Alex a bit incongruous."

"I don't mind that you saw that. It means you already know me better than Alex does." Mary stopped and then said, "He thinks he can know me by painting me, by just making me up out of things he's seen on a wall."

"You give me too much credit. It's just intuition."

Mary saw Turner's hand, the ivoried and timeworn claw, hovering over the demitasse, and she watched as it cleaved upon the handle and raised the cup to his lips.

She wondered if she would stay with Alex or live alone or find a new lover. At any rate, she thought, it's my choice, this person and not that one. Maybe that's what love is, merely choosing. And then, like that graffito said, "Love shapes our purpose."

As they entered her mind, as she composed them, these words seemed inexorably true to her. And she realized that in every case, the word "art" could be substituted for the word "love." She was in the grip of that stunning clarity of mind, peculiar to artists and lovers, in which the connectedness of everything is obvious.

Tom was sitting at the table in the kitchen eating lunch, poking at ramen noodles with his spoon, when the phone rang. He heard Alex answer it, and then Tom went back to his lunch, to the style magazine from the London paper and the broth in the sump of his bowl.

Alex came in ten minutes later. He was crying. Tom had never seen him cry. Perhaps no one had. Tom supposed things with Mary has finally shattered his cool.

"Jens died," Tom heard him saying. "In Seattle. He'd come back from Astoria. I didn't even know that. Peter, my friend from Seattle Art Supply, called. Nobody really knew who else to call."

"I'm really sorry," said Tom.

Alex was pacing, or rather he was circling the kitchen table as though it were an armature he were tethered to. "I guess I'm going back," he said. "He didn't have anybody, family. Even friends, really. I owe him. I should get his work and put it somewhere safe. He was good. I should get it shown. A retrospective. That's the least I could do."

He stopped and looked at Tom, his damp red face just floating, so it seemed to Tom, just hanging in space. "You know he was like my teacher, like my dad? You know that?"

"Sure I do."

"People thought he was just this failed painter, this drunk, but he taught me things. He taught me how to be an artist. He really did. You know how important that is."

"Sure. I kind of thought that for me Wright—"

"Oh, fuck Wright. What a fucking asshole." Alex stopped, and then he said, "I'm sorry, Tom. I'm really freaked out. Okay?"

"I know," said Tom. "Don't worry about it."

Alex nodded, and then he paced off a hemisphere and a little more. "Now how do I get there? Through Milan?"

"Maybe London. Frankfurt, maybe," Tom offered. After a while Alex stopped pacing and nodded and went to the phone. He took out the little notebook that was always stuffed into his front pocket, consulted it, and dialed a number. It must be a travel agent, Tom decided.

Alex was on the phone for some time—put on hold and transferred and given numbers—and after a while Tom went out into the *salone* and sat by himself. On the couch next to him was one of Mary's Victorian novels, and it seemed to him that that was the way it would be from here on out at the villa, that it was a house in mourning. There's black crepe hung up. We're stopping our normal lives for an interval to keep company with the dead. We're all going to be ghosts for a while.

Mary came home a little after two in the afternoon. She found herself hastening to the gate of the villa, and she slowed to consider what precisely she planned to do when she came in, when she saw Alex.

She decided, in fact, that she would do nothing. So everything would remain as it had been: herself writing; Tom at his books, frittering away the day; Alex in his little bubble of contentment, of paints and self-regard. For now.

As she reached the door, she realized that she was unafraid—not simply unafraid, but without the least taint of worry—and this affirmed her conviction that she had chosen the right course. Her actions and her conscience were in accord. Her epiphany was what it seemed. Art would not imitate life, nor would life imitate art. They were indistinguishable.

Mary opened the door. The house was, thank god, cool, at least cooler than the air outside. Tom or Alex had had the good sense to batten the shutters in the morning, before the heat rose from the valley and city below. She went into the kitchen and found Tom there, drinking coffee as he thumbed through the style supplement that had come with last Sunday's London paper.

"Hi," she said.

Tom looked up. "Hi," he returned.

"So what's up? Where is everybody?" Mary looked back over her shoulder into the *salone*. "Is Alex in his studio?"

Tom gazed at her as if confused or alarmed, and his words came in a sputter. "He's gone. I mean, he's left. Jens died. So he's going home to kind of look after his stuff. Some friend of his called from Seattle. He said no one else would do it."

"So he just left? When?" Mary said, standing rigidly. "I mean, when did all this happen?"

"Late this morning. Maybe noon," said Tom, and put his cup down. "While you were out."

"He's flying to Seattle?"

"To Milan, then Chicago, then Seattle."

"For how long?" Mary stared at the floor, and then at her hands. She shook her head and looked back at Tom. "I mean, did he say?"

"Not really. I suppose a few weeks. He said he'd call when he got there."

"It's not very considerate," said Mary.

"He was kind of in shock. He was crying. He called the airline and packed his bag and called a cab and left," Tom said. "I tried to talk to him, but he wasn't really all there."

"Christ," Mary said. "How fucking bizarre. Jens—I haven't thought of him for a year. I suppose it was his liver. Or a stroke."

"I don't know. Alex didn't say."

"So did Alex leave me a message? A note?"

"Not that he mentioned," Tom said.

Mary frowned and, just as quickly, she smiled. "So here we are. Just the two of us. Just like that. It's not how I'd pictured things."

"I don't suppose it'll make that much difference. Maybe it's a good thing, really. In a way."

"How is that?"

"Well, I mean things have maybe gotten a little . . . over-stressed in the house. Among us. I mean, last night . . ."

"Oh, that," said Mary. "I thought that was just what you called critical discourse."

"It just seemed like maybe nobody was liking each other very much."

"I was too hard on you?"

"No," Tom said. "Not so much that. More—"

"You know Alex and I argue. It's not a big deal." Mary entwined her fingers and thrust her palms downward towards the floor. "I mean, we have differences. Some major ones. So there are tensions. Sometimes they kind of leak out, erupt."

"Sure. I know how it is." Tom paused, and then added, "I mean, even between you and me. Maybe you get annoyed, or whatever."

"I suppose it's happened."

"Or I wonder what you're really thinking."

"I thought I was supposed to be kind of outspoken," said Mary.

"Well, I mean what you're thinking about me and all of us together here. In the house. Or with Wright."

"Oh, Tom, you worry too much. Sure, I like Wright. I like *you,*" Mary said. "You brought us together."

"What about Alex?" said Tom.

"Really, just now, I don't know. But it'll be okay." Mary untangled her hands and spread them apart. "But I mean, really, we've been together forever, and he just gets on a plane and disappears."

"He's going to call."

"I'm sure he will," Mary said. "And you and I will be fine. Kind of marooned here together. We'll have fun. We can have Wright over without worrying about Alex getting his nose out of joint. It'll be like it used to be in Seattle. We'll do whatever we want. We'll play."

"Play?"

"Yes. Because it's struck me—just recently—that we came here to work and live in a certain way. And we've all been working very seriously, which is fine."

"Or trying to get started working seriously," Tom said.

"Sure. That too. But the whole ethos here is meant to be about pleasure *and* labour. But we've been worrying about what we think we *need* to do instead of what we want to do."

Tom said, "So you—we—haven't been doing what we want?"

"Not in the right way," said Mary. "But don't worry. I've had a sort of epiphany. It's all very clear to me. I'll show you." And with that she stepped closer to Tom, put her arms around him, and gave him a hug. And then, unaccountably, she felt tears on her face, her own.

9.

Flaming June

It was a little after nine o'clock the next morning when Alex called. Mary picked up the receiver in the kitchen as Tom fiddled with the coffee pot. She forgot to answer with the salutation *"Pronto"* and merely said, "Hello?"

"Hi," said Alex. "It's me."

Tom was pantomiming at Mary from the stove, mouthing some question. She ignored him. "Where are you?" she said.

"I'm here. In Seattle. I got in a couple of hours ago. It's late." Alex paused. "It's like . . . midnight."

Now Tom had moved towards her, gesticulating and silently forming words that Mary realized were "Is it Alex?" She nodded and then waved him towards the door. He returned her nod and left.

"You must be tired," Mary said into the phone. She was not sure she wanted to be seen to express concern. She was still angry, but they would get to that.

"No, not really," Alex replied.

"Oh," Mary said. "So where are you staying?"

"This new corporate-hip place they were building on Fourth Avenue when we left. It's open now. The whole staff dress in black, even the maids and the bus boys and janitors. It's like being at art school."

"Everyone's an artist now, right?" said Mary offhandedly. They were, she knew, only circling one other before they engaged.

"Right."

"So how long are you staying?"

"I don't know yet. I just got here."

"Well, I mean, roughly. Days versus weeks."

"At least a week, I guess," said Alex. "I need to find Jens's canvases. Then give them to somebody here to look after. Or maybe send them to Italy. That might take time."

"I suppose." Mary stopped and then said, "You left in kind of a hurry. You could have waited an hour or two. Or at least left a note."

"Sorry. I was just totally freaked."

"You kind of vanished."

The line from Seattle was silent for a moment, and then Alex spoke again. "Frankly, after the business the other night and then—what was it?—yesterday morning, or the day before, I didn't think you'd care one way or the other."

"I care to know where you are. If only because you do live here."

"Tom was obviously going to tell you," Alex said.

"Still, you don't just walk out—"

"Exactly what you did, the same day. After we . . . talked."

"I wasn't leaving the country."

"So where did you go?"

"I went . . ." she began, and paused in order to fabricate something. "I went to the Maria Maddalena de' Pazzi church." Mary's truth was now her own to bestow or withhold.

"Did that help?"

"With what?"

"With your novel. What else would it be?"

Mary stopped to consider where she and Alex were going with this line of discussion. At last, she said, "Yes, it helped. Or at least it helped more than your disappearing did."

"I didn't disappear. I left for a good reason. Which was not about me. It was about Jens, about his work. I'm trying to do something good here, okay?"

"Okay," Mary yielded. "But vis à vis us, you did it in a bad way."

"If you want," said Alex, with a suppressed yawn. "Look, I'm fried. I'm going to have a drink and go to bed. I'll call you tomorrow. Or maybe the next day. We can hash all this out. If there's any point in it."

"I'd at least like to know whether you're coming back."

"Please, Mary. I can't do this right now. Please, okay?"

"Whatever."

"Okay. I'll call tomorrow. Or the day after," Alex said. "Goodnight, okay?"

"Goodnight," said Mary. She could see out her window that it was scarcely mid-morning.

Tom had gone upstairs, but Mary knew it would only be a matter of time before he appeared before her, wanting to know what Alex had said, and what they were going to do next. Tom was the perennial sidecar attached to Mary and Alex's relationship. Where other couples had, say, a home renovation project or a pug, she and Alex had Tom.

But it occurred to Mary, as she indeed heard his footsteps on the stairs, that Tom was for the moment—and perhaps indefinitely—her sole responsibility. As he appeared before her in the kitchen, it struck her that his dependence went beyond the merely doglike into the realm of creator and creature; of her being the author of his character, the plotter of his next move, without whom he was nothing more than a loose end.

"So what did Alex say?" Tom asked.

"Not much," responded Mary. "I'll tell you. But let's go out, down the hill."

"Where to?"

"Maria Maddalena de' Pazzi's church."

"Okay. Where is it?"

"Just up the street from the Paperback Exchange."

"Can you wait a minute? I've got some things upstairs to trade in."

Tom ran upstairs and returned a minute later with a stack of books. Mary opened a drawer, got a plastic sack from it, and handed it to him. "So what are you disposing of?" she asked.

"Some Foucault. *Adorno for Beginners. Best American Short Stories of the Eighties.*"

"Good riddance," said Mary.

They left by the garden gate, and as they walked down to the city, the heat rose to meet them. In three-quarters of an hour they reached the Paperback Exchange, and in all that time it seemed to Mary that they had scarcely spoken, that they merely trudged along, falling, as by gravity, down the slope towards the Arno. Tiny reptiles bolted from their path, disappearing into the million cracks in the walls and pavements of the crazed and fractured city.

Mary stood near the entrance while Tom traded in his books and, armed with a small credit, began to search for some new volume. It was Mary's opinion that Tom was too well read, or read, in any case, too much, for he retained nothing save the need to read more, as though if he kept at it, he would finally stumble across the book that explained it all.

Tom approached her, holding out a fat paperback. "Auden. *The Collected Poems.* Wright's been after me to read him. With my credit and ten thousand lire, I can swing it."

Mary dug in her bag and withdrew a blue banknote. "Here," she said.

"Come on, Mary. I've got it."

"No, take it. I want you to have it. From me. Maybe I'll look at it sometime."

Tom simply stood there before her, and then a smile took possession of his face. This makes him really happy, Mary thought.

"Okay. If you insist," he said. "It's really great of you."

He genuinely seemed to mean this, although she saw he must at some level be aware that she could easily buy him the entire stock of the store and it would scarcely register on her bank statement. Yet, she marvelled, I can make him happy with this little thing.

Tom returned from the cashier. "Hey, thanks again," he said.

"It's my pleasure," Mary replied, and together they went out into the street.

Two minutes later, they stood before the Maria Maddalena church, entering through an unexpectedly spacious and handsome cloistered courtyard.

"It was a convent," said Mary. "It still is, I think."

"So this is where she lived?" Tom said. "Where she had her visions and stuff?"

"I don't know. I think this was built later. Anyway, there's a mural of her life inside. And her relics are here, in the altar."

Mary led them across the courtyard and they went in. The door gave out a rasp and, as it closed, a thunderous slam. These sounds conspired to make Mary feel herself an interloper here, which, she supposed, she was, being neither a believer nor a resident of the neighbourhood nor even an aficionado of religious architecture and art. She was simply an author in search of a character.

Mary and Tom walked a little way down the centre aisle, and then Mary pointed to the high, flat painted ceiling. "That's her," she said. "She's being presented to the Trinity. When she went to heaven."

"She's floating on the ceiling. That's a nice trick," Tom said. "But I don't quite understand this Trinity thing."

Mary looked up again at the robed figures and angels swimming on the ceiling. "I don't think it's that there are three gods," she began. "It's that the one god has three aspects. Or qualities."

"He has," Tom offered, "multiple personalities."

"Or it's just an interpretive scheme to get around the problem of God walking around on earth as Jesus at the same time as he's supposedly running the universe from heaven."

"A theory of God, then."

"I suppose."

"Cool," said Tom. "So really, they were doing theory back then—unpacking God, unmasking the constructions He's based on—"

"I don't know if Maria would have seen it that way. I think these abstractions were totally real to her. She could touch them, feel them, almost make love with them. It wasn't just belief. It was like she could handle the idea of God."

"Kind of weird, really."

"Well, let's just say she was really intense."

Mary and Tom walked down the centre aisle towards the altar, and Tom said, "So she's in there? Her bones or hair or dust?"

"That's what they say." Mary stopped by the altar rail.

"It's kind of fetishistic, isn't it?" said Tom. "I mean, this ritual hoarding of saints' toenails or whatever. It's like they don't really believe in the spiritual. It's the material world that turns them on."

"It's very carnal, isn't it? It's not the way you usually think of religion, but that's what it boils down to."

"I don't get how it would make anybody happy," Tom said.

"I don't know that it's supposed to. I don't claim to understand it."

They began to walk a circuit of the outer aisles.

"So how are you going to get inside Maria's head?" Tom asked

"Through her having passions, being sexual. The carnality, really."

"Even though she was celibate."

"Especially because she was celibate," Mary said. "It's like her celibacy—her aiming all that erotic longing at God—was her art."

"Okay. That helps."

They had come to a triptych and Mary stopped. She said,

"Now here's something you can explain to me," indicating the Saint Sebastian in its centre, porcupined with arrows. "Why is this a gay icon?"

Tom looked and said, "Yeah, I guess it kind of is. I mean, I've seen it before."

"So what's the deal?"

"Well, he's got this great torso, but not too butch, and nice hair. Scantily dressed. And he's being penetrated by all these darts, or whatever."

"So, is he gay?"

"I guess. Maybe he's the patron saint of gays. I don't know if there is such a thing."

"I really doubt it."

"Well, I'll ask Wright. He says Florence has been a gay centre since the Middle Ages."

"Really," Mary said, and began to walk in the direction of the door and the cloister.

Tom came alongside her. "Yeah, that's why Dante has all the gays in the Inferno come from here."

"Maybe Dante was gay. I've always thought he protested a little too much about Beatrice. Who really is an abstraction, just a bundle of virtues."

"I don't know," Tom said. "I haven't really read Dante." They went out into the courtyard and towards the outer door and the street. "I know he's a big deal," he continued, "that he's the hometown hero and all, but I could never get anywhere with him. Well, really, I never even tried, never started."

"There are worse things. It's not the end of the world."

"And now I've got all this Auden to read." Tom held up the fat paperback.

"Maybe there's a poem about Dante in it."

"That would help."

It struck Mary that it would not help; that Tom's brain was a sieve with very large holes indeed, and he was enamoured of theory because he could not, for all his efforts, get any traction with particulars; with saints' bones or the living hell of Dante's Florence or simply being Wright Turner's lover.

"Anyway," Mary said as they stepped into the street, "let's go get gelato."

They walked only a little farther than Santa Felicità and its Pontormos (which Tom, busy with his little cup and spoon, had the wit not to mention—or so Mary assumed) before they decided to take a taxi home.

There was a rank of taxis near the Pitti Palace, and they got inside one. Mary directed the driver to Bellosguardo, and the driver, uncharacteristically voluble for a Florentine, began to question Mary.

So, you're staying at the hotel up there, then?

No, we dwell therein. I will show you its position. It is tangential to the Villa Castellani.

And you've lived there quite some time? You speak excellent Italian.

Truly, entirely since three or four months. But we have been nine months in Florence.

And Florence agrees with you?

Oh, very much.

But you come from America, no?

Yes. Seattle.

Seattle. I've heard of it. Noumena, correct?

Yes. It exists there.

Now I have to wonder why anyone would leave such a place to come here. To such a dusty and decrepit old place where one can scarcely earn a living.

But Florence is the incubator of the Renaissance.

That was a long time ago. So, you are working here? There are more and more Americans and English here these days, renting out villas, teaching cooking, arranging things for their countrymen. Americans like to fly over and get married in our old churches and then have the Bella Toscana honeymoon, for example. It's a good use for these old places.

Tom broke in. *"Noi abbiamo stati alla chiesa Maria Maddalena de' Pazzi,"* he blurted, but the driver appeared not to have heard him. He continued speaking to Mary.

So what is your line of work?

I am a scribe. My husband is a lacquerer. My friend here professes to be a—I don't know—a sage, a prophet.

He looks the part. So you are all artists and thinkers. Once, Florence was full of such people. Now everyone's out for a buck.

"Oggi," Tom offered, *"siamo artisti, tutt'e due."* The driver looked back at him in the rearview mirror. Apparently he had understood.

Good for you Americans. Here, we're all entrepreneurs now. We're all Americans, I suppose. You can be the Italians. Or at least the artists.

Mary thought this proposition deserved to be gainsaid, but she saw their turn in the road was coming up and that she ought to apprise the driver of it.

Here, at the fork, go right. Our house is ahead. The wall is pendulous with wisteria.

Oh, just before the Villa Castellani?

Yes.

That is the home of your fellow countryman Turner, the great aesthete.

Yes, we know him.

I've brought many people to see him. Many handsome boys.

Here the driver laughed and brought the taxi to a halt before the gate of the Villa Donatello. Mary looked for the fare in her bag as Tom loosed the sentence he had composed. *"In fatto, lui conosce tutto il mondo."*

The driver looked at Tom and smiled. "*Il* Turner? Yes, he is—as you say in English—a man of many parts. *Vero?*"

"I suppose," said Tom as Mary handed the driver three banknotes. She and Tom exited the taxi, and as it drove away, Mary said, "I don't know about that one. He's a little presumptuous."

"I got the impression he made some kind of homophobic comment about Wright. But I couldn't really understand him."

Mary decided it was better not to offer an exact translation, insofar as she was capable of rendering one. "I don't think it was anything offensive. But he was a little full of himself, condescending, playing the worldly-wise European, like he has this secret knowledge we don't even know exists."

Tom considered asking if there was, in fact, such secret knowledge (for certainly he'd missed out on it), but as they came to the gate a small figure emerged from the shadow of the wisteria.

"Hey, hi," she said. *"C'è Alessandro?"*

"Alessandro?" said Mary. "There's—*non c'è Alessandro qui. Siamo tutti Americani.*"

"*Anche Alessandro. Un pittore Americano. Anche* good guy."

"I think she means Alex," Tom offered.

"All-ex," the girl added. *"Essato. M'ha detto veni' qui."*

"Well, he's not—*non è qui.*"

"Pero arriva, Alessandro?"

"No. *Non lo so. Quando arriva*. Maybe not ever."

"Never?" said the girl, and then what seemed to Tom a torrential admixture of dialect and incipient sighs and sobs racked her face. She was small, perhaps twelve or thirteen, with long dark hair in loose curls, her frame bony and angular, her nose a porcelain bud, her mouth pink and almost swollen. As to her attire, she wore a sort of peasant skirt of orange and blue, a T-shirt adorned with the words "Stupido Hotel," and much-scuffed pink sneakers with stacked soles. For all that, she was, Tom saw, not a little formidable.

Mary retreated. "Well, perhaps not never—*non mai. Però non lo so.*" And here she firmed a little more. "And you—you can't hang around—*non è possibile che tu restai qui*. No."

"Dunque, mi dice 'fuck off'*?"*

"No, no," Mary said. *"Ma tu dovresti andare—tua casa."*

"Non ho—"

"Or whatever, then," Mary said as calmly as possible. "And I will tell Alex—Alessandro—*io dirò Alessandro che tu eri qui. E lui*—will contact you—*ti troverà.*"

"He finds me?"

"Yes, *promesso*."

"*Allora*, okay," said the girl. "Fucking awesome." The girl began to walk away down the road, back to the smouldering city below, but she turned back, and said, *"Dunque, tu gli dirai?"*

"Promesso," Mary said. And with that, the girl strode off in a manner at once determined and unsteady, receding into the blazing distance of the road.

Mary was looking skyward. "Shit," she muttered. "This is all I need—urchins banging on the gate."

"I thought she was kind of sweet," Tom said. "Angelic."

"You're out of your mind. You can't even understand what she's saying. She's a mouthy little hustler."

"She just wanted to see Alex. I suppose she's his model."

"Oh, god, I guess that's it." Mary opened the gate and she and Tom walked along the path towards the door. "No way is she coming in this house. Alex can deal with it when he comes back. If he comes back."

"He said he might not come back?"

"No, not in so many words. But I'm not sure he's welcome anyway."

"Shit, Mary. That's how things are with you guys?"

"I don't know," Mary said, "how things are. But this doesn't improve them."

"I'm sorry."

"There's nothing for you to be sorry about. Maybe I should be sorry for dumping it on you, for being a bitch."

Mary was putting her key into the latch. "You're not a bitch, Mary," said Tom.

"Thanks. I appreciate that," Mary said, and pushed open the door to the house and its dark rooms, their shutters sealed tight against the afternoon. She turned back to Tom. "Really, I do. Sometimes I don't know quite what to make of myself."

* * *

Tom decided that on a number of counts it would be a good evening to visit Wright Turner. He had not seen him since Alex unveiled the double nude—only two nights ago, in fact—but it seemed a long while since they had simply sat together in his apartment, drinking wine and talking and making love.

Turner greeted him in his customary manner, giving an impression of amused surprise, of perhaps having been busy or of having better things to do, but none of them so pressing or attractive that he could not happily stop just here, just now.

"So, Thomas, how stands it at the Villa Donatello?" Turner asked, motioning with his hand towards the couch.

Tom seated himself. "Kind of fucked up, actually," he said. "Alex's old art teacher or mentor or whatever died, so he left for Seattle, but without telling Mary. So she's pissed about that, and of course she was pissed at him anyway."

"Because of our little tiff the other night?"

"That, and something—I don't know what—else, something bigger. Like's she's preoccupied, or planning something really big. Some big change."

"'You must change your life.' That's what your idol, Rilke, says."

Tom considered for a moment. "I don't know if I feel so Rilkean any more."

"Well, that's not an entirely bad thing. Let me get us something to drink."

As Turner went about his business in the kitchen, it struck Tom that, in attending to the crisis in Alex and Mary's relation, he had forgotten the one between him and Wright: Wright's inexplicable inattention and lack of support the night of the unveiling.

Turner came back bearing a tray holding glasses, bottle, olives, and nuts. After he had set it down and filled their glasses, Tom said, with as much indifference as he could muster, "I was wondering about the other night, about why you said you didn't remember telling me about Mary's novel."

"Doubtless because I didn't remember."

"But you did tell me. You told me that you'd given her Jeremy's translation of Maria Pazzi, and that she was writing something based on it."

"Well, you must forgive me, Thomas." Wright drew some wine into his mouth with his mouth almost closed, as though through his teeth. "I'm an old man. I forget things."

"I know, I know. But it caused a lot of misunderstanding, what with Mary thinking I must have been snooping."

"Which I'll bet you have, being such a curious boy."

"That's neither here nor there."

"I'd say it's entirely here or there. So had you?"

Tom found himself bending forward, bowing his head, assuming the posture of shame, of readying himself to receive the *coup de grâce*. "Yes," he said. "But just by accident."

Tom was not enjoying this—Wright treating him as a parent when Tom himself was trying to address their issues as lovers—and sat up straight again. "Maybe that was wrong," he allowed, "but I feel like you're evading what I'm trying to get at."

"Which is?"

"That you didn't back me up, that you didn't think about supporting me, taking my side."

"So," Turner said, putting down his glass, "I should have lied for you."

"No, not lied. Because you said you didn't remember anyway. So you could have just given me the benefit of the doubt."

"I gave everyone the benefit of the doubt. I simply told the truth as I recollected it. Which was to say, I didn't remember."

"Well, you being so evenhanded made things kind of difficult for me. When you could have made them easier," said Tom. "I have to live with Mary and Alex, you know. I kind of depend on them."

"Thomas, I cannot and will not attempt to negotiate all the

little intrigues that transpire in your ménage. That you live in it is your choice."

"I'd like to depend on us, on our being together. But you rejected that."

"Now that's not fair or correct, either," Turner said, taking up his glass again. "The kind of arrangement you envisioned was never on offer. You would have liked it to have been, but it isn't possible."

"That's *your* choice."

Turner drank. "I suppose it is. For very good reasons which we needn't rehash."

"Don't my feelings matter? Don't I get to speak?"

"Oh, you rather insist upon it." Turner drank, put his glass down, and leaned forward. "And instead of having a good time together, the evening is spoiled. All because of a hypothetical problem between you and your . . . landlady."

Tom was a little flushed by the wine he had been drinking, but still more by the insulting turn Wright's language had taken. "That's kind of a shitty thing to say about people who like you, admire you, who invite you into their home," Tom said. "But never mind. Just tell me how your being, like, *indifferent* to me is a hypothetical problem."

"Because in the end it was of no consequence."

"No consequence?"

"Absolutely no consequence. Because Alex said *he'd* told you about what Mary was writing."

"Yes," said Tom. "But he hadn't really told me. He lied for me. Which is exactly my point."

Turner picked up his glass again. "I'm afraid it's a point I'm missing."

"I guess it's just one more thing you can't see."

"Oh, this action of his that you interpret as loyalty," Turner said. "If that's why he did it."

"I don't know why he did it. Maybe it didn't have anything to do with me. Maybe it was just a way to get back at Mary."

"Or perhaps he's a secret admirer. Perhaps he loves you from afar. Although he strikes me as rather grossly heterosexual. But then Mary's unhappy with him, so I may be wrong. Perhaps he could offer you this 'relationship' you profess to want so much."

"That is so fucked, so wrong," Tom said. He sat upright, rigid. "I mean, why are you saying this shit? To drive me away?" He feared he was going to cry.

"No, of course not," said Turner. "If I wanted you to go, I would say so."

"But you're not. Not right now."

"I admit," Turner said, "to being on the verge of it. When you hector me like this."

Tom stood, unsteady but, in his own view, towering over Wright, who sat far below him, hunched on the couch, staring into his wineglass. "Let me save you the trouble," Tom said.

Turner looked up at him. Wright's eyes, Tom saw, were sad for once, his face less ivory than blanched, his lips bloodless, violet gone cold or mixed with grey. "Perhaps that would be wise," Turner said.

Tom waited a moment for Wright to append ". . . just now" or "for a little while." But Turner sat in his silence and Tom walked softly to the door and let himself out, as though Wright might have been napping, as he tended to do after they had made love.

Tom recounted all of this to Mary when he got home. They sat in the *salone* and drank a bottle of wine and, as Tom swung between the poles of his rage at Turner and his self-loathing, Mary found herself thinking, and at least once saying, "Poor baby."

"So," Tom said, "I guess we're just a couple of widows now, you and me."

"Like I told you the other day," Mary said, "we can have fun."

"We can play together. Without Wright doing his glare."

"He can be supercilious," Mary agreed.

"He's not so grand as he'd like people to think. Know what?"

"What?"

"He has to take Viagra to get it up."

"Really?"

"Oh, I suppose with somebody his age it's normal, but he'd die if anybody knew. He said it was the one thing he didn't want me to put in my journal."

"But you did?"

"Well, I will. When I get around to it," said Tom. "It's not like it's going to be published any time soon. But when it is, I think I might just leave that in."

"I'd like to see it sometime."

"We'll see," Tom said.

Mary saw that Tom wasn't convinced he wanted to do this. She thought she might make some headway if she offered a confidence of her own. "You know, Alex takes anti-depressants," she offered.

"Really? I think he said something about that. But I'm not real clear."

"It's not a big deal—kind of like a daily vitamin for the brain. A neurological supplement."

"So how long has he been taking it?" Tom asked.

"Maybe three months."

"Do you think it's changed him at all? Made him even mellower?"

"I didn't think so. But then I realized it kind of coincided with this whole . . . headlong plunge he's taken with his painting."

"Then he's done some good work because of it," allowed Tom.

"Maybe. You know how I feel about it. But I've been wondering if it's all coming out of some manic state he's in."

"I don't think you can be mellow *and* manic."

"Maybe he's the first case."

"I wonder if that kind of invalidates the art, if he only produced it because of the Zoloft. Wright would say no, it's irrelevant. But to be consistent with his own position, Alex would sort of have to say yes."

"I don't know, Tom. Right now, I think I want to get some sleep. Hey, thanks for commiserating."

"Sure. It's mutual." And with that they climbed the stairs together and went, alone, to their respective beds.

When the phone rang the next morning, Tom was in the kitchen making coffee as he attempted to fabricate the conviction that he would not much miss Wright Turner. The phone, however, disrupted that process twice over; once in interrupting it and secondly in producing the hope in Tom's mind that it must be Wright himself on the line.

"Pronto," Tom said, coolly but also a little breathlessly.

"Hey, hi Tom, it's Alex. Greetings from Seattle."

"Hey, it's great to hear your voice," said Tom, and to his surprise found that he indeed felt this.

"So how are things there?"

"Hot. Really hot."

"It's about sixty here," Alex said. "And how is it otherwise?"

"Not so good. Wright and I broke up."

"Hey, I'm really sorry. But you know he's an asshole, right?"

"I do now, I suppose."

"Well, here's something to buck you up. I ran into a guy I know from Noumena who knew your old boss, Michael Sullivan."

"Yeah."

"Well, they let him go. Not that that's not happening to a lot of people, apparently. Still, it ought to give you some satisfaction."

"It's a great consolation, as Wright would say," said Tom. "So what's he doing now?"

"Don't know. He moved to Portland."

"I like that part."

"It's the elephant burial ground or whatever, I guess," Alex said. "Well, hey, I'm sorry about Wright. But it'll work out. He was an asshole. Right from the get-go. I saw it. Takes one to know one."

"Oh, come on, Alex."

"Well, all right. I won't go that far. Okay, you take care. I better talk to Mary now."

"Sure," Tom said, and called Mary's name. She had been in the *salone* in her bathrobe, reading the *Herald Tribune*. She took the receiver and Tom began to leave the kitchen, but she shrugged to indicate it was no matter to her if he stayed. So Tom went back to preparing the morning's second pot of coffee as Mary and Alex started to talk.

"So," Alex began, "how's it going?"

"How do you think? It's just *groovy*. Please, Alex, let's be big kids, let's call things by their names. So when are you coming home?"

"I still don't know. I don't get the feeling I'm very welcome."

"That's not entirely inaccurate. But we need to talk in person. At a minimum."

"Well, I'm going to be at least another week. Probably more. At least ten days, really."

"So is that it?"

"Shit, Mary, you're really turning on the charm."

"If you don't have anything to say, I don't really care to listen to you right now."

"What am I supposed to be saying? I'm trying to sort out Jens's stuff and see a few people and it's taking a little time, okay?"

"You could start with an apology."

"Excuse me, Mary, but what fucking for?"

"For the day you left. For the night before."

"I'll grant you the first one. But the other, no way," Alex said.

"Tom told me about him and Wright. I'd say it just confirms my opinion that he's an old witch. If anything, I was too polite with him."

"It's more complicated than that. With them. And with us, obviously. If you can comprehend that."

"I guess I can't. It's late here."

"So I'd imagine. I better go."

"Wait," said Alex. "There's one other thing. You should phone the accountant. He heard I was back and called me here. He says he needs to talk to you before he files your taxes."

"April fifteenth was a long time ago."

"If you live overseas, it's June fifteenth. Anyway, he said to call him right away, okay?"

"Okay."

"So I'll phone in a couple of days, all right?"

"Sure." This, Mary thought, was the part where they were each supposed to say "I love you" to the other. Except they never had done that. There hadn't been any need to.

"So, goodbye," Alex said.

"Goodbye," Mary said.

Mary and Tom spent the remainder of the day alone in the house together, Mary in her studio, Tom variously in the kitchen, his room, and the *salone*. They met only in passing, in the halls or the kitchen, and exchanged looks of mutual commiseration as fellow sufferers of love's agonies and caprices.

At six, as if by unspoken agreement, they met in the *salone* and drank wine together. At seven, Mary took up the telephone in order to call her accountant in Seattle. Tom began to excuse himself, but Mary waved him back to his seat. "This is just some tax-return shit I need to ask about," she said, briskly punching in the fourteen or so digits.

All told, Mary was on the phone some twenty minutes, and although he could not discern the exact subject matter, he clearly saw that it prompted alternating waves of anger and disbelief in Mary, punctuated by withering imprecations.

When she was done, she let the receiver fall from on high into its cradle so it clattered. "Fuck," Mary said and sighed. "Shit and fuck."

"What's going on?" Tom asked.

"It's insane, just totally insane." Mary had craned her neck back and upward, as though to stare at the ceiling or simply collapse backward. She let rip a further sigh.

"But what happened?"

"It seems," Mary said, still addressing the beams and *cotto* above her, "that I owe all these taxes which I can't pay."

"Can't pay?"

"Well, I can pay them, but I wouldn't have much left afterward: just the house and a little extra to live on for a while."

"How can that be?" Tom said. "I mean, you're—"

"Rich?" Mary interrupted, now looking straight at him. "Not any more."

"I don't get it. I mean, I know Noumena's down a little. But it's not like it tanked, right?"

"No. But Critic.com's apparently a different story."

"But they got bought, right? By—what it's called?—Floozy.net."

"Woozel. Which is, as we speak, pretty much, worthless."

"Shit, I'm sorry. But you mainly had Noumena, right?"

"Yeah," said Mary. "But there's a certain weird chain—a conflation, if you want—of events. I have to pay the taxes on what the stock was worth when I received it, even if it's pretty much worthless now."

"Even though you didn't spend the money or anything?"

"Or even sell the stock. It's some weird thing in the tax law." Mary paused. "I hate America."

"So what are you going to do?"

"Fire the accountant. Alex can keep him if he wants."

"So is Alex . . . in the same situation?"

"No," said Mary. "I gave him stock and he sold it last year. At the peak, I suppose. Now it's in Swedish treasury bills or whatever."

"So he could . . ."

"Bail me out? No way. I don't want his charity."

"It was your charity that he got it from."

"I don't care," Mary said. "You know what the accountant said? I guess it was after I flamed him. He said, 'Well, it's not like you *earned* this money.'"

"What a dick."

"And the point is, I did earn it. I ate shit for it, for three whole years."

"True," said Tom. "So what are you going to do?"

"I don't know. But you know what? That . . . epiphany I had the other day? I feel better prepared to handle this because of it. It'll work out."

"It's still very sad. This, and everything else."

"That it is," Mary allowed. Tom wanted just then to comfort her, and, truth to be told, for her to comfort him. Mary felt this too, or something akin to it. At any rate, they put their arms around one another and exchanged a great embrace like long-parted siblings, like fraternal twins.

They pulled apart and Tom said, "So, what now?"

"I think we should get very drunk."

"Okay. That seems reasonable."

By ten o'clock, every light in the Villa Donatello was burning, as Tom and Mary floated, talking and drinking, through its every room, not least the cantina, from which Tom had lately fetched a fourth bottle of Pinot Grigio.

They had washed up ashore in Alex's studio, sitting before the double nude on the couch upon which they had once posed together.

"It's really not bad," Mary said.

"No, it's not," said Tom.

"But at the level of relationships it's neither here nor there. Whether he's a good painter or not."

"I suppose so."

"I mean, all you have to do is sit here and look around this room, Alex's little holy-of-holies. It just reeks of self-satisfaction. It's not even messy, like a painter's studio is supposed to be. There's no paint on the floor. Do you think there was no paint on Pollock's floor?"

"No," said Tom.

"So there you are. It's so fucking pretentious, pretending to be Mr. Casual, when he's full of these . . . *overweening* ideas about himself, about his fucking talent. I can't live with that. I don't need it. Does that make sense?"

"Sure. I guess."

"Because that's why we need to be apart."

"But you're apart because of Jens. That was just . . . the precipitating event. The serendipitous . . . whatsits."

Mary stood and went to Alex's table, where Tom had put the bottle down. But rather than refill her glass, she picked up Alex's camera, switched it on, and scanned through the pictures it contained. She brought it over to Tom. "Here's that little bitch of his," she said.

"That's a bit strong."

"Well, I don't know her name."

"We can call her Angelina."

"That's such a piece of . . . male sentimentality."

"Whatever," said Tom.

Mary looked over to the double nude and scowled. "Hey, we can do better than that. With this." She held out the camera. "Come on. It'll be fun." She stood on one leg and pulled off a shoe. "Wait till he comes back and finds these on his camera."

"Mary, I don't think this is a good idea."

"It's a *wonderful* idea. And so postmodern. I mean, commenting on the painting with the camera that took the picture that made the painting." Mary gestured for him to get up. "Come on, Tom, it's transgressive." Mary was now removing her jeans.

"I don't know. To be really frank, I don't feel comfortable naked."

"Well, you should. Wright says so. I say so. It's not like we haven't seen each other." Mary put her hand under Tom's chin and smiled at him. "It's *okay*. We're best friends, all right? Besides, it's hot out."

"All right," Tom said softly.

"So get undressed and stand over there, by the window. Do a pose." Tom complied as Mary continued. "Something classic. The David. The Donatello—what's his name—the Medusa guy."

Tom now stood as Mary instructed, utterly naked, seeming very large to Mary but very small to himself. "Wait," she said. "I've got it—Saint Sebastian. It's perfect."

"What'll we do for arrows?"

"Those you have to imagine. But you can do the pose. You have to act it. Put your hands behind you. I could find some rope and tie them behind you."

"No, really, that's okay."

"All right, just pretend. Now you have to kind of slump from the waist. Hang your head."

"Jesus, Mary."

"Jesus *and* Mary," she said. "We'll get to that." She raised the camera to her face and said, "Ready? Say Oscar Wilde."

Mary took two shots and lowered the camera. She reviewed them on the screen at the camera back. "Superb," she said. "Now you be the photographer."

"So how do you want to pose?"

"That's your decision. You're the artist. I'm just the model."

Tom walked towards her and he realized he no longer minded

being naked, that the context in which they were naked together just now was not sexual but merely recreational, almost athletic, like being at the gym. He considered his options and at last said, "The angel. Rilke's angel."

"What does she look like?" asked Mary. "What does she do?"

"She's beautiful. But terrible. Awe-inspiring. It's like the beauty that kills. Or almost."

"Sounds like more weird boy-think to me. But what the hell."

Mary stood very still, feet just apart, closed her eyes, and shook her head and wrists as if to clear her mind in preparation for some great feat. Her eyes remained closed but she slowly raised her arms up, level with her shoulders, and then a little higher. Her hands were outstretched, palms downward, in the manner of some priest or magus casting a spell or bestowing a blessing. She stood in this way, stock still, for some time.

Tom was stunned, so stunned it took him some moments to remember he was supposed to take a picture. He had expected Mary to treat his idea for a pose as a joke, but she had taken it seriously, more than seriously. She was awe-inspiring, and very beautiful. He pressed the shutter once and then again. He realized he was becoming aroused.

"That's good. It's great, in fact," Tom said. "You can stop." But she did not, not right away. Then she opened her eyes, as if she were awaking from a trance. She smiled, broadly and angelically.

"How did you do that?" Tom said and, turning his back to Mary, began to look for his underpants.

"I just did it. Or maybe it comes naturally. Because I really am the angel." Mary caught sight of Tom clutching his underwear, and said, "Hey, hold on. I want to do one more. Together. With the timer."

Tom dropped the underpants. He thought Mary might be right, that she might indeed be the angel, Rilke's and his own. "You mean do a pose like we did for Alex?" he asked.

"No, that's a little obvious. And unoriginal. Let me think."

Mary strode over to the couch and sat down. "Could you get me some more wine? For yourself too, of course."

Tom fetched their glasses and filled them from the bottle on Alex's table. He walked over to Mary and handed her her glass. He was not anxious to sit down beside her, but he was less comfortable still with the thought of remaining standing there, his genitals exactly at her eye level. So he sat down, feeling that at least if he did so, the shaking in his limbs and breathing that he was sure must be visible would be a little less obvious.

"So do I get to see?" Mary said suddenly.

"See what?"

"The pictures, silly."

"Oh, yeah." Tom stood up and went back to the table to get the camera. He returned and began to fumble with the controls. "I don't know how . . ."

"Let me," Mary said. "Oh, this is really kind of *good.* I mean, the light's terrible. But it's very flattering." She stopped, and patted Tom gently on his thigh. "Thank you."

"It's you, the pose, really. That makes it."

"Well, thank you."

Tom did not immediately reply. Then he felt that at this particular interstice of the night—the heat, the light inside, the dark outside, their sitting together just so, having achieved this photograph, this one beautiful thing, together—he might make a leap.

"I've always," Tom said, "seen you that way."

"As an angel?"

"As what you are. In the photo, in that pose." Tom knew his voice had begun to quaver. He did not care. He only feared that Mary would laugh, that she would say something like she might normally say.

"Well, that's hardly—" she began, and then halted. "I'll just say thank you. That's very . . . kind. I won't say any more.

Because, under the circumstances, I might cry. I don't feel very beautiful or good. Not really."

"You are to me."

"You'd better stop now," Mary said, but in some way she did not want him to. "So you really saw me that way, all this time?"

"Well, since coming here. And before, in other ways. But you must have known that."

"No. I never imagined."

"I guess I thought you'd just know."

"Well, I'm not very observant," Mary said. "But what about your reading my stuff? You didn't think I was going to believe what Alex said?"

"Actually, I did."

"Well, sorry. And I don't mind either. It seems kind of trivial now."

"Why now?"

"Just because of all that's happened. Disasters. Crazy things. Things I never thought would happen."

"You mean the money?" asked Tom. "You and Alex?"

"That and more."

Tom was silent, and then he put his hands on his naked thighs, looking at the floor. "So are you fucking Wright?"

"Please don't say fuck," Mary responded. "And no, of course not. Even though it's none of your business."

"I thought we were talking openly. And, anyway, it *is* my business," Tom said. "Would it be your business if Alex was fucking little Angelina?"

"So is he?"

"I don't know. It kind of occurred to me."

"I wouldn't be surprised, at this point," said Mary.

"Well, then to hell with both of them." Tom stopped to consider, and then went on. "Anyway, now we're closer. That's seems more important."

Mary looked at Tom as the angel might have done, were her eyes open, were she not so forbidding. She said, "And what if we were closer still?"

"That would be good," said Tom.

After they were done, Mary raised her face up to Tom and pressed her lips to his ear. She began to giggle, and then she said, "You know, when I met you, I thought you were cute, but I was sure you were gay."

"I was, in retrospect. I'm gay now. But I make exceptions. For close friends."

"I'm glad you did. It was nice."

"I'd wanted to for a long time," Tom said. "But of course I never thought it would happen."

"Because of my being with Alex?"

"That, and thinking you'd never be interested in me that way."

"What way is *that* way?"

"Sexually."

"Well, I'm interested in you in every way. This is just another . . . aspect."

"It could make things kind of . . . complicated," said Tom.

"Oh, I hope so," Mary said. She moved from underneath him so that they were now adjacent to one another on the sofa, still lying tightly bound together, Tom's head cradled on Mary's arm. "That's what makes life interesting," she said. "'You must change your life,' right? Make it into art."

Tom was not sure he wanted to hear this from Mary just now, although he felt it remained a great truth. He was considering voicing his perplexity (for what else are lovers' post-coital conversations for?), but he felt Mary's hand on his penis. "This is nice," he heard her say.

"*That,* or *this,* in general?" asked Tom.

"In general, I suppose. But this"—and here she gave his penis, already puffing itself up, a gentle squeeze—"is *very* nice, too."

"So is it as big as Alex's?"

"God, Tom, do we have to do this?" Mary said, and laughed.

"Sorry."

"Oh, never mind. Just let me see." Mary slid her head down Tom's chest and onto his belly. "Bigger, actually."

"But I don't have a big dick."

"Well, neither does Alex. So there you are." And with that she took his penis between her lips.

Mary let it loll in her mouth, let it bob upward as it sprang to full tumescence, and then she pulled away. "Hey," she said, "we forgot to take the other picture."

"We got diverted."

"Well, I still want to. Maybe not just now," said Mary, "But it ought to be part of our collaboration."

Tom began to offer some assent to this, but Mary held her finger to her mouth and said, "Wait. Listen. Somebody's out there."

After holding themselves still for a moment, it became clear that there was indeed someone out there, someone apparently banging a hard object against the front door with increasing impatience.

"Shit," Mary said. "Quick. Get dressed."

They thrust their flushed and damp bodies into their clothes and bounded shoeless down the hall to the *salone*. At the vestibule, Mary took a deep breath, and cracked opened the door. Tom craned for a view over her shoulder.

Before them stood two police officers, *carabinieri,* wearing tight-waisted tunics and jodhpurs with high black boots to match. Their peaked officers' caps bore a medallion, what seemed to be a globe with flames erupting from it

"Yes?" said Mary, and then remembered to speak Italian. *Good evening.*

And to you, madam. We are sorry to disturb you, but there has been a call registering concern about your home. You are the proprietor here?

It's of me, yes.

Good. And everything is as it should be?

Without doubt. There is a chaos?

Well, with all the lights ablaze and at this hour of the night, there was concern that something might be amiss.

No. Nothing entirely.

And then, things were seen—through the windows, I suppose, on account of the illumination—that also raised concern, that were unusual, out of the ordinary.

Well, I can make you insurance. Everything is fine. Stately. Banal. As it always transpires here.

There are just the two of you residing here?

Normally, there is another. My . . . husband, yet he is away. In Seattle, in America.

Oh, Noumena.

Yes, it is there.

Then your husband works for Noumena corporation of Seattle?

No. He was doing there once. I also. Also my friend.

And why did you come here? It's rather odd, isn't it?

We come to paint. And write. And for the beauty. To live in beautiful Tuscany.

The officer appeared to ignore this remark, and turned to Tom, began to question him in Italian; but, as Tom's incomprehension made itself apparent, he switched to English.

"So you also say that everything is okay here, in the villa?"

"Oh, sure. It's fine," Tom said. He thought he should say something offhand to reinforce the air of normalcy he was attempting to convey, even as he practically shook in fear of this man and his silent back-up (darkly handsome specimens of Tuscan butch, Tom had to admit, less like cops than leather fantasies). "It's still really hot, isn't it?" Tom added.

The officer ignored this and turned back to Mary. "Let's just continue in English," he said. "So, let us recount and consider."

"I don't understand," Mary said, her confidence bolstered by being able to converse in English. "You see that everything's fine. So has there been a complaint? Or can we finish?"

"No complaint. Merely an inquiry."

"So there's no problem. The matter's done with."

"Of course, madam. It is of no consequence. This is not America. Everything is permitted. I have just only one word for you: discretion."

"Fine. *Capito*. But who called you?" Mary said.

"That I cannot disclose. A neighbour perhaps, wanting assurance that you were safe, that all was as it should be."

"So what's not permitted is to know who one's accuser is?"

"Oh, there is no accusation. Merely our wanting to *controllare*—to chuck out the situation, as you say in America."

"Fine. I guess."

"So merely remember, discretion, all right?"

"Of course," Mary said.

Then we bid you goodnight.

And we are the same.

Mary closed the door. "Shit," she said. "Shit and shit."

"Do you think they'll come back?"

"Probably not. Unless they have nothing else to do. Now that they've satisfied their curiosity."

"So do you think they saw us," said Tom, "through the studio window?"

"No, they said somebody called. So I suppose somebody did."

"Wright can't see over to here, can he?"

"Not at that distance," said Mary. "But I wouldn't put it past him."

They said nothing more. They did not recommence what they had started just before the *carabinieri* arrived, nor, as Tom had rather been hoping, did they sleep together in the same bed that night. And although Mary was surely right that they would hear no more from the authorities, it seemed to them both, as they lay awake in their separate beds, that the villa had been in some manner rendered less safe, was now exposed to elements more unnerving than the beating down of the heat and malign stars.

In the morning, Tom lay awake a long time before deciding that it would be okay—not *inappropriate,* given their new intimacy—if he went into Mary's room; if he perhaps even climbed into her bed and napped with her a while.

He opened her door as quietly as possible, but a voice came from the bed, saying, "Who's that?"

"Me. I mean, Tom."

"Oh, yeah."

Tom walked over to the edge of the bed. "Can I get in?" he asked.

"Uh, sure," Mary said. "The more the merrier."

"Okay." He climbed in next to her, sidling up against her hip and back, draping his arm over her. He had held Wright this way, but Mary's body contained some opposite principle to Wright's; not merely the softness of female skin and subcutaneous padding, but a kind of yielding and expansive depth that went on extending itself almost infinitely, whereas Wright's body was sharply focused, contained and boundaried, austere as a tower.

Tom was thinking these things (or at least forming their impressions) and was beginning to fall off to sleep when Mary spoke. "Hey, did all that happen? The *carabinieri* and all?"

"I think so. That," Tom added, "and everything else."

"Oh, yeah. It was quite an evening."

This remark displayed a neutrality that made Tom a little anxious, made him wonder if for Mary their having sex had "ruined our friendship" as women were wont to say.

Mary meanwhile spoke no more, merely lay there as Tom held her. Finally, he could no longer contain himself.

"So, you and me," he said, "what have we done?"

Mary loosed herself and rolled over to face him. "I don't know," she said, "but I want to do it again."

So they did. Later, as the day and the days thereafter took on a little of their customary form and business—of drinking coffee, of reading and writing, of going down the hill into the inferno to shop, of watching the gardener go about his endless labours outside—Tom had some time to reflect. Of course, he and Mary were also making love two or three times a day, more at her instigation than his.

Still, he began to think, to see if there were, like a shirt-tail hanging out, ramifications trailing him. Mary, in contrast, was past worrying about Alex, but Tom had never before thought beyond the point of the leap, the declaration of his feeling and whatever resulted from it. He had never calculated the equal and opposite force that would recoil on him and Alex when he and Mary came together.

Tom knew Mary was her own master, that she had been determined to sever her bonds to Alex. So technically he could not be said to have betrayed Alex, although he could not but admit that Alex was unlikely to be pleased by what he had done.

When Tom was with Mary, this preoccupation disappeared; indeed, it almost seemed that one of the aims of their lovemaking was to rub away every trace of Alex that clung to Mary. But, as soon as they were done, it reappeared and sometimes itched uncomfortably, as when Alex, with great joy and satisfaction, called to report he had located Jens Hammershøi's canvases.

At some point, perhaps five days after their first sexual encounter, Tom came to the conclusion that the only way his and Mary's affair could justify itself in his mind was if it genuinely was a relationship; if love, or something like it, were involved. But the truth was, while he liked Mary as much as ever, he did not love her. In fact, the fascination and longing he had felt for her from a distance were pretty well spent once they had been intimate a half-dozen times, once he had seen how her beauty's effects were achieved, once he had unpacked the constructions of her body.

Tom did not mind when Mary came to him, as she did frequently and of her own volition, but the form and content of their fucking was increasingly abstract for him. Mary wanted to open new avenues, follow rivulets and caves to their outlets and depths, but Tom's curiosity about what they might discover together was waning. Her body, in fact, was a problem. Her breasts and bottom, their florid, baroque overripeness, perplexed him in particular. He thought there was something he ought to be doing to or with or about them, but he didn't know what. He wanted parts and appendages more contained, the Bauhaus line of a man's lean ass, the pointed assertion of a hardened cock. He wanted, he feared, Wright Turner's in particular.

Meanwhile, Mary was by every measure as content, even happy, as she had been since her arrival in Italy. Tom swore he had heard her singing to herself, and when Alex called, as he did every five days or so, she was even cordial. The dolorous telephone conversations with the accountant and the stockbroker, which revealed that after taxes she would be left with the villa and little else, did not touch her optimism for any great length of time.

She had, in fact, taken psychic as well as corporeal shelter in the villa, had wrapped it around her tightly like a shawl in the deepening conviction that, as long as it was hers, she was safe—she and the baby and Tom and her book. Just in the last week she'd put aside Wright's de' Pazzi manuscript and returned to her original project, the novel called *The Villa Donatello,* the immense, essential thing.

At the end of the month, Alex called to say he was finally coming back. He had attempted to get a Seattle gallery director noted for representing painters of Jens's school and generation to mount a retrospective exhibition of his paintings, but to no avail. ("That fucking old queen said, 'Essentially, they're *trite.* I simply can't do anything with them,'" Alex fumed.) Tom had heretofore believed that Alex's homecoming would mark a natural end to his and Mary's affair, but when he asked her outright what she thought might happen, she only said, "You'll see. It'll all work out."

This only alarmed Tom more. He wanted to ask Wright to help him figure out what to do, but saw that Wright would only laugh, that he would needle him about the irony, the poetic justice. Beyond that, without any need to consult Wright or anyone else, he saw most of all that, to save himself, he would have to break Mary's heart, the existence of which he had only just lately discovered. And with that he went down to Alex's studio and erased the pictures he and Mary had made on the digital camera.

10.

Purgatorio

Alex came home about seven in the evening the first week of July, shattered by eighteen hours of flight (during which, supine in business class, he drank vodka heedlessly), layovers, trains, and the grinding taxi ride up the Bellosguardo hill. As soon as he entered the Villa Donatello, his ears began to ring. It seemed to him this must the echoing residue of all that forward motion, of turbines and wheels, but then he thought the house itself was vibrating, shaking from the day's heat or thrumming at an unaccustomed frequency.

Alex set his bag down in the hall by the door to the *salone* and called out, "Hey, hi. Anybody home?"

There was no reply. He looked into the kitchen. A mug sat on the table; the aluminum coffee pot stood on the stove.

He returned to the hall and called out again. Then he heard footfalls in the corridor above him, growing louder, turning to scuffs on the stairs. He took himself to the bottom of the steps and looking up saw, now halting on the half-landing as their eyes locked, Tom Hirsch.

"Oh, it's you," Tom said. "I'd been sleeping."

"Didn't mean to wake you."

"Oh, it was just a nap. Anyway, you're back." Tom put his hands into his pockets and began to descend the remainder of the steps. "Do you want something to eat?" he continued. "Do you want a coffee or a glass of wine?"

"No, that's okay," said Alex, and reached out to shake Tom's hand, which Tom slowly prised free from his pocket and offered, bending forward, as though he were pitching it at a ring-toss post.

Alex let the hand fall and said, "So where is everybody?"

"You mean Mary?"

"Yeah, I guess. Unless anybody else has moved in."

"No," Tom said. "Well, the girl that was going to model for you came by."

"Maddalena?"

"She didn't give her name. We were calling her Angelina."

"Well, it must have been Maddalena," said Alex. "Shit. I suppose Mary was put out by that."

"She wasn't thrilled."

"Oh well. I'm already pretty deep in the doghouse. Or dog shit. Whatever."

Tom said nothing. "So where's Mary?" Alex continued.

"I think she's at Wright's."

"That figures. She's been over there a lot, I suppose."

"No, not really. Not for a long time, maybe not since you left."

"Oh," said Alex. "Well, yeah, I guess she wouldn't want to be pushing you off your own turf."

"Actually, Wright and I aren't together any more."

"Oh, I guess you told me that. But I'm sorry."

"It's okay."

"So you're all right with it." Tom nodded, but offered nothing more. Alex went on. "I suppose I ought to wait up for Mary. Is she going to be late?"

"I don't know."

"I'm so fucking tired. But I ought to eat something. Is there some cheese or something in the fridge?"

"I think there's some pecorino and some prosciutto, San Daniele, I think."

"That sounds good," Alex said. "Then I'll go upstairs and get some—" Alex stopped. "This is stupid, but everything is stupid lately, okay?" Tom nodded. "Do you think Mary's going to be pissed if I sleep in our bed?"

Tom shook his head from side to side as if he were trying to clear his ears. "I don't know. That's too complicated for me."

"But her mood—is she lightening up a little? Towards me?"

"I don't know. Maybe. Maybe not."

"So," Alex pressed, "maybe I'd be better off sleeping in the studio? If nothing's changed."

"I don't know, Alex. She's full of surprises. That's all I know."

"Okay. Sorry. But it's tricky, you know?"

"Sure."

"Well, I guess I'll get a snack and crash for a while. So, hey, I'll see you in the morning."

"Yeah," Tom said, and turned and began to ascend the stairs. He turned around. "And welcome home, okay?"

"You bet," said Alex.

Alex went to the kitchen and found, as Tom indicated, cheese and prosciutto. He made himself a plate and took it, together with a glass and an open bottle of Montepulciano, down the long hall to his studio.

Everything was as he had left it a month ago. The double nude stood on the easel. It's still good, Alex thought. It's a fucking good painting. Mary was really pretty in it.

He looked over to the couch and realized he would need some bedding, or at least a pillow. So he set down his plate, bottle, and glass on the painting table and returned to the corridor, back towards the kitchen, to the stairs. At the landing, the notion struck him that he ought to take his shoes off to avoid disturbing Tom; to avoid, he could not but feel, detection. That, despite the fact his shoes were his customary Italian sneakers.

Still shod, he reached the upstairs. To his left, he saw light—the thin evening light of a summer evening, abetted by a lamp—

under Tom's door; to his right, opposite his and Mary's bedroom door, was the wardrobe where the linen was kept.

Alex crept down the hall towards the wardrobe. He opened the door and found a pillow atop a pile of winter blankets. It was a cheap pillow, filled with some artificial crud, not down. They'd bought it at Ikea when they first arrived in Florence, when they'd rented the apartment in the Oltrarno. Alex tucked it under his arm as a boy carries his teddy bear, and turned around. He looked into his and Mary's bedroom.

The shutters were opened as well as the windows. Mary must have opened them before she went out, in the late afternoon, before she walked over to the Villa Castellani. The bed was unmade, or rather, the sheet that constituted the bedclothes was tangled and knotted at the bottom of the bed. There were two empty wineglasses, one on either nightstand.

Mary must be changing, easing up, Alex thought. It wasn't like her not to make the bed, to let dishes accumulate.

Back in his studio, Alex tossed the pillow onto the sofa and went to the painting table to retrieve his meal. He filled his glass, drank a sip from it, and then picked up the camera. He switched it on. There was Maddalena. Or Angelina.

He toggled through the shots on the camera until he came back to the first, the one posed most closely to Ruskin's description of the Turin girl. Might as well get started soon, Alex thought. Get painting right away. Best way to ride out the impending shit-storm that would begin when he and Mary saw each other in the morning.

Alex switched off the camera. He took his plate and glass to the sofa and sat down. The studio was getting dark. The light outside must be beginning to fade, to go orange and lavender as it did here; only here, as far as Alex knew, the clean Florentine light of noon became the streaky pastel light—Pontormo's light, he thought—of the guttering sun. After he ate and drank a couple of glasses of wine, he lay down. His ears were still ringing, but in only a little while, the noise blended with the cicadas outside, and Alex fell asleep.

It had been nearly a month since Mary had seen Wright Turner. She had not, it was true, even so much as called him, but one did not call Wright, one called *upon* him, knocked on his door. That was how things were done at the Villa Castellani, very much as they had been done one hundred and twenty years ago.

But Wright had called, on the telephone. Not the least bit sheepishly, he remarked it had been some weeks since he'd seen anyone from the Villa Donatello and that he merely wondered "what had become of you all." He then suggested that Mary might drop by and bring him up-to-date.

Mary agreed. She had questions, grievances, and perhaps a revelation of her own. And by seeing Wright at the very hour that Alex was due home, she would avoid giving Alex the impression that she took any interest in his return.

Wright greeted her with apparent warmth, in an almost courtly manner, steering her to the couch with a hand lightly beneath her forearm. On the coffee table the wine, the nuts, and olives were already attendant in their places.

"So good to see you," Turner said. "I'd almost feared something had happened to you all. To you and Thomas and Alex."

Mary wasted no time. "So did the *carabinieri,* apparently."

"Oh, you've been investigated?" Turner filled their glasses.

"They came by a few weeks ago. In the middle of the night. Tom and I were up late. They claimed they were concerned about all the lights being on." Mary picked up an olive. "Of course, you really can't see any lights from the road. So I suspect someone—a neighbour, perhaps—sent them." With that, Mary decapitated the olive with her front teeth, flayed it of its remaining flesh, and set the pit down on the edge of the coffee table.

"How curious," said Turner. "Of course, they do tend to drop by unexpectedly, simply to make their presence felt. Generally, one slips them fifty thousand lire and they go away happily enough. But I suspect there was nothing to it."

"I suppose so."

"And better them than the *Finanza*—the fiscal police—digging through all your private affairs. You are being a good girl about your taxes and so forth, I hope?"

Mary did not want to get diverted from the business at hand, but this reminder of her difficulties left her feeling a little weak. "I'm having a little difficulty with the IRS back home," she admitted.

"Oh, nothing dire, surely?"

"It's a major hassle. They want a lot of money. But I have the villa," she said quite firmly. "We'll get by."

"Perhaps you should send Alex and Thomas out to work. You've supported them all this time," said Turner with an upward lilt at the end of the phrase that was almost tender. "It's rather the least they could do, don't you think?"

This blend of pity and praise, of noting her past magnanimity while lamenting her present undeserved plight, was a powerful solvent against Mary's resolve. "Oh, perhaps," she said. "Anyway, I think there are going to be some changes in the . . . composition of the household."

"Oh, really?"

"Well, Alex and I . . ."

"I can't say I'm surprised. Or only that I'm surprised it hasn't happened sooner."

"He's been away. In Seattle."

"Oh, he fled?" said Turner. "Desertion *and* mental cruelty."

"Not exactly. He needed to go settle the estate of an old teacher of his. Or that's what he said. In a way, it gave me a chance to think things through. To see that I'm really better off without him."

"I suspect you will be." Turner paused. "And what of Thomas?"

"Oh, he'll stay."

"Oh, of course. You know, I've missed him. He went off in a huff three weeks ago and I haven't heard boo from him since. But doubtless you know all that."

"He said you two had broken up."

"'Broken up.'" Turned smiled. "How very much like him to say that. With his adolescent conception of love. That's what created the breach really. He couldn't let us simply be friends and lovers. He wouldn't let it be." Turner shook his head. "He insisted on formalizing it, on calling it love."

"Amore perchè anticipare la nostra fine," Mary said, not quite knowing why.

"Well, exactly," said Turner. "That's exactly the point. Which was lost on him, of course."

"It was a graffito. We all saw it on the wall outside the Porta Romana. Months ago."

"Tom didn't exactly take it to heart. He just threw himself into it."

"Into what?" asked Mary.

"Into the pursuit of love. Despite what your graffito said."

"Despite? I don't understand."

"Well, what did you take it to mean?"

"Oh, I just took a guess at translating it," Mary said. "I came up with 'Love shapes our purpose' or whatever. We liked it, as a kind of motto for artists. And lovers, of course."

Turner had sat back, but now he leaned forward, shaking his head. "I'm afraid your Italian isn't quite solid yet. I think I'd render it 'Love anticipates our end.' In the sense of 'hastens our death.'"

"Well, I'm sure there can be multiple interpretations."

"Perhaps. But I've lived here fifty years. And it's more colloquial my way." Turner folded his hands. "You shouldn't feel badly. It takes a long time to learn the ropes."

Mary felt stupid, shamed. But she fought against it and said,

"You know, just when I'm getting to like you, you say something condescending."

"I don't think I condescended. I think you bristle easily."

"Well, you certainly are condescending about Tom."

"He rather invites it. So earnest and cocksure on the one hand and so utterly feckless on the other."

"He doesn't claim to have all the answers," said Mary. "That's kind of refreshing, if you ask me."

"He's an innocent."

"He's just open to things, to not knowing, to being awestruck, to falling in love with things."

"So he's a wide-eyed American," Turner said, "and you admire that. I thought you all came over to become Europeans."

"We came here to do our art."

"It's rather the same thing, I'd say."

"I wouldn't."

"Well then, why come here at all? Surely there's something here that's more conducive to making art. You can't have come here simply because you could—because you have the money."

"Well, apparently I don't have it any more," said Mary. "But yes, there's an atmosphere, a Jamesian atmosphere, I guess. I thought it would inspire me. And Alex likes the light."

"If it's Jamesian, then you came to lose your innocence, didn't you?" Turner said.

"Or to be ruined."

"You see, you're already talking like a European. You can't help it. The dust in these old place infects one with it." Turner paused, and Mary saw that he was taking up his glass for the first time. He gazed off towards the window where the evening was gathering itself, and said, as if to the setting sun, "Thomas, though, is incurable. He's more enamoured of all this than any of you, but it will never penetrate."

"Perhaps that's fortunate," said Mary. "He's good, you know. I would have said you really didn't deserve him."

"You could be right. I probably didn't," Turner said. "So what are you going to do with him? If he stays. If Alex goes."

"Oh, Alex will go. Maybe back to Seattle. It suits him—drinking and watching it rain, watching mould grow on everything. Or he could stay, set up housekeeping with his little Turin girl. He has the money."

"You told me. And how will you and Tom manage?"

"There'll be a little money left," Mary said. "There has to be. Then we'll figure something out. We'll plant a garden."

"And the child? The one you said you were determined to have?"

"It'll happen." Mary took up another olive and regarded it, adding very casually, "It may have already." She looked at Wright to see if and how this latter remark had registered.

It seemed to Mary that he was definitely off balance, a tarnish of surprise overlaying the silver of his customarily serene face. But he smiled, and with that was himself again. "Really?"

"Well, I'm not absolutely sure yet."

"Really? Now who—" and there Turner broke off and then, with a kind of rhythmic and escalating deliberation, began to laugh. "Oh, dear, dear Mary. This is so . . . piquant," he said, and resumed laughing.

"I suppose it's a little ironic—"

"Oh, just consider," Turner continued, as though Mary had said nothing, "Thomas is going to be a father. I suppose I could be the auntie. Or the grandma. Granny Wright. I suppose I should start knitting something." And here he tittered once more.

Mary tried to reassert herself. "I see the humour," she said (although she did not in the least), "but it's serious work, raising a child."

"Well, you'll doubtless need help," Turner said. "Thomas isn't the least bit maternal, never mind paternal—a complete narcissist."

"That doesn't mean he's selfish. Not intentionally."

"Even granting that, what will keep him there, with you? He *is* gay, after all."

"That's what I heard about you."

"As I said, I made exceptions," said Turner. "But trust me, this was just an experiment. He had a certain fascination with you which he found an opportunity to explore. That doesn't change his basic modus vivendi."

Mary was recovering a measure of the equilibrium she had lost in the gale of Turner's laughter. "You're being condescending again," she said. "Or at least presumptuous. I think I know Tom a little better than you. I've known him for six years."

"And I've slept with him. I know what he likes and wants. It's very clear."

"I've slept with him every day for the last three weeks. I'd say I must know a bit more."

"About his sexual tastes? Please, tell me," Turner said. "Tell me what you two do when he wants to be fucked, when he wants a cock in his mouth."

This seemed very cruel to Mary, and all the responses she was capable of mustering would, she knew, give Wright the satisfaction of branding her a homophobe. So she held, with great difficulty, her tongue. Finally, she said, "There's more to our relationship than that. Much more."

"Oh, now he's in love with you?" said Turner. "And here I thought it was me. He's certainly fickle. But then that was my original point."

"You can think what you want. I don't have to justify anything to you."

"Oh, please don't. But you ought to listen to me. We *are,* at least in my mind, friends. And there's something very sad about these situations where a straight woman conceives an interest in a gay man and thinks she's going to reform—"

"Now *that,*" Mary interrupted, "is really so fucking condescending. I don't care about these categories. Neither does Tom.

You don't get it. You think in these rigid ways, where everyone's sexuality is like . . . predestined, and they don't have any choices. When your own life proves just the opposite."

"I doubt my life proves anything. Except perhaps that the exception proves the rule."

"What about you and Mary McCarthy?"

Turner smiled very slightly. "I'm afraid that, strictly speaking, that never happened." He paused. "There have been women, of course, but not that particular woman."

"So you just said that to impress me?"

"It made rather a good story. A fair number of the things in my books fall into that category. It's postmodern, I'm told. Very avant-garde. Actually, Thomas explained that to me."

"I feel a little betrayed," Mary said.

"You feel betrayed? After taking up with *my* lover, without so much as a word."

"You're connecting things that aren't connected."

"'Only connect,' Forster said."

"I suppose you knew him."

"I met him," said Turner. "Well, I saw him at a party once." Turner took a drink from his glass. "Which is neither here nor there."

"No, it's not."

"All right," said Turner. "And I'm sorry if I overstepped somewhat in my remarks. But I would never want you to seem foolish. Or pathetic. It's the worst thing in the world, I think: being or seeming pathetic—I can't quite say which it is, being or seeming."

"Don't worry. It would never occur to me to be."

"It would never occur to anyone. That's the problem. All of a sudden, you are." Turner stopped. "Look," he said, "at me."

"It's not true. Why would you think that? Because you're old?"

"That's half of it. That, and having accomplished so little of what I thought I would when I was your age."

"I think that's the way it is for everyone. I suppose life's inevitably a disappointment. We die."

"Which is the most pathetic state of all," Turner said. "I think I thought I could avoid it, be above it. Because I didn't deserve it. Because my life would not be an ordinary life."

"It wasn't," said Mary. "It isn't."

"That's kind of you to say," Turner said. "May the same be true for you."

"I hope so. I'll try."

"Just don't be pathetic, please. Don't embarrass any of us, least of all me. I'll be watching."

"Like you were that night."

"Yes. If you insist."

"It's a bit pathetic to be looking in your neighbours' windows."

"I only saw the lights. In the distance," Turner said. "It was very late. I was worried. And bored."

Mary came home to a silent house. She saw Alex's bag in the hall. The light was on in the kitchen. She looked in. On the table, there was a piece of unfolded wrapping paper from the *salumeria* and a cork. Alex had been here.

She climbed the stairs, fearing she should would find him in their bed. He wasn't, of course. He was sleeping in his studio with his paintings.

Mary went into the bathroom and began to brush her teeth. She observed herself in the mirror, watched the foam of the toothpaste seep from the corners of her mouth. Wright Turner thinks I'm lovely, she thought. Lovely. That's what loving is to him. Looking at lovely things. But he doesn't love anyone.

But Tom adores me. And he's my friend, my only friend, really.

When she was done, she lay in bed and tried to sleep, steeling herself for what was to come.

* * *

Alex woke up at five in the morning, his body jolting to life, aware that by Seattle time it was well into happy hour. He lay on the couch for over an hour, watching the dawn bleach and then tint the ceiling.

His mind was activated. He wasn't worried—Alex did not worry, not ever—but he was much preoccupied, first, by what would transpire when he and Mary met; second, by an urgent need to paint, to get the Turin girl underway. Thus, he plotted the remainder of the day: he would fight with Mary, and when they were done, he would go down the hill and locate Maddalena.

At six-thirty, he rose from the couch and went to the kitchen. He made coffee and found last Sunday's London paper, with which he spent the next half-hour. Alex was, if not an Anglophobe, wary of English culture, of its dread of social and class embarrassment, which in the arts manifested itself in a terrible fear of being seen to like the wrong things. In the last dozen years, the infection had spread to New York, carried by English magazine editors and writers, and was now lapping at the West Coast, even at Seattle. That, more or less, was why he couldn't get Jens a show, why he had failed Jens.

Then Alex realized that Maddalena would have to wait, that first of all he needed to pick up Jens's canvases, which would now be at customs in Milan. He would have to drive up there, perhaps not today, but tomorrow. He could take Tom with him, and together they could load everything onto the roof rack of the car.

Alex looked up just then, and there, rising before him like a basilisk, stood Mary. He took her in with almost a gasp. She merely stared at him.

"Hey, hi," he said.

"Hi," she returned.

"So," Alex said, now breathing again, "how have you been?"

"Fine. Can I get some of that coffee?"

"Sure." Alex got up and went to the stove. There were mugs

hanging on the wall. He took one down and poured coffee into it. He saw that his hand was shaking. Jet lag, he thought. Just then, Mary's voice shot out, into his back, or so it seemed. "So how was your trip?"

Alex turned around and brought the coffee to her. "Fine," he said, and retreated a little towards the stove. "Long. Uneventful."

"Did you go in coach?"

"Business."

"It's kind of expensive," Mary said. "Kind of a waste."

"It's comfortable. And the booze is free."

"I doubt you could drink enough to cover the difference between that and coach."

"I'll have to try harder," said Alex, and he realized he must be feeling a little better; that he and Mary must be slipping back into their old groove, getting in synch with each other. He took a few steps forward.

"We better talk," Mary said.

Fuck, Alex thought, and began to move backwards before he took possession of himself and said, "Yeah, I suppose we should."

"Not here," said Mary. "Not with Tom around. Outside, in the garden."

Alex followed Mary down the steps leading from the kitchen past the cantina and out under the pergola where they ate in warm weather. The vegetation had filled in immensely while he'd been away, but the wisteria was no longer in bloom. Mary sat down at the table with her mug, and Alex took a seat opposite her.

"Look," he said, taking a large breath, "I'm really sorry about everything. About dissing Wright. About leaving. But I was . . . incapacitated. I mean, I *loved* Jens. I had to go."

"More than you loved me, apparently," said Mary, then realizing that she had offered a motion that was, for her, no longer under debate.

"It might have seemed that way. But it didn't mean that at all," Alex responded. Mary was more than dimly aware that Alex was trying awfully hard, but from that she extrapolated that he must be open to reason; that he would see, without protest, the point of the case she was going to make.

Mary proceeded. "Alex, it's all moved beyond that. Too far beyond that to just say 'Oh, I'm sorry' and go back to how we were."

"Why?"

"Things got set in motion. Things aren't the same. I'm a different person."

"I'm not," said Alex. "I'm the same guy. The one that loves you. A couple of weeks away doesn't change that."

"It was more than a couple of weeks."

"Okay, a month if you want. What's that out of six fucking years?"

"It's neither here nor there—"

"What's with this 'neither here nor there' shit?" Alex broke in. "*Everything's* either here or there. Or someplace. Otherwise, it doesn't fucking exist."

"Maybe that's it. It doesn't exist—you and me. Not any more."

Alex's penitence had transmuted to anger. "And you get to decide that, unilaterally."

"Keep your voice down," Mary said. "Yes, I get to decide that, for me."

"This is totally fucked. I mean, you've taken one or two trivial incidents and turned them into this whole . . . indictment."

"They were just symptomatic, Alex, of how things really were between us. It was a wake-up call."

"That's just the spin you put on it. It's just a point of view. You're not really *looking*. At all the years of being great together, of what we made together."

Mary had put down her cup and rested her hand on the table,

halfway across, towards Alex. She withdrew it a little, in case he tried to take it. "I don't think it really amounts to all that much," she said, more quietly than she might have intended. "I mean, we had fun. We amused ourselves. We were good consumers."

"Oh, come on, Mary. What about this? This house. The whole thing here. You're writing a novel. I'm painting. Tom's working on something or other. At least he's come out. So how is it so lousy? What's missing?"

"This doesn't matter now either," Mary said. "But you know what was missing."

Alex looked away, and when he returned his gaze to Mary she saw that his eyes were tearing, or at least were red. "Look, okay. We'll do it. I'll get the thing reversed. Or we'll adopt. Or you can get inseminated, okay? So now what's missing?"

Mary looked down at the hand she'd retrieved, that was sheltering by her breasts. "Don't make me say it, Alex," she said.

"Say what?" Alex's voice was rising again. "Do I have to guess? Is it fucking here or fucking there?"

Mary's hand tightened against itself, made a fist. "It's here. Right here," she said. "I don't love you any more, Alex."

"Oh, Mary, that's beside the point. You don't love anyone, not really. But we were perfect. We were art."

"Maybe that's the problem. For me anyway," Mary said. "Or maybe I want to try . . . the other thing."

"What—love?" Alex laughed.

"Don't laugh at me."

"I'm not laughing at you. It's just the whole situation." Alex paused. "So, what's the deal? You're going to meet someone else? Or you already did?" Alex had thrown this last phrase out as a piece of incredulity, a far-fetched hypothesis, but even before Mary could speak, it was taking shape before him. "So you are . . ." he began.

"It's neither—it's my business. It doesn't affect us—how I feel—either way."

"Well, I think I'm kind of entitled to know."

"You're not entitled to anything like that. From me. Or of me. Trying to control me."

Alex gave a great and bitter laugh of disbelief. "Control you? I have never fucking controlled you for one fucking minute. This is just bizarre."

"It seems that way from your point of view, like you said. From your fucking *perspective*."

"No, come on, this is way past that. This is—"

Mary stood and said firmly, "No, this isn't getting us anywhere, Alex. We should stop. Or talk about practical matters."

"For example?"

"Well, about living arrangements. About you moving—"

Alex stood up. "Are you trying to make me hate you? Is that the deal here?"

"Look, let's just stop. For now."

Alex continued, smiling oddly, self-mockingly. "I don't think I've ever really hated anybody before. It'd be something to try. I never had the opportunity, I guess."

Mary meant to merely walk away, but she said, "Maybe you lacked the conviction, the guts."

"That's so fucking cruel, Mary. But what the hell. It proves you haven't changed. It's something to hang on to." Mary had reached the steps that went back inside the house. "It's a little thread of hope," Alex called to her. "You'll see."

Tom had been lying awake in his bed and heard voices, rising over and disappearing beneath the ticking sound—birds, insects, cars and *motorini,* the rustle of brittle leaves against lizard scales—of the Val d'Arno on morning simmer, with some hours to go before the hiss and rattle of the midday boil. He heard isolated words, but no sentences or real complete phrases, and so they floated up to him, contextless, and popped just outside his window like bubbles or balloons: "loved," "everything's," "sixfucking," "love," "long," "missing," "anyone," "perfect," "control," "perspective," "hated," "hell," "thread," and, at the very end, one whole phrase that Tom made out as "you'll see."

So Mary and Alex were talking already, about their issues. They hadn't wasted any time. Maybe they'd even pretty much resolved things. Not to stay together, of course, but to negotiate Alex's peaceful withdrawal from the Villa Donatello.

As Tom imagined this, it made him feel more and more comfortable about going downstairs and getting some coffee. He and Mary had agreed that she would not mention their new intimacy to Alex, at least not immediately; and he concurred with her that Alex was not the sort to beat up a guy like Tom for cuckolding him. When Tom entered the kitchen he found Alex sitting at the table. "Hey, good morning, Tom," Alex said, cheerfully enough.

"Did you sleep okay?" Tom asked.

"Oh, reasonably."

"No jet lag?"

"Oh, that's just an illusion. You have to ignore it, move right through it."

"I guess that's a good attitude to take."

"Well, I think so," said Alex. "Hey, I've got a proposition for you. What about a little excursion? Up to Milan."

"Today?"

"Sure, shouldn't take more than six or seven hours round-trip."

"But you just got home."

"So? It's something I want to get out of the way. Picking up Jens's paintings."

"I was really sort of planning on writing or something," Tom said. "I've been wanting to get back on a schedule, you know?"

"Well, delaying one day isn't going to wreck anything. And I really could use some help and some company. I really could."

Tom realized there was no escape. He was in debt to Alex for all kinds of reasons. It would be weird to go, but just as weird to stay, to insist to Alex that, for vague reasons, he couldn't go, and then, once Alex left by himself, to finish up in bed with Mary, fucking dispiritedly and then doing an autopsy on the events of the last eighteen hours. "Okay," Tom said.

"Cool. It'll be fun," said Alex genially. "Couple of dudes on the road."

"Sure."

"So could you maybe be ready in half an hour?"

"Sure. I guess."

"Great. I just have to get a few things together," Alex said. "So I'll see you in a little bit."

"I'll just make myself some coffee," said Tom.

"Sure," said Alex, and turned and exited the kitchen. He saw Mary through the door of the *salone* reading her paper, and continued on, walking briskly down the hall to his studio. Inside, he fetched his wallet and keys and rifled inside his bag, retrieving a large envelope. He walked back down the hall, into the *salone,* and stood before Mary.

Mary did not react. She continued to read.

"Oh, come on," said Alex finally. "You can at least look at me."

Mary raised her eyes from the paper. "There," she said.

"I'm going to Milan to pick up Jens's paintings. With Tom. We'll be back tonight."

"With Tom. Why with Tom?"

"I need some help. Jens painted big."

"Does he really want to go? I mean, did you ask him?"

"Of course I did," Alex said. "He's fine with it."

"Oh," said Mary.

Alex handed the Mary the envelope. "The accountant said to give this to you. He doesn't trust the Italian post office."

"Hasn't he heard of . . . couriers?"

"Yeah, and I'm the courier. He just gave it to me yesterday, or whenever. Just before I left."

"I suppose you read what's in here."

"No. And you know I didn't. That's our deal—that we don't nose around in each other's financial stuff. And I *honour* that, Mary. Still," Alex said. "Even now."

"Then maybe you should think about honouring my ... wishes about the situation here."

"I'll think about it. While I'm driving. But you should think about it too. Because I don't think this is what you really want. Not really."

"It's not what I wanted, it's just how things have turned out," said Mary. "And how they have to be."

Alex shook his head. "Jesus, Mary. Fucking Jesus. You're just a runaway train, aren't you?" Mary did not reply, and Alex went on. "Look, I'm not going anywhere right away. I want to finish this one last painting before I have to go looking for another studio."

"How long will it take?"

"Maybe a month."

"That could be a long time," said Mary. She was trying not to blink, to remain impassive, and this made her eyes look large. "If you want to live in the studio—sleep there and everything—I suppose you could."

"Oh, I wouldn't want to be anyplace else. Under the circumstances."

"That's true enough," Mary said. "Okay." She began to open the envelope and Alex turned his back to her and left. She heard Tom in the kitchen. She supposed he'd overheard everything. Which was fine. She was telling him everything these days. He was her lover and her friend. He was, among other things, a good listener.

It seemed to Tom that the last time he had been in a vehicle with Alex was back in March, when they went home from the

Convento San Marco on the bus, and without quite knowing it took an oath together—*amore perchè anticipare la nostra fine*—that had sealed their fates.

They were, it was true, still together, but the constellation of their relations had been rearranged, and now Tom would have given most anything to have it return to its earlier condition.

He and Alex drove in silence for the first fifty or so kilometres, north from Florence, upward through tunnel after tunnel into the Apennines and then onto the plain of the Emilia Romagna. It was here that they began to talk, as the landscape flattened brutally and the light turned hazy and diffuse and the road followed a line of hulking high-voltage pylons marching northwestward into the heat and atmospheric crud.

"You never think of Italy as ugly, but this comes pretty close," Alex said.

"I guess a freeway is a freeway."

"It's not quite so bad from the train. I went this way yesterday, on the way home. But still, it's like this is the backstage of *bella Italia,* where they hide all the machinery and grease and fumes that make it run."

"The ugliness that's behind the beauty," said Tom.

"Or alongside it anyway." Then Alex's voice brightened. "That's kind of what the new painting's going to be about. You know, this beautiful girl who's surrounded by squalor, by junkies and devastation."

"So you're starting soon?"

"Oh, yeah. Maybe tomorrow. If I can find Maddalena."

"Can't you just work from the pictures you took?"

"Oh, I could. But I've really gotten to like having the model right in front of me. I really think that's what made *Flaming June,* you know, the double nude—having you guys there doing it together all that time."

"You mean doing the pose?" Tom asked.

"Yeah. Of course."

"Sure," said Tom, nodding his head. "So if you're so anxious to get started on the new one, why do this today? When you just got back?"

"Three reasons. I want to get everything else, all the distractions, out of the way. Two, I don't want to leave Jens's paintings with the freight people any longer than I absolutely have to. I mean, I would kill myself if anything happened to them."

"What's the third?"

"I just wanted to get out of the house. The atmosphere hasn't been very welcoming, if you know what I mean."

"I suppose not," Tom said. "I mean, I suppose so—that it hasn't. Been welcoming, or whatever."

"Must be pretty obvious."

"I guess. So how was Seattle—"

"So, just between you and me, as guys, as friends, what's going on?"

"Where?" said Tom, thrown that Alex had not taken up his question. "In the house?"

"In the house, and with Mary. I mean, I can't get anywhere with her, with what's happened to her. I come home, and it's like she's been taken over by fucking aliens."

Tom thought, and then replied, "She said she had an epiphany, that she felt like she needed to change her life."

"When? I mean, when did she have this epiphany?"

"I don't know exactly. Maybe a month ago."

"So the same time I left, when we were fighting," said Alex.

"I guess."

"Do you think she could have met someone, a lover?" Alex drummed his fingers on the steering wheel. "She wouldn't tell me whether she was or wasn't. Fucking anybody, that is."

Tom began, "Alex, I don't really—"

"Could she be fucking Wright? No offense, but he's bisexual, or claims to be. With you guys not being together, the two of them . . ." Alex halted. "No, I don't think so. I just don't see

Mary being attracted to somebody like that. Old." He paused again and then added quickly, "Not that he isn't attractive, Tom. But he's not Mary's type, don't you think?"

"No," Tom agreed. "I wouldn't think so." Tom was beginning to think he might be able get through this conversation using only evasion and the odd half-truth, as opposed to genuine mendacity.

"So you didn't see anything . . . weird going on, then?"

Tom had to say something to distance himself, or at least gain a little time. He said, "Like what?" which was pretty much the wrong thing to say.

"I mean, like Mary going out a lot, maybe without saying where. Maybe being distracted. Not being herself. I don't know."

"Well, you already said she's not her old self. But I don't know. I was busy. Working. She was working, too, I guess."

"So you guys really didn't hang out together, didn't talk?" Alex had his eyes on the road, his fingers fluttering up and down on their perch atop the steering wheel. His face bore no expression that Tom could take measure of. "She just didn't say anything, right?"

Of course Mary had said plenty to Tom, about herself and Alex and about herself and Tom and about how the latter combination was vastly superior to the former. While Alex was away, such talk had been idle summer chat, a temporary habitation, a vacation rental Tom and Mary were sharing. But now Mary was talking about year-round occupation, about breaking her lease with Alex. The fact was, he and Alex wanted the same thing—to have life go on as it had been a couple of months ago—but Mary wouldn't let them.

This last thought helped Tom believe that, even though he had, well, betrayed Alex and was just now misleading him, the bond between them held. "No. I don't know, Alex," he said. "I'm kind of uncomfortable being—"

And Alex interrupted, told the lie for him, just as he had that other night when, really, this whole thing began. “Sure,” said Alex. “I'm really putting you on the spot, making you the meat in the sandwich. Which is unfair. Hey, I'm sorry, okay?”

“There's nothing to be sorry for.”

“No, there is. I've been so freaked out by this whole business that I can't think straight. But it doesn't make it right to put you in an impossible position, just to make myself feel better.”

“Really, it's no big deal.”

“Sure. Let's forget about it.” Alex pointed to the radio. “Why don't you find us some tunes.”

Tom spent the next five minutes scanning the frequencies for bearable music, but could find nothing but Italian pop songs. In resignation, he gave up searching and sat back and listened, and in this way the remainder of their journey passed.

As they approached Milan, Alex threaded a path among various bypasses and ring roads, and a little after two o'clock they arrived at a warehouse near the Linate airport. Alex went inside and returned a few moments later, announcing that, much to his surprise, the place was open and its staff prepared to expedite his business.

“You can wait out here if you want,” said Alex. “Probably take a little while to hash things out. Import fees and licences. Baksheesh to be distributed to the relevant people.”

“I brought a book,” Tom said, holding up his fat collected Auden.

“Smart move. I'll come get you when we're ready to haul the stuff out here.”

Tom sat in the car with the windows rolled down. It was hot, though not as hot as Florence. He read, but without concentration. There were moments of silence, or at least sustained notes of the pure white noise of motors and industry, broken by the bomb bursts of jets leaving the airport.

Tom was just finishing “Another Time” (“No wonder then so

many die of grief"), and thinking that it reminded him of something Wright had told him, when Alex reappeared. "That was quick," Tom said.

"Amazing what a couple of million lire placed in the right hands will do," Alex grinned. "I told them I thought it was a little unfair to impose the import tax on the work of a dead artist, a old grandpa who just liked to play bocce and drink a little grappa."

"Jens didn't play bocce or drink grappa."

"Oh, he would have if he'd known about it. Grappa, I mean. Anyway," Alex continued, "I said that if it was all the same to them, I'd just as soon make a donation in kind to their fraternal order or whatever *festa* they liked. And they thought it was a worthy proposal. So we can go ahead and load."

Alex led Tom into the warehouse and over to a stack of six or seven long tubes, each about six feet long. "So this is it? All his paintings?" Tom said. He lifted the end of one, and found it surprisingly heavy.

"There's a bunch of canvases in each one, all rolled up together," said Alex. "Maybe seventy, all together. With the import tax at six hundred thousand lire each, it would have kind of added up." He moved to the other end of the stack. "So let's get started."

It took no more than ten minutes to load all the cylinders onto the roof rack, but Alex spent a further quarter-hour lashing them down with an elaborate skein of hitches and double knots. "There," he said, "that ought to hold."

All told, they were back on the road by three. "Be home in time for dinner," Alex said, although Tom could not imagine he could take any pleasure in sitting down to the communal meal that had once been the custom of the household. Tom asked, "So do you think you'll be able to exhibit Jens's work in Florence?"

"I don't know. Actually, it might be easier than at home. He's sort of an exotic by Florence standards. A dead Scandinavian from Seattle. And I don't think there are all these intellectual hoops to jump through like there are at home. You know—'Is this artist hip? Is it okay to take him seriously?' That kind of thing."

"Mary"—her name leapt from Tom's mouth before he could stuff it back—"said you were pissed at the attitude you got."

"Yeah, this one gallery director said Jens's work was 'trite.' Can you fucking believe it? I mean, it's his fucking gallery that's trite, selling 'investment grade' art to start-up millionaires and Noumena retirees."

"So you're kind of down on Seattle."

"Yeah. At least I don't think I'd want to live there now. It's funny. This—Italy—was Mary's thing. I just came along for the ride. But I like it now."

"There's nothing you miss?"

"I don't know," said Alex. "Maybe the Emerald. I was in there every night when I was back. It hasn't changed. Sure, this year's crop of assholes and poseurs is lined up at the bar, but behind it, it's still just Kevin and those guys pouring drinks and cooking fish. It's like Seattle a long time ago, before grunge or Noumena. Or at least before anyone understood what grunge and Noumena meant."

"I don't see the connection. They're totally separate. Except maybe that Noumena was one of the things that killed grunge."

"Despair killed grunge. Not old-time northwest despair, despondence with a sense of humour. But junkie despondence. It was like the European diseases the Indians had no resistance to. Same thing with heroin. People in Seattle couldn't handle it. It made them want to die."

"It's not like people exactly thrive on it in other places."

"Yeah, but most of them can cope a little. At least maintain. But in Seattle, it was the end: it's already too grey, too spongy and amorphous and sad. Heroin just pushes people right off the edge."

"Into the inferno," Tom offered.

"I don't know. Into a big black nothing. Or else they work for Noumena and shop and wait to get vested. Or take Zoloft, like me."

Tom had not wanted to risk uttering Mary's name again, but found himself saying, "Vesting wasn't so great for Mary."

"Oh, the tax thing? She's got to pay the piper, I guess. Frankly, I don't have a lot of sympathy just now. Maybe she'll learn something from it."

"What's she going to learn from being broke? It's not like she was a spendthrift before, like she was spoiled."

"Maybe not spoiled vis à vis money," Alex said. "But she's just kind of walked through life with all the doors opening up for her, one after the other. She didn't notice—didn't look down to see those mats and electric eyes—they were all automatic."

"It's not like you struggled so much."

"No, I'm the least struggling artist I know," said Alex. "But I don't struggle because I don't give a fuck. I don't get frustrated. But Mary gives a fuck. Deeply."

"So are you going to help her?"

"If she asks, sure. She'd say it was hers to begin with, of course."

"And if you guys don't stay together?"

"I haven't thought that far ahead, Tom." With that, Alex struck a note that Tom understood to mean that the subject was closed, and said, "Hey, we're nearly halfway. There's an Autogrille up ahead. Let's get something to eat. And drink."

They exited, parked the car, and hurried across the blistering asphalt. The building, happily air-conditioned, straddled the *autostrada,* and contained several restaurants and news and gift stands. They ordered pizza slices and Alex got them a bottle of wine. "Just the one, okay?" Alex said. "I've got be careful with Jens's paintings."

They ate and drank, and afterward browsed in the shop, filled mostly with soccer regalia and Baci candies packaged in varied guises: tubes, cubes, pyramids, hearts, and transparent figures. Alex picked up one of the latter and said, "You know it's all I can do not to get one of these for Mary? It's the kind of thing where we'd both know it was corny and know that we both knew it was corny, and enjoy it anyway. She'd know it was a joke and that at the same time it meant I totally loved her." He put the candy down, and began to walk with Tom towards the exit and the car. "But if I did it now," Alex added, "she'd take it as something weird. Or as an insult."

As Alex found his keys, he said to Tom over the roof, over the scream of the cars on the *autostrada,* "That's the shit that really breaks your heart, you know. Not the big gestures, but the little things you realize that you can't do any more—that don't *do* anything any more. The inconsequential shit that you realize adds up to the whole thing."

Mary read and reread the letter from her accountant outlining the details of what he called "your final accommodation" with the Internal Revenue Service. She read it twice on the couch in the *salone,* and then, arming herself with calculator, paper, and pencil, went through it again at the kitchen table. Then she went upstairs, undressed, climbed into bed, and lay wide awake in the dark.

She heard Alex and Tom come in about ten. They must have stopped somewhere for dinner. She heard a single set of footsteps climb the stairs and turn down the hall in the direction of Tom's room. After a decent interval, after the faint shuffling about in the kitchen and hall below her finally ceased, she slipped out of bed, donned her robe, and went to Tom's door. She didn't knock. She had given up knocking weeks ago. She merely turned the knob quietly, entered, and slid into Tom's bed.

"Hi," Mary said, and nested her body against Tom's back. "Were you asleep?"

"I don't think so," said Tom.

"So how was it today, with Alex?"

"Weird. Weird, but okay, I guess."

"Did he say something to make you feel that way?"

"He didn't have to say anything. It was . . . inherently weird."

"So he didn't tell you about what we'd discussed?" Mary asked. "I mean him and me?"

"Yeah. Not in detail. But I already kind of knew."

"So what was he specific about?"

"He thinks you must be having an affair. He asked me if you were fucking Wright."

A small, light bark issued from Mary's chest, which Tom imagined was a sort of laugh. She said, "Well, he's half right. Did you get the feeling he might have been thinking about you and me, too?"

"No. I got the feeling he must think I was too decent to do that to him," Tom said slowly. "That he thinks I'm his friend."

"You don't need to say it that way—like you're guilty *and* wronged at the same time," said Mary. "Wronged by me, I suppose. Like I put a gun to your head and made you sleep with me."

"That's not what I meant. But no, I don't feel good about betraying him."

"That's the way you're interpreting it. As though it's about *you,* instead of about *my* choices about the relationship I'm in and who I sleep with."

"You don't think there's some deception going on, some element of duplicity?"

"Not in my mind," Mary said. "I've told him I want to live separately. And he's already asked me if I'm sleeping with anyone and I said it wasn't his business. I refused to discuss it. I haven't lied to him. About anything."

Tom was disinclined to challenge Mary on this. It seemed to

him that, for his part, he had lied to Alex, both by denying any knowledge of Mary's activities and by omission. He told lies quite a bit, he supposed. Today's were just a slight further accretion.

Mary meanwhile took Tom's silence to mean that he had understood her point. To confirm it, she added, "I wouldn't be here with you now, in your bed, if I didn't have a clear conscience."

"I guess I should just let you worry about it for both of us," Tom said flatly.

"I think you should. I know what you're like, that you're very reflective, prone to a certain . . . refractoriness. And that's fine. So you just let me handle it. For both of us." Mary wanted to add, "Don't worry—I'll take care of you."

Tom rolled over. "Refractoriness," he repeated. "Okay. I'll accept that. I'm not sure I know exactly what it means, but it feels right. Like you made up a word just for me."

"I kind of did," Mary said. "It's one of your unique qualities." She pulled Tom close to her so she could whisper into his neck, his hair. "It's one of the things I love about you." There, she thought, I've said it.

Shit, he thought. She's said it.

Mary began to tongue around Tom's ear, and then she rolled the two of them over so Tom was on his back. She pulled herself up so her breasts were brushing Tom's face, insistent on being admired and venerated by his tongue and lips. She felt his cock lengthening and hardening, ambling upward against her thigh.

Tom felt it too, felt it responding to her even as Tom found himself at some level revolted by Mary's breasts, by their mass and intrusive curve, which were coming to stifle him, to bury him alive.

Yet his cock went on blithely growing, and when it achieved its full stature, Mary, still atop him, reached down and threaded it inside her.

Tom thought, "Refractory. That's what I am. She's nailed it—me. She always does."

Mary meanwhile had writhed and twisted herself towards a powerful orgasm, into which Tom's penis inadvertently joined by ejaculating as she cried out. Then, as she lay upon him, breathing long contented breaths, she whispered it again, the dreadful phrase.

Mary didn't tell Tom about the other things until later, until they both woke up, simultaneously it seemed, a little before dawn.

"I've got some good news and some bad news," she said. "I know that's a really lame construction, but it's actually true. So which do you want first?"

Tom was a little distracted—or refracted, he supposed—by the thought of Alex being just downstairs as he and Mary lolled together in bed, but he finally reached a decision. "Let's get the bad out of the way first," he said.

"All right. The tax thing is worse than I thought. All that's really left is the house and maybe a roll of nickels—about what I would have gotten in severance pay if I'd been employee number one million and gotten laid off at Noumena."

"So, like five thousand dollars?"

"About that," said Mary.

"What happened?"

"Well, there's basically no market for the stock I have left. And there are some penalties due. Then the accountant and lawyer take their fees, and there you are. Jarndyce and Jarndyce."

"Jarndyce and Jarndyce?"

"*Bleak House*. Never mind. It's not important," Mary said, though she found herself thinking for an instant that perhaps there had been a time when it had been nearly the most important thing on earth for her.

"So what are you going to do?"

"I could sell the villa, maybe go back to Seattle. But the villa is worth less than what we paid for it. Because of the exchange rate. I'd be okay. I could get a job, maybe even buy a little house. But I don't want to. It's like too much has happened—even this thing—to just roll up everything backwards and start where we—I mean I—left off."

"So then what?" Tom asked. "I suppose I could get a job here and—"

"That's really nice of you, but I don't think you're even allowed to work here. Not without a visa or a permit." Mary turned on her side, raised herself on her elbow, and propped her chin on her palm. "Actually, I'm hoping Alex will see that he has some obligations here."

"Because you gave him all his money?"

"That, and the other thing. The good news."

"Which is?"

"That I'm pregnant," Mary said.

Tom did not gasp or say "shit" or "jeez." After only a moment, he said merely, "Are you sure?"

"Pretty much. I've thought I might be for the last few days. I'm way over a week late."

"Oh. I mean, oh that's great. If you think it's great. Under the circumstances."

"It's great."

"Well," Tom said very deliberately, "that's great that it's great. It really is." Then he lay quietly on his back, looking at the light beginning to bloom on the ceiling.

"It's yours," Mary said.

"Yeah, I'd thought of that."

"And how do you feel about it? Because I suppose it might seem a little weird—"

"I'm still just kind of taking it in. I don't know—"

"But it doesn't . . . entail anything. On your part. Obligations,

I mean. It's what *I* wanted. So it's my responsibility. Totally."

Tom nodded, still looking up. "And you, how do you feel about it?" he said.

"I'm really happy. As happy as I've ever been. Even with everything else," Mary said. "So, hey, thank you. For your part in it." She leant down and kissed him gently on the lips. "For everything."

Tom was moved by this, and also relieved. It seemed that Mary loved him because she was happy, because he had helped out with giving her the baby she wanted. It was simpler than he had imagined. She didn't *need* him; nothing was required of him.

They both must have been silent for nearly a minute. Then Tom said, "Hey, maybe I can be the uncle."

"Sure," said Mary. "You can be whatever you want."

11.

Maddalena

It was not long after Mary and Tom had fallen back asleep in Tom's bed (where they remained until some time after ten o'clock) that Alex awoke, dressed, made himself coffee, and drove down the hill. He stopped in the Oltrarno at the framer's workshop (whom he persuaded, over *caffè corretto* in an adjacent café, to round him up a set of stretcher bars by noon) and then at the artists' supply shop, where he bought three metres of linen canvas. At about ten-thirty he found parking behind the Santa Maria Novella station.

Alex walked up the southern flank of the station and entered near platform one. He pressed though the mob of travellers across the forecourt and into the station café, where he ordered an espresso, which he drank standing by the window. From there, he could survey both the north entrance of the station that led out to the bus depot and the long queue for the left-luggage room. Maddalena and her friends circulated in this general area, congregating around the bus platforms between forays into the station to cadge spare change or sneak onto empty trains.

Alex looked and waited. He finished his coffee and went out to the bus depot, then returned to the café and ordered another. He knew she would come. He needed her. He had a month to paint this painting. And after another three-quarters of an hour, she did, efflorescent in pink sneakers and her Hotel Stupido T-shirt, her walk a compound of motions, variously spinning and skipping like a girl, swivelling and striding like a woman. Alex saw he would have to paint her even more quickly, before the bloom was off her.

Mary was sitting in the kitchen and heard them come in, up from the garden and through the cantina. The girl, *la Angelina,* looked at her straight-on as they passed her in the kitchen. "Hey, hi Signora Alex," the girl said, smiling immensely. She seemed about to offer something more, but Alex steered her on, down the hall to his studio.

Mary did not see them again for three-quarters of an hour, when they re-emerged. Alex carried a large pad and his camera. "We're going to work in the garden," he said as they passed by the *salone,* where Mary was reading *Middlemarch.*

Looking up from her book, Mary wondered whether Alex was having the girl pose naked for him. The original Turin girl had been clad in rags, albeit with her incipient breasts visible. Of course, there was no guarantee Alex was going to follow Ruskin's description closely. In the double nude, he had taken liberties with Pontormo and with Mary herself. It was Alex's way, to take liberties.

Mary went to the window and looked down into the garden. Alex was standing over the girl, who lay on the grass. Her arms were cast above her head as though in exhaustion, her body turned slightly so her hip was raised, with one leg straight and the other cocked at the knee. Alex gestured and the girl raised her knee a little more. Then Alex took a picture. Mary went back to the sofa and *Middlemarch.* When she went to the window five minutes later, Alex was sitting, the pad on his lap, sketching the girl. She was still clothed.

As Mary returned to her seat, Tom came in, looking sleepy and abstracted as though his mind were a balloon on a string that he carried before him.

"Hi," he said.

"Hi," Mary returned. She was conscious that she could not just now muster the warmth that had informed their relations last night and early this morning, and, as if in explanation, added, "He's brought her up here. He's sketching her outside, in the garden."

"Who?" asked Tom. "Angelina?"

Mary nodded. "She looks the same. Brazen. Like the Sicilian Pippi Longstocking."

"Is she Sicilian?"

"God, I don't know, Tom. It was just a metaphor."

"You're kind of tense."

"Sorry. I'm really stressed out. I mean, he's got this girl in my house and I don't have any say about it. She's one of these station *ragazzi,* precocious, streetwise. Probably a petty thief, maybe a junkie or a child prostitute. And I'm a pregnant woman now."

"You have to look after yourself."

"Yes, so do you see—" and just then Alex and the girl strode by the door. Alex looked in at Tom and said, "Hey, hi Tom," and continued towards the studio. The girl, just behind him, waved at Tom and Mary with her little finger. "Hey, hi dudes," she beamed.

Mary stood silently for a moment after they'd gone, then collapsed onto the sofa, and Tom sat down next to her. "What am I supposed to do? It's still *my* house."

Tom said, "You just have to talk to Alex and ask him. I mean, you have rights. You guys can come to some agreement."

"I don't have any leverage with him."

"Well, he's already agreed to move out when he's done with the painting."

"That was before I knew how bad things were. Now I kind of need him to stay if I'm going to keep the villa, at least until he agrees to return some of the money."

"I wouldn't worry," Tom said. "I mean, he's not an asshole.

He's generous, actually. And none of this is your fault. He can see that."

"Don't count on it. These days it's just paint, paint, paint. He's obsessed."

"Well, when he finds out about—"

"That's kind of tricky."

"Even so, he's not going to let you just live on the street with a baby," said Tom. "I mean, look at Angelina. He cares about homeless people."

"I hope you're trying to be funny. Otherwise—"

"I just meant that he's a basically decent person. Plus you guys have a history. Of friendship. He's not going throw it all away."

"He didn't used to care so much about his painting. I suppose that's my fault, making us come here. And now I'm an obstacle."

"I'll really think he'll be okay," Tom said, and put his arm around Mary. "You just have to talk to him."

Mary returned to *Middlemarch* and Tom went to the kitchen. After some minutes she rose and walked down the hall to Alex's studio and stood by the door. Through it, she could hear the voices of the girl and Alex, the girl's rapid-fire titter of what must be some street dialect, interrupted now and then by responses in Alex's languid baby-Italian. No way am I talking to him while she's still here, Mary thought, and retreated down the hall.

But five-thirty came, and the girl remained in the house. Then, around six, Alex ambushed Mary in the kitchen. He sidled up to her and said, "Hey, let's have a little glass of wine and talk." Mary simply looked at him and he smiled back at her. He wants something, she thought. From me. This is good.

"Okay," Mary said. "Outside."

"Sure." Alex took a bottle from the refrigerator and glasses and a bowl of nuts from the sideboard. They descended through the cool of the cantina and out into the blaze of the garden.

"So?" Mary said after they had sat down a short distance from where Angelina had earlier sprawled on the grass.

"I need to modify what I said I'd do yesterday."

"What do you mean?"

"Oh, I'll still move out in a month. Or when the painting's done. But for the next couple of weeks, I'm going to be having some pretty long modelling sessions with Maddalena. And frankly, it's a pain to have to drive down and get her every day. Plus she really doesn't have any place to live anyway. Not any place that's decent."

"Yes?" Mary said, trying not to allow her voice to tremble.

"So I thought she could stay here—in the studio—while we're working together."

"She'd stay in there, with you?"

"I guess. Or I could sleep in the *salone*. Whatever."

Mary took a breath. "I never pictured taking in boarders, Alex."

"I'd say 'a temporary guest.'"

"She's hardly what I'd call a normal guest. This little hottie from the station."

"She's a child, Mary."

"Whatever. Either way, it's problematic. Not to say a little weird."

"Look, let's put it on a business basis. I'm paying her for the modelling—"

"Oh, good. That'll keep her in lollipops and Barbies—"

"So I'll pay you for her room and board. Isn't that fair?"

Mary stood up, set her hands on her hips, and looked down at Alex. She thought she might merely walk away in silence. But his proposition—so vastly insulting yet a perverse variation on precisely what she hoped to obtain from him—bore consideration.

Before Mary could respond, Alex added, "Just as a gesture, whatever amount you think is right."

"How does a thousand a week sound to you?" Mary came back, and she was not sure whether she meant this in mockery or in earnest.

Neither was Alex. "That's a little steep. Unless you're kidding."

"It's on the low side for renting a villa in Tuscany."

"Maybe for a whole villa, but not for a fucking couch in what's still my studio."

"In my house."

"Mary, this is really fucked."

"Frankly, I think it's fucked that you want to impose this kid on everyone just because it's convenient for your painting."

"Who's everyone? You and Tom? I imagine Tom's perfectly okay with it."

"Did you ask him? Or just assume?"

"I know Tom. Who, to be equally frank, has been living here rent-free for months."

"Tom's a friend. Our best friend," said Mary. "This urchin of yours is a total stranger."

"So really, this is about your comfort level."

"I suppose. But anyone would say it kind of reeks of inappropriateness—you and the girl. Are you going to paint her nude?"

"I don't know," Alex said. "Probably not. It's too open to misinterpretation. By people like you."

"And what is a person like me like?"

"I don't know."

"So that was just a cheap shot," said Mary. "Like, oh, this small-minded person from Woodland Hills can't understand my oh-so-important work."

"Maybe, but not the second thing. About knowing what you're like. Because I really don't know any more."

"And you're really, really, really trying hard to understand, I suppose, hiding out in the studio with your paints and your minx from the station."

"I came back here ready to pick up where we left off. To be

normal with you," Alex said. "And you told me you wanted me to leave. Do you remember that? I mean, if I misunderstood you, please enlighten me. Or has something changed?"

"Lots of things have changed. They're changing all the time." And with that, Mary decided she had to unburden herself a little; that although she had been holding her own rhetorically against Alex, her very success was taking them in a direction she did not want to go. "I'm broke," she said, and then sat down again on the grass.

"I know. You already said."

"No, I mean really broke. It's all gone, everything but the house. They can't take it, apparently. Or they just can't be bothered. In dollars, it's worth maybe two-thirds what we paid for it anyway."

"It's still a nice asset. You could live here—"

"I couldn't pay the taxes, the utilities, the upkeep. Never mind the groceries."

"I guess you'll have to sell it, then," Alex said. "It's too bad."

"I don't want to sell it. It's the last thing I have left—of everything I worked for."

"So what are you going to do?"

Mary looked at Alex. She wished she still loved him. "I was thinking you could help me out," she said.

"Well, sure. The offer about the rent for Maddalena staying here still stands. And I guess it's only fair that for the weeks I'm here I should chip in for groceries, utilities, whatever."

Mary was digging her fingers into the turf. She looked away from Alex, up towards the house. She could just see, at Alex's studio window, the girl looking out.

"But I guess," Alex was continuing, "that doesn't really do much for your long-term situation. After I'm gone."

"You know I gave you three times what this house cost before we even came here. I just gave you that. Now—"

"That was then. Everything was different."

"Everything is different now," Mary said. "I never thought I'd lose—"

"But the whole point of doing it was to even things up between us."

"They're not even now."

"And I'm sorry about that. But the whole point of your doing it was so I'd come here and I'd be protected if things didn't work out, if they turned out like this."

"I never thought they'd turn out this way," Mary said. "I never imagined it this way." She wished she could love him again; or, since that was impossible, could have never loved him in the first place.

"Neither did I," Alex was saying. "But I didn't even particularly want to come—"

"So you really wouldn't mind going back. You could let me have maybe half of what I gave you, and you'd still be ahead. Half is fair. It's always done that way in these situations."

"I don't know what this situation is," said Alex. "And you're missing the point. I don't want to go back. It's like you think I should just accept everything. You end our relationship. You take the house. You take our life here. And I make all the sacrifices."

"The money I gave you was a fucking gift. I sacrificed it to you, for you."

"It was supposed to be no strings attached. That was central to the whole thing."

"So basically, you don't give a fuck. No strings. Our history together doesn't mean anything—"

"You ended it. You told me to go."

"You were already gone. I just formalized it." Mary held fire for an instant, then continued. "But that doesn't mean we don't have a past. It doesn't mean you don't have an obligation to even consider being maybe half as generous with me as I was with you."

"You weren't being generous. You had money to burn. It was play money," Alex said. "You wouldn't know generosity if it came in and sat on you—"

"That's as lame as it is fucked, Alex."

"Well, I didn't love you because of the money. But you talk about me not being here. It was you who walked away from us. You'd rather be hanging out with that faggot bag-of-bones Turner."

"That's really offensive. I'm just sorry he threatens you so much," Mary said.

"Not really. You took his side against me—"

"What, like we're choosing up teams for kickball? Grow up, Alex. Just try to consider what I'm saying, what's really fair in this situation."

"To me this situation feels like a mugging," Alex said. "Twice over. First you cut me off at the knees, then you come back two days later for my wallet."

"You're being a total asshole."

"And what are you being?"

"I'm just trying to survive."

"So you're a little desperate."

"Maybe."

Alex looked at his glass and then at Mary's. "Hey, we forgot to drink." He picked up his wine and took a long sip. "Cheers," he said.

Mary frowned, and Alex said, "Come on." She lifted her glass and said "Cheers" flatly.

"What, no 'to art and friends and shit'?" Alex said.

"No." She saw that Alex sensed some advantage, or, at a minimum, was trying to charm her. She pressed on before he could consolidate his position. "So," she said, "will you consider it?"

"Consider what?" he said, and drank. "Oh, the money thing?"

"Yes."

"Can Maddalena stay?"

"I suppose."

"Then, yeah, I'll consider it."

Tom saw Alex only in passing that day. For the last twenty-four hours, he had been pretty much within Mary's gravitational field (whose pull, given her pregnancy, was now considerable). But that was not the same thing as being close to Mary, as being able to tell her everything, as he had during the first thirty-six hours after their very first bout of lovemaking. Now they were not so much close as simply deeply entangled.

Tom thought he ought to check in with Alex, if only to avoid suspicion, and he found an opportunity the next morning. Coming down the steps into the hall, he heard voices—Alex's and the girl's—coming from the studio, whose door was open. It would be just the thing for Tom, by-the-by, to stick his head in. The presence of the girl would preclude Alex from raising any awkward matters.

From the doorway, Tom saw the two of them regarding a large canvas that was unrolled on the floor. Alex was gesturing at it, apparently offering a commentary which was now and again punctuated by what Tom understood to be various affirmations and superlatives from the girl.

The girl's voice, glassy and high, was climbing staves of exclamation, offering *"Che colore, che luce"* before returning to the major chord, *"Bellissimo."* Here Tom tapped on the door.

"Hey, come on in," Alex said. "We're looking at some of Jens's work. I'm showing Maddalena what real art looks like. You know Maddalena, right?"

"Sure," Tom said, joining them. "*Buon giorno,* Maddalena."

"Rise and shine, guy," the girl returned.

Alex had unpacked one of the largest canvases, perhaps seven feet wide and five feet high. Tom had seen a few of Jens's paintings at Alex and Mary's old house in Seattle, smaller pieces that had never made much of an impression in comparison to the fact of Jens himself, a cloud bank of oblivion stalled over the living-room couch.

"It's something, isn't it?" Alex said. Now Tom was prepared to admit this on grounds of being agreeable or even in connection with the painting's scale, which opened up before them like a pool set into Alex's studio's floor, deep and broad, its surface ashimmer with lappings and roils. But then the painting more or less came after him and pulled him in, fully clothed.

"Shit, yeah, it really is," Tom said as he went under. He was immersed for some time, and when he surfaced, sputtering and flailing, he began to search for something to hang onto, some buoyant device, a category or genre or hermeneutical life jacket to keep him afloat. But he could find nothing; he could not even say whether the thing was abstract or figurative, and down he went again, into the maelstrom of forms and light, into the depths which, when he failed to hit bottom, he knew must be beauty.

Recovering himself, seeing this was only a large piece of cloth, stiffened and incised with pigment, laying on the floor of a villa in Bellosguardo, he realized he was neither drowning nor, as he feared, panting. Finally he was able to say, "It's just . . . fucking beautiful."

"Yeah," Alex said. "I think maybe this one's his masterpiece."

"Che stupendo," said Maddalena.

"Stupendo Hotel," Alex returned, and he and Maddalena laughed.

This was lost on Tom, who was lost to everything save the canvas. "How could those fucking idiots in Seattle not want this?" he said.

"I don't know. Maybe I forgot to show them this one," said Alex. "Or maybe everything just looks better here, in this light."

That light was just then giving up its morning indigo and lavender, gathering itself into the saturated honey yellow of noon. It was falling on all of them, and, Tom saw, particularly the girl. She, too, was beautiful; perhaps, in the eye of some beholder, unbearably so, and you might very well fall into her and never come up, but drown.

Tom realized he must have seen Mary in this same light at some point, formed an unshakeable intention about her, and clung to it long after the light had moved on, the effect still driving him after the cause had vanished.

Tom looked back at the canvas on the floor. Its effect had not diminished. It took possession of him, and then he felt an overwhelming longing. Now he would have given any sum to own this thing, to possess it. It contained no universals, embodied no gods. It was no more than itself, distilled down to its own essence, complete in merely being itself. This, Tom thought, is what love feels like.

So wasn't love the only true response to beauty? Love, like the graffito said, that shapes our end? And as we are shaped, so we shape the world, changing matter into art, into yet more beauty?

No, because that doesn't explain me and Wright, Tom thought. Because Wright isn't beautiful. You could say he's even ugly, inside and out, soured and old. But what I finally loved was him. And I miss him a lot. So I suppose I still love him. Oh shit.

Tom came back to the painting, which still seemed to him like a body of water. He heard voices over it, the light and the swells running across the painting, and he saw that Alex and the girl were still talking, but that he himself was speechless.

"I better get back upstairs," he managed. "Kind of working on something."

"Sure," said Alex. "See you later."

"Rise and shine, guy," the girl said.

"No, no," Alex said to her. *"Solo per svegliare, per la mattina."* He turned towards Alex. "I said that to her this morning when I got her up and now she wants to use it all the time, like it's the standard greeting in English."

"It's okay. It's cute."

Tom went up to his room and closed the door. He lay down on his bed, which was still florid with unguents of his and Mary's bodies, and began to weep. He was having the big overdue cry that belonged to his break-up with Wright. When he was done, he had another. Because the fact was, he wanted Wright back and there was no way that was going to happen. Because Wright wouldn't ask him to come back and Tom was afraid to say he wanted to come back. It was just another of the cowardice and betrayal chapters in the autobiographical novel of his self-destruction. His heart hurt, and his brain only exacerbated the pain. He should stop doing theory, stop thinking dislocated thoughts about the groundless world. Florence was lost on him. He couldn't see the beauty of it. He was hot for ugly. He should go home and live out the days still vouchsafed to him pulling espressos.

In the following days, Mary continued to come in the evenings to Tom's bed, to make love and wonder aloud about what was going to happen to them all who were in the palm of Alex's hand.

Alex had said he would consider Mary's proposition, but his mind was elsewhere, on and in the new painting. It was coming quickly, even joyfully. He loved painting Maddalena, who for her part loved to be painted, who thought it was the kindest, most wonderful thing anyone had ever done for her. Posing, she smiled too much. Alex had to remind her she was supposed to be devastated, poor, a child of the streets. That didn't mean, she responded, you couldn't be happy a little.

Maddalena would have done anything for Alex, and in fact offered to do some things she had done for money in the vicinity of the station, or other things she had done with her friends. But Alex said no, dismissed her as he might a silly child, and they got back to painting. Alex was himself surprised that he was able to withstand her proposals so easily. She was terribly pretty, and by no means entirely undeveloped. It had been two months since he had had sex. The last time he had attempted to engage with himself mano-a-mano had been a fizzle (coming home from Seattle, slumped in the bathroom of the 767, anesthetized with business-class booze, catching sight of himself in the mirror muttering "We are as gods," as his cock wilted in his hand). But right now, he would simply rather paint.

Moreover, it occurred to him that with Jens dead, Mary dead *to* him, and Tom keeping pretty much to himself, Maddalena was his best friend. That, and a little bit of a daughter to him, although he had no idea what having a daughter might be like. They were, in any case, a happy partnership, artist and model, and the painting they were making together was promising to be Alex's best, full of molten colour, sun and dust, and the beauty, the girl-innocence, of Maddalena's sprawled body. After a week, he had reached no decision about a financial understanding with Mary, but he knew with adamantine certainty that he did not want this—painting this model in this manner in this mood in this room—to stop.

By the following week, everyone but Alex needed to say something to somebody: Mary to Alex; Tom to Wright; even Maddalena, who now that they were so very close to being done with this picture really wanted to go down the hill and see her friends. Alex made no objection, would deny her nothing, and so she boarded the bus—she didn't want to be driven—and said she would be back, the day after tomorrow.

Mary went to Alex not long after Maddalena left. She stood at the door of the studio, intending to have Alex come out and talk to her, but he motioned her inside and invited her to sit down on his sofa. The painting, big as a billboard, was propped against the far wall but oppressed her no less for that. She glared back at it.

Alex was oblivious to everything *but* the painting, and of course to the business at hand, to Mary's plight. "So what do you think?" he said.

"Of the canvas?" Mary understood she had to defer, to humour him a little. She glanced at it again, into the swirl of light and pity, but she had no patience for looking, for the painting's plaintive attempt to engage her. "It's good. The T-shirt and shoes are kind of incongruous. But it's more or less how I imagined it."

"I think Maddalena really nailed it—the pose, I mean."

"I suppose she did," Mary agreed, and then looked up at Alex and said, "I was wondering if you'd given any thought to what we discussed."

"In the garden?"

"Yes, the garden."

"Well, I've been kind of busy," said Alex. "I mean totally. With the painting."

"Well, that's great. But there are bills to pay, Alex. And I can't handle them all."

"It's that bad?"

"Yes, it's that—"

"Well, don't sweat it. Give them to me and I'll take care of it."

"We still need some kind of long-term solution. For what's going to happen after you're gone."

"I don't know," Alex began, "when that will be—"

"You said a month, or when the painting's finished. And it looks pretty much finished to me."

"You really just can't wait to get me out of here."

"I don't want to go on in limbo, in this purgatory, indefinitely."

"But suppose I don't want to go?"

"Come on, Alex. That's not an option."

"Well, I know I don't want to leave Florence," Alex said. "Or even Bellosguardo. I feel like I need this place, this light to work. That everything depends on it."

"Well, I'm sure you'll figure something out. But meanwhile I've—"

"Wait a minute. Suppose I bought the house from you? For the same as you paid for it."

"It's not for sale, Alex."

"Least of all to me, I suppose."

"To anyone," said Mary. "It's a lousy deal anyway. You end up with the house plus most of the money I gave you. All I have is the value of the house, which I already own."

"You couldn't get that for it on the open market."

"Which is why I'm not selling it."

"But I'm offering you that—the original value."

"And I wouldn't be any better off. I'd just have the money instead of the house."

"You could live on the money for quite a while."

"A while," said Mary. "Yes, exactly. And then what?"

"Well, it's not like you couldn't work, like you don't have saleable skills."

"Here, in Italy?"

"Well, you don't have to stay—"

"And in case you hadn't noticed, I am working. I'm writing, which is what I came here to do."

"I mean paid work."

"And who's paying for your work? I don't see the gallery directors and curators lined up. So basically I'm paying for it, with the money I gave you."

"I don't know about that," Alex said. "I have a pretty good feeling about this new stuff."

"Well, dream on."

"I could say the same thing to you. But I won't."

"I'm not interested in your opinion."

"Just my money," said Alex. "Maybe you ought to consider trying to change your own situation. I'm offering you a nice piece of change here. Take it. Go home and get back on your feet financially. Maybe then you could come back."

"As if that were remotely likely. As if there were a remote possibility of me getting another windfall."

"I thought you always said you earned the money."

"Don't start splitting hairs—"

"I don't think it's splitting hairs. It's an important distinction. Because if it was your hard-won life savings, you might have a case for asking for some of it back," Alex said. "But until now, you always said it was found money, money that fell out of the sky."

"It still fell on me. And I could have kept it all."

"And then it fell on me. Maybe by way of you. But why should I give it up? Because the real issue is that there's only enough money between the two of us for one of us to live on, separately at least. And you think it should be you."

"You think it's that simple? That you can just rationalize your selfishness—"

Alex laughed. "You own the fucking patent on selfishness, Mary. And, yeah, it is that simple. Simple bad luck. Life. Welcome to reality, Mary."

"Fuck you, Alex."

"I mean what is so unbearable about going home, buying a house—"

"From what I hear, I couldn't afford a house in Seattle now."

"So move to Portland. Or rent. Invest the proceeds from this place. Do some freelance editorial stuff like you used to do—"

"Christ, you're an asshole, Alex. Just listening to you makes me sick, the condescension, the callousness. 'Why don't you just do this? Or that?' Like it's so easy—"

"It is easy. You still have a charmed life by most people's standards. You have some money. You're single. By choice. You don't have anything or anybody to worry about except your fucking self."

"Not any more."

"How do you mean?"

"I mean I wouldn't be alone. I'd be supporting—"

"Oh, whoever it is you've been screwing," Alex said. "Why am I not surprised? And of course, he's a freeloader. So you fucking come to me and say, 'Hey, support me and my new boyfriend.' This is fucking unbelievable."

Alex stopped. He was waiting for Mary to insult him or defend herself in some way, and because she did not, he was concerned, worried—about her, he supposed. Maybe he'd been too rough, gone too far.

He looked at her. Her face was turned to the floor, and she was sitting more or less where she'd sat when he was painting *Flaming June*. That was a long time ago, but the way she was holding her body seemed to display the same exhaustion as the pose had. She looked up at him, and said, "There's going to be a baby, a child."

"Oh," Alex said. "So you're going to adopt. Maybe not the best time, not that anyone's asking me—"

"I'm not adopting."

"Shit, Mary," said Alex and walked away from her, towards his little table, his brushes and paints. He turned around. "I sure didn't see that one coming. I suppose you're pretty happy about it."

"Really happy, yes."

"So when's it due?"

"March. April. Next spring, anyway."

Alex took a step in Mary's direction, stopped, and put his hands in his pockets. He looked down and then up at Mary. "I suppose you know I'm going to ask—I can't help wanting to know—who the—"

"No, Alex."

"No what? You won't tell me?"

"It's not your business. It hasn't got anything to do with you. It's not even important. I'm raising it by myself."

"It might care. To know who its father is."

"That's for me to deal with," said Mary. "If you care at all, if you're not totally indifferent, maybe you could give me an answer to what we've been talking about."

"I'm sorry, but I need some time to take this in."

Mary said, "There's not much to take in. You can either do the right thing or you can be an asshole."

"You know, I can't tell whether you want me to hate you or pity you, feel for the destitute single mother—"

"Please don't. I've had what you call your love. I can only imagine what your pity would be like."

"You're some piece of work, Mary. I'll bet you'll make a swell mom."

"Just fuck off, okay?" said Mary wearily. "Take your time. Do what you need to do. Like you always do."

"I need to finish this painting. And I need to think. So I'll think while I paint and then I'll let you know, okay? By the end of the week probably."

"Okay. Whatever." Mary stood up from the couch. "So I suppose you're done working from your model now. It would really help me not completely lose it if you got her out of the house."

"She's not here. She went back down the hill."

"But she's coming back."

"She's coming back. I'll talk to her, see what she wants to do."

"You'll see what she wants to do? Like she's running this house? Jesus, Alex."

"Look, it'll get handled. All of it. Just don't hassle me. It's not a good way to get what you want."

"Oh, thanks," Mary said, and walked to the door. She stopped and looked back at him. She said nothing, but simply shook her head from side to side. Then she was gone.

Alex had never intended to go to the Villa Castellani. He had never so much as crossed the threshold, still less gone to Wright

Turner's door. But he had sat on the sofa for a long time after Mary left the studio, drinking wine, realizing that he was already missing Maddalena, and he came to the conclusion that going there was exactly the necessary thing.

When Turner opened the door, he regarded Alex and said, "Well, what a surprise." He guided Alex inside and pointed him towards the *salone.* "I haven't had a visitation from the Villa Donatello for some time. But you—I believe I've never had the pleasure of your company here."

"No, I've never been."

"Well, it's home," Turner said. "Please sit. Can I get you a glass of wine? Some nuts?"

"Sure." Alex sat down on the sofa while Turner disappeared for a minute. He looked around the room, at the painted ceiling, the grave incisions of the cornices, the massive curtains, the vast pools of darkness and light. Turner came back with a tray, and Alex said, "It's like a Caravaggio in here, the shadows and the brightness."

"Oh, the chiaroscuro. And then you have me, skulking about." He handed Alex a glass. "So, how goes the painting?"

"Okay. I'm just finishing something. The Turin girl."

"Oh, from Ruskin? Yes, I put Mary onto that."

"You put Mary onto lots of things."

"I couldn't say. It seems unlikely. She's rather headstrong, a young woman of ideas, of many theories, so to speak."

"You know she's leaving me?" Alex said quickly. "Or she's asked me to move out."

"How sad," said Turner. "I gathered you hadn't been getting along. That last time I was at the villa, things got a bit tense."

"But not just between me and Mary."

"Oh, you and I? That was just a critical disagreement. I took you seriously enough as a painter to be frank with you. But that shouldn't interfere with our friendship."

"It hasn't interfered," Alex said. "I never much liked you in the first place."

"I see. *Tant pis*. But I rather sensed you don't like queers. I suppose that can't be helped."

"I like Tom just fine. He's probably my best friend."

Turner laughed. "Oh, that's charming. 'Some of my best friends are queers.' American hypocrisy is so earnest. I'd forgotten. So what can I do for you?"

"You know Mary's pregnant?"

"Really? Well, *good* for her. And congratulations to you, of course."

"It's not mine."

"Well, I'm sure that stings a little. But, trust me, it's going to change your whole experience of this country. Italians love babies. I can see everyone fawning over you all as you push the stroller through the Boboli—"

"Stop fucking around with me."

"Stop being vulgar," Turner said. "If you can."

"I just want to know the truth about something."

"I'm noted for telling the truth. For self-revelation. It's my art, just as painting is yours."

"Then tell me about you and Mary."

"Mary and I. Tell you what? I wouldn't want to breach any confidences."

"Force yourself. Try very hard."

"Mary and I?" Turned sucked air between his teeth. "Oh, you can't possibly imagine Mary would want to sleep with a wizened old prune like me." A laugh caught in his throat. "Besides, as we were just discussing, I prefer boys."

"You've been with women. Some pretty famous ones."

"Well, there was some . . . embroidery there. Artistic licence."

"But you're capable of it."

"Of improving on a story, for art's sake? Oh, most definitely—"

"Come on. Of getting a woman pregnant."

Turner covered his mouth with his palm, removed it after a moment, coughing. "Really, I don't want to make light of your questions. You're obviously very upset—"

"Just answer, okay?"

"All right. Of course," said Turner. "In theory, yes, I'm capable. But in practice, no. I'm quite old, and there's a certain lack of response on the part of one's organ—"

"So you can't get it up?"

"Yes. So aside from the other factors, your surmise is a bit off target."

"So where should I be aiming?"

"You put me in a terribly awkward position. But there's nothing for it, I suppose," Turner said. "I think you ought to look closer to home, to your immediate circle."

"Oh, Tom? Give me a break. You didn't like him leaving you, I guess."

"You needn't believe me. It's more or less public knowledge. Or at least it's known by the authorities. The *carabinieri* dropped by the villa while you were in America."

"Oh, bullshit."

"No, they did. They were seen to drive up, to go in. Apparently, it was the middle of the night, but every light in the house was ablaze, there was loud music, and some neighbour or another caught sight of Tom and Mary . . . gambolling around the property naked."

"So? That could be totally innocent. They've spent a lot of time naked together, posing—"

"You have a wonderful notion of innocence, you painters," Turner said. "But when they came to the door, it was quite obvious to the *carabinieri* that they'd been interrupted at an intimate moment."

"How was it obvious?"

"Oh, the police have their expertise. And this is the Old World.

People don't blind themselves to ordinary human frailty, to the tears of things. They understand what goes on. They accept it."

"But who told you?"

"Florence is a very small place. I'm something of a fixture here. So one hears things, unbidden. I won't be more specific than that. But I do get out. I'm going up to I Tatti later today for drinks. Doubtless, I'll hear more. People just tell me things. They can't help it."

"Well, you're the last person I'd believe on something like this."

"Suit yourself. I'm not an oracle. As I said, it's only art."

"It's not art. It's gossip. People just can't tell the difference."

"Perhaps," Turner said. "I'm sorry you can't believe in me, in what I say. Not that I do entirely. Sometimes I think I'm rather agnostic about myself, about my life as I've created it." He shrugged, raised his glass, and drank.

"I just believe in Tom a lot more," Alex continued. "That he couldn't do that to me."

"Perhaps not *to* you, but *for* Mary—to oblige her, to satisfy his own curiosity. Thomas is a very obliging and very curious young man."

"I think I know him a little better than you."

"No you don't. That's just another of your smug pretenses, that and saying he couldn't do it. Of course he could." Turner licked his lips. "Wystan Auden—W. H. Auden to you—has a poem where he says—let me think—yes, 'Evil is unspectacular and always human,/And shares our bed and eats at our own table.'"

"It's only a poem."

"It's true."

"I don't know. Isn't Auden the guy who said that art, poetry or whatever, doesn't make anything happen?"

"Who told you that?"

"Tom. Mary. One of them, anyway. I don't know why. But you

can't say it doesn't do anything on the one hand and that it tells the truth on the other."

"I don't see that as an insurmountable problem."

"Then you're having it both ways."

"Yes, I suppose I am."

Alex confronted Tom in the most oblique manner he could. He found him in the kitchen alone (Mary was outside, in the garden) making his lunch. Alex got himself a glass of wine and leaned against the counter. He said he'd been to Wright's.

"Oh," Tom responded. "Why?"

"To see what he could tell me about Mary—about what's been going on."

Tom stepped sideways along the table and turned a little away from Alex. He rested one hand on the half-cut loaf of bread, and then he set his other hand, palm down, flat on the table by the knife, as though he was going to pick it up and slice himself another piece. His back was now to Alex. "And what did he say?"

"Mostly his usual effete bullshit."

"Well, there you are—"

"And one really crazy thing. About you."

"I guess he feels the need to be catty, now that we're—"

"No. About you and Mary. That you're lovers."

Tom made no response for what seemed to him like twenty or thirty seconds. He slid his hand off the loaf so both his palms were on the table and he pressed down. "Well, yeah, we were," he said quietly. Then he let his weight back down on his feet.

"Can you turn around and tell me that? I'm not going to hit you."

Tom turned around. His face was already flooded with tears. It was red and contorted, Alex saw, ugly and pathetic.

The mouth opened. "Yeah, we were," the voice choked out.

"Were or still are?"

"Well, *are*—but I've been trying to break it off. I didn't know what to do, to not hurt Mary."

Alex took a long draught from his glass. "That's very thoughtful of you."

The eyes seemed to Alex to have opened up a little, and the face was relaxing a little bit, recomposing itself into something more human. There was sniffling, and then the voice again. "Look, I can't even start to say—"

"So don't."

"We got drunk. It was a big mistake. I knew it was wrong. I wanted to stop, but Mary—"

"She made you."

"I know how it sounds," and here Tom, recognizably Tom again, wiped his nose with the side of his hand.

"Maybe clichés are the only adequate truth at times like this."

"I suppose. But look—why would I want to ruin my life just to pretend I'm hetero? When it's hard enough being gay?"

"Maybe Wright made it too hard."

"Maybe. Anyway, I'm really, really sorry," Tom said. He stretched his hand out towards Alex. "It's the worse thing I've ever done, I guess." Alex saw that there was a snail trail of mucous glinting along the base of Tom's thumb. "Can you forgive me?" he was saying.

Alex drank again. "Maybe. Probably." He went to the bottle and refilled his glass.

"You can beat me up if you want," Tom added. Alex laughed, laughed into his glass so that wine spumed like seltzer from his mouth. He looked at Tom and smiled, and then Tom laughed with a sincerity and hardiness that genuinely surprised him.

When the laughter drained, more quickly than either of them were now prepared for, a long silence ensued, a silence that refused to be broken, that paralyzed both of them even as it insisted that something be done. Finally, it came to Tom to say the obvious thing.

"I suppose I should leave. Go home."

"That might be a good idea."

"I wouldn't be running away."

"You'd be making a mess a little less messy."

Tom put down the sandwich he had picked up during the long silence. It had one bite taken out of it. It must have been from before Alex had come in. "So I'll just go up and collect my stuff," he said.

"I'll call the airline and set something up for you."

"How do I pay—"

"I'll take care of it."

"Well, you shouldn't—"

Alex grimaced. "Don't, Tom. Don't do it. Just fucking go."

It took Tom scarcely fifteen minutes to pack. He tried not to look around or at anything, to take in anything that might cause him to realize he was being thrown out of paradise; that would cause him to lose it completely.

He stood for several minutes at the bottom of the stairs, listening to Alex talking on the phone. Then Alex came out to him. "It's all set," he said, and handed Tom a piece of paper he'd written the flight numbers on.

Tom stood silent for a moment. "Well, I guess I should get going. It's funny. My bag isn't any bigger now than when I came. I didn't really acquire anything. A few new books, but then I sold just as many. So it all evened out."

"It's smart to travel light."

Tom began to pick up his bag, and then put it down. "Hey, just one thing. A question. The night of the big altercation—why did you lie for me?"

"Oh, about how you knew about Mary's nun book? I don't know. Mary was being a bitch. I didn't want her to win, her and Wright."

"That was kind of when things started falling apart."

"And all because I put her in a painting."

"In a way she didn't like."

"What was not to like? You tell me. You know her better now than I do."

"I'm not sure. Maybe that she thought you used her body, her face, her—I don't know—*persona.* But it wasn't her, like she really is."

"It's exactly like her. That's what she couldn't handle. I fucking nailed her in that painting."

"Well, then you and she have different versions of who she is."

"I guess."

Alex smiled. "Hey, before you go, one more favour. Maybe leave off saying goodbye to Mary. I mean, write her when you get home, sure. But otherwise, I'd have World War III on my hands."

"I'd really like to see her, Alex—"

"And a half-hour ago, I'd really liked to have beaten the shit out of you. But we reached an understanding. Let's not fuck with it by—"

"I really ought to. I mean, what's she going to think? She'll think I'm a total—"

"She might have thought that anyway," Alex interrupted. "But don't worry. I'll explain things to her."

"Okay, but maybe I could just *see* her."

"You mean, like, just look at her?"

"Yeah, from the window."

"Be my guest."

"Okay. So I guess we'll talk some day. Or not."

"Oh, we will. Just give it a little time. Then maybe you could come back and visit. Take a vacation in *bella Toscana.* It's heaven, right?"

"Oh, yeah," Tom said.

Tom picked up his bag and carried it to the front door. He went back into the *salone,* to the window.

Mary was lying on the grass in the garden below. She had a few books and a bound journal and her pen and the sheath of pages that Tom knew was her novel. She was propped on one elbow reading them, and then she took up the pen and made a few marks and capped the pen and set it down.

She rolled onto her back and closed her eyes, to take some sun, Tom guessed. She'd become quite tan without even meaning to. So had he. Only Alex was pale any more.

Mary stretched her arms above her head and let them fall. Tom thought, She's still pretty, I guess. It's just not a big deal, a big mystery, for me any more. While he was thinking this, Mary lifted one of her knees and her face tipped to the ground, yielding to the heat. Tom saw how she had arranged herself, the pose, the *exact* same pose; and he thought, how things copy themselves against all human reason or intention, refract into symbols we can make no sense of—derive no truth from—but only arrange into patterns to amuse or bedevil ourselves with how little we know, with how great is our remove from every created thing, even our selves.

So irony really is the only truth now. As this dawned on him and sank in, a slight breeze came up, one of the innumerable breezes that made summer in Bellosguardo bearable. It seized the top two dozen pages of Mary's manuscript and sent them scudding through the garden. Mary jumped up and cried, "Shit," chasing after them.

And that nails it, Tom thought.

Tom walked down the road to the centre of Bellosguardo, to the triangle of grass with its enormous pine. He had planned to take the bus down the hill, get a hotel room, and leave the next morning. There was an open ticket waiting for him at the Air France desk in the little Florence airport. It was all taken care of, Alex had told him.

He was nearly at the triangle when it struck him that it truly was an open ticket; that he had no prior engagements, plans, or obligations; that he was, in short, a person with no place to go and nothing to lose. And with that, he reversed his course, continuing past the Villa Donatello to the gate of the Villa Castellani and Wright Turner's door.

Tom put his bag down on Wright's threshold and rang the bell. Do your worst, he thought. I don't care. Send me away. Or take me in. He followed up with a strong knock. Go ahead, be an asshole. Don't answer. Or open the door. I'm here. Or not, if that's how you want it. It's neither here nor there to me. I'm simply available.

He passed five minutes in this way, alternately ringing and knocking. Then he picked up his bag, and as he did so, he felt a few tears coming. He could not say that he wasn't in some way relieved that Wright had been out. But by the time he walked past the Villa Donatello, hoping Mary wouldn't see him (hoping she would see him), he was sobbing.

He went left at the triangle, down the road that descended through the olive trees and meadows to the city below. A quarter-mile along, a great vista of the city and its valley opened up before him. Their immense heat was already upon him, and would mount as he descended. It was the end of July. Summer was at full boil.

Tom walked on, descending. His tears dried, or perhaps evaporated. Contrary to what he had told Alex, his bag did seem heavier and he stopped to rest for a moment. It must be that immense Auden, he thought. Maybe since Wright hadn't been home—or hadn't opened the door—he might as well jettison it. But no, it had been a gift from Mary.

He looked out at the view. He was a long way from the bottom. And then he realized what he was finally seeing—the inverted cone, the vaporous pit with its terraces and balconies and concentric rings for each species of the abject: the *stazione* and its *quartiere* for the junkies, prostitutes, and hustlers; the via dei Tornabuoni and the Santa Trinità for the vain and avaricious and the usurers who abetted them; the Cascine and the Campo di Marte for the homosexuals; the blocks behind the Ospedale degli Innocenti for the artists, chasing after patrons, models, fame, illumination; the hundred churches, convents, and cloisters for the saints, the sinners and the afflicted, the dead and the grieving; those places and more, infinite habitations for infinite failings. There was even a special perch, Bellosguardo, for the expatriates, who from such a height might imagine they were merely onlookers, tourists at the inferno. But they fell too, and by the gravest sin, pride, by thinking they were above it all.

That night, Tom slept in the Hotel San Remo, in Rilke's room. At first, the clerk said it was already taken. But Tom asked him to double-check, and by some happy turn, it was, after all, available. Tom was a little stunned by the tariff, which was considerably higher during the summer months. But the day had been a perfect chain of perfect ironies—of dislocated consciousness finding form in happenstance—and Tom wasn't going to break it.

So there he was, where it all began, if it began anywhere; of his going too far, of going off the deep end. With Mary, with art and ideas, with letting love shape his purpose, his end. Well, maybe it had shaped his end. Here he was, back with Rilke, who had abandoned and betrayed wives, children, lovers, patrons, and friends, all for what love—the thing he wanted—required of him.

Tom went out and got a bottle of wine and a piece of cheese, and sat in the room eating and getting buzzed just as he had on his previous stay. He had come, he supposed, to discover the essence of the last five months, the thing that had once seemed so important to him. But whatever it was, it escaped him now.

It wasn't that he felt empty. It was that there were so many choices about how to feel, and then there were the feelings about the feelings, which multiplied themselves—refracted—infinitely. He had thought he wanted Wright, and then he'd lost

Wright, and he'd wanted Mary, and then he'd wanted her to go away. Now he wanted both Mary and Wright and it was him that had to go away—or couldn't bear to stay. Now he only knew that there was a hole in his original thesis for the essay he had never written: that not just Baudelaire but Rilke, too, had been superseded by Morrissey. Maybe, because of the way art worked, Morrissey was quietly superseding everything. Heaven knows I'm miserable now. That was the one true thing he knew.

Mary noticed that Tom was gone, but did not ask Alex about it: she and Alex, understandably, weren't speaking, and it seemed to Mary that, under the circumstances, Tom, too, would scarcely confide in him.

So she said nothing, and then at ten o'clock she went to her room, and at eleven she went to Tom's room and climbed into his bed, hoping to find him there in the dark, hoping she had failed to hear him come home.

She lay there until midnight. She couldn't sleep. There was something odd in the climate of the room, not so much cold or damp, but perhaps a drop in the barometric pressure, an absence larger than just the absence of Tom's body beside hers.

She got out of bed and turned on the light as she might have done when she was small to make sure there was nothing in the closet or lurking behind the door. It took her a while to see that all Tom's things were gone, that the room was empty save for the bed, the dresser, the desk, the chair, and her.

Just to be sure, she lay in Tom's bed for the rest of the night, and her mind spun scenarios to account for his disappearance: had he perhaps reconciled with Wright, or met someone new, or had he simply run away from home; run away because Mary didn't love him enough—hadn't offered him a life with her—or because he was confused or threatened by the baby or because Mary had offended him by not acknowledging him as the father, by not asking him to take his rightful place in that role?

In the morning she went down to the kitchen, and she thought she would say something off-hand to Alex, along the lines of, "You haven't seen Tom, have you?" He came into the kitchen to fill his coffee mug not long after her, but before she could put her question to him, he said, "Maddalena never came home."

"Maybe she just went back to where she came from."

"She doesn't come *from* anywhere. She liked it here. She would have come back if she was okay."

"Don't be so sure."

"What, did you say something to her?" Alex stepped forward.

"I have *nothing* to say to her. Assuming we could even understand each other."

"Well, I'm worried."

"So am I. About Tom. He's gone. All his stuff in his room is gone."

Alex stepped back, turned his back to Mary, and refilled his mug. "Well, yeah, he left."

"He told you that? Why? What for?"

"Because it's an impossible situation for him. He's the meat in the sandwich, the third wheel."

"Can you try not speaking in clichés and tell me what happened?"

"Okay. He's neither here nor there." Alex turned around and looked at Mary. "That's a Turner cliché. Is that better?"

"So is he with Wright?"

"I doubt it. I think he's gone home, to Seattle."

"Without saying a word to me. That doesn't make any sense," said Mary. "But he told you."

"He told me. He told me the whole deal."

"The whole deal. What does that mean?"

"You and him."

"He just . . . sort of mentioned all this?"

"I had an idea. A theory. I asked him to verify it."

Mary grimaced. "Where do you get off fucking *investigating* me? Asking questions about me? Putting people on the spot so they feel like they have to run away?"

"He didn't run away. He saw that the three of us couldn't go on here, in this house. So he left."

"I don't believe you. He wouldn't go without saying something to me."

Alex took a sip of coffee. "I asked him not to," he said.

"You asked him. And he just went along?" said Mary. "I don't think he'd do that. He's not that big a jerk."

"I'd say he is. Anyway, he saw it was for the best. I'm sure he'll write."

Mary stepped forward and flung her palm against Alex's face as hard as she could, hard enough so that the recoil of his head was visible. He recovered his balance and, reddening, hissed, "You fucking bitch." He seized the lapels of her bathrobe, lifted her nearly off the floor, shaking her, pushing her towards the opposite wall.

Mary was shouting, "Alex, stop," not hysterically, but evenly, like the car alarms that used to bay through the night on the street where they lived in Seattle. They had reached the other side of the room, Mary's back to the wall, Alex still shaking and lifting her. Here, Mary thought, is where he starts smashing my head against the plaster, the white plaster that he paints with my blood.

But Alex stopped, staggered backward, panting, and Mary realized that she, too, was panting. "You said I'd changed into somebody, somebody"—and here she stopped to catch her breath—"totally different. But look at you. You're just a pig, a violent crazy pig."

"I guess one thing changes and then everything else does." Alex dragged his hand across his forehead and down to the cheek where Mary had struck him. Then he examined the hand. "It's chaos theory."

"Bullshit, Alex. You just lost it. You went violently crazy and abusive."

"And you hitting me, what was that?"

"What you deserved. But what *you* did was assault. You'd be busted for that at home."

"Here they'd have burned you at the stake a few years back for the shit you did with Tom and god knows who else."

"I'm sure they take violence against women seriously now. Maybe I should call the police and find out."

"I hear they were just here."

"Tom told you about that?"

"He confirmed it."

"So you've talked to Wright," Mary said. She was aware that the anger, the incisiveness, was draining from her voice; that she was tired; that Alex must have succeeded in shaking, if not the life, some degree of vitality out of her.

"Yeah. He's not a nice man."

"Neither are you. I should be afraid to be alone in this house with you."

"That won't happen again."

"That's what abusers always say."

"Oh, come on, Mary."

"Okay. But it goes without saying I want you out of here. Right away."

"I can't just yet," said Alex. "And you need me, remember? To pay the bills."

"So you're just going to stay against my will, hold me like a prisoner in my own house?"

"It's your prison. Sell it."

"You think you can intimidate me into doing that?"

"No. You don't intimidate. And here you are, scaring the shit out me again."

"You're scared of me. That's ironic."

"It's not ironic. It's straight-on reasonable. Ask anyone. Ask your friend Wright."

"I don't talk to Wright any more."

"Well, there you go," Alex said. "Look, I have to leave now. To look for Maddalena."

Mary nodded. She was not defeated, not when Alex had shamed himself with his violence. But she saw they were at best deadlocked, chained one to the other, sentenced together to some eternity or another.

It did not take long for Alex to find Maddalena. He saw her and three of her friends on one of the Eurostar platforms, having apparently just emerged from an empty first-class car. He waved his arm high in the air, but she didn't see him. Then, when perhaps twenty feet separated them, he caught her eye. She beamed and began to skip towards him, but stopped and looked back at her friends. She started in Alex's direction again, but now she walked without haste.

"Hey, hi Alessandro," she said in tone of abstracted cheer. "How's it going?"

"I don't know. I was worried."

"What is 'worried'?"

"Preoccupato."

"Di chi?"

"You."

"I? I am great."

"That's good then," Alex said. "Do you want to come back with me now? We can paint you some more."

"Okay." Maddalena looked over her shoulder and indicated her friends. "I am saying *ciao,* okay?"

"Sure," said Alex. Maddalena loped back to her companions from the empty railroad car and spoke to them for perhaps half a minute, and then she returned to Alex's side. "*Allora,* we make to the studio of Alex," she said.

They drove up to Bellosguardo in silence until Maddalena said, "So what way do you paint me now?"

"I'm not sure yet." Alex was grateful they had something to

talk about, that the uncanny sensation he felt of being a father driving a wayward daughter home might cease. He saw she had changed her clothes, that she wore a long flowing skirt. "Maybe *come un angelo. O una ballerina.*"

"*Che bella.* Maybe *un angelo che balla.*"

"Maybe," said Alex. "We'll see." He was still distracted. He had wondered whether he ought to say anything, but Maddalena gave no sign that she had caused him any concern by her absence, offered no excuse or apology. She merely chattered on: about how angels were always beautiful and so he would have to make her especially beautiful in this painting and perhaps they could find something very lovely for her to wear.

As he brought her into the villa, he was relieved to find that Mary was neither in the kitchen nor the *salone,* that he could reinstall Maddalena without her and Mary encountering each other. That would come later, he hoped, when he would broach the idea of Maddalena taking Tom's old room.

When they entered the studio, Maddalena ran to the painting of the Turin girl and regarded it intently, her face scarcely six inches from the canvas. She turned and said, "Can I touch her?"

"If you want. It's dry."

"I will be very soft."

"It's okay," Alex said. "You can't hurt it."

She continued to look intently at the canvas as she raised her hand to it, letting her palm hover just above the surface as though she detected some heat or vibration there. Then, after half a minute, she stepped back and looked some more. She said, finally, "I am not very pretty. I am . . . *sporca*—"

"Dirty. You're supposed to be. You're a poor girl. But you're a beautiful poor girl."

"But this time, I am *splendida,* okay?"

"Okay."

"*Come supermodella,* okay?"

"Much more so. *Assai piu splendida. Promesso,*" Alex said. "But hey, you must be hungry."

"No. I am great."

"So we'll start, then. We'll take some pictures."

"Okay." Maddalena began to walk towards Alex, striding languidly, each leg nearly hooking round the other as it came forward. Her eyes were blank, her mouth a gelid pout.

Alex laughed. "No, not the *supermodella.* Do the angel."

"*Come,* the angel?"

"However you want. Imagine it."

"Okay. I image it." Maddalena stood very still, very straight. She closed her eyes, tipped her head down just slightly, and after a moment she raised her arms up before her, almost over her head.

"That's very beautiful."

"I make the *angelo dell'annunziata.*"

Alex took several photographs from different angles. "We could paint that."

"I need a flower, *un giglio*—"

"A lily."

"—and a beautiful angel dress."

"We'll see," Alex said. "But what about the dancing?"

"You want her a ballerina?"

"Maybe not. Maybe just twirl around a little."

"*Che vuole dire* 'twirl'?"

"Spin. Like this." Alex put his arms out and spun around, raising and lowering his arms, fluttering his hands and fingers.

"Okay, *capito.*" Maddalena began to twirl slowly, and Alex took a picture. She increased her speed, and he took another. Then she thrust out one leg, the leg and foot nearly perpendicular to her body, all the while continuing to turn and spin.

"You really are a ballerina. You dance beautifully."

"And I—me—am beautifully too?" Maddalena asked, a little short of breath.

"Very." He took another picture. "Now a little faster. I want to capture the motion."

"*Come mai?* I don't understand 'catcher.'"

"Capture. Make it look like it's moving in the painting. Even though it's not."

"That also I don't understand."

"It's okay. You'll see. Anyway, go a little faster."

Maddalena began to twirl around. *"Così?"* she called out.

"*Sì*, but even faster, okay?"

Maddalena said nothing, but only spun faster. Her skirt whirled outward, rising so her legs were visible almost up to her buttocks. It was some time before Alex, who normally saw everything, on whom nothing visible was lost, noticed what Maddalena would at first insist were only *morsi,* only mosquito bites.

Mary was surprised that Alex came to speak to her so soon, the very next morning. She had imagined that the most advantageous strategy for him would be simply to stall, to starve her out as she saw her money and her options disappear. But meanwhile, she had conceived a strategy of her own. It would not overcome the stalemate, but it evened things up.

Her confidence increased as she saw, even before they sat down at the table on the edge of the garden, that Alex looked weary, hungover perhaps, but certainly a little preoccupied. "Look," he had said. "I just want to settle everything now. End the suspense."

"That's a surprise."

"Well, something's come up. With Maddalena."

"I saw she was back," Mary said. "So she's doing some more posing for the Turin girl?"

"No, that's pretty much done. We're starting another."

Mary's face tightened. "Excuse me, Alex. Our agreement was for one painting, and then you and her were supposed to be out of here. So what's going on?"

"She needs to stay here, and I need to stay with her."

"Well, that's impossible. It's bad enough having you here. I'm pregnant. I should be avoiding stress."

"I can't leave now," said Alex. "And if I did, where are you?"

"I'm here, in my house, with my baby."

"And how are you paying the bills?"

Mary looked down, released her breath, and said, "This is just the same shit as last time. You haven't changed your mind."

"I could have, up until yesterday. I thought about it. But I need it all now, for—"

"Leverage?"

"For my own needs."

"Which include coercing me to sell my house. Or I have nothing for my child, right?"

"That's not how it has to be. There are alternatives."

"Such as?"

"I thought Maddalena could have Tom's old room. I could go on living in the studio. It'd be pretty much like it's always been, everybody does their work, has their privacy, except instead of Tom—"

"That is just fucking . . . risible. You're not serious. Obviously, you're insane. I mean we're supposed to have this happy little ménage of me and you and your pubescent girlfriend."

"That's really unfair."

"It's really sick, Alex. I mean, I know 'Everything is permitted' here, but you're definitely pushing the envelope."

"That's not it at all. It's giving Maddalena a family for a while, which she really needs. And it gives you and your baby a home—"

"I'm sorry. This is insane. I'm just going to get up and leave and make other arrangements. You've forced my hand."

"What arrangements?" Alex said.

"I'm going to call the police and have them throw you out."

"And why are they going to want to do that?"

"Because you beat me up. I should have done it yesterday."

Alex did not speak immediately. Then he said, "They'd probably wonder why you didn't call right away, what with you being all broken and bleeding. Unless it suited you better to wait until you could use it against me."

"I'm not using it against you. I'm doing the right thing. You crossed a line that a man is never supposed to cross. With a pregnant woman, for god's sake. I don't want you here anyway. But now I am fucking in fear of my safety."

"What a load of shit. You don't believe that for a minute."

"Well, it's what I'm doing."

"And I don't suppose there's an 'unless' in there somewhere. Like if I just happened to slip you four or five hundred thousand bucks."

"Let's say five. Sure, I'd take that as a sign of your . . . remorse. I'd feel the score was more even."

"And I could stay, me and Maddalena?"

"This is getting tiresome, Alex. No fucking way. And I don't think you have much choice, really. Not now."

"So you think if you call your friends at the *carabinieri*—"

"I'll call whoever it takes. *Polizia, Finanza*—"

"And they throw me out, maybe even put me in jail. Why is that going to make me want to give you a bunch of money?"

"Because I don't think you'd like it in jail, being investigated. Maybe being prosecuted, maybe even serving a sentence."

Alex threaded his fingers together. "So I'm down in custody, in the *questura,* I'm going to come to my senses and cut you a cheque. But suppose I decide to call, say, the *Finanza* and let them know that you and I have reached this understanding, that there's this big transfer of foreign funds—"

"Then obviously we haven't reached a real understanding. No point in your writing the cheque. So you just stay in jail. To cut your nose off to spite your face."

"And you stay here until you're forced to sell, and you take whatever sum you get and move to Portland. To cut your nose off to spite your face."

"I should call your bluff."

"I don't have a bluff to call. I'm totally serious about this, about staying, about Maddalena."

"To the point where you're willing to live under some weird armed truce?"

"If that's how it has be," Alex said.

"But why? I really don't get it."

"Oh, shit. I suppose you need to know this. If that's what it takes," Alex said wearily. "Maddalena's using."

"Using?" Mary asked. "What, heroin?"

"Yeah. I saw needle marks on her thighs."

"So this kid you want me to share my house with is a junkie. I won't ask how you happened to be looking at her thighs."

"She was dancing. Twirling. In the studio."

"I see," said Mary. "The mind boggles. I mean, the dance of the sugarplum junkies—"

"This isn't a joke. She could end up with a serious problem."

"Which you want to . . . import into my house. Her habit."

"She doesn't have a habit. Not yet, anyway. But if she goes back down the hill . . ."

"And how do you know she's not an addict already?"

"She was just skin-popping. She and her friends wouldn't know how to find a vein on her thigh."

Mary shook her head. She said, "Why do you know so much about all this? The technical aspects."

Alex forced out a long exhalation of breath. "Jens used. He gave it up before I really knew him. But then, ten years ago, in '91, '92, everybody was. It was the vogue. The *Zeitgeist*."

"Even you?"

"Even me, a little."

"So you didn't have a habit?"

"Not really. But I was getting to like it pretty well. Jens got me to stop." Alex shrugged. "He showed me that drinking was, you know, my true medium."

"That's kind of a mixed blessing."

"Things are always mixed. It's like paint."

"So that's part of why you owed him."

"Yeah. That and more."

"I never quite understood what you saw in him," Mary said. "I mean, I didn't mind having him around. It made me feel less corporate."

"I liked that you didn't mind."

"I might have felt differently if I'd known about you guys using junk."

"We never did it together."

"You should have told me, you know," Mary said.

"And if I had, what would that have accomplished?"

"I think it's a matter of trust. Of me knowing the person I was really with."

"You were with me. The junk was just some lame thing I did once, that everyone was doing, like some stupid music you used to love, like bad art you used to think was really cool."

"I don't know if it's the same thing," said Mary. "But I don't want to argue about it. I just don't want junk in this house. It's sleazy."

Alex laughed. "Oh, it's an offence against good taste."

"Look, I don't even want to hear about it. I don't want anything remotely connected with it in this house. I don't want that girl bringing it with her."

"She won't. I promise. She's a good kid. She just needs a little break."

"For how long?" Mary asked.

"I don't know. Not too long. Not forever."

"That's not very helpful."

"Look, I just want to paint a few paintings and do this one good thing. You can have the money."

Mary stopped. "So if I agree, what are my responsibilities? I'm not going to become her mother. I won't. I can't."

"Just be yourself. Tell her what you like and don't like. She's already really . . . autonomous, living the way she did."

"So you promise I won't have to cook her meals, do her laundry, tell her to take a bath—"

"No, no. Nothing like that. I'd do all that stuff," Alex said. "But, I mean, maybe you could help her with her English. I try, but I've got my limitations as a teacher."

"What somebody should do is teach her proper Italian. Correct grammar and usage."

"Maybe you could do that. She'd love it."

"I doubt it. Anyway, don't cook up any little schemes to get me to bond with her," Mary said. "I'm writing and I'm having my baby. That's it. It's all I want and it's all I'm doing. *Capito?*"

"Sure. You've got it."

12.

Isabella

Within two weeks, Mary received papers in the mail from her bank reporting that securities to the value of a little over one half-million American dollars had been deposited on her behalf. Then, at the end of August, she had a postcard from Tom. He was living with Jason Fiori, the CULTURE.ALT columnist for the Seattle *CityReader*. He was working at a Starbucks. He wondered how Wright was. He hoped she was okay. That was all.

Mary read the card, and read it again, as though it might say something more if she bore down on it. But it was what it was, slight and inadequate, a little like Tom himself. She was not lovesick or heartbroken. Tom had made a perfectly agreeable lover, but he was in no way a partner for someone who was becoming a mother. She felt herself fall out of love with him in much the way she noticed that her breasts had swelled and tightened, yet another transformation dictated not by her but by her pregnancy.

That was not to say she did not miss him, often desperately so. He was her best friend, and under the new dispensation Alex had imposed at the Villa Donatello, Mary had no friends or even (with Wright now embargoed) anyone to talk to. When she did not feel furious about it, she merely mourned it, grieved for Tom and her and how things had once been in this, her house.

In the interim, Alex's Maddalena had settled into Tom's old room, and spent most of her time there or wherever Alex was, following him, Mary reflected, much as Tom had once followed her. When the girl and Mary encountered one another, it was usually in the kitchen or the upstairs hall, as the girl was making her way to or from the bathroom. Mary was relieved they didn't have to share, that she had propitiously insisted on the second upstairs bathroom when they were remodelling the villa. On the other hand, she could not but help wonder what the girl was *doing* in there beyond taking baths that might be measured in hours. More than once, Mary poked through the wastebasket, looking for scorched bottle caps, tiny bags and vials, spent matches and lighters. But after a month, Mary could only conclude that the girl occasionally applied cheap makeup and fragrance, and that she did not yet menstruate.

There had been conversations between them, at first deeply awkward, undermined still more by the girl's defective Italian and rudimentary English. She had no grammar and no concept of number or tense, while at the same time she embraced every catchphrase, cliché, and idiom she overheard and misused them with determined enthusiasm. Mary's intention was, if not to snub the girl, then at least to discourage conversation and keep her at a distance. But the fact was that Mary the editor and author could not help but correct the girl's mistakes and lexical infelicities, which grated on her both on aesthetic and personal grounds: her response of "You bet" or "I am so whatever" to virtually every remark set Mary's teeth on edge, and the girl's habit of calling her "Mrs. Alex" was cheeky, if not deeply offensive. Correcting Maddalena's speech therefore was not a matter of pedagogy but pure survival.

After the first two weeks Mary ceased to bristle and instead resigned herself to the intrusion when the girl appeared in the kitchen or the *salone* or even in her studio with one question or another. She knew that Alex was putting the girl up to this, pleading ignorance and sending her to ask Mary, the house's *dottoressa* of English usage. So the girl would find her four or five or six times a day, and Mary would put down her book or her pen or lift her hands from the keyboard and listen with an openly weary expression.

"So what is 'here' to mean?" Maddalena asked one morning.

"In what sense? *Nel senso di . . . ?*"

The girl looked at her blankly, and Mary tried again, "What do you mean? Like '*sentire*'? Or like '*qui*'?"

"I don't understand. Because they are the same, okay?" The girl put her hands down on Mary's desk.

"They sound the same," Mary said. "But they don't mean the same thing."

"*Dunque,* it is 'here,'" and the girl stamped her foot, "and 'hear,'" and pointed to her ear, "and 'here,'" and tugged her hair. All the same. It's fucked, you bet."

"Don't say fuck."

"I say it wrong?"

"Don't say it at all. It's a curse, *una maledizione*."

"But how do I understand—'here' and 'here' and 'here'?"

"Well, first," Mary said, "this"—she touched her hair—"'*capelli*' is not 'here.' It's '*hair.*'"

"Yes, I know. 'Here.'"

"No, 'hair.' Listen. 'Ha-a-air.' Now you try."

The girl stood very erect and pulled her lips away from her teeth. "He-ar-a."

"Better. Again."

"Okay." She paused, and then breathed out, "Haa-ara."

"Good," said Mary. "That's it. Hear the difference? 'Here.' 'Hair.' 'Here.' 'Hair.'"

"Maybe. But they are still almost the same."

"You'll learn."

The girl came close, reached out and took a strand of Mary's hair in her fingers. "You have beautiful 'he-er-a.'"

"Ha-a-air."

"Ha-ara."

"Good," Mary said. The girl was still holding the strand. Mary reached up, took her hand, and moved it away. "But thank you," she added.

"I want it," the girl said. She was still pressed against Mary's desk, leaning over it.

"What, like a wig, *una parrucca*? You can't. It's mine."

"No, like the same, when I am big."

"So you would like hair *like it* when you are big, right?"

"Yes, I like it very much. Like it."

"You already have beautiful hair. Better than mine. But I'll explain. There is 'like' in the sense of *'come'* and 'like' in the sense of *'amare'*—"

"It is too dark. I want it more light. Like Madonna."

"I think her hair is dyed."

"Her he-era is dead? It's *una parrucca*? I don't think so."

"No, it's coloured. *Capelli tinti*."

"Vero?"

"I don't know it for a fact," said Mary. "But she's Italian, like you."

"Like the same as me?"

"I think so."

"But she is American."

"But her family came from Italy. A long time ago, I imagine."

The girl said, "Why are they left?"

"I don't know. Perhaps they were poor, they wanted to immigrate, to get ahead—"

"What is 'imgrate'? What is 'ahead'?"

"To 'immigrate' is to move to another country, to live. And to 'get ahead' is to have a better life," said Mary. "To have more money, I suppose."

"So you and Alessandro are imgrates. To here." The girl stamped her foot. "To Italia."

"Yes."

"But you are already ahead, having money." The girl leant over the desk and then rocked back on her feet.

"Yes, I guess so."

"So why do you go *here*." She stamped her foot again to clarify her meaning.

"To do my writing, Alex's painting, to have a better—" but here Mary broke off, and then began again. "Because we like it. That's all. Now," Mary said, "I'll answer the rest of your question. Then I need to work."

"Okay."

"All right. So 'hair' is 'hair.' But there is 'hear' like *'sentire'* and 'here' like *'qui.'*"

"So how is the difference to know?"

"By the context," Mary said. "The situation."

"I don't understand." The girl picked up Mary's pen and, before Mary could object, put it down.

"It's the circumstance—the place the words are said. And the other words around them. So if I say 'I hear you,' it means 'I hear *you,*'" and Mary pointed at the girl. "But if I say 'I'm here,' it means 'I am *here.*'" Mary slapped the desk with her hand.

"*Dunque,* 'I am hearing you' is I am *here* or you are here with me?"

Mary felt intruded upon, less by the girl's questions than her body's constant motion. She had, Mary surmised, a capacity perhaps unique to her age group to simultaneously fidget and to be rapt. "I'll try to explain it again. But not now. This afternoon. I have to work now."

"Okay. I go and find you later."

"If you must."

"Thank you, Mary," the girl said. "I understand better. I am not so much so whatever."

"No, you aren't so *lost,* confused. Not 'so whatever.'"

"So I am here you, right?"

"Whatever, Maddalena," Mary said. "I'll see you later." This was the first time Mary could recollect having called the girl by her name.

Later, in September, when the blaze of heat and light was not so intense, it became Mary and Maddalena's custom to walk every afternoon. Or, rather, Maddalena followed Mary out the gate several times, and Mary tried unsuccessfully to drive her off, addressing her brusquely, in crisp, formal Italian.

I prefer to walk alone. It is my custom to make a diurnal excursus.

You shouldn't be alone. It will make you a sad, lonely person.

It is fundamental to my well-being. Otherwise, for your sake, I will come down with dementia praecox.

If you are sad, you will lose your looks.

And if you are so insolent you will turn into a sassy minx.

Actually, you look tired. Maybe you and Alex should visit a spa.

The girl, Mary felt, was unnerving her, trying—intentionally or not—to trip her up. She feared she might make a grammatical slip.

Look, Maddalena, I love you, yet—

And I love you too. So we shall walk together.

Shit, Mary thought. She made the best response she could muster.

If you promise not to speak.

Maddalena liked to walk—she was an active, vital girl and had felt confined inside the villa, to say nothing of Alex's studio—so to remain quiet was not so onerous. Her walks with Mary became a time to observe and reflect on what she saw, rather as Alex did in his studio. She tried, therefore, merely to look, to see, and form an impression of the neighbourhood and the countryside.

Maddalena saw that there were not many walkers up here in Bellosguardo, that it was a settlement composed of villas and their gates, through which the inhabitants came and went mostly in cars and taxis. So she was struck when, not once but several times, they came upon a man on the road, also walking in a leisured and undirected manner.

He almost always wore a white shirt and cream-coloured pants and he carried a stick. Each time they encountered him, Mary talked to him in English for a minute or so, which he seemed to understand quite well. In any case, they spoke together at such a clip that Maddalena could make out few if any of the words. Then the man would speak to Maddalena herself in Italian, quite beautiful Italian in fact, and she might even have thought he also was Italian. But surely not from Tuscany, but perhaps from Milan or Turin for, despite his age, his skin was quite fair, almost glassy. Maddalena imagined that in strong enough sunlight you might see right through him.

Maddalena asked Mary what she and the man talked about, and Mary said they "exchanged pleasantries," which she explained was essentially saying hello and goodbye at some length with an interval between for talking about the weather. Maddalena was not sure this was all they said to one another, for she had noticed that when the man came into view Mary's jaw seemed to slide forward and cement itself in that position until he was gone.

The fair-skinned man appeared three or four days a week for nearly a month, and then, about the time of St. Francis's feast day, Maddalena realized they hadn't seen him for some time. She asked Mary what had happened to him, and Mary told her that she had heard he was sick, that he had to stay inside all the time now, and that in any case he was very old, so perhaps he did not have a long time to live.

Maddalena asked Mary if she was going to visit the man, perhaps to bring him something to eat. But Mary said no, she probably would not. They weren't really friends, but only neighbours. Alex, too, was curious about the fair-skinned man, about how often they had seen him and how long he and Mary had talked. Maddalena told Alex what she could, but that was very little. Her

English was still very basic, and did not extend to parsing the nuances of pleasantries.

Around the same time the fair-skinned man ceased his walks, Alex had a serious talk with Maddalena. He began by noting that Maddalena had been living with him and Mary in the villa for over six weeks, and he asked her if she liked it there. Oh, of course she did: she loved the villa and the garden and Alex especially, and she thought that she and Mary had become friends. So he asked her if she would like to stay "indefinitely," which, he explained, meant for as long as she liked. Mary would teach her not just English but other subjects and then in a little while she could attend the *scuola media*. After Alex had explained all this, he asked her if she would miss her friends or her relations in the city. She said she didn't think so. Then he asked if there was anyone she wanted to telephone or write or perhaps meet. She said she supposed she ought to leave a note for her mother at her friends' apartment, but she didn't really feel like it. She explained why, and it was then that Alex explained to her about the word "maggot."

He persuaded her that she ought to leave a note for her mother anyway; that they could go together and drop off a note. Then, the one last thing, he asked her to promise never to go anywhere near the Stazione Santa Maria Novella.

"So she wants to stay," Alex said. "Are you okay with that?"

"Does it really matter to you whether I am or not?" said Mary.

"Of course it does. We're all living here together." They were sitting in the *salone,* late in the day, while Maddalena was having a bath. Mary could feel it was autumn. Night was coming early. The olives were beginning to be gathered, to fall into nets and onto groundcloths; the olives they'd told Tom he would be picking.

"Living under your thumb. Under whatever conditions you decide to impose."

"That's bullshit, Mary. We hit a stalemate. Each of us had the same amount of power over the other. So we split the difference. It was voluntary."

"Voluntary in the sense that you had a gun to my head?"

"And you had one to mine."

Mary said, "Somebody should have had the guts to pull the trigger."

"We both wanted the same things."

"The same things, but without each other."

"That wasn't how I felt," said Alex. "You wanted all the changes. I was happy with the status quo."

"Which was the problem," Mary meant to say this forcefully, but it came out in a murmur. "Maybe we could have gone on the same. If you'd been willing to change." She wondered if he realized they had been in Italy together for exactly a year this month.

"That doesn't make any sense. I mean you—after five perfect years—just announced you were going to overturn everything."

"Basically, I only wanted a baby. It's a pretty standard thing for a woman to want. Maybe the artists and junkies in Belltown aren't—"

"Don't, Mary," Alex said. She made no response, and he went on. "It was totally . . . antithetical to our life together, to everything. And you wanted me to just turn 180 degrees and say 'Oh, okay. No big deal.'"

"I asked. I tried to discuss it with you. But you wouldn't even consider—"

"What was so fucking awful about what we had?"

Mary wondered what he would do—what would happen to them—if she said, "Nothing. I'd die to get it back. Really, I would." But she said something only a little less true.

"You never get to have what you had. Things change whether you want them to or not."

"You kind of forced them. You decided you *wanted* something, and, like always—"

"No," Mary said sharply. "It wasn't just something I wanted. It was something I needed . . . to complete myself, someone I was becoming. Whether I wanted to or not."

Alex shook his head. "I don't think so. You just wanted to complete the picture: the house and the garden and then the baby. It was just the *idea* of a child. As opposed to a real child like Maddalena. Who really needed us. Of course you didn't have any use—"

"Don't try to shame me about that. She was your project. That you forced on *me*. That was something *you* wanted."

"She needed help."

"There are a hundred kids who need somebody's help. You just wanted to paint this one."

Alex looked away and then said, "Well, that was a factor."

"And this isn't an abstraction." Mary touched her stomach.

"No," Alex said, "It's not." He held fire. He had lost interest or simply run out of arguments.

Mary burst the silence. "You know what really galls me, Alex?"

"No. Tell me."

"That you *think* you love me. And that thinking it entitles you to be smug, to condescend to me. When really, you don't love who I am now. Or even who I used to be. You just made up an image of me and framed it and hung it on the wall and decided you loved it."

"So it's like *Pygmalion* in reverse. I took a real woman and turned her into a statue," Alex said. "That's slick, Mary. Even if it's not true. Because I did love you. I saw you and I loved you."

"But then you stopped looking."

"I don't know. What does it matter now?"

"Not very much."

"So what about Maddalena?"

"Oh, god. I just want her out of my hair—my 'he-are-ra.'"

"Oh, come on. You kind of like her. It won't cost you anything to admit it."

"It feels like it would."

"Because I would have been right?"

"Not exactly. More because it would give you something else to be smug about, to condescend to me about."

"Come on, I'm not going to do that."

"You're doing it right now," Mary said. "You're thinking how nicely things have turned out. You're happy about it."

"So if I'm happy, I'm condescending to you?"

"Happy in that 'everything's mellow' way of yours, yes. Because it's not."

"We're all getting along."

"But that's just an accommodation, a compromise. It doesn't mean I'm happy too."

"Why shouldn't you be? You're writing, you're having a baby, you've got the villa and money in the bank—"

"You see, that—right there—is the absolute essence of condescension."

"I'm just being optimistic. It's the way I am," Alex said. "Maddalena told me something. She told me she asked you what 'mellow' meant, because she'd heard me say it. And first you said something about it being like old wood or wine or something. But then you said, 'Just go look at Alex. That's mellow.' So you see, you understand me. You just don't want to say so. Otherwise you'd have to stop freezing me out, maybe even have to smile once in a while."

"So you think I'm just being a bitch."

"Yeah, actually I do. But only to me. Maddalena says you're nice. To her. Even to Wright Turner."

"It's just small talk. He knows I don't like him. I know he doesn't like me."

"Kind of like us," Alex said.

"I suppose it is."

"Except, really, I don't not like you."

"That's nice," said Mary. "Of course I don't suppose it costs you anything. With your pills, your canned happiness."

Alex turned his head as though dodging something. "Shit, Mary, ease up, okay? This is how I am, how I feel, with or without it."

"Sure. But you ease up with . . . with coming onto me or whatever it is you're doing."

"It's called being friendly, being kind."

"Well, I'm not ready for it."

"Whatever." Alex laughed. "I am so whatever," he said in a high, accented voice. "So, anyway, you're okay with helping her a little with her English?"

"I suppose. Maybe she can learn to read."

"Can she read in Italian?"

"I think so."

"She reads magazines."

"She looks at the pictures, you mean," said Mary. "It's like shopping. She wants the clothes, the hair, the skin."

"She must know she's pretty. Beautiful, in fact. I've told her."

"It doesn't matter. No one ever knows that for sure, no woman anyway."

"That must be hard. Like you can never just stop and look at yourself and say, 'Yes, that's me. I'm beautiful.'"

"I guess so. Not that I'd know."

"Yes, you would. You're—"

"No, Alex. Please don't," Mary said. "So is there anything else?"

Alex thought for an instant and said, "Well, I've had this idea. About doing frescoes—real ones—on the inside walls."

"Here? In the villa?"

"Well, yes. Of course. I think it'd be totally—"

"No, Alex. Absolutely no fucking way."

* * *

Another week passed. It was the middle of October, which is vaunted as perhaps the most beautiful time of year in Tuscany. The grape and olive harvests are underway. The days are comfortably warm, the nights cool enough to sleep deeply. Soon, there will be a snap in the air, the smell of chestnut smoke pressing against the cold.

Maddalena and Mary were sitting in the *salone* reading *The Mill on the Floss*. Mary read aloud, and then she would let Maddalena try. Mary listened, occasionally correcting her mistakes in pronunciation. These were many, but Mary chose not to interrupt Maddalena for most of them: it was important, Mary believed, that the girl get caught up in the story, more important than sounding a particular word correctly or even knowing precisely what it meant.

Thus, more often than not, Maggie and Tom Tulliver were "Moggie and Toam Tooleevere," and Phillip admired Maggie's "here-a." But for all that, the book—the life and the art of it—was becoming Maddalena's, her story, which she took possession of as her eyes trawled the page and the drafts and quavers of her breath spilt from her lips. And as Maddalena read (that being the only sound in the room save the rustle of the gardener at his work outside, the gardener who kept Mary apprised of Wright's condition, of his recent move to the hospital), Mary almost believed herself happy, or content in some manner.

Maddalena stopped reading. She had reached the end of a paragraph, the bottom of the page. "I stop now?"

"If you want. Do you understand everything?"

"I think so maybe. Anyway, I am guessing the end already."

"And what do you think happens?"

"Maggie will have Stephen. They will be *sposati*, okay?"

"Do you want to know what really happens, or would that spoil it for you?"

"You tell me."

"She gives him up."

"She breaks him off?"

"Breaks *up*. Yes."

"For what? The English like to be sad?"

"No, she wanted to be good."

"It's good to be in love, to marry, to be happy."

"But she would have to betray a friend to—"

"What does 'betray' mean?"

"*Tradire*."

"Oh, okay. That is our famous *storia,* here at *Firenze*."

"Your history, your tradition, I suppose. Betrayal."

"But Maggie is good but she is never to be happy. Why does she decide this?"

"She believes it's more important to be good than to be happy. Otherwise, I suppose, you betray yourself."

"And the writer believed this?"

"Oh, very much."

"And the writer is a woman. Even though she calls herself 'Giorgio' when she became writer."

"Became *a* writer. It's not like Italian. It was unusual for a woman to be a writer then. So she used a man's name."

"But that is a betray. To lie about one's name."

"It was necessary. Or she believed it was."

"So she is a woman writer. But can a woman be a writer, since that time?"

"*At* that time," Mary said. "But yes. There were quite a few. Very good ones."

"And now, this day, a girl can also be writ—can also be *a* writer?"

"*To*day. Now. *Attualmente*. Yes, of course. I'm a writer."

"I know him—"

"Just 'I know.'"

"So you are writing a book like this La Giorgio. Or a movie."

"Perhaps. Anyway, I'm writing a novel. *Un romanzo*. Really, I'm working on two of them."

"And what stories are they about?"

"One is about a saint who was a nun. *A Firenze. Nel convento.* Maria Maddalena de' Pazzi."

"Maria Maddalena, *com'io. Anche Fiorentina.*"

"Yes. Like you," Mary said. "But a long time ago, almost five hundred years ago."

"And the another?"

"The *other.* It's about life here, in Italy. In a place a little like this."

"With people a little like us also?"

"Perhaps."

"So I am in this book."

"Not really you. But perhaps someone like you."

"Make me like Maggie."

"That would be nice. I'd like you to be like her anyway, in real life," Mary said. "When I was your age—or maybe a little older—it was my favourite book." It seemed to Mary this was the first time she had ever said "When I was your age" to another human being.

"And now it is also your favourite?"

"I still like it. But there are others I like more."

"What most best?"

"Best of all," said Mary. "I'm not sure. There are two or three. Maybe two, really."

"They are also about girls like Maggie?"

Mary said, "Yes, I suppose they are."

"Are they beautiful also?"

"I'm not sure Maggie is supposed to be beautiful, Maddalena," Mary said. "But, anyway, I don't think either of these women are, not especially."

"So how are they like?"

"*What* are they like. Well, they're both good and smart. Intelligent."

"That is all what they are like?"

"No, not all. One is wise. Or she becomes wise. And—" Mary stopped. She felt a cramp in her stomach, not severe, but surprisingly forceful. "And the other is rich, but perhaps not very wise."

"But it's good to be rich. To be ahead."

Mary was going to correct the girl, but the cramp was taking the will from her. She went on to the important thing. "It's nice to be rich, but not necessarily good. For example, people lie to this woman because she's rich. They manipulate her."

"What is 'manipulate'?" Maddalena asked.

Mary thought. "To try to make someone do something. Something they shouldn't do. Or wouldn't do if they knew the truth. To betray themselves."

"*Tradirsi.* That is very hard, very *complesso.*"

"Complicated. Complex." Mary stopped. The cramp had returned with greater force. "Look, Maddalena, we'd better stop now. I have a pain in my stomach that's distracting me."

"Oh, maybe it is the baby. Her little foot that she moves inside you."

"No, I don't think so. It's too soon. The baby is too little."

"Let me touch, okay?"

"It's nothing."

"Please," said Maddalena.

The cramp eased and seemed almost to have disappeared entirely. "If you want. There's nothing though."

Maddalena lay her palm on Mary's abdomen. "Oh, I think I touch something. Really." She lowered her head and lay it where her palm had been. "And I hear, *hear* something too."

"It's just my stomach," said Mary. She needed to say something to Maddalena (who gave no indication of moving her head or the hand that clasped the far side of Mary's abdomen) about boundaries. But that would require explaining what boundaries were, which was hard enough in English, and probably impossible in Italian, in which culture they did not seem to exist anyway.

So she let the girl's head remain where it was. Her cramp was easing, which made her feel that much less irritable.

"So what do you call it?" Maddalena said, her voice seeming to resonate through Mary's body like a voice in a cavern.

"Call what?" Mary shifted herself a little, and the girl's head now rested on her lap.

"The baby. When she comes."

"I don't know."

"Then you call her Maddalena, okay?"

"One's enough," Mary said, and found herself laughing in a light, unburdened register that had not been used in some time. She patted the girl's head by way of indicating this remark was mere affectionate jest.

"So if not Maddalena, what?"

"I really haven't considered it," Mary said. "Let me think." As Mary pondered this matter, she wove her fingers into the girl's hair, and, when she realized what they were doing, withdrew them quickly.

Mary put her hand to her chin. "What about Dorothea?" she said. "That's a nice name."

"It is very English. Maybe too old-fashion and stuck."

"I suppose it is. You don't hear it much any more."

"Madonna is a beautiful name," Maddalena offered in a near whisper.

"No way. Absolutely not." The girl offered no response, and Mary guessed she might be falling asleep. "What about Isabel?" Mary said a moment later to no particular interlocutor, the girl apparently having dropped off, the room otherwise empty.

"It is a nice kind name," said the cottony voice from her lap. "But too American. Isabella is better, here, in *Firenze*."

"All right. Perhaps Isabella, then."

Mary was made to spend several days in bed when she returned from the clinic, Alex and Maddalena attending to her together, except when Maddalena came alone. It took Alex two days to enter her room by himself. He sidled to her nightstand and picked up the little tray that had carried Mary's lunch, and held it before him, between Mary and him.

He cleared his throat. "I guess there's no way for me to say this without it being, I don't know . . . freighted with all kinds of other things. But I'm really sorry. I really am."

Mary looked at him and nodded. She hoped he understood that it was simply a nod, meaning nothing more or less than a nod, but she could muster no words. It would exhaust her to shape them.

It wasn't that she had no words for him in particular. She could scarcely speak to Maddalena, except in the circumscribed language of benevolent condescension that was customary between adult and child. She lived in dread, even fear, of Maddalena saying what the doctor had said—"You're healthy and young. There will be others"—; making the assumption that Alex was the father; and saying it, unlike the doctor, with utter conviction and unstanchable cheer. But so far, happily, Maddalena had said nothing.

Alex looked back at Mary and then began to turn around. It made her angry (and she was so, so angry already) to think *he* required reassurance and comfort from *her* at this point, but she managed to force out the words "I know. It's okay." He turned around and smiled at her, then took the tray and left.

That night, she mostly lay awake. Her anger struck alternating chords, bitterness and grief, and one offered no rest from the other. They merely fed each other. It was not happening the way Mary had been given to understand this process was supposed to go.

She could not read and she could not sleep, and to write, even in her journal, seemed joyless to her. So she found her old three-ring planner and address book and began to go through it. Alex had given it to her right after she'd first gone to work for

Noumena, and it rather stunned her to see that she had known so many people, performed so many tasks, lived such a manic life as the little book seemed to record.

Mary found the last address she had for Jason Fiori (they had overlapped at the *CityReader*) and after one recording and a brief conversation with one of his former roommates, she secured his current number. She dialed it. It was five o'clock in the afternoon in Seattle.

Tom's unmistakable voice answered, inflecting the greeting "Hello" into a question rather than a declaration.

"It's me," Mary said.

"It's you? Mary? Oh, wow, this is great. I really miss you."

"I miss you too. Lots." Would anyone ever miss her as Tom missed her, miss her so emphatically? "I got your card."

"Hey, I'm sorry I haven't written again. But I just didn't know what would be okay."

"Sure. I understand."

"So," Tom asked, "How is it there? Is he still living in the house? Alex, I mean?"

"Yeah. Maddalena—Angelina—too."

"Really? Wow. I didn't see that happening."

"We settled. I keep the villa. He gave me some money. And he and Maddalena get to stay."

"What for?" Tom asked. "I mean, what are they doing?"

"He's just painting her. Almost every day."

"And what's in it for you? Besides the money?"

"I don't know. It's the best I could do, at the time."

"So does Alex expect you to *mind* her or anything?"

"No. I was explicit about that," said Mary. "But actually, I'm helping her with her English. Reading and speaking."

"So you've got her reading, like, *The Wings of the Dove* or something."

"No, *The Mill on the Floss*. Stuff like that."

"You know, I could have sworn she was one of those little

maggots that tried to mug me at the train station," Tom said. "Anyway, I still don't really get exactly why she's there."

"Because she doesn't have any place else to go. And she's Alex's model. I've learned to tolerate her."

"And Alex?" Tom said.

"What?" said Mary.

"Do you tolerate him?"

"Barely. It's just a . . . truce of convenience. On a really good day we're like roommates sharing a really big house."

"Oh," Tom replied.

"So what's with you? Are you okay?"

"Basically," said Tom. "I was managing to just work part time and crash here. It wasn't putting Jason out. But now I have to go. So will he. He lost his job at the *CityReader*."

"Really? He's been doing that for maybe five years."

"Well, that's the problem. They're kind of retooling editorially. Cleaning house. No one on staff over forty. Except the editor and the publisher."

"He's that old?"

"He will be pretty soon." Tom added, "We all will eventually."

"So what are you going to do?"

"I don't know. Move to Portland maybe."

"What's in Portland?"

"Same thing as here, I guess. It just costs less."

"Well, you'll be okay. You still have most of your severance, right?"

"Most of it," Tom said.

"Well, if things get really tight, let me know, okay?"

"That's really great, Mary. But I'll be okay. So what about you? Getting some writing done?"

"Actually, yes. I'm almost done with a first draft of something. A novel."

"Wow, Mary, that's great."

"I'll send it to you when it's done. If you want."

"I'd really, really like that," Tom said.

"Read anything good lately over there?" Mary asked.

"Just that Auden you bought me. That Wright put me onto." Tom paused. "Do you ever see him?"

"Auden?"

"Ha."

"We—Maddalena and me—used to see him out walking until a couple of weeks ago. But then I heard he was sick, that he's in the hospital."

"Really? Is he okay?" Tom said. "Not that I care."

"Sure you don't."

"Okay, so it's morbid curiosity."

"I really don't know. I'll try to find out and I'll let you know."

"I wouldn't expect you to go over there or anything."

"The gardener knows everything. His wife cleans for Wright. I didn't know that until just recently."

"I wonder if that information channel runs both ways."

"It would explain a few things," Mary said. "So has he ever gotten in touch?"

"No. Not a word."

"Do you miss him?"

"Do I have to answer that?" Tom asked.

"No."

"Okay. So how about you, you know, the baby, whatever."

"I lost it. Miscarried. Just a few days ago."

"Oh god, Mary."

"I was just short of three months."

"I'm really sorry. You must feel awful," Tom said. "I wish I was there."

"No, you don't. Trust me. Anyway, it's pretty common at this stage. It happens all the time."

"It doesn't happen to you all the time."

Mary said, "You know, that's the nicest thing anybody's said to me so far."

"It must be kind of weird being around Alex."

"Oh yeah. And it was just starting to get less awkward. Now I suppose he feels bad for me but good for himself. But bad that he feels good for himself."

"But that's not your problem."

"No, I guess not," said Mary. "But you, is this weird for you? I mean, you were almost a father and now you're, I don't know . . ."

"A mourner? Surviving parent? If that matters."

"It does. It was a real baby, at least for a while. I was thinking of names."

"I'm just really sorry, Mary." Tom stopped. "Hey, you're crying."

It took Mary a moment to recover her speech. "It seems like the thing to do . . . under the circumstances."

"Do you want me to hang up? I can call back. Or you can, when you feel like it."

"No, no. It's better just to talk. With you, I mean. I can't sleep and it's two in the morning here. But we can talk all night as far as I'm concerned."

"That'd be fun."

"Just like we used to. Before . . ."

"Alex came back?" Tom paused. "Before I left," he said, and paused again. "I should say I'm sorry for that."

"You don't have to."

"I didn't even say goodbye."

"Well, yeah, that was a little rude," Mary said, clearing her nose. "Why didn't you?"

"Alex asked me not to. And I was so freaked out and scared—"

"He threatened you?"

"No. Not really. He just sort of convinced me it would do more harm than good. That it would be better to make a clean break. I mean, things looked so fucked."

"He was wrong," Mary said.

"But he always *sounds* right."

"I guess. But then what did you do?"

"That day?" Tom asked. "Well, I tried to go to Wright's, but nobody was home. Or he didn't answer the door."

"Sometimes I'm pretty sure he does that, just hides out in there."

"Anyway, that bummed me out pretty well. So I went down to the Rilke hotel and spent the night."

"You should have called me. I would have—" Mary halted. "Well, I would have done something."

"I was too messed up to think about that. The hotel really sealed the deal. I mean, there I was, not even back where I'd started, but even worse."

"You really know how to cultivate your own misery, Tom."

"I'm sorry."

"No, no. That's not what I mean. I understand. I was just commenting. You know, just talking," Mary said. "Anyway, then what?"

"I used the plane ticket the next morning. I came back here. End of story. So what about you?" said Tom. "What are you going to do now?"

"How do you mean?"

"I mean this—the thing with the baby—kind of changes everything, doesn't it?"

"Everything changes everything," Mary said. "Alex told me that. So it's got to be a tautology, or at least a cliché."

"It's a truism, I think."

"Yeah, that's it. You know, I really miss talking to you."

Tom stopped for a moment and then said, "So why don't you come home?"

"You mean to Seattle?"

"Yeah."

"I've gone to an awful lot of trouble to stay here."

"But it's not a very good arrangement, is it?"

"I guess not. I needed the money, a place for the baby."

"And now that's not . . ."

". . . an issue," Mary said.

"So you can leave. Alex can't stop you."

"But he wants to stay here, in the villa."

"So let him. He can pay you rent. Or you can sell it to him."

"It's my home," said Mary.

"I just thought you might want to be . . . among friends."

"That would be nice. With you especially."

"We could share a house. Be roommates."

"And lovers?"

There was a silence from Tom's end of the line, followed by an exhalation. "I don't know, Mary. I love you. But I think—"

"I'm not your grand passion."

"No, I guess not. But you're my best friend. I think it's better that way."

Mary said, "You know, I bet you're the first guy in history to say to a girl, 'Let's not spoil our friendship by sleeping together.'"

"Maybe. I mean, I suppose if it was really important to you, we could try, you know, getting you—"

"Are you serious?"

"Well, it's not like I minded. It's a little weird, but hey, we're artists, free spirits."

"That's very sweet of you. But right now I'm not even thinking of that."

"But promise me you'll think about the other thing, just coming home," said Tom. "I really think it would be good for you. I mean you don't want to be . . . a captive in your house, with Alex holding you hostage. With Wright spying on you."

"Oh, it's not that bad."

"But still, think about it, okay?"

"I will. I'll be thinking about everything, I imagine."

"Okay," Tom said. "So is it okay to call there? With Alex?"

"Who cares? But yes, I think it is. Alex is mellow again."

"Good. And maybe find out about Wright? Just out of curiosity."

"Sure."

"Well, I guess I should say goodbye. So . . . I love you."

"I love you too, Tom." Mary put down the receiver. She thought that perhaps Tom was the only person she ever had loved, or had loved in this way, where "love" was precisely the right word, the *mot juste,* the one that nailed it.

In the morning Maddalena came in with Mary's breakfast while Mary was still asleep. "Hey, hi," she said. "Rise or shine."

Mary rolled over and opened her eyes. "Rise *and* shine," she said.

"Rise and shine," the girl repeated, a little dispiritedly. In the shuttered half-dark, she put the tray down. "You want me pour *caffè*?"

"*To* pour," Mary said. "No, I can do it. I think I'll get up today."

"So you are best now?"

"Better. Yes, I think so. And you? *Come stai?*"

"I am sad. For you. For Isabella."

"So am I."

The girl stood silently, her gaze apparently intent on her sneakers. "It was bad . . . *sfortuna—*"

"Bad luck."

"—bad look, maybe that I try to touch her. Maybe I hurt you inside."

"Oh no. No, no, Maddalena. That didn't have anything to do with it. This happens all the time, *gli aborti spontanei.* I'm okay. I could have a baby another time, if I wanted. But we won't worry about that now."

"*Un aborto,* that's in English 'maggot.'"

"No, no," Mary said quite sharply. "That's wrong. It's . . . offensive. *Molto brutto.*"

Maddalena reddened and seemed almost to shake. "*Mi dispiace*—I'm, so, so very sad—"

Mary collected herself. "It's okay. It's a mistake. But who told you that?"

"Alessandro."

"Well, that's a crazy thing to have told you. You shouldn't listen to him. Alex can't really speak Italian."

"But he can."

"He thinks he can. It's all to do with what he believes about himself. He has real issues."

"Itch you's?"

"Issues. Things inside him, in his mind, that make him do and say bad things. I don't know if there's word in Italian—"

"Peccati?"

"I don't know. Maybe a little like that."

"Alessandro has done ishyoos against you?"

Mary thought. "Yes. I suppose he has."

"But you forget him?"

"Forgive him?"

"It's the same, no?"

"Maybe. But not exactly. Not in English."

"So you have forgetted him?"

"I don't know."

"And me?"

"Forgive you? For what?"

"Maybe for hurting your stomach."

"No, no," Mary said firmly. "That had nothing to do with anything."

"But maybe for wanting too much. For thinking to have her be like a little sister. Maybe that made a *sfortuna*."

"No. That was perfectly fine. It was sweet," Mary repeated.

"It was good." And then she was struck by an impulse or perhaps merely a need. She patted the bed next to her. "Here. Come sit next to me."

"Okay," the girl said. She climbed onto the bed and sidled up close to Mary. "It's okay?" she asked. "Not a crowd to you?"

"No. You can keep me warm," Mary said, and put her arm around Maddalena, not with any special intention but simply so it would have someplace to go. "I was cold. I didn't know it until now. But I was."

"Okay," Maddalena said, and they sat together for some time in silence.

The girl spoke. "But Isabella—I wanted, I wish . . ."

"You wished."

"I wished her."

"So did I. Very much. *Volentieri.*"

"How do you say *'volentieri'* in English?"

"Freely. Willingly," said Mary. "Gladly."

"So maybe you will again—"

"No. Don't say any more. Everything's fine. I'm just going to get up and dress and perhaps I'll read, in the garden. So you go see what Alex is doing. See if he wants to paint you today."

"Okay," Maddalena said, standing, and went out.

Mary swung her legs out of bed and poured milk and coffee into her cup. She spread apricot jam on her bread. The house felt a little cold, the stone floor colder still. It was already nine o'clock. There was light seeping in through the shutters. Mary went to open them, and the day flooded in, very blue, shuddering second by second towards deep yellow, afternoon, a lily's gilded tongue.

This was all merely quotidian, unremarkable, this being Tuscany, but Mary just then had, if not an epiphany, an inkling of her future course. It seemed to her a very straight path, and a long one. She did not know where it led, but, for all that, she chose it.

* * *

"So is he the same?" Tom asked when telephoned. He asked this straight on the heels of five or six other questions, none of which he had thus far given Mary a chance to answer. They all boiled down, more or less, to, "Did he say anything about me?"

Mary began in a slow and measured way to recite what she had learned. "He had a stroke, a very small one—"

"So he's normal—"

"His mind's just fine. He was very adamant about that. He laughed about it."

"But there's no—"

"His voice is a little different. More deliberate. Less . . . acute."

"And that's all the—"

"He walks a little more stiffly. I think he needs to rest more."

"So really—"

"He's pretty much the same. Slower. Older."

"Well, that's good, isn't it? He's fine," Tom said, as though repeating something by rote. "But did he say anything, anything—"

"About you?"

"Yes, me. Me. And *him* and me."

"He wondered where you'd gone. So I told him."

"Everything? I mean, did you tell him that I'd gone to his place, that he wasn't home—"

"I did. He said he was sorry to have missed you. That he must have been out."

"That was *all*? I mean, did you tell him we'd talked? That I'd asked about him, that I was curious?"

"Would you really have wanted me to say that?"

"Maybe not."

"I thought so. I just said you sent your regards."

Tom seemed to ponder this. "Maybe he'd think that was kind of lukewarm, kind of weak."

"Well, isn't that pretty much how you feel?"

"I suppose. It depends on how *he* feels. Did you get any sense of that?"

"Come on, Tom. He's not going to say. You know that."

"So that's it?"

"More or less. He did say he hoped to hear from you."

"He *hoped*?"

"I think that was the word he used."

"That's pretty strong for him. Don't you think?"

"I couldn't say, Tom. But the ball's in your court, if you want to pursue the matter."

"And you think it would be okay with him. If I did."

"He says he wants to hear from you."

"Well, that's kind of weak."

"It's something."

"I guess. So did you tell him what had been going on with you and Alex at the villa? I mean, since June?"

"Pretty much. Of course, he already knows most everything. He has his spies. And the gardener's sort of a double agent."

"So what did he think about it all?"

"He commiserated, in his fashion. He said I'd come to Italy to be happy, to avoid suffering. Which he told me was a terrible mistake on my part."

"Wow."

"I told you he hadn't changed. Anyway, he said that maybe some good would come out of all this. That I needed 'seasoning' to become a real artist, to stay the course."

"That is so fucking condescending. I'd forgotten—"

"Really, from him it's not," Mary said. "It might even be true."

"Well, anyway, what about you? Are you going to stay there?"

"As opposed to what?"

"What we talked about. About you coming here. Coming home."

"I don't know. I really don't."

"I guess it's a tough thing. But I want you to think about it. It could be really great. Anyway, I'll call you in a week."

"Okay," Mary said. After they'd said goodbye, it wasn't all that late, or at least she wasn't sleepy. She thought she could do a little work on her novel. Since she'd first gotten up from bed after the miscarriage, she'd written steadily, and the book was catching up to where it should be.

It seemed to Mary she was nearly done, at the end. Yet she also felt that in some way her novel didn't "add up." It was a phrase she herself had used in reviews for the *CityReader* about other people's novels, long before she'd ever attempted one herself, and perhaps she'd used it naïvely and even unfairly. Because the truth was, things didn't add up—never, of course, in real life—or even in stories. The trick, the great thing, as the Master himself had said, was to make them seem to add up, by shining one's lamp only into certain rooms and not others; it was in framing—and she had to give Alex credit for this, if only for this—one's objects and the light that fell upon them within the picture they appeared to make. So she would just have to keep at it, persist; be prepared, as Wright Turner had proposed, even to suffer for it.

A little over a week later, the telephone rang at the Villa Donatello, a rare thing since Alex and Mary knew so few people in Florence. It was Tom Hirsch, calling from Seattle.

He and Alex had a perfectly pleasant conversation. They even laughed once or twice. They commiserated about the firings at the *CityReader,* the headlong descent of Noumena stock, Tom's Nazi supervisor at Starbucks, Alex's recent news of Wright Turner, and, briefly and with many silences, the mischance of Mary's pregnancy.

And with that, Tom asked if Mary was home, if he could speak to her. But he was told that she was gone for the day, that she and Maddalena had gone to Rome to buy books and clothes for the girl, to buy Mary a new desk, one that would fit perfectly in Mary's studio, which Alex was going to repaint in a more agreeable colour as soon as he had completed the first of the frescoes inside the villa.

13.

Lee Street, 2001

There is a house on a hill in Seattle, and if you crane your neck from one of the upstairs windows, you can—on a clear day—just make out a slash of the ash-grey Puget Sound. The house has had five owners, three of them in the last past five years. The first, who bought the house new in 1915, was a family that ultimately grew to six persons. When the children were grown and became parents themselves, one of the grandparents died and the other was taken in to the home of one of the children and her spouse. At that time, in 1949, the house was sold for the first time.

The new owners, then in their mid-twenties, raised three children in the house, and when the youngest of these went off to college in 1978, the owners remained there alone another ten years, until they retired permanently to Tempe, Arizona. They retained the house as a rental property until June 1996 when, under much pressure from their eldest son, it was put on the market for $350,000. It sold quickly and was subject to multiple offers, of which Mary Bruckner's (for $375,000) was the highest.

Mary sold the house in June 1999 for $648,500—$28,000 more than the asking price. Alex and Mary had accomplished great things with the interior (the previous owners had scarcely done a thing to mar its original Craftsman features) and updated the kitchen with quasi-restaurant appliances and grey-brown granite counters.

The new owners were a childless couple not so very different from Mary and Alex. In fact, the husband worked at Noumena (although Mary had never met him: Noumena had become a very large company), and the wife was a genetic microbiologist at a new company called BioMorph, whose stock ultimately proved no more attractive than its name. The house had to be sold, and one supposes it would have been anyway, as the couple decided to divorce.

Now the house—it's just after New Year's 2001—is vacant, awaiting its new owners, who are coming from the East Coast later in the month. No one knows anything about them except that they probably earn their money by one or another of the more traditional means, such as a law or medical degree or a trust fund.

Were you to look inside now, the house would seem disconsolate, to say the least—a few bare bulbs burning in the hallways, the occasional click or thrum of the furnace, set at fifty-five degrees to keep any pipes from bursting. But doesn't every house have its ghosts, empty or occupied? Doesn't Henry James still inhabit the upstairs apartment at the Villa Castellani, and doesn't Isabel Archer rustle through its rooms still more, art being infinitely more powerful than any guest register, deed, or leasehold?

So imagine, if you will, that it is the holidays over three years before our story began, Christmas 1996, Mary and Alex's first Christmas in this house. A week before Christmas Eve, they decided they ought to have a few people over—friends and co-workers: by and large ex-humanities majors working as dronebots, artoids, and coffee-and-muffin wageslaves—plus Alex's elderly painter friend, Jens Hammershøi. At this time, Mary scarcely knew Tom Hirsch, whom she had met in a writing class, but his existence struck her forcefully for some unknown reason at five o'clock. She phoned him and, as she guessed, he had nowhere to go; and it must have been that very night or shortly thereafter that Mary began to think of him as "The Great Loose End."

Tom arrived around six, the silent electric trolley bus—made more silent still by the snow that had started to fall—having dropped him off within a block of their door. He found the house easily. He only felt lost once he came inside. There were many more women than men, and they seemed to Tom to be universally like Mary—dark-haired, clad in black or brown, wearing speculative expressions—but much more grumpy; their conversation focused on the useless and passive men they knew, men, Tom could not help but feel, like him. Alex was busy either making, serving, or drinking drinks, and Jens Hammershøi looked entirely too alien and formidable to speak to, assuming he spoke English, or spoke at all.

By seven, in any case, Jens was "shitfaced," as Alex delicately put it to Tom, with whom he was just then having his first conversation. By eight it was snowing hard, and the guests began to leave, fearful of getting stuck, or having other social functions to attend. Only Tom, Jens, Mary, and Alex remained, and with Jens now passed out on the couch, the three of them talked happily before the fire for another two hours. The snow was mounting on the windowsills, and they talked about their work—not their jobs, but their work: the paintings, fictions, and essays they wanted to make. At midnight, Alex manhandled Jens into an adjacent guest room ("Santa will never come with him on the couch," Mary observed), and they offered Tom another bedroom upstairs, as if it were his, as if he always slept there.

When Tom came downstairs and into the kitchen the next morning, he found Mary making cappuccino and Alex griddling pancakes. Jens shuffled in, silent as a stump, took a cappuccino and fortified it from a vodka bottle. Even he, Tom decided, was no longer so dreadful and gelidly Nordic, but merely another member of what felt uncannily like a family.

When they all had their breakfasts and coffees in hand, they carried them out to the living room. And there they found stockings hanging from the fireplace mantle, four of them, big bright-coloured polypropylene hiking socks from REI stuffed by Mary and strung by Alex just after dawn. Tom's had a Morrissey CD and an edition of Baudelaire's poems, interests Tom could not just then remember having ever mentioned to Mary. Tom might have wept.

"They're sort of pre-owned," she said. "It was a spur of the moment thing—not knowing you were coming." And then Alex motioned to Jens to take his stocking down. Inside there was a purple tube. Jens fumbled to get it open and finally Alex helped him. There was a drawing inside. Alex unrolled it and passed it to him. Jens just stared. Alex said, "It's a Clyfford Still," almost—it seemed to Tom—like he'd screwed up and was trying to apologize.

Jens held it in front of him and finally said, "I know that. He was my friend." Jens's hand was shaking and the drawing was trembling in it. Tom thought Jens was going to cry, but he just held the drawing, and with his other hand he reached over and touched Alex lightly on the back. It seemed to Tom he even smiled.

There were, of course, two more stockings. Mary's had an antique fountain pen in it and a first edition of James's *The Portrait of a Lady*, in three volumes—all from Alex, of course. In his, Mary had put what she said were Victorian glass chemist's bottles—three of them—with glass stoppers. Inside each one she'd put a different ground pigment—pure blue, pure red, pure yellow, utterly concentrated and intense.

You see the beautiful things good people can do with money, Tom had thought.

After that, Alex made fancy hot drinks. Jens sat contentedly on the sofa and Mary, Alex, and Tom sat on the floor, between the fire and Jens's feet. They persuaded each other to sing Christmas carols, and Jens sang something in what Alex later told Tom was Danish.

Of course, even as it was transpiring, Tom had decided that it had to be unreal, this first idyllic Christmas of his life. It was like nostalgia for something that had never happened, for times that never were. He might have admitted for all his longing and hunger for exactly such a Christmas, it was illusionary or artificial; or he might have confessed that it was merely art and left it at that.

That, you would suppose, was the real beginning of Mary, Alex, and Tom's friendship, which only prospered all the more once Jens moved down to the "Finnish Riviera" on the Columbia River for what he called the winter drinking season. You would be right. And you might also suppose that, were you to visit Bellosguardo today, six years after that Christmas, you would not find all three of them in residence, or at least not all on speaking terms. But you would be wrong.

Perhaps they had already done all the terrible things they were ever capable of to one another. They had gone native, taken on the local coloration and learned the Florentine arts of *tradire* and *tradirsi.* Between Mary and Tom, these had taken the form of crimes of the tongue or crimes of silence—things said or left unsaid—and perhaps words lose their force, just dry up and blow away after a certain amount of time, or alter their character, changing from arrows and slights to dust bunnies. Of other things—one person's heart's desire refused to him or her, yet freely, even carelessly, given to another—perhaps time turns these to memories and then to words, and these, too, are scattered. Alex, of course, is better than Tom and Mary at setting such things aside, but then he also knows he has yet to meet anyone with a heart as black as his.

In any case, Mary and Alex live together with Maddalena in the Villa Donatello. Go and see for yourself. If it's not a school day, more often than not you'll find Alex painting Maddalena, and he's very productive these days. There's going to be a show at a gallery not far from their old apartment in Oltrarno, and he's on the verge of taking on portrait commissions. (There's a urologist whom Alex has approached about reversing his vasectomy in exchange for a large family grouping.) It's Mary, of course, whom Alex really wants to paint again, but she's not quite there yet. And, should you go in Alex's studio, you'll see there's still a blanket and a pillow on that sofa, which suggests that at least on most nights Alex sleeps alone. But he bears that and all the rest—the time these things take—quite well. He has all that time to get through, but then he has all the walls of the house to paint. He's going to fresco the lot (that was part of his deal with Mary) and he imagines it could take him into his late middle age to do it properly.

Upstairs, Maddalena has Tom's old room. It's full of clothes, magazines, and too many cosmetic products for Mary's taste, but there are also more and more books. She and Mary still read together, and for her part Maddalena understands that Mary needs her solitude, her boundaries and limits. She will never be Maddalena's mother. That is just the way Mary is. It's sad, Maddalena thinks, but then she also thinks it might be sad for Mary too. It is not *facile* to be Mary. Anyway, Maddalena's English is on the verge of fluency, and this coming autumn at the *liceo,* she's beginning French. Soon she'll read Manzoni, *I Promessi Sposi,* and she'll learn about love *fra adulti,* how it's bartered and betrayed.

Next door, of course, is Mary's studio, and there she sits, five days a week, until she's written her daily five hundred words. Despite having less—Alex now pays the bills—she is doing, she believes, more. She's well into a big novel by now, a virtual "three-decker." No one knows what it's about, though doubtless it's Jamesian. ("Henry James—talk about 'issues with penetration,'" Tom likes to tease her when they see each other, generally every other day or so.) She loves this room, to look out from of course, but also simply to be in; and for that, she must concede, she owes Alex. When she looks at the walls, which appear to anyone else to be simply mottled and washed in layers of colour, they seem to contain figures; figures, in fact, from the very story she is writing, Alex's unbidden gift to her, and it is all she can do not to run down to the studio, and embrace him and tell him, Never mind about everything, Let's go back to where we were. But she knows—knows it because she does love him that much—that it cannot be so easy yet.

But from Alex's studio you can see the windows of the Villa Castellani, and if you had binoculars, or perhaps just looked through the zoom on Alex's camera, you could almost see into the rooms, except that it's so very dark in there. So you will have to use your imagination. Tom has been back since November, all because Wright Turner simply called him up in Seattle and asked him to come. Tom knew about his illness, and when he'd gotten over the shock of hearing Wright's voice, he asked him how he was.

Turner told him, Oh, he'd had the tiniest little stroke, that it was nothing grand, that his speech and, thank God, his facial muscles were intact, but he did get a little tired. Then he asked Tom how he was; was he *really* going to stay in Seattle, of all places, what with him being a boy like, well, *him*.

They talked things through—Tom's various miseries and agonies and their insufferability, Turner's hauteur, malignancy, and devotion to the superficial in both relationships and life—and then at some point, Turner just came out and said, Why didn't Tom come back?

"Where?" Tom said.

"Here."

"I don't think Alex and Mary would quite be up for that."

"Oh, not there," Turner said. "You'd think they were running some sort of an orphanage up there. That awful man is putting his vulgar, trashy stuff all over the walls, I hear. No, no," he said, "I mean here. Here. With me."

And so Tom came back to the Villa Castellani. You might say he acts as Turner's aide and nurse, and it is true that Turner needs help with some basic tasks and, increasingly, with bathing and dressing and the like. But that would be a one-sided and rather uncharitable way to describe their relationship. Because Turner has, as he would put it, "taken Thomas in hand," to educate him after a fashion; to wean him from theory onto things themselves, onto particular paintings, music, and books; and, not least, onto his own failing body.

Tom seems to understand it's a fair bargain. One day Mary was pressing him about whether he would ever take up the project he'd started at the Hotel San Remo or do something with his writing and critical studies. Tom said, "Really soon. Or maybe later. Wright says it would be fine with him if I wrote a memoir of our time together. Actually, I think he'd love it, even posthumously. I hadn't understood this before, but Wright's not vain: he just wants to be on *exhibit*. He's his own artwork. He wants to be seen, heard, read."

He also told Mary that at least Wright had gotten him reading again—really reading. Auden, for example. "Auden says love is mutual need, none of that other stuff you thought it was," Tom said, and from that he explained his arrangement with Turner. "And Wright needs me. He needs me to talk to, to listen to him, to entertain him, to adore him, to help him move around, get cleaned up, get him hot (or let him watch me get hot), and be generally 'lovely' for him. It's pretty much a full-time job."

Mary was either so taken aback or merely wise enough that she let the matter drop. But Tom wasn't done. "Wright showed me another poem of Auden's. It says 'Hell is neither here nor there/Hell is not anywhere.' And all this time, I thought Wright used that phrase as a cliché. Or just an evasion of pretty much everything that was difficult or inconvenient. When really, 'here nor there' was where he found me, the place he guided me through and out of."

"Like Dante," Mary put in very quietly.

"I don't know. I still haven't gotten to that."

Of course Mary, like anyone, wanted to know what they were doing for sex these days, but Tom refused to be drawn. Finally, later in the year, when the wisteria was in bloom again and it was warm enough to eat dinner outside under the pergola, three empty wine bottles on the table and nothing left in the way of light but a citronella candle, Tom told her and Alex.

You could imagine it, or even see it, if by chance the curtains at the Villa Castellani were left open at night. It would be no surprise to know that Wright Turner tires more easily and the pills he once took no longer agree with him. But he and Tom do other things.

Now, of an evening, Turner will say, "Let's make a *tableau vivant*." You know, striking the poses from a famous painting. It perhaps goes without saying that the ones he chooses are mostly nudes, or become nudes. So Tom undresses and adopts these poses, and it seems to give Turner every bit as much pleasure as any of the things they used to do together. He says, "Oh, let me watch you, let me see you," and you can probably picture the rest.

Not that it's done carelessly or haphazardly. Turner is, of course, very particular about the precision of the pose, about its art-historical veracity. He'll say, "No, no. Not that way. Move a little this way, a little that way. Now raise your arms." And Tom will rearrange himself until Wright's satisfied. Then Turner says, "Now, *there* you are."

And yes, so at last, Tom is.